Wave Rising

A Phoebe Thompson Story

E.L. Phoenix

Wave Rising

Publisher's Note
This is a work of fiction. Names, characters, businesses, places, events and incidents either are the product of the author's imagination or are used fictitiously, and any resemblance to actual persons, living or dead, or to actual events is purely coincidental.

Published by St. Mark's Publishing Co.
Front Royal, Virginia and Jackson, Wyoming

Edited by Jacques Rouen
Cover Design by Brent Meske

ISBN: 978-0-9897483-6-0
Printed in the United States of America

Chapter 1

"Stack it up," she said.

"You sure, Pheebes?"

"Oh hell yeah, 175. I can bench 175. Let's do it." Phoebe Thompson glowered, not at Jamie Eddington, just in general, and she caught the reflection of it in the old gym's mirror. It almost made her laugh, because in that moment, she kind of looked like her mom. Helen fucking Thompson, the original badass, at least in the courtroom. In the weight room, she ruled; well, at least when the blockers skipped lifting. This morning, it was just her and her captain and even if the blockers showed up, Phoebe could outlift them or just about anyone pound for pound.

"Okay, go get 'em, and don't go pulling a muscle or something, just because you're mad," Jamie said.

Phoebe finished her set of one-arm pushups, 25, on top of two sets of 50 pushups, and jumped up from her supine position. As soon as she landed on her toes, she shadow-boxed once or twice, not too fast, nice and gentle. Plenty of time for Jamie to get her hands up; anyway, if there was one person who would take Phoebe out, no questions asked, no harm, no foul, it was Jamie. Hell, Jamie had clocked her once or twice, at least during practice bouts. All was in bounds during derby. Honor among friends, and hard hits of course.

Once the weights were lined up, Jamie put her hands on the bar.

Phoebe stretched out on the bench. Her sweat was pouring out and made her back stick to the leather or fake leather or whatever it was. Old-school, so probably leather. "How do you know I'm mad?"

"Well, I don't know, I think you were cussing under your breath when you were walking in from the back." Jamie patted the bar. "Ready?"

Phoebe closed her eyes and centered on it. Let it take her. If her rage was like an ocean wave rising, higher and higher, spreading deeper and deeper until it reached every nerve, every muscle, from head to foot and all places in between, then she was a helpless, tiny creature riding the surfboard that was her brain, searching, searching, but never finding, a safe shore. She breathed in, a deep, furious breath really, but the air, or its molecules, felt like ice crystals, each one cutting her windpipe as it cartwheeled, windmilled, fluttered, *aw fuck it.*

Phoebe's eyes popped open. "Yeah, let's do it. Ten reps."

She got the first one. What was thinking she thinking? No, what were they thinking? This time was the same as last time, and last time was the same as the next time would be. Another ice crystal broke inside her.

The second one wasn't hard. Before she got here, she wanted to break something, and if she didn't calm down, it would be the oversized TV screen blinking at her from the side of the main room. Not blinking. Madly gyrating. The way men did when they were—she winced. Another ice crystal.

Three. Easy.

She squinted as the sweat hit her eyes. Another ratbastard. She didn't know him. She didn't know the little girl he'd raped.

Four.

But the judge had apparently known them both well enough to assign no prison time. 30 days, suspended. It was, after all, a special situation.

Five.

The girl was mature for 15.

Six. Didn't hurt. Nothing hurt.

She'd sashayed practically—for all intents and purposes, really—nude in front of her teacher, a family man *if the judge had ever seen*, asking for it, yeah, she might as well been.

Seven. She could kill someone.

Victimless crime, really, because the victim was no innocent. Victimless really, because it was not a typical crime.

Eight. Easily kill someone.

It was a complicated, messy, sinful, sick, nasty, dirty, dark crime. Dirty dark crime, like the crime she carried inside of her, a modern version of Eve carrying a piece of Adam's rib, a crime that made her what she was.

Nine. She could do this all day.

Yeah, right. Victimless. If only she could break that rib, tear it out of her.

Ten. She could keep going.

"Phoebe, stop. Ten. That's great. Come on. Let go now."

Phoebe was squeezing the bar so hard, her hands were numb. She rolled out from under the bar, and threw a few punches at the mirror. The woman who threw the jabs back at her would never be touched, felt, tapped, molested, raped, or otherwise interfered with ever . . . again.

"So, you gonna tell me why you're mad?" Jamie passed her a hand towel, and stood there, in charge, not imperious, and hell bent on getting Phoebe to talk. This is how this usually went. Jamie would just wait her out, patient, no rushing, as Phoebe went around breaking shit, until Phoebe would relent and start talking. And a few hours later, Jamie would still be listening, and Phoebe would have calmed down a little.

But today, she didn't have a few hours. She told Cass she'd pick up Zander, and she had just enough time to get over to their house before he blew a door off a car or put a bazooka-launched potato through a neighbor's window. With a wry smile, Phoebe punched Jamie in the shoulder.

"I'll call you later," she said.

"And tell me what's wrong?"

Phoebe shrugged, and waved over her shoulder.

Chapter 2

Zander White careened around a pen oak, feinted left, sprinted right, and with the Nerf football tucked into his chest, he barreled past one of the neighborhood kids. The soles of his feet scraped the just-greening grass beneath him. With a stutter-step, he spun 360 degrees in the air and dove into a much-dented Azalea bush.

"Score!" He stood up with dimples rising on both sides of his light brown cheeks.

Phoebe jingled her keys. He was making her late, and she had a lot of homework. "Ready?"

Zander spiked the football, and started off in the other direction, as if covering a punt.

"Bye, I'm leaving," she said.

"Aw, come on, just—"

"—Bye."

"Later, Ronnie, Garrett, later," Zander said. He gave fist bumps out with an insouciant nonchalance that made Phoebe work hard not to smile.

Without saying *hi how are you or anything like thanks for the ride*, Zander took one more galloping step, then flipped the football into the trunk. "Pheebes! When are ya gonna get rid of this hunk o junk anyway?"

Phoebe shook her head and caught her reflection in the small side view mirror on her Bronco's mint green door. The unfortunate color choice just made it more lovable. "Get in."

Already up to her shoulders, Zander had big hands and feet; he reminded her of a colt, or, she realized, a bronco. *Of course.*

"Time to ride the Peppermint Sled! We should test it on the snow slopes this winter."

"Insult the ride, don't get inside." She slammed the door shut and stared straight ahead, with only the slightest movement of the muscles around her mouth.

Zander missed that, which was just as well. He moved real quick so that he wouldn't have to take a long walk to his mother's office. He jumped into the passenger's seat and sat very still for thirty seconds.

Phoebe nodded, flipped on the engine, and took in the deep-throated burble of her old vehicle. With a practiced application of foot to medal, she rocketed forward and took in the outline of Zander with her peripheral vision. She liked the throat on this old beast, and she kept the radio down nice and low so she could hear the symphonic growling. *Mmm.*

Zander leaned forward and started tapping the dashboard.

"St—"

"I didn't mean to insult your peppermint sled," he began, drawing out the name with a lilt. "Maybe we should rename it. You know, like abbreviate it! That's what we'll call her Pheebes!"

"Shut—"

"P.M.— "

"—Up!"

A loud burble tumbled up and out of Zander, and Phoebe tried to reply about five times before she gave up and with a reluctant half smile, waved her hand and then turned the radio up. Just a few minutes of peace . . .

"Oh. Yes." Zander closed his eyes for a second, and clasped both hands together. A bubblegum saccharine song emerged from the rusting SUV's tinny speakers, but he didn't notice the sound. The twang was pronounced; the words, absurd, but as Phoebe knew, Tyler Slow was sacred to Zander.

"We'll just listen now, 'kay?"

For a few minutes, Phoebe kept her eyes on the road, with a frequent check of the rear view mirror. Her mom had taught her some of the rules of driving, but Phoebe had learned how to drive stick shift from her riding coach, Anne McCaffrey.

Left foot, shift knob, left foot release, right, right, yes, child, very good.

Phoebe could hear Coach like it was yesterday. Whenever Anne called her "child," Phoebe's heart would leap forward, because the very first time she'd met her coach, when Phoebe was just a kid really, and brand-new to Bryson House, Anne had said to her, "*Ah, Phoebe. You're named after the goddess of light.*" And from thereafter, whenever Anne had really wanted to make a point, her gray eyes would twinkle, and she'd murmur, "Now see here, child of light," and it would make Phoebe feel like there was a point to it all, a point sometimes even to her living, when the pain got too bad. Just hearing that there was light, and she was in it, and maybe someone could see it even when she couldn't, well, that's what being called child of light did to her.

Eyes closed for an extra moment, Zander sighed. "I'm in love with Tyler Slow." His eyes popped open, and for a moment, Phoebe could see a younger version of him, perched on top of the barn roof and murmuring strange ditties to his stuffed animal, "Chickie."

She shook her head and grinned at the same time.

"In love with her, eh?"

"Yeah." He inclined his head. "I'm going to marry her."

"Really?"

He hummed the last few bars of the song, which were exactly the same as the first few bars. "You think she lives in a big mansion? Maybe with horses in the country? I wanna live in a big mansion with horses and a pond and maybe I'll have a little house so that mom can live there and Cat can come and visit . . ." Zander kept going, and after a few sentences, Phoebe's mind fell into a moving version of the picture he was painting with his words. It was like she was watching a movie of the Bryson House, where her new life had begun.

She was sitting on a fence post watching, just watching, and Anne McCaffrey asked her, "Are you watching or are you riding?" Then she was lying on a cold table as the nurse administered the rape kit, and her mom's mellifluous words rolled and she held mom's hand and while it wasn't great, it was all right. Then she was screaming, "Where were you when he was fucking me?" And her mom crumbled and fell, and was lying on the floor, and she hadn't meant to . . . Phoebe winced and shook her head. No, not that memory. She fast-forwarded, which Cary had taught her during one of their earliest therapy sessions, as if she were holding the movie projector that displayed the pictures that together, constituted her own life, the patchwork, the signature pieces, fragments. Phoebe froze. Fuck. Parkings in the barn. No. He was behind her, laying claim to her, his breath on her, his tongue on her neck, and it was hot but she felt cold all over.

What the hell? Why am I thinking of him? He's locked up tight for life. Phoebe startled and looked around. She gripped and re-gripped the steering wheel. Hands. Driving. Bronco. Smells? Slight scent of cigarettes. Whiff of musty old vehicle.

And then the music was playing and she heard the words again, words that must have summoned Parkings like a Ougii Board summoned a long-dead relative:

My brown-eyed girl

Phoebe shivered.

"How may I help you m'lady?"

And then she could hear his belt unbuckle, and she knew then that it was all up to her, and she'd never wanted it, never deserved it, and she wasn't put on this earth to be a victim, so she pivoted and swung with all she had and—

La la la la la la

Phoebe took a deep breath. "Zander. Zander." Her words came out like a puff of air, barely above a whisper. "Please change the station. Anything else. Please. Now."

"What's up with that guy and his brown-eyed thing anyway? We need more songs about white mansions and horses, and lots more songs by Tyler—"

Phoebe gritted her teeth. "Change. Station." Her words sounded harsh, so she added, "Please," and that sounded kind of mean too, but Zander didn't seem to notice. He moved the radio dial until he found another suitably screechy whiny teenager singing something stupid . . . Phoebe shook her head. *Damn, I hope I didn't say that out loud.* She glanced over at Zander and he looked happy. She took a deep breath and surveyed the damage.

She'd lost some time, and when she lost time, she often got lost, or at least misplaced her exact location, without getting off whatever route she'd taken. Sunlight, shadows, *no don't go there . . .* with a relieved sigh, she followed the shadow to the white line on Route 123. She'd just crossed Route 29, and to her left was an office complex that was composed of cozy 1970's era townhouses. In about another mile she would reach downtown Fairfax city. Keep going past the Starbucks, past the Irish bar, and then she'd be at mom's office. It was safe there.

A few minutes later, Phoebe arrived at the driveway leading to 10000 Chain Bridge Road. As she wrenched the wheel to turn past the rust-colored stone building several stories high, she frowned. Her Bronco was not responding the way it should. She fought to keep it under control, because a big cement wall was rushing toward her and she was rolling downhill, fast.

Chapter 3

Phoebe leaned against the front door and waited for Zander. She could see Cassandra White pacing from one end of Thompson, White & Hansen's main conference room to the other, her feet just scraping the polished wood floor underneath. Ms. White paused only to pivot and turn when she got within a half-stride of the taupe walls. Of course she was wearing Levis. Phoebe snickered. Ms. White was badass enough to dress however she wanted. After all, she was one of the best-known criminal defense attorneys in Northern Virginia.

The setting sun reflected off Ms. White's long, silver-blonde hair, and while she wasn't young anymore, her smile was young. The only person bothered by her Levis was her aging secretary, Janice.

"Cassandra, really, must you wear those striped socks to work?" Janice was grousing.

Without taking her eyes off the sheet of paper she clutched in her left hand, Cassandra waved absent-mindedly. "You got the witness notebooks ready?"

Janice flipped her half-moon, dark-rimmed reading glasses off her nose, and crossed the room, where a stack of thick, black plastic binders sat on a side table. "Check."

Cassandra tapped her fingers on her belt loop. "Exhibits list ready?"

"Check."

"Jury pool?"

"Check."

"Excellent, thank you." Cassandra made eye contact with Janice and moved her right hand in a quick, horizontal motion. They'd been working for so many years together that they could speak almost in code and with hand signals.

"Well then, I'd best be getting over to the courthouse and file the witness list before it closes."

Cassandra nodded.

Zander's voice skidded around the corner in front of him. Phoebe was laughing now, because his shirttail was untucked and his hair was sticking up on one side of his head and none of this was out of the ordinary. Almost every time she dropped him off at the office there was a kerfuffle, and she could only imagine what it was like to live with Zander. It would never be boring. She rolled her sleeves up, and took a deep breath.

"Mom, mom, Pheebes almost crashed the peppermint sled!"

"Don't call it that—I'm warning you—"

"Mom, Mom, you should've seen it! It was epic! We were flying down the ramp!" Zander raised his arms and made a loud explosive effect with his mouth, his entire body leaning backwards as he described the scene. "And the edge of the sled came within—"

"—Bronco, damnit—"

"—Inches of the yellow pillars. And then Pheebes swerved, and it almost hit the other side, and we almost were flying, and then . . ."

Cassandra's eyes narrowed. "And then?"

"Ms. White," Phoebe said, "Really, it was nothing. I had it under control. Master cylinder's busted, I'm thinking."

Something about Ms. White had always seemed comforting, kind of like the old Levis she often wore. Phoebe had first met Ms. White more than five years ago at the Bryson House, a shelter for victims of domestic violence. It had been her job to make sure Phoebe's mother Helen stayed out of prison after killing Phoebe's rapist, who had also been Phoebe's father.

Phoebe contemplated Ms. White and for a few moments, barely heard Zander. Ms. White felt safe because she had kept them safe, somehow. Well, no one was ever totally safe; there were no guarantees. But she owed a lot to her mother's partner.

Cassandra shook her head and fingered the sheet of paper in her hand.

Phoebe caught sight of the pink and orange tattoo on her upper arm and she rubbed the skin around it. Her muscles were already feeling a little sore, but she'd lifted 175. That was almost worth a smile.

"So, your truck's busted, you've probably got a test to study for, and your mom's in Chicago and isn't getting back into town until late tonight. Sounds like a pickle."

Phoebe frowned and rubbed her bicep and shoulder muscle. The phoenix moved underneath her fingers. "Yes ma'am. It would appear so."

Zander disappeared into the kitchen, still talking and making explosion sounds.

Cassandra leaned over and let the sheet of paper she'd been reading fall softly on the conference room table. "Tell you what, Phoebe—do you have a garage that usually looks after your truck?"

Phoebe shook her head, and made her face not move. *She'd sooner sleep in the Bronco parked in the garage parking lot than ask for a ride.*

This would have worked with anyone else, but not with Ms. White. Cassandra hit the speaker button on the phone next to the sheet of paper she'd dropped on the table.

"Yes?"

"Janice, would you please call Triple-A and ask them to tow Phoebe's green truck to Ronnie R's gas station?" Cassandra suppressed a smile and let the receiver rest on her shoulder. "Best mechanic in Fairfax," she murmured to Phoebe. "Hope that's all right."

"Yes ma'am."

"And after we swing by Ronnie R's, if you wanna hitch a ride home with us and hang out with us until your mom gets in, we'd love to have you. I'd offer to drive you out to Middleburg but

I got a trial in the morning and a ton of prep to do still, but we'd love to have you."

Phoebe looked away, her eyes following a sparrow in flight through the bank of office windows that lined the conference room wall, and didn't say anything.

Holding a bottle of red Gatorade in one hand, and a chunk of beef jerky in the other, Zander, all elbows and knees, careened around the corner and stopped just in front of his mom. He grinned and waited for her to rest her head on the top of his head.

Cassandra chuckled, and wrapped an arm around him. "And if everything gets too loud, you can grab some privacy and get some studying done in Catherine's old room."

Phoebe was in the middle of answering, of agreeing without really agreeing, when the front door to the law firm banged against the back door jam. Shoes clacked on the wood floors, and the sound carried to the conference room. Only one person slammed doors into door jams like that, and that was Helen *fucking* Thompson.

Phoebe's mom took three long strides before she registered anyone. She towered above all of them, and looked regal in a dark green suit and black high heels. Not much had changed in the way Helen worked a case since she'd been ushered out of her "white-shoes" law firm in D.C. five years ago. Her firm's partners viewed the entire incident involving Richard Thompson's death as a potential liability, one not befitting a partner, and not worth holding onto Helen Thompson's immense book. What they hadn't counted on was Helen retaining a large percentage of that book. When Helen joined up with Cassandra White, their law firm instantly became one of the most profitable boutiques in Northern Virginia.

With a reputation for hard-nosed courtroom excellence that had not been diminished by the circumstances surrounding her husband's death five years ago, Helen was known in the hallways of courtrooms all over the country as a "fixer." Handed a mess, a multimillion-dollar sinkhole of a case, she could add a motion, call an expert witness, create a novel legal argument out of disparate or apparently nonexistent facts, frighten opposing counsel, and make the impossible appear easy. And with a price tag of $1,000 an hour, and a ten million dollar book, she could afford to pick and choose which messes to fix.

"Hey, Partner." Cassandra was grinning as she greeted Helen, and it occurred to Phoebe that no one made her mom smile as much as Ms. White did. Everyone else saw her mom as a badass, a stern, downright scary presence, but Ms. White wore better boots and took no shit from anyone. Phoebe was grinning now too, because she was, well, really happy to see her mom.

Helen nodded, stiff and proper as ever, and then her eyes crinkled when she saw Zander.

"Ms. Thompson, guess what?"

Helen gave him a curious shake of her head and held up her hand. "Hold on a minute, Zander." Letting her eyes settle on him just long enough to take the edge off her peremptory tone, she then hoisted her black leather briefcase beside the wall leading into the conference room. Then she turned, and with both arms wide open, she beckoned to Phoebe.

A beam of light fell on the space between Phoebe and her mom, and Phoebe stared at the light, watching as if it was melding or bonding her to her mom. Helen held on for an extra moment and then, with a brisk pat, let Phoebe pull back a few inches. Then they stared at one another and Phoebe felt like crying but she didn't know exactly why.

> *She was seeing her mom talking to Ms. White at the Bryson House, outside by the front door, but neither one of them knew Phoebe was watching them. Ms. White had wrapped one arm around Helen's shoulder, in a loose way, and they were both smoking a cigarette, and she could hear Ms. White promising that they were going to figure things out; they were going to be all right. She hadn't heard what her mom said, but she could see her mom stand up a little straighter. A few more scenes flashed past. Riding with Anne. Being wrapped inside a blanket, curled up next to Helen in the kitchen the day Parkings came for her. And the look of relief in Helen's eyes as Cassandra explained that the case against her would never make it to trial.*

Oh. And now she felt like crying, because the last thing she saw was Helen, draped in black, standing beside Ms. White at Anne's funeral. And the grief written on Helen's face made Phoebe almost able to feel it too.

"Zander! Where are your shoes?"

Zander wiped his mouth with the back of his hand and slipped away from his mother with a subtle sidestep. He bounced up next to Helen. "Phoebe almost crashed her truck, Ms. Thompson. It's stuck in the garage. Blown master cylinder." As Zander finished speaking, he gave his mother a peek from under his long eyelashes and ducked out of the room before Phoebe could get disentangled from Helen.

"Did not!"

"Did too," he said.

Helen's face registered nothing. Ms. White gave Helen a quick "sitrep" on the Bronco, and then paused long enough to shut the door behind her.

"Listen, both of you, while we're going over sitreps, I need to give you an update on the perps from your case."

Helen, meanwhile, leaned against the wall and folded her arms. "Please. Go ahead, Cass."

"Well, it's just not good news, you know?"

"He's got parole?"

Phoebe already knew the basic outline so she was only half-listening. The final perp, who had at first received a ten-year sentence for conspiracy to commit deviant acts with a minor, had been conditionally approved for parole during his third and final hearing. Ms. White had submitted detailed and updated victim impact statements. They'd attended the parole board hearing back in October.

"Oh for fucksake." Helen slapped her thigh with her right hand. "So he's fulfilled the pre-release conditions?"

Ms. White nodded, and they both turned and looked at Phoebe.

She didn't have anything to say. She glared at her hands without speaking, until the muscles around her jaw and chin contracted and then it was all aching and cracking and hurting.

"Yeah. Exactly, Mom. Fucksake. And fuck them." Phoebe didn't knock the hair out of her eyes as she stalked from the room, but she slammed the front door really hard into the door jam. She would have broken it if she could have. As she hit the elevator button, she could hear her mom saying something, and then she could also hear Ms. White murmur, "Let her go."

Chapter 4

Phoebe stood next to one of the massive concrete pillars holding up the building from the garage floor and stared at the spots on the ceiling above the rusting air conditioner unit and tried not to count the drips. Lots of drips were cascading from it and she sort of wanted to touch the water and see if it was hot or cold or something in between. She wanted to fall like a drop of water from the cold cement ceiling too.

One of her arms was holding the other one up and she wasn't sure which one was doing the holding.

It's another day and another body has passed
I'm weary of it all, won't stop, can't turn away
It's another day; Another was set free
I'm weary of it all, besieged, misaligned,
Pieces are broken, pieces of me.

With a sigh, she shifted her weight and leaned against the cold concrete. The corrugated wheel on her Zippo pressed into her thumb as she flicked it, once, then twice, and then she was inhaling. She shut her eyes and for a moment it was all still inside.

The smoke swirled around her and she held it deep in until she felt the nicotine; then she felt nothing.

> *If then, that she was numb,*
> *If then the space was parted and fell*
> *Back in against a man, a prison cell,*
> *winding, dripping, dark catacomb.*

She repeated the words a few times in her head. *Numb, cell, fell, dark catacomb.* It would become the line in a poem if she could ever remember to carry a pen with her.

CLANG. Phoebe startled and then cringed. A man. Heavyset. Short-sleeve blue workman's shirt. *Coming toward. Coming toward me. He could just be working on the HVAC system.* She checked his hands and his pockets. He was carrying a wrench in one hand. *He could hit me with it. No.* She was ready. Without making it obvious, she repositioned her legs so that they were spread about eighteen inches apart and tightened her quads so that when, no, if she needed to spring forward, she'd be ready. She let her arms drop to her sides and glared over in his direction. She contemplated his weak points, and got *ready to crack his fucking head open.*

He disappeared for a moment, his shadow reappearing from behind a dark blue Ford Explorer a split-second before the tips of his scuffed, brown work boots followed, and she caught a reflection of the mousse in his hair in the side window of the SUV. And just when she was sure he was coming for her, he pivoted and swung around toward the door leading to the electric room.

CLANG. The door slammed shut behind him. Phoebe felt the tension grip her even tighter for a moment, and then she shook her head twice and tried to relax her muscles. *Smoke. Smoke will help some.* She let her eyes drift shut but *then he was grabbing her from behind and she was counting the dust particles as his belt clicked and then—*

CLANG. The engine room door slammed again. The HVAC man was now carrying a toolbox in one hand and a clipboard in the other. And that sick bastard Parkings was in jail. *I'm safe now. I'm safe. It's all right. I'm safe and it's safe and I will be okay.* Phoebe took another drag of her cigarette, and then flicked it toward the trashcan. That probably sucked but she didn't really care. At this rate humanity was going to blow the damn earth up in a another decade or two and damned if a cigarette butt or two was gonna make a fucking difference.

Phoebe clicked her Zippo again and tried not to count that this was her ninth cigarette of the day. *Too much time left to worry about having too little*; too *little worth seeing to worry about this body passing on before its time.* One body just passed, and now another body's been set free; and the pain of it was her prison.

She saw the flashing lights reflected off the far gray *almost black in the shadows* wall of the garage ramp, and then she was shivering a little because of the crashing almost thrashing echo of the tow truck. It was so loud, its metal shaking and scraping, its reverse beeping mechanism then screeching. She was out of control. She had to calm the fuck down. She inhaled another harsh draft of her cigarette and watched the full-size tow truck drive down the ramp backwards. If it went too fast, would it smash into her peppermint sled? Phoebe couldn't contain the start of a smirk. Zander wasn't around, so she could go ahead and call it that.

It didn't take long for the tow truck driver to get things sorted with the Bronco. Phoebe studiously avoided eye contact under the guise of studying the orange tip of her Marlboro Red not Marlboro light *because lights are for wankers* cigarette, and yet out of the corner of her eye, she observed everything he did. That close observation, that studying of what someone else was doing without them knowing it was one of the many things she'd learned from Anne. Phoebe winced. *Whiskey for your men; beer for your horses.* Her eyes were starting to burn. *It hurt too damn much. Why did the people you love with every fucking piece of your soul have to go?* Phoebe gritted her teeth and shut her jaw. She couldn't be crying in the garage parking lot of Thompson, White & Hansen.

Between the rattling of the chains and the clicking and whirring of the HVAC system, Phoebe didn't hear her mother until Helen cleared her throat and made an exaggerated tapping sound with her ridiculous black heels on the cement. Phoebe let one of her shoulders drop so that she could confirm it was her mom, but

she knew her mom's footsteps, and the sound of heels on cement
had the odd effect of calming her down.

> *Mom's even making sure I hear her and won't be scared,*
> *which is too damn sweet of her, but I wish—fuck it. I wish it*
> *wasn't necessary. I wish I could calm the hell down and*
> *stop chasing shadows when it's not even dark out.*

With a naughty glimmer in her eye Phoebe flicked her
cigarette so that it landed a few feet in front of Helen. Without
missing or altering her stride, Helen brought the front of her shoe
straight down on the butt, and with a roll of her eye, and a raising
of one eyebrow, Helen managed to communicate undying love and
annoyance and disapproval with nary a word spoken.

"Mom?" Arms still akimbo, Phoebe twisted around and
nodded at the tow truck, which was now edging up the ramp.

"Need a ride to derby tomorrow?" Helen spoke in her
clipped, New England accent, and Phoebe wanted to close her eyes
and just listen to her mom talk for an hour or two. Her mom's
voice may have scared most people but it felt like home to Phoebe.

Phoebe nodded. "Yep, probably, if you don't mind."
Phoebe suddenly dropped her arms to her sides and then shifted, as
if skating toward Helen. Then she ducked her shoulder and glided
in fast, and just shy of colliding, pulled up and issued just the
gentlest of taps to her mom.

Helen chuckled and wrapped an arm around her daughter.
"I suppose I could bring some work with me while you skate."

CLANG.

Phoebe froze, all muscles stiffening, and she knew her
mom felt it, because she pulled Phoebe in a little closer, until
Phoebe could relax her muscles a little.

Phoebe rested her head against her mother's well-coiffed
auburn hair for an extra beat, no longer feeling like a cocky
menace to Twenty First Century civilization. She needed to rest
her frightened mind for just a little while. It wasn't the world that
was too much with her, as Wordsworth once wrote. It was her own
fucked-up brain that turned a simple clang into a cascading
massive monster coming for her and she was tired. So tired of it.

Chapter 5

Jim McMahon shrugged and set down the old gray rag on the workbench. Right, so if I understand what I read this morning in Jeremiah, *before I formed you in the womb I knew you.* So before Mom bore me, He intended that I'd be what—that I'd be a car and truck mechanic? Or should I have been reading this bit:

> *Before you were born I set you apart; I appointed you as a prophet to the nations.*

Nope, not a prophet, but maybe something more than what he was, right now. A what? A poet-mechanic? Jim felt a smile tugging at the sides of his mouth and tried to remember not to reach up to scratch an itch with his greasy-crusted fingertips. It might take all day to get the grease off his jaw. Not that anyone would be able to tell, because he'd stopped shaving every day since he'd left the Army.

Jim lifted a drill, and let his chiseled, much chipped fingers wrap around it.

> *God's going to measure me not according to what I do, but according to whether I fulfilled His purpose for me.*

So what was his purpose? His mom and his sisters told him this was just a stopping point for him. Ronny called it his way station. But Ronny also signed the checks and they weren't for a bad amount; after all, fixing old vehicles kept his hands busy and his mind off the past. He didn't want to think about the war and he didn't have anyone he could talk about it with even if he did want to think about it. He had old friends from high school, and a few from college, but if they hadn't been over there, in the dusty mountains of Afghanistan or the sands of the Iraq he couldn't talk about it with them. Not without wanting to shoot holes in walls.

At least shooting holes in walls was better than shooting heads. When the lights went off and left only shadows flickering on the walls, Jim could see Christopher. Sometimes he was laughing; more often he was trying so hard not to laugh. But most often, what Jim saw in the shadows was Christopher with pieces of his head scattered beside the latrine, with not even a note to remember him by.

> *I don't want to think about him like that. So I'm going to grip this wrench and finish this job and get out of here before the sun goes down and the shadows start climbing the walls of Ronnie's garage.*

Jim let his hand rest on his lower back again. That was another casualty of Afghanistan, a reminder that kept on giving. But it was easier to live with than the shadows on the wall.

"JJ?" Ronnie's deep Southern drawl dripped into Jim John's head like a smooth finger of bourbon. Jim winced and shook his head with an inner groan. One year four months twenty-three days and he could still smell it rich and harsh in the back of his throat. But he was a better man without it. *Yeah I am.* He straightened up, but not too fast, because even a sneeze or a cough could jack him up, make it even harder to sleep at night.

Jim's eyes shifted down, in the direction of his nametag, which clear as day gave his Christian name: Jim John, *friends call me Jim*. Ronnie didn't mean anything by it, but JJ was a Brooklyn boy, a guy with slicked-back, greasy hair and a toothpick hanging out of a loosely-flapping lip. JJ's hair was the color of oil and he'd sooner hang out at the corner of what they used to call the five and dime than grab a wrench and twist a rusted, busted bolt with it. But he wouldn't go saying anything like that. He was many things, but never rude.

Ronnie caught none of that. He was a mess. There was forty pounds too much of Ronnie. He walk-swaggered around the shop with a dun-lap to match the sets of tires mounted on the side wall. Jim thought of a puppy with huge feet and shook his head. Ronnie had a complete unawareness of the size of his own feet even as he was stepping all over the sensibility of his best mechanic, because that's what Jim, *not JJ*, was. It rankled at him just a bit, but so had Christopher, before he'd gone and blown—

Jim shook his head. *Enough. Enough of that.* One bad thought took hold like a puff from a kid blowing a dandelion, careless, carefree, and that almost invisible puff would lay down all these seeds all over the neighbors' yards, until the whole street was choking from the same weed. That was what bad thoughts about the war were like. Dandelion seeds that landed then scraped then scraped away at parts of Jim's brain, until the entire working CPU was filled with more and more bad thoughts. Once it got like that, he'd wanna drink so bad his hands would shake. But he was a better man than that; and that wasn't an option. *Not again. No.* So no thoughts of Christopher's dying.

"Yes?" *When in doubt what to say, keep it simple*, his mom used to say when she was bustling about the big, yellow kitchen.

Ronnie leaned over with a groan and picked up a half-drunk Big Gulp. He was always leaving half-drunk Big Gulps all over the shop, and Jim studiously refused to touch them, because grown men didn't clean up each other's messes, not unless they had good reason to. Sloth and bad habits didn't count as good reason.

Ronnie rearranged his loose fitting blue uniform shirt, which had pilled up around his mid-section, and heaved the red cardboard cylinder toward a trashcan a few feet away, but it smacked against the edge and tumbled out of the metal bin. The top came undone, and some of the medium brown liquid squirted out, puddling up on the floor. It took all of Jim's self-control not to chuckle as Ronnie groaned, grabbed one of the ubiquitous gray shop rags, and leaned back over to clean up his spill.

Of course Ronnie's butt crack showed. *That's what you get when you rush something,* grimaced Jim.

"So, where were we?" Ronnie wiped his hands on the shop rag and looked around, as if trying to figure out where it went.

Jim put his hand out. "Here. I'll toss it into the pile of 'em and sort it out later. What were you going to ask?"

"Can you stay late tonight? Just got a call from my lawyer's office."

"Lawyer?"

"Well, they're not actually my lawyers, too expensive, but one of the partners there brings her car in here and she always answers my questions, so I kinda think of her as my lawyer."

Jim nodded.

Ronnie waved his hand and issued a quick shake of his head. "Anyway, she just called. She needs someone to look at her partner's kid's old Bronco. It's being towed over here and I gotta get off in time for practice." Ronnie coached his son's football team and never left the garage any later than 4:45 p.m. on Thursdays.

Jim's eye ticked, which was the first sign that something wasn't sitting right with him. He didn't mind staying late most nights, but he had a paper due in the morning and he was somewhere between ten minutes and ten hours from completing it. He sighed and ran his hand through his hair. Ronny was a good dad. A *nine to five dad* who didn't miss games and practices. So if there ever was a reason to cover another man, this was a good enough one.

Jim made brief eye contact with his boss, long enough to nod and turn the eye twitch into a pronounced almost-wink, the way Clint Eastwood always did it in his Dirty Harry movies when he was agreeing or assenting, in that laconic, hard bitten way of his, with someone who was asking him to do something that he was going to do it. He might not be happy with it, but he was too much of a man to complain about it. He would help because it was the right thing to do, not because he was too scared to say no. After all, Jim was one of the best mechanics around. He didn't need to do anyone any favors to prove it.

"I will. All right." Jim paused. "But why is the lawyer's kid or whatever coming here? I'm not going to be able to get under the hood until tomorrow afternoon at the earlier. I gotta get this old Chevy limping on out onto the road again." Jim chuckled. "And no doubt Parker will drive it down some ravine and knock the bearings loose all over again, just because—"

"—He can," Ronnie finished, with a loud belly laugh. "No, no, seems she left something in the trunk that she needs tonight. Something like that."

Jim tried to keep his shoulders from slumping and had no idea what that was about. With a grunt, he nodded and focused on the work at hand. One bolt, one turn, one minute, one day, at a time—*damn clichés are clichés for a reason*, he thought.

Chapter 6

The office door slammed open again and Cassandra heard a gasp from Janice, which was so unlike the unflappable iron-ax. Cassandra was pretty sure she knew who it was, and it made her heart beat a little faster. Catherine had graduated from Oregon in December, and now she was living down in Quantico, near the Academy. Training to be a special agent. It was as unlikely as it was beautiful.

Cass set her file folder down and almost collided with this tall woman who was also her daughter. *My daughter, my grown-up, incredibly gorgeous, and righteous when indignant, yet still unflappable and cheerful 23-year old daughter.* Cat had grown at least three inches these last few years, and it might just have been the worst thing that could have happened to her running career, and yet Cat had still won two NCAA Cross-country titles. An amazing accomplishment for a Virginian, but that's not the only reason Cass was so proud of her.

Cat's freshman year had been undistinguished. She'd barely clung to a 2.5, but then she'd been friends with this kid, a junior, who was interviewing with the FBI. At about the same time, something tragic had happened to Cat's best friend. A date rape, a football player, some photos taken on an iPhone, and then the girl had gone to the campus authorities, who'd said that it was a case of his word against hers; and the local police had said the same thing.

Oldest story there was, and of course Cass had known it, had lived it as a student and later as a young lawyer, but all this had been new to Cat. And Cat? She'd responded in an unexpected but really glorious way. She'd gotten serious about changing the system. She'd started reading books by this modern prophet, and then she'd started actually reading all the books her teachers assigned, and then reading more books, and then she'd changed her major to political science with a theology minor.

Cassandra chuckled and shook her head. She had no idea where the theology came from, but it suited her daughter. Cat started writing gospels on her arms in Sharpies, or having her roommates pen verses on her back shoulders, "Just so they know why they're running in my dust, Mom," Cat had laughed when Cass first asked her about it.

"So you're getting to be like that QB from Florida?" Zander said, twirling a football in his hands.

"QB? No, they're a bunch of fucking assholes," Cat had snapped, and it had caused a kerfuffle, even made Zander, who had been eight during all this, cry. He never asked Cat to get him football autographs again, or even mentioned RG3 to her. Football was off-limits around Cat from there on after.

But politics, God, running, and locking the rapists and abuser bastards up? Cat was always more than happy to talk about that, and always with a smile and a light in her eyes. There always had been something special about her daughter, but Cass would have never pegged her for an FBI Agent, or a religious-political activist. Somehow Cat pulled all this off without ever seeming embittered or shrill, and maybe that's why Cass had trouble figuring out how to describe the woman her eldest child had become.

No matter.

Cass leaned into one of Cat's athletic but warm hugs. Her daughter smelled so good. Like she'd been outdoors and out in the fresh air most the day, hopefully handing it to the men she was training with. Cat could out run any of them by at least 15 seconds in the standard 1.5 mile run, and she usually challenged the top guys in the 300-meter sprint; same thing went for situps. But pushups were an issue and so was Hogan's Alley.

It wasn't like she was gonna fail PFT. She was one of the fittest ones there. But she couldn't get pushed around or intimidated or God forbid mocked when making arrests during the training sessions at Hogan's Alley. All the bulking up and competing on upper strength had been taking all Cat had, and a little more. In fact, that's one of the things Cass had been meaning to talk to Cat about, but she sort of wished Phoebe had been in the office.

"Cat!" Zander body-slammed his sister just as Cass was letting go, and she damn near almost fell over.

"Zander, you gotta stop doin' that," Cass said. "You're getting too big." She raised an eyebrow and took her son in with just a hint of annoyance. He was going to be at least as tall as Frank, maybe an inch or two taller. And just a couple years ago . . . Cass caught hold of her thoughts before she got to thinking how fast he was growing up.

"Hey Mom, you gonna feed me something?" Cat put an arm around Zander's shoulder and then laughed as Cass's shoulder moved into a shrug. "Just joking Mom. I'll ask Dad when I see him—he's home right?"

Frank White was still an attorney with a big firm in DC, and he traveled at least a week out of each month.

"Yep, he's home, and I'm sure he'll feed us especially if you ask him," Cass said. Frank did most of the cooking, usually with Zander acting as his not so helpful wingman.

"Good. And I got your hint about bulking up with the roller derby girls, thanks a lot Mom, maybe I'll drop in and check out their gym, sounds hardcore."

Cass nodded. She hadn't thought she'd said a word to Cat about Phoebe and Jamie. Must have been Zander, who never could keep his mouth shut about anything. But it was okay. Cat didn't seem annoyed.

"Oh sweet," Zander said, "I know how to get there and Pheebes always says I can't work out with her but I can work out with you can't I Cat?"

"Work out with me? Oh hell no, no way Zander, not the kind of stuff I have gotta be doing."

"Then will you take me to the range?"

"No." Cat's voice had gotten steely in a way Cass wasn't used to, and she was trying to figure out just what it all meant, or who her daughter was becoming, but it was late, and she had a trial to prep for, and there was nothing wrong with her daughter's steely tone. It was just new. Maybe that's the kind of seriousness Cat had always had in her; maybe it had just taken time for Cat to grow into the woman she was . . . becoming, or if not becoming, already was.

"Gun range, huh?" Cass smiled at Cat. "I reckon you have to put some serious time in to qualify?"

Zander had a gleam in his eye that Cass was trying to ignore.

"Actually, the shooting comes pretty natural to me, but it's all about making it totally rote so that when you find yourself in a situation, you fall back on your training, you know what I mean?"

Cass nodded, and turned to grab her briefcase. As soon as Cass shoved a few file folders into her larger legal briefcase, which looked more like a suitcase, Cat leaned over and hefted it on her shoulder, not pausing to ask if Cass wanted help. It was one of those wonderful moments that was also a little sad too—when a mother finds that her children will carry the heavy bags.

With Zander circling them both, Cass said, "Sort of like running, I mean, you run the miles, the killer long long miles just so you can fall back on all that training when you're racing and you're up against a couple of runners who seem like they are gonna take every last ounce out of you, right?"

Cat smiled and her smile lit up the hallway. "Yes, Mom, that's just how it is," she said.

Chapter 7

"Hey, God, you there?" Jamie was alone now, pacing up and down the kitchen floor, the wood boards underneath creaking every fifth step or so, kind of reassuring when her head wasn't killing her, and for once, it wasn't.

"Yes, Jamie."

She talked to him all the time. It was hard to explain, not really believable really, so she didn't talk about it with anyone. Her Aunt A had known, and maybe that's because she could hear Him too. Not that Anne talked much about it, but that was probably because her mission was at least sort of getting done. Phoebe was safe and the Bryson House was thriving. Souls were getting the help they needed.

"Not sure I'm getting through to her, you know?"

"She's fine. Something's about to happen. Things will change now."

Jamie bent over and reached out for her coffee cup. It was almost ten PM and pretty soon, she'd be making her rounds around the stables. Now that Anne was gone and Phoebe wasn't riding, some of the joy had gone out of it, but she was a shepherd of sorts and she had a job to do.

"You sure you should be drinking all that caffeine?"

Jamie thought about it. Her headaches weren't getting worse, not exactly. Holding stable. Stables. Time to get to the horses.

"Jamie?"

"Oh, right, caffeine? Course I need it," she said. And she thought about all the cups she'd drank of it lately. Since Anne had gone Home, she couldn't sleep much. It was too quiet, so she'd been up until all hours more nights than not. It wasn't that she couldn't bear to be alone; and it wasn't like she couldn't talk to Anne anytime she needed to. She visited with Anne sometimes, floating on up to talk to the woman who raised her after her mom had passed on. *Damnit. No.* It wasn't the same, talking to souls in heaven when you were still on earth. She was missing her.

"I know, Jamie. I know it's quiet."

Jamie waited for the coffee grinder to finish whirring until she replied in a hoarse whisper, "Yeah." Her voice caught a little, so she closed her eyes and let the images caress her. Anne. Anne on a horse; sitting strong and steady; then leaping through the air, in control from liftoff to landing. Anne. Anne folding the newspaper a little too sharply and mock-glaring at Mimi up at the Bryson House. "Shush," Anne cracked, and waiting for Mimi to launch into one of her ribald ripostes. *Anne. She missed Anne.*

Jamie sighed. "So, what do you mean things are gonna change? With Phoebe? She okay? Or is she about to lose her shit again and bust a head, get herself in the middle of something I gotta get her out of?" Jamie's main objective, as far as she knew, was to ensure the safety of Phoebe Thompson. She wasn't sure if there was much else to her mission, but maybe there didn't need to be, for Phoebe was as certain to get into trouble as a spark was to fly upwards.

"Ah, well, trouble, always, yes, but other things are coming down the avenue for her."

"Wait, now what kind of trouble?"

"Don't worry, Jamie."

Jamie smiled. God always said that to her, and it usually came right after He told her something that was worth worrying about. Like 9/11, which she had known about, well, sort of, just enough to change an appointment with her neurologist who had an office close to the White House . . . this whole not worry thing was ridiculous; shoot, why tell her if not to get her to worry?

"No, don't worry. Just pay attention, make sure she doesn't get hurt, not now, because she's about to meet someone."

"What?"

"Yes," God said. "Not just anyone. The one who bears her mark."

A shiver ran down Jamie's arms. "Phoebe's gonna meet her soulmate?"

"Make sure she doesn't go off and kill that bastard, okay?"

"What bastard?"

God put an image of one of the perps from Phoebe's trial in Jamie's mind. Jamie sighed, and crossed her arms over her chest. *Damnit. So that's why Phoebe was so angry today.*

"Yes."

"I don't blame her for being angry, you know? I'm angry too."

"He's not going to get away with it, not when he comes back Home he's not," God said.

Jamie nodded. She knew there was justice in heaven, and someday, when it was right, she would explain all this to Phoebe. Just not . . . yet.

"Just keep her focused on getting whole, okay? Not breaking stuff, because it's almost time for her to get her mission."

"Her mission?"

"Yes," God said. "And speaking of missions, don't you need to go walk the grounds?"

Then God was gone, leaving Jamie alone to try and figure out how to keep Phoebe around long enough to . . . "Receive what mission?" Jamie said aloud.

God didn't answer.

Chapter 8

Phoebe took a deep breath, trying to tune out her mom's turn signal as it click-click-clicked in the background submachine gun style. She could last a five-minute car ride without snapping at her mom. Maybe. To get her mind off it, she swung her neck around and checked the backseat, as if taking inventory of something, but she wasn't really seeing the tight stitches on leather seats of the Range Rover. Her eyes and then her mind got stuck on the light waves from the red stoplight that shimmered and reflected against the wet rear windows. There was a verse or two in the red photoelectric waves, the merest fraction of a poem, *if only the fucking turn signal would . . .*

"—Can you turn that thing off?" It came out much more terse than she'd meant. *Story of my life.* Helen raised one eyebrow but didn't remark. Or turn off the fucking blinker. Phoebe crossed her arms.

If Anne were the driver, she'd get one of those half-smiles of hers and she'd manage to contain her laughter while quietly assenting, "Yes'm," taking her damn time all the while to make the clicking stop, and by the time she did, I'd be laughing and then she'd be laughing too.

Phoebe felt it rising inside her, this thing she couldn't describe to anyone else because it was too dark and ugly for the spoken word, choking, stifling—

Rage.

Her old mate, lodged so long inside her head. She gritted her teeth and hoped her mom couldn't hear her teeth grinding, because when she got mad, she wanted to cut. *Herself.* And she wasn't going to do that anymore. But she was shameful and sick inside, all angry about a turn signal, and about a woman she missed, who left too soon, *oh why, damnit why, why God did she have to leave me now?*

Phoebe had committed Anne's note from her deathbed to memory.

> *"You don't need to say goodbye, dear friend. Just know, know dear child, know that light inside you will never go dim. Protect your light. Let nothing and no one dim it, not even for a moment. Know that no one can ever touch that beautiful place deep inside you, no matter what part of you they ravaged, no matter what they made your body do, no matter what your body did and had done unto it. Please know, dear Phoebe, that I'll be with you always, right there, right there where you feel your heart beating and your pain rising, and when it rises, when that pain and anger and urge to hurt yourself rises, dear child, let it shine. Let your light shine.*
>
> *"Oh and child? Watch out for horseshit. It's everywhere.*
>
> *All my love, and with you forever,*
>
> *Anne.*

Phoebe felt a warm touch on her arm and only startled a little when she looked up. *It's mom and I am safe.*

"You okay?" Helen's accent had softened the tiniest bit over the last few years, but it had never seemed harsh to Phoebe, not even when she'd been a kid and Helen had been barking out orders, more ship captain than mother. Phoebe shook her head.

"I know I don't always say the right thing. And I wish I knew what to say right now."

Phoebe glanced at her mom. Helen Thompson had never been the type to second-guess her delivery, right up until the moment when the golf club had ripped more than her husband's skull apart.

Phoebe really didn't want to think about that today. It was funny. She could be sitting in a car minding her own business, and then one thought would touch the very edge of another, or a frame from a video would intrude on another image, leaking; leaking, as if radioactive isotopes, harmless image mixing with an invisible measure of evil more pure than Colorado mountain water. And she'd be gone, right on back there, in bed with him, but before she got there, she could throw up this shield, she could, and she would. She would.

With a flipping, semi-circular motion of her left hand, Phoebe shut it down. *Mechanism engaged.* She focused on Helen's ship captain's voice, which was saying something else, if only Phoebe could stop listening to ghosts and entertaining phantoms.

"So after we grab your journal, we'll swing past Freshfields, grab something for dinner—"

"—You're going to cook something?"

"Yes. I was going to grill some tuna or some salmon. Toss up a romaine salad, Pheebes, and we'll be golden."

Phoebe gave a satisfied grunt and tried not to smile. Ever since Helen had been working with Cassandra White, she'd started peppering her speech with words like "golden" and "reckon." *Not that she reckoned she minded.*

Her mom's Bluetooth rang, and Helen answered on the second ring.

"Hey Brian." Helen paused. "Yeah. Just got back to DC. My secretary is faxing out a proposed Order and we should be able to wrap things up, perhaps next week."

Phoebe tapped her fingers and converted lawyer-talk almost as if it were second nature. Her mom's case was settling and this must be opposing counsel, calling to talk terms. And the order, once signed by both parties, would have to go to the judge.

"—In person? Sure, that would be fine. Yeah, we could make it lunch . . . maybe Friday? Okay. Yep. Call me when you get the order." Helen glanced over at Phoebe when she hung up. "Looks like the AirCorp case is settling."

"Rocket docket?"

"Yep."

Phoebe chuckled. "And that was opposing counsel? Brian Williams from Hunton and Clark?"

"The one and only."

"He's a hardass."

"Hmm." Helen almost smiled. "I think he's top-notch, actually."

"Damn, Mom. I thought he was taking you to the cleaner's on this case."

"He negotiated a good deal for his client. And mine is ready to focus on the business—"

"—Will you give me a ride into school tomorrow? I've got Lit 515 at 9 a.m. Can you get me over there too, Mom?"

Helen finally turned the fucking blinker off, and after glancing in her rear view mirror, cleared her throat. She didn't say anything about how rude Phoebe was being, which made Phoebe almost feel bad. It must have been painfully obvious how sad she was. "Check on the ride in during the morning. I'm happy to have you with me, Pheebes. Are you absolutely sure you don't want to swing by the Bryson House and get Anne's old pickup truck? I know it's hard for you, but I have a client coming in at three."

Phoebe felt it gripping back up inside her and instead of just saying, *I hurt Mom,* she did much worse. "Hard? Hard?" She spluttered. "What the hell, Mom? What do you know about hard?" As soon as it came out of her mouth, she knew how absurd she sounded, and gave a quiet mental thank you to her mother's "cold containment," which was how she thought of her mom's personality. Helen was pretty much unflappable, and as frustrating as that was to most people she came in contact with, it always had a calming effect on her daughter. Phoebe could bluster and bust about, as Anne used to call it, and Helen would ignore all but the most extreme or downright rude manifestations of it. And even then, when Phoebe went too far, Helen would freeze her with "the look," which could freeze anyone.

Phoebe checked Helen's reaction out of the corner of her eye. One Mississippi. Two Mississippi's. *Damn I hate Mississippi's.* Three—"

"—So I guess now would not be the right time to talk about your legal case?" Helen's eyebrow rose as she ended her sentence, which ended not so much on a high note, but on a droll low tone.

"Aw, wha—, aw—damnit!" Phoebe, despite all efforts to remain angry, couldn't hold back laughter.

The side of Helen's mouth, rose, and for a moment, her face looked wrinkle-free and youthful again. *She looks kind of pretty when she smiles.* Phoebe wanted to hold, hold tight to the moment, just as tight as her mom held to the smile. And then the 19-inch tires on the Land Rover almost laid waste to the fresh-painted white curb that dipped a few inches too late at the ramp to get into Ronnie's gas station.

"Easy there!"

Helen swung the wheel to the left and leaned toward the window as the tires made a ker-plunk sound, and Phoebe crossed her arms, frowning. "Jeez, Mom, this ain't a sports car. You're going to ruin a perfectly good set of alloy wheels driving like that."

"Hmm."

Phoebe hated when her mom did that. It made her wanna laugh, sort of, but seriously, *what the hell did she need a damn Range Rover for?*

"I could buy a new engine for my truck for the cost of a new set of tires for your Rover," Phoebe persisted as Helen wove between the gas pump closest to the shop floor and came to a stop a good eighteen inches from the raised pavement that abutted the wide garage doors.

"Hmm. Well, I suppose you could. But I'll take care of that for you, okay sweets?" Helen grabbed her purse and made eye contact with Phoebe before she dismounted. Phoebe wasn't sure if she was annoyed or amused. Her mom looked somehow graceful as she hopped out onto the oil smudged concrete . . . and her heels were ridiculous, almost as ridiculous as the Range Rover.

Phoebe tightened her jaw and the tendon clicked twice before she remembered to *stop it stop doing that*. She was both mad and not mad; she was annoyed and yet laughing. She was churning, boiling, and conflicted. *A mess. Certifiable. Still.* She needed to see Cary more often. Like every day at this rate. Tens of thousands of dollars in therapy. She always had worried that Anne thought she was spoiled for it, but she'd never asked her coach, and now it was too late. Click. *Stop it stop doing that.* Phoebe rubbed her jaw, then fell in step behind her mother.

Chapter 9

He flinched.

Hellfire! It's just the side door slamming Jim, and there you go flinching like the bolt's been snapped backwards and the magazine's done been loaded up, locked and loaded and . . . and it's nothing.

He straightened up and smacked his head on the underbody of Parker's old Chevy and was about to reach up and rub it when he saw her, and then he felt like a high school baseball player all over again, hit by a pitch, running to first, and as much as it hurt, he'd be thinking, don't rub it until it don't smart. He didn't usually care what women thought, but there was something so fierce in this one's brown eyes, so warrior-princess like, that it would take an artery spurting to make him pause when her eyes were on him.

She didn't scare him. In fact, something about her looked vaguely familiar, like a smell he couldn't quite place, or a vision reminding him of a place he hadn't seen enough of. She made him want to stand up taller. She made his fingers itch to create verse. And something about her jaw line and spiky brown hair and camouflage cargo pants made him restrain a smile. She looked like she was going to war. And if that's where she was going, well, Jim was going in after her.

He shook his head at himself.

Maybe you need to make her acquaintance first, before, you know, you're writing poems about going into battle after her. That must be her mom right next to her.

They were a strange pair in a way. The mother, in her hair not out of place, threads in perfect alignment corporate costume; daughter, decked out like Linda Hamilton's fictional little sister in T2. And yet daughter belonged to mother and mother to daughter in some inchoate way. Maybe the set of jaw, maybe the steady, fierce glare, maybe the military-stiff posture. *Mother—daughter, for sure.*

The mother took three strides toward him and then directed a nod in his direction.

Jim returned the nod, and then waited.

"Evening. My daughter's truck was towed here, I think?"

"Yes ma'am."

"If it wouldn't be too much trouble, my daughter left something in the trunk, and—"

"—And I need to get it out, now, please," finished the daughter.

Jim started walking before the words could get ordered in his brain. "Yes. Sure. Follow. Yes. Follow me, please." *What? Am I nervous?* He shook his head, trying not to smile, as if at an inside joke. No one made him nervous, at least since Basic. *Remember, son, we McMahons bow to no man.* Jim could almost smell his mom as he thought of her words. She was lilac and honeysuckle, his mom was, and these two? Something different altogether, maybe campfire and burning leaves, and he couldn't get enough of it. *Get a grip man.*

Without checking to see if the mother and daughter were behind him, Jim said, "Cold for March, isn't it?"

He led them outside and the side door clanged shut. This time he didn't flinch.

"Yes."

"Yeah, it's good and cold," the younger one murmured, and then he realized where he knew her from. Maybe.

"Whoa," he whistled in appreciation, as they came beside the old Bronco. "She's something else."

Warrior princess's eyes lit up a little, and she gave, yeah she did, she gave him a smile. Well, maybe a half-smile, or maybe not even half. *Come on man, pull it together*.

She crossed in front of him, inserted her key and twisted the trunk open. An odor of tack and sweat and grease and old vehicle emerged from the trunk. *It was glorious.*

Jim leaned toward the Bronco and put one hand on the top of the tailgate lid. As she removed a duffel bag, something fell out of it, and he reached down and grabbed it before it could roll away. It was a single pair of roller skates, black, and they'd landed wheels down. When he started toward her, to hand her the skates, she leaned in, fast, grasped the skates by their laces, and almost danced backwards, like a scared dog who'd been beaten a few times taking a scrap from a stranger. He didn't know what to say, because he knew in that second why she did that, but anything he said would make it worse; anything, almost anything, except maybe something real gentle.

First he stepped backward a half-step. And then in the same voice he'd always used with the dogs he and his mom and his sisters were taking in, and with eyes not fixed intensely on her, murmured, "There you go."

He couldn't see her expression behind her sunglasses but it seemed like her shoulders relaxed a little.

She shoved the skates inside her burlap bag and with her free hand, she took hold of a black spiral bound notebook. Then she waited for him to step away from the trunk, which he did, before she slammed it shut.

CLUNK.

Before she pivoted and walked away, Jim leaned away from her to give her space and asked, "Are you taking a lit class at Mason? Either you or your doppleganger's in one of my classes."

And then she smiled. It was for sure a smile. And in that split second between her smile and him smiling back, he realized he'd been waiting for her smile. And he'd done stop waiting for any woman to smile back at him. He'd been done with that, but *come on Jim. This is just a smile.*

"Lit 515? Monday nights?" She was shoving the bag under her arm and was gripping the spiral notebook between strong-looking fingers and her palm.

"Yep. One of my last electives before I get my degree."

She glanced at his nametag. "You're Jim John McMahon."

"I am. Nice to meet you."

She grunted, and finally, it seemed reluctantly, she replied, "Phoebe Thompson."

"English major?"

She didn't answer, and with a sinking feeling he realized that he cared. He wanted her to say something. *Well, try again, mate.* By this point, the mother had stalked away and he realized how slowly he and Phoebe Thompson were walking. "You want to teach?"

She shook her head, then shrugged one shoulder. "Don't know. Guess almost all I wanna do is write."

"If it's all you want to do, and all you care about doing, then it's really what you should be doing." Jim could see that hint of a smile toying with the muscles around her jaw line, or maybe he was projecting it. "Or so my mom always said."

"Wise."

"And she's a writer too. She never told me to get a real job that paid well. Just told me to write, and well, and it would all work out."

"She's a writer?" Phoebe Thompson's voice rose at the end of her sentence, and she paused, almost making eye contact.

"Yes."

Phoebe looked off to the west, where the sun was sliding toward the horizon. Then she let her face turn to meet his. "Someone once told me to strive for excellence in whatever I did, and to only choose those pursuits that were worth giving all I had to, and that's what I'm going to do, you know?"

Jim let his eyes take in Phoebe Thompson, who was now a few strides away from her mother.

"Yes. I do. Nice to meet you Phoebe Thompson." He smiled with his eyes only at her mother. "Evening, ma'am."

Phoebe replied over her shoulder, "See you," and he stood a few feet away from their SUV until they drove away, toward the sliding sun.

With a smile in his heart, Jim turned up the volume on the greasy shop radio. *Maybe I've left the country, but the country never left me.* Jim worked steady on Parker's Chevy for another hour, not rushing, because there were some things that got broken when a man rushed. And Jim sung, slow and steady, just like he worked.

Chapter 10

The door to Cary Matterly's office slammed shut and the bell, the one announcing visitors or clients *as if it didn't matter, as if a client really was just a visitor* . . . clanged. Phoebe winced and glanced around her to make sure she was alone in the vestibule.

> *I can't ever leave. If he's in hell, then I can't go there too. But if he's in heaven, then I'm better off in hell. Can't. Won't risk it. No thinking about it, about the blood and the pain and the letting go, not even a little knick to the wrist, because who knows what could happen, but no praying, either. Who would I pray to, anyway?*

She ran her hand through her hair and rested a finger on her dark sunglasses. She'd leave them on so that Cary's client wouldn't see her eyes. She could just nod or maybe pretend she was fixing a thread on her shirt. She saw her mom do that all the time, and no one had figured out yet it was how the high-powered trial attorney bought time when no words came to mind.

Unbidden, a smile tugged at the edges of Phoebe's mouth. Over the past five years she'd seen a lot of her mom in the courtroom. When Phoebe was in high school, Helen would only leave her home when Phoebe had a show to compete in; the rest of the time, Phoebe trailed behind Helen to Chicago, San Francisco, and up and down the east coast, dressed in thousand dollar suits making her look a decade older, and often acting as a de facto legal assistant. Her choice, never Helen's. It wasn't like Phoebe wanted to be like Helen. Phoebe didn't want to be a lawyer. She just wanted to be a part of her mother's life, and Helen could no sooner give up her career than Phoebe could give up . . . Phoebe swallowed. *Riding. No, Phoebe, don't think of that now.*

Her fingers twitching, Phoebe shook her head and pulled her mind back to this scene she'd replayed in her head, over and over again. They were in Richmond, Virginia, before the "rocket docket," and Helen rose from the bench with an authoritative nod at the judge, no extraneous gestures, no excess words, and she commenced talking. And until she finished, no one, sometimes not even counsel for the plaintiff, even when he should have stood up and bellowed, "Objection," interrupted the queen of the courtroom. Helen was spellbinding; almost bewitching, and there was this thing deep inside Phoebe that felt connected to her mother's quest for—what? Phoebe almost smiled, and with Anne's serious voice now entering her head, she almost said aloud, "Excellence, then, is not an act but a habit."

Phoebe shifted her weight so that now she leaned against the wall, caught within the 90-degree valley where she felt safest, and she let her fingers run over the blue and maroon stripes on the walls. If only Anne was still here to quote Aristotle to her. If only Anne wasn't stuck in heaven with one of hell's denizens, dragging, drifting . . .

She heard the bell clanging before she realized a woman of average age, height and weight was walking past her. She tried to look up in time to figure out if she needed to look away first. But the woman was already past her, and the bell was done ringing, before Phoebe could do something to contain herself. Then it was quiet again. Phoebe realized her finger was still tracing the lines on the wall and she dropped her hand to her thigh. Thwack.

God. I'm such a freak. There's no diagnosis for freak, is there? Or freaked out, heaven and hell-obsessed child of . .

.

There was a tight feeling in her throat. Anne always called her "child of light," and now where was Anne? What was heaven like?

Cary's loud-ass bell clanged again and Phoebe used all her energy to control herself. She'd almost jumped out of her shoes, and that was pretty hard, seeing she was wearing combat boots. Her aging therapist emerged from the polished wood office door after the bell finished its metallic ringing. Before Phoebe could push her sunglasses out of the way, because it was pretty rude to wear them inside, Cary smiled in a brisk way and gestured toward her inner office.

Cary Matterly hadn't aged much. When the sunlight hit her forehead straight on, Phoebe could see an extra line or two, but sometimes her 60-year old therapist could still pass for late forties, especially when Phoebe came in at six or seven p.m. She liked the night appointments best, especially the last one of the day, the 7 p.m. appointment, because she didn't have to worry about running into Cary's next client on the way out. Phoebe hated that. She'd be all intense and *into the shit*, and then she'd have to pull it all together before she even reached the elevator.

Phoebe looked around Cary's office and flicked her sunglasses on her head, rubbing her short hair underneath her fingers for a moment, and then she looked her therapist in the eye with a brave gaze. This was the first time she'd seen Cary since Anne passed away and there was something bittersweet about the whole thing. Damned if she could explain what the hell she was feeling, or why, so she just sat there and waited for Cary to start talking.

Still. She wasn't prepared for the first thing Cary brought up. "I am so sorry for your loss, Phoebe. So sorry."

It was too late to look away. To find a place to store her tears, so she didn't even try. She just let them fall.

Cary reached over and put a hand on Phoebe's wrist, and Phoebe didn't move her hand back or flinch. Before she could think what she should or shouldn't do, she reached out with her other hand and with it, she grasped Cary's hand for a moment. And then Cary squeezed again and gently let go and Phoebe brushed away her tears.

Cary reached over and grabbed hold on her notepad and tapped her fingers on the brown leather folio while she waited on Phoebe. There was something so familiar about Cary, so comfortable, and yet so foreign. She was about as different from her mom as a woman could be, and the entirety of that difference was captured in the Birkenstocks.

The first time I met her, I said some sniping remark about the color of her skirt, or was it the pattern on it? It doesn't matter, not really, except now I like her weird patterns. I even like her funky shoes. They're ridiculous but so are mom's dress shoes. And Ms. White's boots. It's all ridiculous. I guess my boots are ridiculous too.

She took a deep breath and tried to stop thinking about her history with Cary. *Shhh. Enough.* Phoebe's mind was racing again. It was time to slow that shit down.

"So." Phoebe paused and took a deep breath. "So," Phoebe repeated, aware of how much higher her voice sounded than Cary's; then she came to a complete stop. She had no idea where to begin.

"How's your week been?"

With a groan, Phoebe lifted one hand, waved it, and then dropped it back to the arm of the sofa.

"That bad?"

Phoebe inspected Cary's office as she contemplated what to say. She liked the esoteric black and white photographs of women that decorated her therapist's walls. One time, she'd asked Cary who all the women were, and Cary's eyes had lit up when she replied, "Those are the people that carved a path through the darkness, and made my career possible." Sometimes, when Phoebe glimpsed one of the women in the photographs, she wanted to write an ode to them, but today, she wanted to take a hammer to them, almost as an act of self-immolation. She didn't resent them. She loved them, or at least she loved them when she loved herself. But today, today was the asshole's release day, and Anne was dead, stuck somewhere, safe, or not safe, with her father, because a woman was never really safe when her father was prowling, dead or alive.

No woman was safe, not really, not ever, and no matter how many woman now obscured by the dust-creating hand of time yelled or carried on about it, that was the truth, and it sucked. *It all sucked.*

Phoebe took a deep breath. "I'm having rage issues." She tried to laugh, but it sounded phony; like she was covering something. Came out closer to a sob. "That man, the one who—" Phoebe waited for the stammering to end. She stammered when she got really angry. "—was in on it with Dad, he's . . ."

Cary nodded as Phoebe looked around and then back at Cary. "He gets released today. And I wanna just break something. Me. Him. Something. I don't, can't live in the same world he's in. It's just so sick. And everything I read, everywhere I look, TV, Facebook, billboards, it's just more, more of the same, same— same shit! I mean, really! Last night, I saw a picture of a woman left, all beaten-up, at the foot of a staircase. You know what the caption said?"

Cary shook her head.

"'Next time, don't get pregnant.' Can you believe that shit? Really. Can you believe it? I am just so sick of it. And then, and then, and then I went and reported it on Facebook. I reported the page that shared that photo—'Fuck all Sluts,' really, that was the name of the page. So I report 'em, and you know what they say? 'Thanks for your recent report of a potential violation on Facebook. After reviewing your report, we were not able to confirm that the specific page you reported violates Facebook's Statement of Rights and Responsibilities.' Can you believe that? And you know what else? It was right next to one of those Dove commercials, the ones about how all women have great bodies, accept yourself, whatever." Phoebe paused and sucked in a breath, waving her hand, impatient with breathing. "So I went and looked up a few groups like the one, like the one . . ." She froze and gazed at Cary, who was taking notes without looking at her notepad again.

"You're thinking of your dad's group? And the man that's getting released?"

"Fucker's out. Today. And you know what I wanna do? I wanna hunt the fucker down. Like he hunted me. Staring at me, fantasizing, fucking me in his head. I wanna take a piece of hell to him." Phoebe leaned forward, chin resting on hand, and looked straight through Cary's eyes. "Know what I mean?"

Cary didn't answer right away. She put her notepad down and held Phoebe's burning gaze, not shrinking, not leaning back.

Phoebe felt the pulse in her neck booming. *Blood. Lots of blood. It could just pour out, pour through me, washing away my pain, my shame. Shhhhh. No.*

"It makes sense that you're angry. Anyone would be angry, Phoebe."

"Really?"

Cary nodded and Phoebe took a deep breath, a painful one, and looked down to see her knuckles white and pressing against her skin. She closed her eyes, and the backs of her eyelids felt hot, burning hot, and all she could see was a barn, with horses in it, and that, oh that was also something she needed to forget. She breathed in again, and opened her eyes as she exhaled the picture, the smell, the sound of horses, and she whispered, real soft, "I miss her. I feel like I let her down. With the riding. And now all I can think of is why I stopped, and I think of him, and her, above me, watching, and is she, is she crying too?"

Cary's eyes filled with tears, and she sat there, not talking, and not taking notes, and listened to Phoebe ask, over and over again, "Are there tears in heaven?"

•••

Phoebe leaned back on the hood of her mom's Range Rover, cigarette hanging out of the corner of her mouth as she flipped through the spiral notebook, passing verse after verse of her poetry. The one thing no one could take away. And then she began.

Nowhere. Not here.
Everywhere,
Faded barn doors,

paint peeling
Off fencepost,
compost wafting, raised, raising.
Has she risen?

Her mouth was burning. Phoebe sighed, and flicked away the butt. It fell, and ashes scattered, orange, then into black.

Him.
His ashes not scattered. But spread, spreading always,
Inside me.
Him, always, inside
Above.
Around.
Him. A neigh.
A whip
of a tail
on a stall.
Him too.
Other.
He's gone,
and he's locked
inside
a jar,
But so am I,
locked,
convicted by his fluid.

She looked around the parking garage she was hiding out in. The concrete was as different from a field as the hard ground was from a soft featherbed. She needed that demarcation as a divider from the life she once lived, and the world she now inhabited. The hay, the damsel flies, the chirp of cicadas and the flight of the blue heron overhead, it all brought him back, and it took her back to the barn, where she was safe, until one afternoon she wasn't.

Phoebe turned the page she'd been writing on. Before she could get a word on paper, a bird started screaming:

Procedure, procedure, procedure.
Phoebe chuckled.

Of course he's following me here. He screams at me every morning. His call pierces me every single time I'm on my way to try, to try to ride again. Procedure, procedure, procedure. The words of a world of lawlessness hidden within the workings of a legal system. Procedure, procedure, procedure.

She'd taken to calling this screeching winged terror "the lawbird," and it followed her even into the world of steel and concrete.

It figured. Just when I was going to write about him. Fucker's taunting me. The lawbird, singing the sad song of the sick. Singing the jailbird's tune.

Parkings. It seemed pointless all of a sudden. Verse. Poems. What would that do? She shivered. How soon would he get out? How fucking soon?

Phoebe shook her head and slammed her notebook shut. Time to bust some fucking heads. Time to skate.

Chapter 11

Phoebe Thompson flung a duffel bag over her shoulder and jumped out of her mom's Land Rover. She kicked the door shut with her left foot. Something tugged at Phoebe when she leaned back into the lowered window to say goodbye. Her mom had already reached for her cell phone, but then she stopped, and got a funny look on her face. Well, not funny. Concerned.

"You're sure you got a ride?"

"Yeah, it's no problem. Jamie can give me a ride back. It's on her way home."

Helen took her sunglasses off and fixed her eyes on her daughter until it was all Phoebe could do not to fidget. Helen would have stuck around for practice. She wouldn't complain about bringing work with her or having to type all scrunched up on her laptop. Phoebe didn't feel abandoned, not anymore. And Helen Thompson had never, would never, could never, make Phoebe feel crowded. So it wasn't that.

> *Hell. I don't know exactly why, but I want to spread my arms and just be, be . . . well, without her now. I love her, and I don't want her to want to leave, but then again, I want her to leave. Just as long as Mom isn't happy to run back to work, or home without me. That would suck.*

Phoebe had no idea what her mom was thinking, and she tried not to put thoughts in her mother's head. She and her mom were so different. Helen, when silent, was usually lost in her work; Phoebe, in her poetry. *Or maybe we aren't so different after all?* And then the weight in her chest got heavier. If she wasn't like her mother, than who was she like? *Not her father? No, please God no, not like Dad.*

Phoebe sucked in air, and then started to cough on the pollen. It was early Spring in Northern Virginia, and the oak pollen was on the rise.

"Got your inhaler?"

"Yep." Phoebe reached into her duffel bag and closed her fingers around a hard plastic cap, which she flipped up in the air, opening with just one hand, and swallowed a gulp of water before she nodded, and then, when the look on her mom's face strayed from concerned to worried, and right back again, Phoebe slapped her hand on the window sill. "I'll be fine. Really. I promise."

Helen tapped her finger on the steering wheel, and Phoebe, while twisting the cap back on the water bottle, added in an almost brusque voice, "I'll call or text if my ride falls through, k?"

Helen's head bobbed up and she nodded, and without saying another word, she pulled away, waving her hand as she drove off.

A cold late March wind brought goosebumps to her forearms, and Phoebe thought about the jean jacket that was tied around her waist. It was too much trouble to untie it, so she rubbed both arms and with eyes half-closed, let the smell of the asphalt and gasoline and cherry blossoms and grass waft over her. It was a different smell than manure and Virginia red clay and tack and horse. And different meant not remembering what she didn't want to remember. And that—that was safe. Sane.

Two things she's rarely felt when anywhere near the stables at the Bryson House. Not since Parkings had—

"Pheebes! Get a move on!" Jamie Eddington, the niece of the late Anne McCaffrey, Phoebe's riding coach, leaned her head out the back door of Steve's Arena, which was where Sick City held its roller derby practices.

Phoebe couldn't contain a grin. Jamie Eddington, as usual, wore a pair of jeans two threads away from falling into pieces, and her upper arms bore so many tattoos, the tanned skin underneath was almost invisible. Jamie towered above Phoebe and almost any other woman who skated, and her brazen disregard for anything remotely feminine did very little to bely her badass persona. Underneath the tattoos, Jamie was threaded together by equal parts devotion to the Holy Spirit and an abiding unwillingness to please anyone or anything in this, as she would shrug, "meaningless material world."

Hitching her duffel bag on her shoulder, Phoebe easily jogged to the back door, and grinning so hard it hurt, she punched Jamie on the shoulder. Jamie grabbed Phoebe's head and wrapped her in a choking hold, and for a moment, they grappled, until the edge of the thick metal door caught the heel of a boot, someone's boot, and Phoebe was twisting free and with one last lurch, one extra push, toppled the much larger Jamie over.

"Jamie? You all right?" A flicker of something she didn't want to acknowledge made the grin on Phoebe's face fade a little. Jamie had suffered a traumatic brain injury fifteen years ago, and it had effectively ended her competitive riding career. In truth, she had no business skating, but she did it anyway, and it was something Phoebe knew better than to bring up. *But still, still what if—*

With wild, wavy blonde hair billowing underneath her, Jamie spread her arms out on the concrete floor, almost like she was a kid making angels in the snow, and caught the outside of Phoebe's knee, and with the fading grin now turning to that inexpressible feeling she always got in that moment between trying not to fall and trying to fall gently, Phoebe turned all serious long enough to turn her shoulder and get her hands out in front of her. She landed lightly, like a cat jumping down from a stonewall to chase a mouse, and then, only then, she starting grinning again. At least the first fall, the one you worried about, was out of the way now. It was just like getting the first hit out of the way on a football field, or so Phoebe had heard Zander earnestly explain, in that sometimes squeaky, invariably annoying little voice of his. As if Zander knew what it was like to really take a hit. Phoebe imagined him running down a sideline, shirt untucked, and just out of reach of a linebacker, and for just a moment, she missed the little guy.

"What are you smiling about Pheebes? You damn near killed me." Jamie stood up as she issued one of her imperial-sounding questions. *No wonder she skates by the name Queen B*, chuckled Phoebe, suddenly overcome with an almost painful touch of hilarity. The vision of Zander and the collision with Jamie was just too much . . . joy. She couldn't contain it.

"It's good to see young Phoebe smiling." Big Bertha, one of the blockers for Sick City's much-feared Laydiators sidled up to Phoebe and Jamie, knee and elbow pads adding to her already imposing girth. Big Bertha was a social worker for the Prince William County court systems, and at five-ten and a half, and 200 pounds after skating a hard bout, she dished out more punishment than anyone else on the Laydiators. *Perhaps more than anyone else in all of Sick City*. But that wasn't the only reason lead jammer Phoebe loved Big Bertha, who in real life went by Beth Hudson. Beth spent her working hours taking kids from abusive assholes. Beth was a hero in a way. *Kind of like the women from Bryson*.

Phoebe took Beth's outstretched hand, and hopped a little as Beth's yank jolted her forward. "Sheesh, Beth, easy."

Beth leaned backwards, placing both her hands on her wide, bulging belly, which almost looked like a beer gut underneath her tight, tye-dye muscle shirt. Beth nodded at her biceps. "God gave me these gun for a reason."

Beth's voice had a flat Midwestern accent and her black hair was folded back against itself in double braids. And her eyes most definitely did not twinkle. And yet almost everything that came out of her mouth made Phoebe smile.

"Oh, really? So lemme get this straight." Phoebe tapped Beth's biceps and then jumped out of reach. "God told you to beat the shit out of Ivana the Terrible in last week's bout? Kinda like a skater's version of Win One for the Gipper. Hail Mary Full of Grace, this head is busted, amen?"

Without warning, and moving much quicker than Phoebe was expecting, Beth bent down, caught Phoebe at the waist, and hoisted her up over her head, like one of the hay bales Beth had grown up hurling into her dad's flatbed, and then she spun around and around.

"Put me down, damn you!" Phoebe was laughing so hard she could barely speak. "Jamie, make her put me down." Phoebe felt like a cricket trying to get out of a lizard's mouth, and the thought of being a cricket just made her laugh harder.

A whistle echoed off the cavernous walls of the arena, which looked like a combination airport hanger and stripped-down high school gymnasium.

"Beth, line up. Pheebes, in front. Make sure your panty's fixed on right. Joannie, Bellitzer, Corinne, Marie . . ." Jamie snapped off several names of skaters, and in less than a minute, Phoebe had pulled on her custom built jam quad boots, clipped her helmet in place, locked, and shoved her mouth piece just above the clasp knotting her helmet. Now she was all business, just like her captain. Before Phoebe got to the line, she ran through the thoughts in her head, and prepared to discard them, to shove them into an imaginary metal box, which she could pick back up after she was done skating. Most of her thoughts didn't fight back, but there was one, and it didn't, he didn't, want to get back in the box. He was getting out the bastard was getting out, and she wanted to slam his head into a board until it fucking bled. *No,* she whispered, *not now.*

"Pheebes," whispered Beth.

Phoebe held her hand up, and without turning her head all the way, murmured, "Tell you later." At the last bout, when Beth had taken out Ivana the Terrible, it had been to protect Phoebe. Beth knew Phoebe, unlike all other jammers, actually looked for contact, and that night, Phoebe had railroaded several of the opponents before they could lay a hand on her. And in one of the last jams, she'd flung an elbow directly in Ivana's tender left breast, not so much on purpose, but with absolutely no concern, or radical disregard, for anyone or anything. Phoebe had been skating angry, and when she skated angry, she got in a lot of trouble. Or she got her teammates, her hulking blockers, in a lot of trouble. In the next jam, Ivana had a hit lined up on Phoebe, and it would have fucked her up real bad, so Beth had done something she didn't usually do: she'd punched another jammer, knowing Ivana would come for her, and not Phoebe.

"Just remember, we're on the same team, sister."

Phoebe, with a slight incline of her jaw, shoved her mouth piece in and then Jamie clapped her hands real loud.

"Okay, the entire point of today's practice," Jamie sought out Phoebe's eyes and held contact while she continued, "Is to get Firebird in and out of traffic with minimal contact. Everyone got it?"

A few of the skaters started to laugh, but then everyone waited for Phoebe's reaction. Jamie didn't play favorites, but she didn't believe in showing anyone up, either. As sensitive as Phoebe could get, as easily enraged, there was no telling how the youngest woman on the team would take this gentlest of corrections.

"Minimal?" Phoebe smirked.

"To win the bout you gotta stay in the bout, eh?" Jamie set her clipboard down, and only then did she take her eyes off Phoebe, who was shaking inside, just a little. *What if Jamie kicked me off the team?*

With a gulp, Phoebe rolled her eyes dramatically. "Yes'm." And then, helmet tied and tightly bound under her chin, she got real quiet and waited, which took all of about ten seconds, for everyone to *stop fooling and fussing around*, as Jamie always was saying.

Get through. Phoebe clicked a mental switch on, and as she whispered *get through* aloud to herself, the hair on the back of her neck stood up. *Get through.* She bit down on her mouthpiece and felt something building, something inexpressible, something part joy, part freedom, part bird in flight, taking hold, and the only words she had left were: *get through.*

Phoebe leaned forward, and as soon as the whistle blew once, long, she accelerated to the left of the pack of blockers and pivots, and with the slightest of shifts right, squeezed between Murderous Marla and the other jammer, team B's black-haired, Joan Jett lookalike Slacker Kay. Phoebe easily drifted away from the pack, and with several brisk strides, she was around the circle and approaching the pack again as Lead Jammer. She concentrated on drafting behind the team B's pivot, Minute Mayhem, and just when Mayhem was about to spread her legs and slow her down, Phoebe lifted one foot, hopped over the near line so that she wasn't out of bounds, and grabbed hold of Queen B's outstretched hand for a gentle, firm whip-it forward.

"Good!" cried her captain. "Get em' Pheebes."

Now she was collecting points, five per lap, and her mind was clear, absolutely clear, of anything but points, and blockers and pivots and trajectories and hips and buttocks and it was . . . it was glorious. It was so different than riding. On a horse, the world passed by too slowly. And when the world passed by slowly, her mind went too fast. Images, problems, memories, names of people, snippets of dialogue, a remembered smell . . . a sound that should have been safe, had it not summoned a similar, scary one, like a neighing horse. *Ginger. The barn. Parkings.* She never knew when it would happen, the shifting from safe to unsafe, so whenever it did, she'd flinch, or clench her muscles, or grasp hold too tightly of the reins, and that show would be done. It didn't take much to transfer her anxiety to her mount. And the worst thing? It only seemed to happen in shows. She had no idea why.

Maybe it was her mind's way of being heard. Maybe it just got too quiet, all eyes on her, including her own eyes, when she approached the judges, circled the ring, and tried to perform in front of others. If everyone else was staring at her, waiting, assessing, judging, and there were no other distractions, she had no choice other than to gaze inward. It seemed so unfair. So unfair. Riding had been an escape, but it turned into a padded cell inside a paddock. And the harder she tried to break free, the tighter it gripped her. And that was something a rider couldn't be: tight.

But here, and now, flying around the corner, crossing from left to right, arms raised at the last possible fraction of a second to avoid team B's pivot, it was all if not forgotten, at least temporarily forgiven. The failure. The moments she couldn't hold off the memories, the involuntary flinches, and the string of non-shows, failures to place, to win. And the unending patience of her coach, who never criticized the flinches, the tight grips, the no-shows, or the failures to place.

It's meaningless, really, dear child. It's just a show. There'll be other ones. Other days. Other chances.

Phoebe never understood what the hell Anne meant. How could it be meaningless? But in the space between pivot and lead jammer, she found not so much meaning, but the suspension of all searching for it. *Maybe that's what Anne was talking about?*

Phoebe coasted past team B's pivot and jammer. Then she stood up, placed both hands on her hips to signal the end of the jam. A practice jam. Maybe it was meaningless. Maybe it wasn't. But it sure felt good.

After grabbing her water bottle and gulping down a few swigs, Phoebe was wiping her mouth with the back of her forearm when Beth, after skating backwards, braked to a stop next to Phoebe in the sprints lineup.

"Trying to make me look good, huh?"

Beth chuckled and shot her jammer a good-natured glare. "Sugar, you don't need help looking good," and she gave Phoebe a swat on the butt. "Anytime you wanna sample some more of that—"

"—Fuck off," Phoebe snapped, and before Beth could respond, Jamie blew the whistle, and Phoebe raced off, sliding with one knee to the midline, and easily gliding forward at least ten feet ahead of anyone else. As soon as she hit the end line, knelt, and turned, she wished she wasn't so touchy. And by the time she'd come to a sudden but somehow graceful stop where she started, she felt sick to her stomach. *Damnit, why do I have to be such a bitch? Everyone knows Beth is harmless.*

So Phoebe did what made sense at the time, which was never a good idea. She slid in front of Beth, almost taking Beth, Minute Mayhem, and another blocker down, and then somehow, like a swan dipping down to tap pond water without really landing, took her pantie off and, mouthpiece hanging out and head bowed, quipped, "At your service, sexy lady."

For a moment, Beth tried to look away, but it took all her concentration not to bowl into the Minute Mayhem, and so she fixed her eyes on Phoebe. Her initial hurt gave way, as best as Phoebe could tell, to amusement, maybe even, gulped Phoebe, attraction. Which Phoebe so didn't want, not from Beth, not from anyone, man or woman, as best she knew, but who could be really sure, but sometimes you gotta take a hit for the team.

Once she had Beth almost smiling, and perhaps even salivating, Phoebe lifted her skirt and flashed her real panties, and the entire team whistled. *Fucking wolves.* She'd gone too far, she realized. Because in that moment, nausea and revulsion flashed through her; the words, *I'm a slut* started replaying in her mind on fast-forward, and yet with a smile etched like hard plastic on her high cheekbones, she kept moving straight to the bathroom. Barely slowing down as she crashed through the black door, she ripped off her helmet and went straight to the sink.

Her heart was racing and she was sweating. *What the fuck is wrong with me? She flirts with me, I tell her to fuck off, and then I go showing her my ass?* Phoebe turned the water on, and she thrust her head as close as she could get to the filthy spigot. *Filth is as to Phoebe as Phoebe is to . . .* She shook her head, and then ducked it under the water. No, no poems now. The cold water flowed over her spiky hair, and then trickled down her neck, and she just stood there, for at least a minute, neck cooling down by degrees until she shivered. Without looking, she reached over to turn the water off and sighed. Her hand was shaking again, and all because what? A woman was hitting on her? Someone was attracted to her? Someone bigger, someone stronger?

"Fuck! Fuck everyone and everything! Just . . . fuck!" Phoebe raised her helmet and then hurled it as hard as she could, straight down on the hard porcelain. "I hate . . . FUCK!" Her helmet shattered, and the pieces exploded like a bomb. One of the pieces of her helmet sliced into her finger, and at first, she was too surprised, swallowed in, and swept up by her rage to realize how bad it hurt, or how copiously she was bleeding. It took a moment for the sound wave to pass, and for the pain to arrive, which it did at the exact same second the door burst open, and through it skated Slacker Kay.

Phoebe looked up, and was about to explain, to apologize, to someone, and then she realized that there was a disconnect between her voice and the words in her head. It was getting dark, but the lights were on.

"Phoebe! Wait! Look at me!" cried Slacker Kay, who was a EMT during her non-skating hours.

And somewhere between nodding and saying "Okay," her peripheral vision disappeared completely and Phoebe was falling, and so was Slacker Kay.

Chapter 12

It was not early, not for a runner. Catherine repeated that to herself when she rolled over and took in the alarm clock. It was 4:39 AM. There was plenty of time to grab an ill-advised cup of coffee, for drinking coffee was always ill-advised before an early morning run but damn near impossible to give up was not so much the coffee as the idea of it. It was one tiny vestige of normalcy, maybe even a bowing to that human need for no no not weakness. Maybe habit? Then again, running seven miles every morning except race days was a habit.

Catherine shook her head. Philosophy was never her thing, not when it meant finding ways to get out of doing hard things. That was the modern way. Philosophize, harmonize, strategize . . . ways to achieve the venalities and vices and pleasures of our animal natures. There was never enough pleasure, not when the body was set before humanity's altar to itself.

Catherine stood up and smiled. There was still plenty to be grateful for, and when she was off running in the wilderness, knucklelights blazing only just ahead of her footsteps, she could hear angels whispering, sometimes singing, and it made her heart want to sing with. Human souls liked to sing with, and it was all about finding the right songs. If only there were more songs, more singers, who could hear the now-ancient seeming ditties of goodness, of God, of another world that once was our home here.

A half-hour later, Catherine was on the trails in the forest near Quantico. She took it easy, especially at the start, just a gentle jog, seven, maybe eight-minute miles, nothing to it, and she was certain that she wasn't going to have arthritis because of it. She'd been listening politely the other night at the local Wegman's; some little old lady had seen her stretching in the vegetable aisle, and had lectured Catherine on the aches and pains that were coming if she ran for fitness.

"Yes, ma'am," Catherine had said, "I hear your concerns and I thank you," and she'd walked away as soon as the lady took a breath. It had been a long wait, or so it had seemed. She was tired of people telling her how to live. Enough of the judging what you didn't understand, judging all that's different than you. That's all it amounted to really. The old lady's comment was just a little thing, but Catherine was tired of being condemned, tired of it, tired of a world that looked for reasons to cast others outside, tired of a world that elevated the fallen and cast out the risen or those who were giving it their all. And that's what Catherine was all about: giving her all, always, and running was just one way she gave all she had. Just one way. There were others, and she was trying to figure it out, but why get on her case for stretching in a grocery store?

Catherine shook her head and chuckled. This was a silly way to spend the first five minutes of her day. She needed to look to the light, deep within, and go there to figure out what was really bugging her. It had something to do with the early wakeup time, and how much kids at school had given her crap about it when she was leaving the dorm at the same time many of them were coming back home.

What was she tired of? Being different, not because she wasn't like them, but because they weren't more like her. That was the truth, and it sounded maybe a little prideful. In high school, then in college, she hadn't spent her weekends and weeknights drinking and sleeping around with everyone else. Even if she wasn't a runner, she wouldn't probably have wanted to, but the

4:39 AM wakeup times made partying a . . . well, another near-impossibility.

And after Marcie had been . . . destroyed, yep, pretty much, by that bastard, star running back, *go OR football*, Catherine had wanted to blow something up, blow it all up, root it out, every bit of the system that did nothing to make better people out of the students who (eventually, once the student loans stopped getting deferred) footed the tab. Yes, even the football players paid the bills but their checks were written in spiritual tender.

That was the problem. Or one of them. It was a corrupt system through and through. Student-athletes were no longer students, and they both used and got used by the system. Coaches? Trainers? University Presidents? Penn State—'nuff said. Ugh.

Catherine took a deep breath and tried to reorder her thoughts. The running was about the only thing that made her thoughts ordered, sort of like a meat slicer at a delicatessen. Throw all these wild thoughts into the holder, and the steady fall of feet on dirt was like a rhythmic slicer. After a few miles, what would be left would be an ordered stack of solutions to problems that seemed incomprehensible at the start of the run.

But the college life was damn near incomprehensible to her, no matter how many miles she ran, no matter how much she studied, how long she tried to understand the past few years. It just didn't make sense. There was so much wrong, so much wrong with it all, and it wasn't just the way the university spoiled the football players, both spoiled and exploited; players selling their bodies, universities selling out, giving up on the charters; students supporting the whole corrupt structure, all for a fuck and a drink and a t-shirt and a "good time."

How do you define good? What is a good time? Plato defined good as virtue, or as the pursuit of wisdom. Catherine felt her jaw tighten. She'd argued that in a poli-sci seminar once and one student had said, "Virtue doesn't pay."

"That's not the point. It makes the soul better."

"What's a soul? How can you prove it exists?"

"Just look inside you. No proof is needed."

"Superstitious, perhaps? About this whole soul concept?" the professor had said.

Catherine had almost sputtered at that point. "Souls are not superstitious . . . anyway, the issue was virtue, and why society should encourage it, why political frameworks and systems should be built to create more of it. Instead of making the full-throated pursuit of animal pleasures the end of all social planning, instead of allowing the sexual exploitation of minors—"

"—Oh, is this one of those feminist attacks on the right of each individual to enjoy the fruits of his labor in the privacy of his own bedroom?" Roger, the student who had said virtue didn't pay, leaned forward and stared into Catherine's eyes, thinking he would intimidate her.

"Plato also said that too much democracy, too much liberty, could hurt the individual as well as the political good just as much as excessive tyranny. And I'm thinking that what you're speaking of, your right to watch men screw under-aged women in their own bedroom, falls into the category of too much liberty. After all, who gives these men the right to violate other individuals—and yes, Roger, women are individuals just as worthy as respect as men— who gives men, who gives society, the sanction to violate the liberties of these children?"

Roger had kept arguing, and Catherine's face had kept getting hotter and hotter, so much so that she almost started to cry. But she hadn't cried; she hadn't stopped arguing with Roger or with the wrinkled-khakis professor. She never stopped arguing for the good, for the virtues, for the possibilities and potentialities of the human soul, never, and she never would. Not after Marcie left the world a few decades too early. She wouldn't stop fighting; she wouldn't then, she wouldn't now.

Catherine glanced at the trail marker. She was somewhere around the six mile mark, running a loop that started and ended on a one mile stretch of asphalt. She should be hitting it in another minute or so. Now wasn't the time to figure out how to stop the sex trade. That was setting herself up for a tree root, and she didn't need to be spraining an ankle or tweaking a lower back muscle, not now, not so close to graduation, and so close to the final strength test.

She didn't mind the stringency of it. She damn well expected to be able to lift the same weights, perform all the same physical tasks the average male agent could perform. To be honest with herself, maybe not the average male agent, at least not the pure lifting. She was struggling to hit the bottom quartile for pushups, but she was the fastest runner and in the top twenty-five percent in the shooting tests. She wanted to be judged fairly, that was all.

Catherine smiled. God was with her. She'd be fine, she'd find a way to lift more in two weeks, when she needed it most . . . He'd be with her. She was doing His work, and He'd be with her.

Chapter 13

Jim pushed the fridge shut with his elbow and sat down at the kitchen table with a bottle of Seven-Up in his hand. The fizz tickled his tongue and the back of his throat, and it was refreshing in a way that beer was not. Jim shook his head. That's not what the ad men wanted you to believe, and it wasn't what his brain would have him believe, but it was true. And he wouldn't forget it. He shook his head. There was irony there, this trying to remember some things, and wishing he could forget others.

He couldn't get the image of Christopher's casket out of his mind. It just wouldn't let go of him. And when it let go of him, he saw something else. He couldn't stop seeing the kids crouching behind the black Mercedes. They were just kids. It looked like they were handing clips over to the men who were carrying AK47s. One of the men was holding a cell phone, and about two seconds after the Arab raised the phone to his ear, an IED went off in the middle of the highway, about five feet away from an Army supply truck. That's when he and Christopher had started shooting in the direction of the black Mercedes. They took down the men, and it wasn't like they were trying to shoot the kids.

A couple days later, they drove past the burnt-out hulk of the black Mercedes, and almost nothing but the one kid's red and white Coca Cola t-shirt was recognizable. The kids were laying by the side of the road. Shreds of them had been torn out of their bodies by birds of prey. Christopher had insisted they pull their Humvee over and he'd tried to grab some rocks to cover up their bodies, but there were a soda can next to one of the rocks, and that's one of the things rebels used to build incendiary devices, and finally, Christopher had taken his pistol out of his holster and started screaming, "Ahhh!! You bastards" as he shot at the vultures until he'd shot through one whole clip, and was about to grab another one.

"No, shhh, buddy, we gotta get back," Jim had said, and he'd gently taken Christopher's hand and helped him secure his pistol. Jim could see a group of men coming closer, and their dark robes, as usual, freaked him out. You just never knew what they were concealing, and all one of them had to do was call a cell phone number, and that soda can, if it was more than a soda can— it would be lights out.

"Come on, Christopher, please get in our ve-hic-le," urged Jim, and he gave his buddy an extra shove that he didn't mean. You did and said a lot of things you didn't mean when you were scared. As he checked behind them one more time, Jim could feel his heart beating out of his chest and could see the birds circling closer and closer, and then all he could see was dust, and the heat shimmering on the road, as he floored it and drove back to their base.

They hadn't talked about it much on the way back. Jim had tried, but the words got stuck coming out, so finally, he'd just let the whooshing sound of the air sandblasting them as they hurtled past say all that really could be said. He'd meant to talk to Christopher. After all, Jim was his best friend. And it wasn't certain they'd shot those kids. Even if they had, the whole situation had been impossible, really. Impossible. Or so Jim had told himself about a thousand times since . . .

Jim took a deep breath and a big gulp of Seven-Up. The ice cubes clinked together and the liquid burned a little going down, like gin but without the warming feeling.

You see I pull the trigger when I have to, I do Uncle Sam's
will. I can never show any weakness, I'm only meant to
kill.
I think of all I've done.
Will it be praised or thought as sins?
A son becomes his father,
A body rots under an Arab sun.

Jim poured more soda into his glass until it bubbled up and almost over the top. He sucked the foam off the tip of the thick, clear glass just in time, right before it hit the edge and slid down the sides and onto his keyboard.

He wiped his eyes with the back of his hand. It wasn't that he was crying. It was like wiping his eyes would somehow induce the tears to fall. Why couldn't he cry? There was no shame in crying, was there? Jim wrote another stanza:

I wish I could erase the memories.
Tell my brain it's all a lie.
I wish I could just break down.
but I was trained to never cry.

The anniversary of Christopher's death only came once for sure each year. He wished he could say the same for the nightmares. They weren't all the same.

Sometimes he and Christopher were driving on the base,
laughing, and then he looked over and he saw parts of his
best friend's brain leaking into his collar. Sometimes, they
were playing catch and then, when Jim blinked, a skeleton
wearing a Coca Cola t-shirt stared back at him. He'd blink
again, and it would be Christopher, dressed in shorts and a
white t-shirt.
"Fuck that, I'll play buck-naked if it gets a degree hotter,"
he howled.
Then, Jim heard a helicopter going overhead, and when he
looked down across the sandy square, there was no one
there, no one at all. The barracks were all gone, and in

their place was an army of boys wearing red and white coca cola t-shirts, and they were bleeding from these massive head wounds, and parts of their bodies were missing, and the birds of prey were circling closer and closer, and please God, please . . . save me.

Jim always woke up screaming from that one. He called it *Birds of the Undead*. There was no reason why he had to name his nightmares, but it made him laugh a little, and that was a lot better than drinking a lot.

The phone rang and Jim contemplated whether he felt like talking to anyone. He reached over to read the caller ID and an easy smile came on his face. It was Anne, his big sister.

"Hey sis."

"Jim John!" He could tell she was smiling from the way she let the second "J" carry into the receiver. She made his name sound like part of a chorus from a folk song.

"How ya doin'? How are the kids?" Jim could hear the din of children's voices in the background. Anne had two kids, and a third was due in the summertime, but it sounded like a lot more than two kids were with his big sister, probably in her kitchen.

"I'm exhausted, and baby Jim is killing me right about now. I swear this one's going to be hyperactive."

Anne and her husband, Bill Winters, already had two boys, and like any good southerner, they'd named their firstborn son after the daddy. By the third one, they were grabbing whatever relatives' names they could, and Jim was as good as any other name. Still, he loved the thought of it.

"Sounds like you named him right." Jim took another swallow and then he blushed apologetically, because for sure she could hear that on the other line. "Just Seven-Up I'm drinking."

"Oh, hon, I didn't—wouldn't—think anything but, you okay?" Man she sounded so kind, and he was about to say something incredibly bland in response when he wanted to say something awesome, but the call waiting was beeping, and it was his Mom.

"Mom's calling—you were just calling to check on me, right?"

Anne laughed, and the peal of a toddler laughing echoed in the background. "You got me. Yep. Tell Mom I said 'hi.'"

Jim clicked over. "Hi there Mama. I'm fine. I promise."

"Now Jim, really." She drew her words out a little longer for emphasis, but though she lived near Charlottesville still, she didn't have much of an accent left over. Her years in Boston had taken care of that. "Is that how a man should greet his mother?"

Jim cleared his throat. "I'm sorry Mom. It's a hard . . . thing. I'm writing some, but every time I come up with a stanza, I feel like I'm back there, and I can't shake it. Don't want to . . . you know." He sighed. If anyone knew, she knew. She'd lived with it for more than 15 years, before his dad had died young. Sometimes he thought, not soon enough, but that wasn't the kind of thing you were supposed to think about your dad.

"Well, first, about the writing—just keep at it. The words will make the images not burn so deep, I think. At least, that's how it worked for me." Mary Madeline McMahon was a well-respected literature professor and head of the English Department at the University of Virginia, and more often than not, she and her son spent most their time talking about their craft. In some way, poetry and literature was the family business.

"Okay. Right. How's your current crop of students, anyway?"

"You know how it is." She sounded like she was outside, probably in her wildflower garden. Jim could hear the shrill trilling of a robin. "A bunch of people want to see their name in print. A few maybe have some talent. But except for maybe one, two tops, no one wants to put in the hours crafting, rewriting, reading, and then, worst of all, submitting."

"You ever tell them to work harder?"

Mary Madeline laughed, not quite so melodiously as Anne. "Every time any writer, particularly my students, ask me my secret, I ask them how many words they've written today. Most of them stop asking me for advice after that."

Jim grunted. The truth was he never seemed to write enough words, not since he got back home at least. The words once tumbled out, like water busting through a broken dam, but now it was a damn desert, his writing was.

"You doing okay?"

"Yes."

"Are you going to meetings?"

He gritted his teeth. AA meetings depressed him. Made him want to drink more, or made him pity the people who were talking. "You mean AA?"

"No, Jim. I know those don't work for you. Veterans. PSTD. People who've been there."

"No." He barked the words out, and tried to slow it down, talk nicely to his mother. He sounded angry, but it wasn't anger. *At least, this time it wasn't.* "Can't. I gotta go Mama. Love you lots." He was already starting to hang up the phone and she was adding a sentence about coming up to see him soon. He thought he replied, "That would be great," but the concussion of the bombs exploding in his head made it hard to concentrate.

Jim stood up and counted to ten before his nerves kicked in and he felt his leg through and through. One of the main things the last tour left with him was a couple of bulging discs in his back, and he'd given up waiting for the pain to go away. The VA kept blowing off his disability claims. They denied his first claim, then granted him 15% disability on appeal. He'd appealed that. They'd asked for more paperwork. He re-filed. This process had been going on for eighteen months, ever since he'd requested and received his honorable discharge.

Effective the first of this year, he'd gotten them up to 30% disabled, and were it not for the nightmares, and what his grandfather had called "being Scottish," he'd have long since stopped sending letters. He'd have walked away, or limped, a long time ago.

But it isn't right, not after all I gave them. The miles sweating in the convoys, the bright flash of an IED, always shocking, no matter how much you were expecting it, the two Purple Hearts, the pieces of shrapnel still buried in his thigh, too close to the femoral artery to risk removing at a military hospital, too much trouble to remove now . . . he'd given them too much to receive so little. Being disabled could seem like being less of a man. Suck it up and shut up, dad would have told me.

Jim realized he was holding his muscles all tense when a shiver of pain shot up his leg. He'd never run or even walk pain-free again, and that wasn't right. Nor was shutting up about it, burying it in a special box like the one his daddy used to store his medals and his service pistol in. You can't shove your pain in a box like that because it finds a way to eat away at you, and that's when a good man turns into a drunken bastard.

And Jim wasn't going to be the same drunken bastard his daddy and his daddy's daddy had become. *Vietnam War; World War Two . . . a long line of proud Southern warriors turned drunken bastards.* Jim took a deep breath and tightened his jaw. He stood a little taller, almost without realizing it. *He wasn't that guy.* Once a month, he drove to see a VA psychiatrist, and those visits usually just made him want to punch a wall, but he still kept going back, and he wasn't going to quit getting the care he needed. He wasn't going to start drinking again.

Jim walked over to the window overlooking the kitchen sink. His townhouse overlooked Route 66, which sounded kind of awful for a country boy, but in the distance he always got a glimpse of the Shenandoah mountains, and that made him feel at home. It spoke to him of vistas and voyages. He could almost smell the cooler air swirling among the mountain mists. And after the first few nights living at 5346 Mossington Place, he'd grown accustomed to the traffic from the Interstate. Most of the time, it sounded like a protective layer of white noise, almost like a river's waters drifting past.

Out of the corner of his eye, Jim saw two deer standing on the edge of the thin layer of woods that separated his small development from the freeway overpass. Growing up in the country, he'd started going hunting when he was still too young to drive a car. He'd shot his first deer with a shotgun his uncle Timmy had given him for his sixteenth birthday. He remembered the smell of the blood and the sticky feeling of it on his hands. The way it made his camouflage pants stick to his leg after the blood got caked on it. His uncle had taught him how to prepare a carcass, and it was the first of many Jim had killed. He didn't like the taste of venison, so after dressing the dead animal, Jim would drop it off at the local food shelter.

As his Uncle explained to him, "We don't hunt for sport anymore than you use a knife as anything other than a tool. Don't you ever forget that JJ. No deer ever asked to be killed, but if you're going to use it to feed someone who otherwise wouldn't get enough to eat, then you can go to bed tonight proud, having done a man's job." So Jim didn't feel bad about having killed deer. Killing was complicated.

But he didn't like seeing the deer standing there so close to the interstate. If he wasn't stuck in the suburbs, if he wasn't afraid of getting arrested, he'd grab his shotgun from the locked gun cabinet and lay those beautiful animals down to sleep. It seemed a lot more merciful than waiting for a semi tractor-trailer to do the job.

Chapter 14

Cassandra glanced over at Zander, who still wouldn't stop talking. He was bleeding from a gash to his temple, or just below it, right next to an old scar from a bash to the same damn eyelid from a friend's toy truck. He was sitting in the passenger seat so that she could keep an eye on him the whole way to the ER. She wished he'd be quiet for just a blessed second so that she could think and figure out which hospital she'd rather go to. Sometimes Fairfax INOVA was best, but that was for the scary stuff, like seizures and detached eyeballs.

Cassandra giggled to herself. *Okay, it wasn't that bad. No detached eyeballs.* But at the rate Zander was going, nothing would surprise her. Since his eyeballs were still attached, INOVA Gallows Road was overkill; anyway, it was rush hour, and the only way there was via I-495. And driving anywhere on I-495 at this hour would make a miserable trip even worse. The closest ER from a geographical standpoint was INOVA—Fairfax, but they had the longest wait times during the weekdays.

Cassandra ran her hand through her long, silver hair and pulled her sunglasses down to shade her eyes from the setting sun. As she started up the engine to her Volvo SUV, she sighed. Fair Oaks Hospital it was. *Only twenty more minutes of a Zander-ologue to endure.* Her head was killing her; the bright sun was only making it worse, and perhaps worst of all, she wouldn't have time to run tonight. And man, she needed a few miles, maybe more, to sort through the details of Phoebe Thompson's case.

It wasn't like, realistically speaking, there was anything else she could do. Wayne Toller had served his five years. She'd filed victim statements, written letters to the parole board, met with the Commonwealth's Attorney twice, which was two times more than most attorneys could have finagled. She'd spent hours reading up on child porn, and her junior partner, Natalie, had billed even more. Not that cost was a factor. Helen approved all the bills without a moment's hesitation.

Crap, I even leaked stuff on Twitter to several child porn advocates. There was the University of Michigan law review article, the DOJ studies, the compilations of perv interviews . . . all pointing to the sheer sickness, the unvarying recidivism rates. Once a pedophile, well . . . nothing worked on these sick bastards. Nothing except for chemical castration, as the University of Michigan article recommended. Cassandra shook her head. It had sounded awful when she first read about it, *but if nothing else worked . . . well, crap.*

The statistic that had made her shudder and had induced a frozen look of shock on the Commonwealth Attorney's face was the one about the percentage of child porn users. Somewhere between 65 and 83 percent of these so-called victim-less criminals had also committed an act involving a minor. They simply hadn't been caught. It was a persuasive statistic, but it wasn't a persuasive legal argument. What do you do with a porn addict who won't admit to committing worse sins, sins that could buy a longer prison sentence? Torture them? Charge them with thought crimes? Prescribe, sentence and require the criminal to receive testosterone-deadening pills for the rest of his life? Cassandra had no good answer to it all. And now—now Toller was free. And there wasn't a damn thing she could do about it.

"—So can I, Mom, can I?"

Cassandra shook her head absent-mindedly and massaged the side of her head with her right hand. She had no idea what her son was talking about, and for just a moment, she contemplated fudging it. *No, just fess up and be done with it.* "I'm sorry, love, I missed a little bit. Can you back up a few paragraphs?"

Zander was chewing on his fingernails and Cassandra found herself wondering, without emotion, about where he was spitting the pieces of broken-off nail. Twenty years ago, this would have just killed her, but now, well, it was just another thing.

"Thinking about work?"

"Yeah. Got a case that's really bugging me."

She swore she heard a nail breaking between his front teeth, and she cringed but didn't react to it. Reacting to all the things Zander did was crazy-making.

"What's it about?"

"Can't say."

He started humming, and then interrupted himself again. "Phoebe?"

She felt her eye starting to twitch. He must have overheard something. "Can't say."

"So it's about Phoebe?"

She clenched the wheel a little tighter. "Really, Zander, stop."

She caught his shaggy head bobbing up and down out of the corner of her eye, and he remained quiet for a full fifteen seconds. "So can I go on Saturday?"

"Where?"

"Mom, really? I already 'splained." Zander started to wave his right hand and then he let out a little scream. "Ew! Still bleeding!"

"Put the damn towel thingie back on it!"

Zander grumbled and managed to drop the t-shirt on the floor mat before he got it pressed back on his temple. Then he was still for five seconds.

Cassandra actually counted. It was maybe a bad habit, because it often made her giggle, but that was better than losing her temper. *And Zander had a way of . . .*

"—To Justin's house. He's building a huge ramp, in his backyard and it's going to be rad, I mean, like, at least ten feet high," Zander raised his left hand really high, and then made a fast, downward motion with it. "It's gonna skate fast!"

Cassandra didn't hesitate. Not for a second. Justin was the youngest brother of the infamous Jason, a friend of her daughter's who was best known for crashing his dad's car and (in a subsequent incident) smashing his Jeep through his neighbor's garage. "No. Absolutely not. Are you . . ." she censored the cuss word she was about to utter. "Kidding me?"

"But Mom!"

"No. Seriously? And how did you hurt your head today? Doing what exactly? Hmm?"

"Doesn't count."

"How do you figure that?" Cassandra pulled into the garage at Fair Oaks Hospital, and she could feel the back of her neck getting hot. *Damnit. Damn damn damn.*

"It was a fluke. If I hadn't snagged the edge of my board on . . ."

Cassandra lost the rest of his sentence to the sound of her door slamming shut. She took a deep breath and set her shoulders. And then when she saw her no longer tiny son climbing out the passenger's seat, with one hand holding a now blood-soaked t-shirt, she wasn't angry anymore. There was something so manlike about her son, something intangible but so very sweet and real, and it made her need to hold him, just as much as she wanted to capture this moment here with him, for a little longer than she could.

With a big smile, and a pang in her heart, she threw an arm around her man-boy and guided him toward the ER.

Chapter 15

Phoebe had only lost consciousness for a minute or so. She'd woken up in Kay's arms. While Kay expertly applied direct pressure to the gash in Phoebe's hand, Jamie had ducked her head into the bathroom and returned holding the Laydiators' much abused medical kit.

"Going to need a few stitches, Pheebes," Kay had murmured while she dressed the wound.

"Stitches?" The words sounded thick to her own ears, so Phoebe let her eyes drift toward Kay, but the florescent lights overhead were giving her a headache so she closed her eyes shut and curled into Kay to make it easier for Kay to reach the wound. Phoebe sighed and listened to Kay talk ever so quietly about her two daughters. They were now twelve and thirteen, and Phoebe was their favorite jammer, even favorite skater.

"They like you even better than me, can you believe that Pheebes?"

A smile had pushed Phoebe's cheeks out, and her eyes flickered open for a moment.

"Shhh. You don't need to talk. I know you're resting right now. You're going to be fine."

Jamie made a gentle tapping sound on the door. Phoebe could feel Kay's arms shift a little as the EMT murmured, "Yeah, Cap'n?"

"Let me get practice wrapped up. Get everyone stretched out. And then I'll take Phoebe over to Fair Oaks. It's on our way home."

Phoebe tried to raise her head to say something but the bathroom door made its three-times squeak sound before it came to a complete rest.

"Shhh. She knows. Just rest, and it's all going to be all right."

An hour later, Phoebe sat on an examining table in one of the pods inside the ER. Jamie stood beside the entrance to their "room," which was really a semi-private space set off with barriers that didn't reach all the way to the ceiling. Anne's niece remained still, stoic, and impassive, with her hands wrapped behind her. Phoebe thought Jamie looked like a fierce sentinel from some distant century, standing guard over her "cousin," which is what everyone on the Laydiators and now at Fair Oaks Hospital probably assumed they were.

"Jamie, um—"

The sound of shoes rapping, tap, tip, tap, on the floor interrupted Phoebe before she could finish her sentence, and the cloth "door" rustled as an Asian resident stepped into their space.

Phoebe shook her head in frustration. Phoebe had a million questions to ask Jamie all of a sudden. But during the ride from practice to the hospital, they'd talked about bouts and tattoos. Jamie had taken Phoebe to get Phoebe's first tattoo on Phoebe's eighteenth birthday, and since then, they'd shared sketches and concepts and an enthusiasm for ink.

"Phoebe Thompson? Hi, my name's Doctor Wong. What exactly happened?"

Phoebe shrugged and glared at a space above the doctor's shoulder. "I broke a helmet and the shards cut me."

"How exactly did you break a helmet?"

Phoebe was getting pissed off. What the fuck did it matter? Her fucking hand was killing her. And now, what, she had to answer to some stranger? I don't think so.

"Doctor Wong." To Phoebe's surprise, Jamie was talking. "It was a fluke accident. Happened during derby practice. Now— can we get her stitched up and back out on the ice, if you please?"

Jamie's voice neither rose nor fell as she spoke; in fact, with its total lack of affect, her voice seemed or felt unassailable. As if questioning it were as efficacious as trying to break through a steel door. Phoebe closed her eyes for a moment, and pictured a massive door, like one in a nuclear containment facility, and she knew she had her next poem. She'd call it "Steel Door."

The bespectacled Asian doctor raised one eyebrow and perused the chart in her hands. "Are you her next of kin? Because otherwise, you know, we don't allow domestic partners—"

"She's my cousin. And that so-called rule of yours? What do you think Pheebes? You're the lawyer's kid."

Phoebe caught a mere hint of amusement in Jamie's voice, but she knew the doctor was missing it. "Hmmm. We are stuck in Virginia. But everyone votes blue around here. I'm thinking the ACLU would be on that like bees on honey, or a pig on," Phoebe paused and she could hear Anne enunciating the word in the barn, "—Shit." Phoebe grinned. "Pardon the expression and all that," she concluded.

The doctor was reading through Phoebe's chart and didn't seem to be listening.

"Phoebe Thompson, right?"

"Right."

"Any relation to Helen Thompson?"

"Yeah."

Doctor Wong murmured, "I see," and for a moment, Phoebe wanted to push further but a glance in Jamie's direction convinced her otherwise. Jamie had spread her legs and with arms crossed, didn't seem to be in the mood for any more messing around. She wondered if everyone looked up to Jamie like she did. Maybe she could ask Kay. *And did Jamie look up to anyone? Maybe to God?*

"So, Doctor . . . Wong." Phoebe waited for her doctor to make eye contact. "How many stitches am I gonna need? Five?"

Doctor Wong set the chart down and the muscles around her mouth tightened. She was doing her best not to frown as she took hold of Phoebe's wrist. "At least that many. And perhaps a couple here, too." She tapped her fingers next to the smaller gash in Phoebe's hand, and there was something practiced, competent, and good about Wong's way of touching her. Suddenly, Phoebe decided maybe she like or at least could tolerate her doc.

So she smiled, and made eye contact, and to her surprise, Doctor Wong smiled back at her. "So you're pretty tough eh? You skate roller derby?"

"Yeah. We skate." Phoebe nodded in Jamie's direction, but Jamie was surveying something in the distance, probably not even in the same room. Jamie had a way of doing that whenever Phoebe was around her. Sometimes, Phoebe wondered what Jamie saw, but Jamie usually didn't hear or at least acted like she didn't hear questions about that sort of thing.

"Tough sport." The doctor grabbed materials from the nurse, who'd floated back into the room without making a sound.

"You ever watch it?"

"Actually, yes, I have. I'm from Texas, and as you probably know, it's pretty popular out there." The doctor spoke quietly about roller derby and the many bouts she'd attended as she stitched Phoebe up, and Phoebe made sure she didn't flinch or whine about the pain. *Not like it really hurt, anyway*. And Phoebe found herself talking about Sick City and their next bout and the whole thing made her heartbeat slow down a little.

"So, Phoebe, what's your skating name, anyway?"

"Firebird. Like the Phoenix here on my arm." Phoebe pointed to her shoulder blade. "And she's Queen B."

Dr. Wong nodded, and a few minutes later, she stood at the threshold, giving directions. Before she turned and left, she added, "When's your next bout? I'd love to come see it if I'm off."

Phoebe realized at the exact same moment Jamie uncrossed her arms and replied, "Next Friday," that Doctor Wong was sort of apologizing in the only way she knew how. There was something about the whole thing that she really needed to think about. She needed to get hold of her notebook. Or maybe she didn't. *Maybe some people weren't all good or all bad.*

"Great. Please give my regards to your mother, Phoebe."

After the doctor's footsteps faded from hearing range, and after the nurse issued Phoebe's release instructions, Phoebe hopped to her feet and promptly tripped on the thick grey wire that was duct-taped to the floor. Jamie put a steadying hand on the back of

Phoebe's elbow, and then wrapped a protective arm around the younger woman's shoulder in a loose, athletic way.

"So what was that all about?"

"You mean, when she asked about your mom?"

"Yeah."

Jamie walked a few steps while she twirled her keys in her other hand, and Phoebe followed along at Jamie's more measured pace. It felt different not to be rushing. Maybe better. Maybe just different.

"You know, some people talk about your mom like she's kind of a heroine of sorts," Jamie said. "She does a lot for the women at the Bryson House, especially for the ones that end up here, at the ER, for treatment."

Just when Phoebe was about to ask another question, she heard a voice, or saw a wreck of a boy with a familiar voice moving fast toward the exit, all elbows and moving body parts. *It couldn't be . . . Zander White? And his mom? Here?* She picked up her pace and caught the last few strains of a Zander-logue on skateboarding.

"See, I gotta try Justin's ramp, Mom! It's at least fifteen feet high, and . . ."

"You said ten feet earlier."

Zander waved his arms as if drawing a ramp from one end of the aisle to the other. "No! Fifteen if it isn't five inches. And his mom and his dad said I could."

"No."

"It will be totally safe. And I'll wear my helmet this time."

Cassandra White gasped and took hold of her son's shoulders. "Wait. You said you were wearing your helmet and that it broke. Are you changing your story now?"

Zander's hand stopped in mid-air, and that's when Phoebe caught up to him. "Really, Zander? Not wearing a helmet is babyish. So uncool." Phoebe rolled her eyes and made sure Cassandra White caught the full effect of it. Cassandra White, after all, was one of Phoebe's favorite grown-ups.

Cassandra took a deep breath, and Phoebe could see the strain in the older woman's eyes. It was like she'd aged overnight. Maybe it was just the hospital lighting.

"Hi Phoebe. And you're right, thanks. Zander, you have one chance to give it to me straight. Why weren't you wearing a helmet? Cassandra made a theatrical gesture with her arm. "You realize this could have been much worse? Like killed you?"

"—Or made it so that you could never skate, play football, or watch a TV show without getting a headache ever again," added Jamie, who had caught up to them.

Zander's eyes tracked from left to right and back again and he stopped hopping and gesturing and talking. He stood absolutely still, except for his right hand, which he kept near his mouth. He wasn't chewing on his fingers, and he had long since stopped sucking his thumb, but in her mind, Phoebe envisioned a younger Zander holding onto his mother while he sucked his thumb and tried hard not to cry. He was tough but sensitive like that, and damned if no one else but Ms. White seemed to know it.

"Hey, Zander?" Phoebe smiled as she spoke so that her voice would have a soothing effect. "I got an idea. Now, it's a good one, and it might even be fun. You ready for it?"

Zander nodded, and Phoebe paused and included Cassandra with her smile.

"I need to buy a new helmet for derby. Mine came to an unfortunate end." Phoebe tried not to chuckle but was pretty sure Jamie caught her smirking. "I know this place out in Chantilly. They sell the sturdiest and the coolest, most bad-ass helmets around, don't they, Jamie?"

Jamie nodded. "Great idea."

"Yep, it is." Cassandra gave Phoebe a tired smile. How do I get there, Phoebe?"

"Oh, well, actually, if I get my wheels fixed, I was thinking," Phoebe was starting to blush all of a sudden. What if she was pissing Cass off? Why couldn't she just keep her mouth shut? Ugh. Well, she might as well just ask. "How about if I take Zander out there this weekend?"

"Oooh, would ya Pheebes?"

Phoebe relaxed. She didn't like seeing Zander all cut up and vulnerable. It was scary, and unsettling, like the moon had switched rotational forces or something, so this was good.

"As long as it's okay with your mom." Phoebe paused and waited for Cassandra to smile and nod. "Good. Well, that's settled. Maybe Jamie can come too. Whaddya say, Jamie?"

"As long as I get my chores down first, yeah, sure."

"Okay. I'll call early Saturday, and we'll get it sorted and I'll pick you up and then we'll grab Zander."

Phoebe watched Zander run a few steps ahead of Cassandra, and then he came back, wrapped his arm around her waist, and whispered something that Phoebe couldn't quite hear. Cassandra took her own arm, wrapped it around her son's shoulder, and kissed the top of his head. It felt good, seeing that.

Chapter 16

Phoebe stretched her arms and yawned. She was sitting in the passenger seat of Jamie's Ford Explorer. They were about to turn off I-66 and head into the countryside, bearing south toward Middleburg. It was a familiar drive for Phoebe. Now she and Helen lived out here. But now she found her mind traveling back to the first day she came this way. Only fifteen at the time, she had been with her mom, and they were on the run from a hell she couldn't bear to think about, and yet couldn't seem to let go of. Her past was like a blanket with a thick covering of burrs. She kept covering herself with it and the result, a tearing away at old wounds, never seemed to change.

> *Why can't I just watch the suburbs giving way to the exurbs? Why can't I just listen to the wheels rolling over the asphalt? Why does it seem like I'm always running from something, someone, stuck out of time and place?*

Phoebe looked out the window. A banner announced a used tire sale.

"What the fuck. Used tires? Is that even safe?"

Jamie lifted a shoulder and didn't take her eyes off the road.

"Well, is it?" Phoebe rubbed her fingers over a smudge on the window. "How can anyone trust what they're buying?"

"Some people can't afford a new set of tires, especially out here in Manassas."

"Yeah but in Middleburg? Which we're headed towards? Come on. This is horse country. Eddie Bauer or Ralph Lauren-burg." Phoebe gestured toward the mountain ranges, which suddenly appeared over the rise in the road. "These folks don't need new tires."

"I don't reckon the sign's for them, Pheebes."

"Don't reckon, huh?" Phoebe sounded like a jerk, she knew it, but she couldn't help it.

"Nope, don't reckon."

Phoebe smiled. Jamie sounded so much like her "Auntie A." Like Anne, Jamie almost never reacted to Phoebe's bad temper or brash pronouncements. It was like Phoebe was forgiven before she even knew enough to feel guilty when she talked to Jamie.

"So who buys these fucking tires then?"

"Hopefully somebody. Or else this sign's gonna stay up and keep annoying you."

"Damn straight. And—"

"—Pheebes," Jamie interposed, "What's really bothering you?"

Phoebe's head swiveled around. *Jamie never interrupts.* "What? So I'm being a bitch? A spoiled brat? A millionaire's kid who doesn't know what it's like to be . . . to be . . . what?" She ended her sentence almost shouting. *The fucking guilt.*

"No, no Pheebes. It's okay. Okay. It's okay. That's not what I mean at all."

"Then what? Because I told Beth to fuck off? Then went and flashed her? Then went and broke my helmet and cut my hand and . . ." Phoebe paused and realized how funny the whole thing sounded. She laughed and when she looked over, she saw that Jamie was chuckling, but not in a cruel way.

"Um, yeah," drawled Jamie, sounding more southern than she really was. "That. And that. And that, too."

They laughed and neither one spoke for a minute. Phoebe remembered the first time Jamie had called her "Pheebes," back when she was living at the Bryson House. It was the first week she was there, and she'd just broken her arm falling off a horse. Phoebe winced remembering the jagged bursts of pain. That afternoon, after she'd gotten "home" from the hospital, Phoebe had run into Jamie while Jamie was painting fence posts, and Phoebe had been almost been too scared to talk to the mighty head of the Therapeutic Riding Program. Still, she'd started up a conversation, probably saying something kind of stupid, and Jamie hadn't been as intimidating as Phoebe had expected.

Five years later, they were best friends. *And to think that earning a nickname that afternoon had felt like receiving a badge of honor.* If anything, they'd gotten even closer when Anne died. Phoebe wasn't sure how to explain it, but having Jamie close made her feel more connected to her coach. It was like they were only one degree of separation apart, she and Anne, whenever she was with Jamie. And Jamie—did she feel the same way? After all, Anne had been Jamie's last remaining relative.

Jamie hadn't cried at the funeral. She hadn't seemed lost or even brave, like she'd done all her crying in private. Her eyes weren't red-rimmed and her skin didn't bear the sick grey pallor of the grieving. She'd spoken an awe-inspiring eulogy in this quiet, straightforward tone filled with grace and dignity and . . . Phoebe searched for the word. *Ah. Peace. What had she said?* Phoebe closed her eyes and concentrated.

My Auntie A, if she were here with us right now, would tell me to keep it brief, and remind you all that our time here is a mere wisp, a minor, sometimes painful preparation for a better time. She'd tell me to skip the metaphysics, fly right past the dogma, steer clear of religion, and tell you that she feels loved right now. She felt loved while she was here among us, and from the distance that is not really so distant, she loves all of you still, oh so very much.

Phoebe gulped. That last line, about Anne loving her, because of course she was talking about Phoebe too, had made her cry at the funeral. Helen had wrapped her arm around her then, and when Phoebe rested her head on her mother's shoulder, her mother had kissed her on the forehead.

"Jamie? How did you write the eulogy?"

"Closed my eyes and listened."

"Listened to what?"

Jamie issued a dreamy sigh. "It's kind of hard to explain. Call it the Hand of God, maybe call it Jesus 'cept Jesus talks different than God does, I don't know. I used to just call it the Holy Spirit. But now I know it's really God talking to me. Been hearing from Him ever since that night. You know."

"When you were raped?"

Jamie reached over and grabbed her water bottle from the center console. After she popped the top open and swallowed a few gulps, she handed it back in Phoebe's direction, and Phoebe guided it back into the semi-obstructed cup holder. "Yeah." Jamie nodded. That night."

Phoebe sat in companionable silence, waiting for Jamie to keep talking. All the times they'd talked, sometimes while shoveling shit in the barn, sometimes in Anne's kitchen, and most often while skating or working out, and never had Jamie spoken of her rape. She'd spoken of it in a matter of fact way that afternoon in the pasture, but nothing since. Not in the five and a half years they'd been friends. Phoebe tried not to think too hard about why Jamie was telling her now.

"Almost 16 years ago, Pheebes. I was just a kid, like you were when I met you. 14. Kind of a toughie. Didn't give a rat's ass for much besides riding. Won every competition, every show, and it was easy. I'd been living with Auntie A since—" Jamie paused, and Phoebe waited.

Jamie started talking again. "Well, since my mom died. Yeah. I know it sounds like my life was hard. Mom was in so much pain those last couple years. She fought so hard, so, so hard, to give me as much time as she could. I didn't wanna let her go. Not until I couldn't bear making her suffer any longer. So one night, I kissed her goodbye. And Auntie A, well, she took me every weekend anyway, since I was at least five. Before I walked out the door of her bedroom, Mom knew it was me letting her go, or trying. She promised me she'd see me soon enough."

"You mean in heaven?"

Jamie nodded. "Reckon. But I see her, I hear her, whispering my name a lot. I know she's gone, but she's with me still. Watching me. Like when the wind's blowing, or when I'm watching the rain drops fall, it's like she's there, trying to tell me something. Don't know what, but it doesn't scare me. Auntie A used to hear it too. She's not there all the time, and I'm glad. She wasn't there the night it happened. I guess God made sure she didn't have to see it. No sense making her suffer when she couldn't stop it."

Phoebe realized Jamie was talking about the rape, and for once, she wasn't all tensed up and sick inside. She'd heard so many rape survivors talk about it in her support group, but this felt different. She was breathing, not holding her breath. "What happened that night?"

Jamie was silent for a few minutes as the miles unfurled in a patchwork of rolling hills and large estates. They were on the edge of Middleburg now, and the shadows had grown much longer as the sun neared the horizon.

"Well, it sounds crazy, but I don't remember most of it. That used to frustrate me so much. Guess they beat me up so bad, I ended up with a lot of short-term amnesia. I don't know how I got there, lying beside a hiking path near Georgetown. I can still smell the canal, the stench of it, which is how it got in the middle of summer. Like carcasses, pigs, rotting. Or human feces. Gosh. I looked up and I guess I'd passed out, because this man was holding me down. Another one was . . . inside me, and another two men were standing by, waiting, or maybe one of them was already done."

Phoebe was shaking a little. She could feel the shock of the penetration and its chafing foreign aching thrusting violation. *Not Jamie*. It seemed unfathomable that it could've been, could've happened to, the peaceful warrior sitting next to her.

Phoebe started to ask, "Then what?" but then she saw the plain mailbox with just the street address and not even the name of the safe house written on it. Jamie held up her hand and murmured, "Once we get home."

Jamie pulled into the gravel road that connected the Bryson House to the country road 615. When she rolled up to the Gatehouse, a burly guard approached her and extended a wave after submitting the SUV he'd waved through a thousand times to an almost-glaring inspection. A barrage of images cycled through her mind. *I'm not ready to be here without Coach. Or am I?* She didn't want this conversation with Jamie to end, so she tightened her jaw to hide her emotions. Jamie steered her truck up the winding hill and veered off to the left toward Anne's chalet, which sat at the top of a hill about a half-mile from the main house. Jamie switched the engine off and inclined her head. "Come on in and drink a cup of coffee with me?"

"Okay." Phoebe struggled to unbuckle her seat belt with her left hand and chuckled. "Reminds me of that afternoon I fell off Ginger, and then I couldn't even get out of my seatbelt. Mom had to do it for me."

Jamie slammed the door shut and appeared next to Phoebe with both duffel bags tossed over her shoulder. "How's your mom doing? You call her and tell her you were at the ER?"

"Thanks," Phoebe nodded at the duffel bag, and fell in step next to Jamie. "Nah. I'm not a kid anymore."

Jamie unlocked the door front door to a modern A-frame country chalet, and as soon as the door gave way, a familiar aroma greeted Phoebe. It smelled like a combination of tack and pine and wood polish, with a hint of coffee, Jamie's favorite drink. Jamie tossed the duffle bags in the corner of the foyer on top of a stack of boots and a barn jacket. Jamie continued into the family room and stopped in front of a mahogany gun cabinet.

"It's yours whenever you wanna toss it in the back of the truck, the one I keep starting up every few days for you," Jamie paused and pretended to glare at Phoebe, "and I'm hoping tonight's the night you get your stuff outta here."

Before Phoebe could crack a joke, her hands started to go a little numb, and she could feel a vise tightening on her throat. She reached out as if to lean on the edge of the cabinet, but mid-motion she put her left arm around Jamie and rested her head in the crook of Jamie's shoulder. Jamie rested her chin on Phoebe's head and wrapped both hands around her head jammer. Phoebe closed her eyes and didn't move for almost a minute. She waited for the tightening in her throat and the numbness in her hands to pass, and when it did, she patted Jamie on the back and silently moved away, toward the kitchen, where she sat down in one of the chairs.

With one knee pulled on to her chest, Phoebe was trying to clear her mind so that she could listen to Jamie.

Guns. Wayne Toller. Horses. Parkings. Coach. Heaven. Dad.

Phoebe let her chin settle on her knee and sighed a little. It felt so comfortable to be back here in the kitchen. Anne's chalet was her second home. It had always been as much Jamie's home as Anne's, but with Anne gone, little things had changed, like the smell of coffee, not tea, and the missing black riding jacket that once had hung on the back of the front door.

Once Jamie had finished grinding coffee, she got the pot brewing and pulled up a chair next to Phoebe.

"So, anyway, it hurt. I had the worst headache of my life, at least up until then." Jamie paused, chuckling ruefully. "The really bad headaches didn't go away until a couple years after all this. And it hurt. Worse than anything else. You know what I mean, right?"

Jamie had that faraway look again in her dark eyes, and Phoebe wondered how a woman could seem so grounded and yet detached from a story like—like *this*. Phoebe gave a bleak groan and whispered, "Yeah."

"I wanted to die, then and there, Pheebes. It was really bad. And then, then when I got a fix on the man who . . . who was on . . . me, well, it was the weirdest thing. This bright light, brighter than anything I'd ever seen, shone from inside him. I was sure I was dying then. And it was like I could see into him, straight to his soul, and I saw all these things, like a movie of his life, from the time he was a baby to a college student, which is what he was, at least in the vision. A Georgetown frat guy. And you know what I saw?"

Phoebe shook her head.

"I saw all the good things he'd ever done. I saw him giving his mom flowers. I saw him taking care of a worm that was about to die from the hot sun on the pavement in front of his house. I saw him kissing his grandmother goodbye in a hospital bed, and a tear drop falling on her cheek. And then I saw his pain. I saw his dad hitting the shit out of his mom. He tried to get in the way, and his dad was screaming, 'Shut the fuck up, you little bastard! You ain't even mine!' And I saw him putting a gun in his mouth and pulling the trigger, and crying when he realized there weren't any bullets in the chamber. And the whole time I was seeing his life flash before me, I wasn't feeling what was happening to me. I felt his pain, not so much my own, and I wanted to tell him it was going to be okay. There were words. But I couldn't speak. Then he went away, I mean, he was still there, but the white light billowed all the way up to the sky, and got wider, bigger, until that's all there was. Just light. I guess I passed out then.

"I kept passing in and out of consciousness I guess. Saw a woman and a man. Another woman and a man, and some loud noises. When I woke up, I was lying in a hospital bed, staring up at a bright florescent lights, you know, the ones that kill you when you wanna sleep." Jamie leaned forward and the lines around her eyes crinkled. "Then Mary came to visit me."

Phoebe shook her head. "Um, Mary? Like Mother of God and all that?"

Jamie tapped Phoebe on the knee and grinned. "Mary Magdalene. World's first rape counselor. She didn't talk to me. Just sat beside me for a little while, kept my mind off everything. I'd lost a lot of blood, and my head was cut open right through my skull. Funny. It didn't hurt while she was there. And I could hear some music, like chanting, and when that ended, and Mary left, my mom came by. At first I wanted to cover up and hide from her, but she kissed my hands and told me I was safe, and . . . well, I don't know exactly what she told me. Just made me feel like I, or it, was gonna be all right."

"You saw your mom?"

Jamie rose to her feet, and from where Phoebe was sitting, she seemed even taller than six feet. "Yep." With her usual quiet efficiency, Jamie poured two steaming mugs of coffee. After setting them on the table she handed Phoebe the half and half from the fridge. Phoebe found the hint of a smile creeping around her mouth and she hoped Jamie wouldn't be offended. This was all so comfortable. It would be like Phoebe to mess it up by smiling when she was trying not to cry.

Jamie tossed the creamer back into the fridge and slammed the door shut in one quick motion. Phoebe took a long sip of coffee and observed Jamie as wisps of steam wound their way from the top of the brown liquid in Jamie's mug. Phoebe felt something she couldn't really put a finger on. It was powerful, whatever it was. Like . . . love. Whatever that felt like. Phoebe grimaced. Hopefully not that kind of love. That would make things way too complicated. But if it wasn't that kind of love, what was it? All she knew was that she didn't want this conversation to ever end. And if something ever happened to Jamie, she'd break through a brick wall to save her.

"How long were you in the hospital, anyway?" Phoebe almost dropped her mug when she grasped the handle. *Damn hand,* she mumbled. Jamie reached over, and with a calming hand on the other side of the mug, repositioned it until it rested more securely in Phoebe's aching hand. Jamie murmured, "There, now. Better?"

Phoebe nodded. She wanted to smile but she was too tired. Then she repeated, "How long?"

Jamie leaned back in her chair and put her feet up on one of the other chairs. She almost looked like a man, the way she was sitting, or at least like a woman no one would fuck with. "Few days. They had trouble getting my seizures under control. In fact, turns out that wasn't all there was, you know, wrong. Well. A few days later, they had to rush me back into surgery. Brain was bleeding."

Phoebe gulped. The idea of Jamie having her head shaved and cut open scared her. She pictured a kid, and Jamie must have been just a scared kid, lying in a hospital bed. Jamie would have been wrapped up in and there must have been blood everywhere. And flowers—were there flowers? Did anyone send her flowers? She shook her head. It seemed crazily unfair all of a sudden. Because if anything ever happened to her, Mom would be right there. Cass too, probably. And Zander. He showed up everywhere.

But Jamie didn't have a mom or a dad. *It was so awful. Really.* The back of Phoebe's throat felt raw, like she'd been screaming, but it was probably just spring allergies.

"Were you all alone?" She blurted out.

Jamie closed her eyes and took a deep breath, smiling, and opened her eyes only when she began speaking again. "Course not. I had Mary. And my mom from time to time. And of course Auntie A was there the rest of the time. I wasn't even alone during the surgery."

"They let Anne be in the OR?"

"Nah. Mom was there." Jamie took another sip of coffee and then rolled her head, like she was stretching her upper back muscles. Phoebe tried to remember if she'd remembered to pack her helmet in her duffel bag, or whether she'd been wearing it in the hospital. Helmets, hostiles, and hospitals. That was the phrase of the day.

Chapter 17

After they sat sipping coffee in an almost reverential silence, Jamie stood up and stretched. Then she poured the rest of her coffee down the drain and put her mug into the dishwasher. She was just as neat and orderly in the kitchen as she was in the barn, Phoebe noted.

"Come on, Pheebes, wanna go on my rounds with me?"

"Fuck, I don't know," Phoebe blurted, and then she gulped.

"Time to rip the bandaid off, kay?" Jamie strode across the kitchen, and as she passed the gun cabinet, with Phoebe on her heels, she paused ad handed Phoebe a thick, black metal flashlight.

Phoebe nodded.

"Longer you put it off—"

"—Yeah. I know." Phoebe looked around for her jacket and realized she'd left it at practice. She wrapped her arms around herself, and Jamie issued an imperial nod.

"Guess you need to borrow a jacket."

"Yeah."

"On the other side of the door—think there's one." Jamie gestured toward the alcove between the gun cabinet and the front door.

Phoebe swallowed and then grabbed the collar of a dark red barn jacket. It smelled like tack and leather and Iberians. She smiled to herself. *That was ridiculous. Iberians smelled no different than any other horse.* And then a chill ran down the back of her neck. Iberian. Ginger. Ginger in the barn. Parking.

> *Here I go again. Been over this. Been over this a million times if I've been over it once. Trauma consult. EMDR. But nothing got rid. Got rid. Got rid of him. His smell was like a poison she couldn't find an antidote for, and every time she rode, she got jumpy. And you can't get jumpy, feel jumpy, be jumpy, around an Iberian, or almost any horse really. Well, maybe not a quarter horse. Sheesh. Here I go again slamming on quarter horses. Here I go again. Yep. Here I go again.*

Phoebe shrugged into the jacket, easing it over her bandaged hand with a grimace that turned into a bark of laughter.

Jamie leaned on the door, with one hand on the knob to the screen door. She didn't ask why Phoebe was laughing, and that made Phoebe laugh a little harder. Then she stopped, as if bringing a horse to the fence after a gallop and then pulling up just short of the jump, and she stood there, thinking about what her life would have been like if she were still riding with Anne.

"Ready, Pheebes?"

"Fucking A."

They stepped outside and the stars and the moon shone bright above the looming mountains, which cast a shadow of sorts over the gravel driveway that ended at the side of the chalet. Phoebe could hear the miniscule stones crunching underfoot and when she glanced down she realized she was wearing her combat boots. Man, Jamie remembered everything.

"Hey, Jamie, I'm wearing my boots." Phoebe sounded cocky again, at least to her own ears.

"Yeah? Funny that."

Phoebe worried that Jamie was annoyed. *Nah. It's just Jamie. She's always like that.* "Thanks for bringing them to the hospital."

"Hmm." Jamie glanced at Phoebe out of the corner of her eye. "You should thank Beth. She's the one who grabbed your duffel bag."

"Beth did?"

Jamie took loping steps toward the path that led to the main house, and Phoebe had to jog a few steps to catch up.

"Think I should—"

"—Yeah." Jamie's didn't stop moving, but she held her cell phone out over her should. "Call her. Her number's in my contacts."

"Under 'Beth?'" Phoebe chuckled as she scrolled through the list of names. "No, no, of course not. You got everyone's derby names in here. Man, it's like the whole lineup's in here."

"That's because the whole lineup is in there." *Jamie's voice wasn't cold, was it?* Phoebe shook her head. Then she smiled a little, when she saw Beth's derby name, Big Bertha. But before the smile reached her eyes, she felt *chickenshit scared* all over again. *Fuck it.* She hit the green symbol.

"Jamie! How the hell are you sister?" Beth boomed.

Phoebe smiled in spite of herself. "It's me. Pheebes." Phoebe dropped her voice and tried to sound as hardass as she knew she looked, at least when she was on skates. What would the girls think if any of them saw her with her dad? And then she was wiping a tear from her eyes, because she cared what they thought.

She never could get free, could she? Of him, of what he'd made her, of being scared, being foreign, being visible, being seen—by anyone.

She wiped the tear away before it stung her eyes too bad, and then she waited for Beth to say something so she could talk right.

"Pheebes!" Beth's voice boomed just so loud, Phoebe held the phone a little away from her ear. "How the hell are you sister?"

"Aw, shit, Beth. Not bad. Not bad. How are you?"

"Just sitting here watching some hockey, drinking some cold beer." Beth put the emphasis on cold, and it made Phoebe laugh real hard. Beth always did that. She could make a plate of spaghetti sound funny.

"Hockey, eh?"

"Yessiree, sister. Hockey! You should see the hits they're laying on one another. Y'all should come watch a game here at Bessie's Joint with us this weekend. I got some moves I wanna try out, and some strategy—and hey! Bill! Gimme another one, all right? Good man!" Beth paused and made what sounded like guzzling sounds.

"Hey, Jamie! Wanna go watch some hockey with Beth this weekend and talk derby?"

"Oh hell yeah, put her on the phone, Pheebes! Lemme yell in her ear for a sec."

Phoebe started to pull the phone away from her ear.

"Oh hey, wait. Pheebes. Listen. I'm sorry, sister. Won't do that ever again, promise."

"Me too. I'm sorry too."

Phoebe handed Jamie the phone and walked several feet away so that she wouldn't overhear their conversation. Seemed rude, and surely Jamie was still fixing whatever Phoebe had gone and fucked up. Without looking back, Phoebe reached into the pocket her jacket, in search of her pack of cigs. Too late, she realized she was wearing Jamie's jacket, and all she felt was a key ring. She didn't need to look at the keys to know what they were for: she'd driven Anne's old Ford pickup truck enough times to recognize the feel of the metal against her finger tips.

Maybe tonight she'd drive it. Maybe there was no way to stop forgetting it all. Maybe she just needed to drive through the wave right before it swelled and fell in on her again.

She swung her arms out behind her and spun around, eyes fixed on the stars. It seemed really late because the air was still and everything was quiet, but she had no idea what time it was. The frogs and the cicadas and the nighttime insects hadn't woken from winter yet, so all she could hear was the thumping of her heart and the wind moving the leaves and the fir tree branches. The grounds at the Bryson House weren't that different from her own home, but at home, it was simpler, or at least her memories were.

Here, on the grounds of a safe house that had been anything but at times, she tripped from joy to fear to peace to heartbreak to panic to gratitude, and that was all in the first five minutes of setting foot on the soft grass underfoot. No matter where she moved, she thought of someone or something, and then immediately of its opposite, or its nemesis. She thought of Anne; she thought of Parkings. She thought of mom; she thought of dad. She thought of cantering with a quiet competence; she thought of gripping too tight, and Anne correcting, right before she snapped, "Fuck it," in her most vulgar voice. She thought of watermelon; she thought of vicious stinging flies.

Pain, pleasure. Happiness, sadness. Loving, losing. Phoebe began to laugh. She turned faster and faster, spinning wildly, a little out of control, then even faster, and laughing harder still. After all, "It's better to love and lose than—"

"—Never love at all." Jamie came up behind her, and finished reciting the line from a poem they'd both learned from Anne.

Phoebe stopped turning. "Okay if I don't do rounds with you?"

Jamie's eyes glittered in the darkness, as if illuminated. "Wanna take the truck?"

"Yeah."

"Yeah." Jamie nodded. "Why don't you get it started up and I'll grab your duffel."

"Kay."

A few minutes later, Phoebe gunned the engine one more time, and as she released the parking brake with her foot, Jamie slapped the rear panel of the blue Ford. Phoebe tapped the accelerator and with one hand over the back of the seat, reversed, and drove off into the night.

•••

Helen Thompson flicked her pen and checked her watch again. It was past 9 p.m., but she wasn't worried about her daughter. As long as she was with Anne's niece, Jamie, Phoebe would be all right. Helen gripped her mug of Earl Grey tea and leaned against her top floor balcony. Much like The Bryson House, her own home had a top floor alcove, and she found herself spending more and more time outside, not so much just sitting still, but working. Nothing really was much more enjoyable to her than her work.

Except, of course, her only child. As cocky and difficult and tender and downright messy and mixed up as her daughter was, she was, of course, the light of my life, mused Helen.

And that's when the phone rang. Of course she had both her cell phone and the home phone with her. Just in case McCormick needed her. And just in case Phoebe got stranded. But it wasn't McCormick and it wasn't Phoebe. It was Cassandra, and Helen answered it as soon as she saw who it was on Caller ID.

"Hello, Cassandra." Helen took a sip from her tea and then just waited. Cassandra was a fast-talker and a loud one, too. Their conversations always went by quickly, and they'd been talking everyday for more than five years.

"Hey, Helen! You wouldn't believe who I ran into at the ER today. Seriously. I'll give you one guess."

Helen didn't answer right away. It wasn't like Cass to talk in riddles, so it would have to be an obvious answer. "And why were you at the hospital?"

Cassandra laughed in the background.

Helen heard a child's voice asking a question.

"Hmm, not right now Zander. Give me a sec, and I'll—no, really, just wait. Or ask your dad. No, really, I'm on the phone. Enough." Cassandra sighed dramatically and laughed again. "Excuse me Helen. Sorry about that. He's been quiet for the last few minutes, so I thought I could talk in peace." Cassandra sighed again. "You know. *As if.*"

"That's fine." Helen looked out toward the side of the house, and then into the dark, where the slightest hint of a mountain rose into view, only to vanish into the foreground. She didn't mind waiting for Cassandra to tell a story. These hospital visit stories were always quite amusing.

"So," Cassandra continued, "For some reason I let Zander skate."

"Not derby?"

"No. Skateboard. Bought him a skateboard. And a helmet. And some Vans."

"Vans?"

"Yeah, as in the shoe brand, not conversion."

Helen smiled to herself. Cassandra was the smartest woman Helen knew. When they talked Helen never felt impatient.

"Right. You bought your attention deficit hyperactive son a skateboard, a helmet, and some Vans shoes. Sounds prudent, under the circumstances." Helen smiled again, and pictured Zander swinging from a school swing set upside down, which had resulted in one of Cassandra's ER visits.

"Prudent? Oh my gosh. I don't know about that. Because apparently," Cassandra drew out the word, "He went skating with Justin—"

"—As in Jason's little brother?" Helen knew the back story on Jason.

"Yep. Justin, brother of Jason. Same Justin, brother of Jason who's building a ramp, a really, really big ramp. But I get ahead of myself."

Helen chuckled.

"And then Zander kept getting his hair in his eyes, or he couldn't see well enough with the helmet blocking his peripheral vision, or maybe he just fucking missed the ER, I mean, right?" Cassandra laughed.

"ER's a hopping place on a Thursday night." Helen took another sip of tea, feeling content. And then she remembered Cassandra had started the story off with a riddle. She still didn't have the answer figured out.

"Funny you should mention that." Cassandra was snickering.

"Mention what? That the ER was hopping? Come on Cass. Who'd you run into? And is Zander okay?"

"Well, lemme put it this way. Zander isn't the only child related to you or me who had helmet issues today."

Helen put her hand to her throat. "Phoebe?"

"You got it counselor." Cassandra murmured something unintelligible into the receiver, and then added, much louder, "No. To bed." After another moment, Cassandra's voice returned to its normal volume. "Yeah. She was there too. She's okay. Jamie was there with her, and I think they were driving out to the Bryson House. Why? Phoebe didn't call you, did she?"

Helen shook her head and then remembered to add, "No. Oh, wait, I take it Zander's okay too?"

"Yeah. Zander's okay. Phoebe's okay. And Phoebe and Jamie are taking Zander helmet shopping on Saturday."

"I see."

"Yeah, Justin, not Jason, is building a ramp. And against my better judgment, I said he could skate again." Cassandra giggled. "On a ten-foot high ramp."

Helen shook her head. "No worse than my kid brawling on skates with women twice her size. Oh, wait, they call it derby."

Both women laughed.

"So, just thought you'd wanna know, I don't know, that the kids are all right."

"Or in this case, they're all right after they weren't."

"Quite right."

They both chuckled again.

"Thanks for calling."

"Yep."

After she hung up, Helen thought about her partner, who'd started off as her lawyer, and now had become her best friend. Maybe her first real friend, at least since undergrad. And with a sense of peace than ran deep, she sipped on her tea and waited for Phoebe to get back home.

Chapter 18

Jamie took a final look around the barn and then zipped up her parka. Padding behind her came Charlie, her dog. Anne had gotten Charlie after Parkings attacked Phoebe. Charlie slept with the horses, which was not anything she or Anne had planned.

One night, when Charlie was still a puppy, Jamie had spent the night in the barn to keep an eye on one of the Iberians, who'd come down with a virus. Charlie had followed her down to the barn and had paced all night, not nervously. Just as if he were guarding. The next night, even after Jamie had headed back to the chalet, Charlie had stood sentinel, not budging, snout turned toward the trees, as if waiting. She hadn't questioned it. Apparently, as Anne later mused, Charlie was where he needed to be.

The temperature had dropped several degrees in the last hour, and she'd worked up a sweat fixing a few broken slats in one of the stalls. She couldn't be catching a cold. No one else could run the program, not really, and the Bryson House had several families staying at it. Not only moms, but moms with little kids.

Most of the kids didn't know enough to be scared. They weren't scared of the horses, not so much, and that was the first lesson she taught them. Not to be scared, but to respect the horse, much like even the strongest swimmer respected the ocean. The thing was, some of these kids were almost fearless, but not in a good way. As their inner cargo, they carried recklessness. They fled from fear, stared it down, swore it off, refused to own or be owned by it, not even for a second.

For the fearless ones, God had chosen her as their minister. For in running from fear, or from caring about anything enough to fear it, they were running from love. From Him. And so in a way, Jamie was their shepherd, sent to teach them to face their fear with love. He told her these things, just as He was talking to her now.

When He spoke, it came like a thought, a direct thought, not a spoken voice, but a kind of certainty, with words, more formal than any she ever used. And the thought felt like light, a whiteness, a warm glow inside, when it came. Like now, she heard Him.

"Teach her now. She must not fear. Teach her not to fear. Not to strike out with anger."

"You mean in Derby?"

"That's one arena; life is an arena, is it not?"

Jamie let the barn door close shut behind her, and as she moved toward the perimeter of the Bryson House, she double-checked the safety on her pistol. This was when God spoke to her most of the time. When she was on her nightly rounds. Protector. Shepherd.

"You mean Phoebe, right?"

"She is much loved," God said. "She will be tempted to hurt, even to kill. She will strike out. But she must learn her own way."

"What am I supposed to do?"

"If you keep trying to save her, you will be hurt, my daughter."

"Hurt?" Jamie asked.

"You must be strong for your flock. You must be strong for her. There are many ways to be strong; many ways to protect the one you must protect."

"Phoebe?"

"As I was saying, be strong for her without taking it on the chin. If you have ears, hear."

Jamie let her boots sink into the Virginia clay under foot. She could smell smoke rising from a distant chimney. Hopefully not the main house's chimney. The smoke bothered Charlie. He always pawed at the ground and shoved his snout into the grass, sneezing extra, whenever Mimi lit one of the fireplaces. Of course, Jamie only had to ask, and Mimi, kind heart that she was, would put it out.

"Hear? My flock? You mean the kids? Or the derby team? Or just Phoebe?"

"Be strong and lead; being strong and fearing not is different than flying into a hurricane. Your plane has cracks in it; a squall it will endureth not. Be guided by love more than bravery."

"But derby? Is it okay for me to keep skating? I know it's not so safe," Jamie said.

"You fly with cracked wings and you ask me if the wind shear makes flight unsafe? Really Jamie, you ask this of me?"

Jamie shook her head with a rueful smile. He was hilarious. Wind shears and hurricanes and cracked wings. He loved talking in riddles. He would never tell her not to do something. It just wasn't His way.

Since she was talking to Him, she wasn't fudging it. If she were talking to anyone else, she would not have admitted that maybe derby wasn't the safest sport in the world. *But deep down . . . well, deep down she knew*. In fact, she knew it so well, she'd hidden it from her Aunt.

When Anne got too sick to leave the house, she camped out downstairs. Until the very end, Anne had insisted on remaining by the gun cabinet, on the sleep sofa, close enough to the kitchen to make her own tea.

Jamie smiled. She could feel Anne with her sometimes, especially in the early morning hours. Jamie never liked waking before dawn, at least before Anne passed away. Now, it was a special time.

One morning, Anne had pulled Jamie aside. Her grip was still firm, and she'd guided Jamie by the elbow toward the kitchen table. It would be their last cup of tea in the kitchen together.

Anne had never wasted time or minced words, and this morning had been no exception. "I have one thing to ask of you."

Jamie had swallowed, hard, and then had reached over and held Anne's hand. "Anything."

"Watch over our child of light."

"Watch over Pheebes?"

"Aye." Anne inclined her head, and when she saw how hard Jamie was working her jaw, she'd added, "And lay off that damn derby. For cripes sake, Jamie Anne, you know you're one good hit from another brain bleed."

Jamie had been stunned. She had kept derby a secret from her Aunt. How could she turn down what was feeling like a deathbed request? On the other hand, how could she stop skating?

And just when she'd opened her mouth to make a promise she didn't know she could keep, Anne had grinned. For just a moment, Anne had looked almost young again. "Aw, shucks. I almost had you. I know you love it. I know you lost riding, and I know it almost killed you, not being able to ride all these years. Just be careful, okay," and with her grey eyes crinkling, Anne had tapped her fingers on Jamie's wrist.

Jamie pulled her parka up higher, so that her neck was covered as she approached the tree line. The Bryson House still had professional guards. It wasn't like they saw the two dead ones and threw their hands up in the air.

To the contrary, Mimi and Miranda asked Anne and Jamie to research the house's security. They got in touch with one of Anne's eccentric, specially talented old friends, Paul, who had once worked out of Langley, or possibly still did. Paul went through a security assessment, and for months, he met with Anne and Jamie every Monday night. He taught them tactical awareness and risk assessment, more than anything.

Jamie became the liaison between the Main House and the guards. She even played a role in hiring guards, who now were all ex-military. She helped establish new security procedures; for example, the guards did not follow set hours. Sometimes two served at a time; sometimes, three were on duty. Sometimes two staffed the guardhouse; sometimes one watched incoming traffic and another watched the perimeter or kept an eye on the grounds.

And Jamie, who never slept more than four hours or five hours a night, took on something she never told anyone else about. At night, but without a discernible pattern, she walked the property, again, with no pattern, and she always armed herself. Usually she carried a pistol, which lacked total firepower, but she didn't want to alarm the guests. She didn't feel angry when she patrolled. Or scared. She was a shepherd. No more. No less.

On this night, Jamie decided to check out the south side of the estate, which bordered on the Lawrence winery. Mrs. Lawrence wasn't so bad. A bit of a wine snob, but she never had a nasty word to say about anyone. That was one of the best measures of a person. How they talked when no one they knew so well was listening.

Jamie reached the pond, and paused to see if the frogs were out yet. It was one of the surest signs of spring. The forsythia bloomed, a not quite pale yellow, and the frogs made their frog noise. She chuckled. It didn't really sound like a *ribbit*. That's what she used to say to her mom, back before her mom took ill. *Pain, so much pain, my mom, for so long, just holding on. She was holding on for me.*

Jamie took a deep breath, and then she walked a little faster. She swung her arms high and closed her eyes, walking blind, but feeling the earth, grounded in it, steady. She could sense the hill rising, and in a few strides, it would start sloping down again. And she concentrated on the air, and her feet, and the other sense, *the one we humans lost too easily, when we saw with our eyes, not with our souls*. And once she connected with her soul, all her cares and her memories faded and the light ruled.

It didn't seem dark outside anymore. She felt a lightening coming from inside. It wasn't that she could see what was around her as if it was illuminated from within. It was more that she wasn't looking outside. She was looking, feeling, almost touching her inner essence, and in finding that, she felt like she was on her way Home again.

Jamie opened her eyes, and she thought about derby. When she skated, she felt this lightness of being, a freedom, a freedom from needing, or wanting anything of this or from this world. It was almost like she was riding again, but it was even more freeing, being part of a team, part of something, connected, moving, always moving, no reason, no good reason, not needing one, not really. Just going Home. Home again.

Chapter 19

Wayne Toller turned his hat over and over in his hand, and then, with a final, awful sigh, he strode into the hallway of his parents' Methodist church. They were waiting for him, to welcome him. That's what they said. It was a likely story.

He was supposed to thank them all, and keep his eyes glued to the ground, and just maybe if he didn't stare at any of the girls, no one would mention the whole affair. A big mistake was all it was. That's what his mom had told all her neighbors.

He overheard her talking sometimes, when she was leaning over her hedges, explaining the *whole unfortunate affair* to her neighbors. *Tragic.* That's the word she used. "Tragic," and "Oh heavens," she would cry, hands to throat, "to think my son was with those hardened criminals." Then she'd wipe her eyes on her apron, and blink a lot.

He was free. That's what they said. A freed man. But they didn't understand. None of them could see that he'd never be free.

He leaned forward a little bit, until his body slanted and then he would either have to fall or move. He wondered sometimes if he'd ever fall, trying that. He used to love playing chicken in his dad's Charger. The hair would stand up on the back of his neck until the other guy's elbows would jerk, like a lever, at the very last minute. He was playing chicken with the ground, well sort of.

Damnit that made no sense. Wayne shook his head, and shuffled his feet right before he went horizontal on the grimy, gray church carpet.

The shuffling felt comfortable. He held his hands out in front of him, almost as an instinctual sacrificing of his dignity. *Number 287-98013*, he almost murmured. That was his three-five, as they called it on the inside. He followed the dots and the coffee stains from the atrium all the way into the chapel, where the carpet turned into plusher, blue material.

E-F-W niner five oh.

Wayne had that stuck in his head. It wasn't his three-five. That he'd memorized. It meant more inside than his social security number. For real. But E-F-W niner five oh rolled off his tongue. Felt right. He'd memorized it and kept it close, within reach of his thoughts, almost at all times, for five years now. It didn't mean anything to anyone. Just some letters, and some numbers. He liked it. He pretended that it was the code for a safety deposit box or a password for a secret bank account. He played games like this, late at night, when all he could see was the vertical stripes on the bunk bed above his.

Wayne lifted his ankles a little higher, to make it over the entranceway, and then the sound came rushing in. The organ, the saccharine greetings, the muffled exchanges. He lifted his eyes from the polished brown leather shoes he was wearing. Some old people. Like his mom. And a few families, ones with little girls wearing pretty pink dresses. He tried not to stare at her. She looked at him; he glanced to her left, and his eyes met with a glaring set of heavy-browed ex-military *daddy's got a gun* eyes. *Oh shit.* He shivered a little, shrinking away from the thought of shaking hands, his hands, even the little girl's hands, during fellowship. Her hands would feel soft, warm, so soft . . . *oh shit.* He's need to get out of the atrium before that, maybe hit the head.

He took eleven more steps, and ducked in behind the pretty little girl wearing the frilly pink dress. She was too far away for him to touch, but she was close enough for him to catch the air conditioner vent blow the fringes of her skirt up toward her thigh. *Ahh.* He'd been away too long; not long enough. He'd never be free, truly free, of it.

He sat down and bowed his head and prayed. Well, he thought about praying, but it didn't sound right, what he wanted. So he sat still, and moved his mouth like he was saying something nice. And he tried not to smell his mother's perfume, or the slight whiff of mothballs that was coming from his suit jacket. It reminded him of kitty litter, which made no sense, because they smelled nothing alike. *Mothballs and kitty litter?* He'd been a three-fiver for too long.

They stood up again. And sat down. And stood up. And sat down. He didn't mind the steady drumbeat of minutes ticking past. Peppy used to say time was all a man had, and some other good-sounding stuff, while he was cutting potatoes with a dull knife. But Peppy was a bit of a fool sometimes. A man had a lot more than time, as long as he didn't let it get the measure of him.

Wayne heard the rustling of his mother's thighs against the seat bottoms and the scritch-scratch of her fingernails on her silky, light purple blouse. He fumbled through the unwieldy church bulletin, and then the pastor cleared his throat and announced, "Today's reading is from the Book of Genesis, Chapter 18, verse 13:

> *Then the LORD said to Abraham, "Why did Sarah laugh and say, 'Will I really have a child, now that I am old?' Is anything too hard for the LORD? I will return to you at the appointed time next year, and Sarah will have a son."*
> *Sarah was afraid, so she lied and said, "I did not laugh."*
> *But he said, "Yes, you did laugh."*

Wayne wrinkled his forehead. Sarah conceived a baby and the baby became . . . he paused and skimmed ahead. He should know this stuff. Been too long since he'd last read it. He got to chapter 19. He had to stop and reread it again, while still remembering who Sarah gave birth to. He had to figure that out, but he read:

> *Lot went outside to meet them and shut the door behind him and said, "No, my friends. Don't do this wicked thing. Look, I have two daughters who have never slept with a*

man. Let me bring them out to you, and you can do what you like with them. But don't do anything to these men, for they have come under the protection of my roof."

So really, that's all Richard had done. He was taking care of his guests, and as Richard's guest, it would have been wrong to turn down an offer to sleep with his daughter. He did nothing wrong, then? According to this?

Sarah gave birth to who? He had to focus. Wayne kept reading, and a few lines farther down, he came to the story about Lot and his daughters. Genesis 19:30. He'd read this story before, and it really wasn't suitable for church. The first time he read the story, he'd laid hands to himself. He really shouldn't read this in church, damn his eyes.

But he read it anyway:

That night they got their father to drink wine, and the older daughter went in and slept with him. He was not aware of it when she lay down or when she got up.
The next day the older daughter said to the younger, "Last night I slept with my father. Let's get him to drink wine again tonight, and you go in and sleep with him so we can preserve our family line through our father." So they got their father to drink wine that night also, and the younger daughter went in and slept with him. Again he was not aware of it when she lay down or when she got up.
So both of Lot's daughters became pregnant by their father.

And then it was happening. Not here. "Be right back, Mother," he whispered. He didn't shuffle his feet this time. Not with the evidence of Genesis 19's effect on him growing more obvious by the second. No foot shuffling. No one could see him— see it. It wouldn't do.

Wayne flicked the bathroom door open with three fingers, and tried to avoid seeing his face in the mirror. He caught a glimpse of someone who looked ordinary. Thick glasses, thinning hair, a strong chin. No one would know, just seeing it, that it was a face marked by guilt. He sighed, and retreated into the bathroom stall, one hand reaching through his open zipper, the other hand on the lock.

He'd never be a free man.

Chapter 20

Catherine pulled the Volvo crossover into a nice and wide, *you know you're out of the city when* . . . type of space and tried to relax her shoulders. She lifted better when she was relaxed for some reason. Same thing for running. She never did anything well when she was angry or hepped up, and she'd never jammed to loud music before a meet or before lifting or before a session at the range. Catherine wanted to have all her senses, especially when she was needing to push her body. In fact, she didn't try and get psyched up even for her sparring sessions, which she'd started up as a sophomore at Oregon, about when she decided she'd follow Mike into the FBI.

Mike had been her sort of boyfriend who she'd never actually dated. Catherine started to laugh. It just had never been the right timing: either he was coming off a relationship, or she was grieving Marcy, and later, when he signed up with the FBI, he'd known that he'd be leaving and probably not coming back, not ever, not if he could help it, to Oregon or anywhere near the Pacific Northwest. He'd been oddly set on that, and she never understood why, other than it had something to do with his family.

Ahhh, Mike. Maybe she'd run into him at some point. Maybe they'd still have that funny thing between them, best of friends, everyone was sure they were destined to be more, and so were they, so sure neither one really dated much, at least as far as she knew since he'd left two years ahead of her. He'd come back to the East Coast. Stationed now near Richmond, and he kept saying they should meet up maybe on the weekend, once his current detail settled down just a bit.

He wasn't just saying that . . . damn timing. No idea why she was thinking of him just now . . . oh right. He'd taken her to self-defense classes with him, let her tail right along to Judo and then to the firing range. And after Marcy . . . went back Home, Mike had held her all night. He'd even lost his girlfriend at the time because of it. She'd walked in on them, and it was totally innocent, it really was, but she'd been too into Mike, too into herself, too into Mike and herself . . . to understand that Mike had really just been holding her.

Catherine felt a surge of desire and she shivered a little. Truth? She wished they'd made love that night. It was the closest they'd ever come, and now? Now she missed him; she missed all they'd had together, and she missed even more the one thing they'd not had. Maybe she should just call him, tell him how she felt. Catherine groaned. She'd only cared about two people like this, and one of them was dead. It was all so confusing.

Enough. It was time to see what Phoebe Thompson's gym was about. She didn't see Phoebe's famous Peppermint Sled. Maybe it was still in the shop. Zander swore Phoebe would be here and he seemed to have her schedule memorized. Zander didn't just have a crush on Phoebe: he worshiped her in that innocent, adorable way of little boys who still cuddled their mamas. Catherine smiled tenderly. She had almost brought him with her. Almost. But she needed to focus and that was impossible when he was circling her. And though having him there would probably have given her some sort of protection or comfort or whatever . . . Catherine shook her head in disgust. She was past needing any of that.

Down a few dark hallways and underneath a series of dingy drop ceilings, all smudged with the grease and grime of years and bodies, she passed until she came to a large open area, almost 30 yards long from the looks of it. Catherine breathed in the dank air, the smell of hard work and guts, and she forgot for a moment about finding a workout mate. She wasn't here to fuck around, and the only way to start was to drop and start.

So without much thought about where her bag landed, Catherine dropped and did 50 pushups. She rested and did 50 more. She could feel the pulse in her temple during the last fourteen or so, and it wasn't a great feeling, that anaerobic complete and total loss of control really, no air, none getting in, and sudden, no real warning, so different from running. She always knew, maybe a minute, a quarter-mile ahead of time that she was losing air, but even then, she could slow down, drop to three-quarters speed for a minute, maybe even glide to a few clicks slower than her mom's marathon pace.

But reaching that can't breathe threshold while lifting was a precious process. It was not a matter of guts. It was more a matter of knowing exactly when you were gonna black out if you didn't back off, and all Catherine knew was she'd not blacked out, not yet, but she needed to push it someday, why not this day, why not find out here, without any men she was competing against, why not?

So she dropped and she was thirty-three pushups into the third set of fifty when she wasn't seeing right, and after that she wasn't too sure where she was, not sure, not completely. But she knew how many. She kept up the count, thirty-five, then forty, then forty-five, then forty-six, forty-seven, forty-eight, forty-nine, and fifty. She couldn't see anything, not during the last five, but she could hear, and what she heard was a very loud, very sharp voice, shouting out insults, and she was pretty sure she recognized the voice.

There was only one Phoebe Thompson.

And Catherine was aware of eyes on her, aware of a consciousness watching over her, but it wasn't Phoebe. It was— she was someone, something . . . familiar, but strange too, and the last thing Catherine felt like doing was meeting someone new, except this didn't feel like someone new. It felt like someone she just hadn't seen in awhile, in too long, someone . . .who? *Damnit, Catherine, get up now and don't faint.*

Catherine jumped to her feet and that's when she first made eye contact with the woman who had been watching over her.

"Hey, name's Jamie Eddington."

Catherine shook hands with a tall woman with grey eyes. Eyes unlike any other, eyes that were closer to white than to grey, with a halo effect from all the light, and she almost couldn't find the words to reply. She almost said, "How long's it been?" Because she knew this soul from somewhere. Instead, Catherine leaned back against the painted white cement wall. And then she let her eyes show the smile she was too tired to fully form.

"Catherine White," Catherine said, "And you're—"

"—Hey Cat," Phoebe said, her voice neutral, "Zander said you might come lift with us."

Catherine rubbed her hands together. "Yeah, reckon I could use the extra work." She had to force herself not to tell the rest of the story, about the FBI and all that. It wasn't like she needed to brag, show she belonged. *I belong anywhere, anyhow,* was how she'd gotten to the podium so many times in the NCAAs. It was and it was how she'd held herself after she testified against the running back and then the entire football team had catcalled her for the rest of her time at OR. None of them had touched her or any of the other runners; they just called her that *crazy white bitch* and that was just fine.

"You been touring downtown?" Phoebe nodded at Cat's FBI t-shirt, grey with blue letters.

Cat had the sudden wish to slap Phoebe upside the head. There was no way Zander hadn't told her . . . Catherine took a deep breath and thanked God her face was already red from the three sets of fifty. And then she saw the grim look on Jamie's face, somewhat grim, but also a bit amused, not at Catherine's expense though . . . Catherine could read that. Jamie had a calm way about her; she was no-nonsense and somehow in charge—as if anyone could be in charge of Phoebe? Yes, Jamie was in charge. At least that's how Catherine read it.

And sure enough, Jamie said, "Hmm, Catherine, are you with the FBI? That looks more like one of their official training shirts."

Catherine crossed over to the pull-ups bar and closed her eyes for a moment, counted to three, made sure she was focused in on what she needed to do. She needed to clear twenty-five, full extensions on each. "Yep. Training." Then she commenced, and while she worked through her reps, she kept God there, kept asking Him to hold her, praying, Please Lord give me strength, please Lord give me strength.

When she dismounted, Jamie gave her a sober nod, and that's when Phoebe clapped her hands and walked in Catherine's direction, shadow boxing and talking trash.

"So Cat, I didn't take you for a FBI Agent type, I was thinking you were this runner, running over hill and dale and all over the state, the states of the Pacific Northwest, so what do you say, spar with me a little? I got some ladies I'm owing a couple of hard hits, fuckers got me good last bout."

"Bout? As in roller derby?" Derby was huge in Oregon, and Catherine had been to a few bouts with Marcy their freshman year.

"Yeah, best sport ever, maybe you wanna come skate with us sometime," Phoebe said.

One thing about Catherine is she didn't think before she said shit sometimes, and this was one of those times. "Sport's too dangerous. Not worth the concussion risk. Almost as many concussions per bouts played as in football and you know what percentage of NFL players have shown brain damage when their brains have been autopsied?"

Phoebe kind of scoffed, and kind of got in Catherine's face without really moving that much closer. "What, you don't like getting hit? Guess running doesn't have much hitting, much real danger, does it?"

"You asked me if I don't like getting hit, and the answer's 'No,' I don't really like getting hit, but I don't mind delivering one when it's needed." Catherine paused and stared at Jamie, then she faced Phoebe, holding eye contact as she continued, "As far as running not being dangerous, have you ever been to a cross-country meet, or a marathon, ever seen a runner collapse at the finish line, pretty near dead, having given all and a whole lot more? Dangerous?" Catherine was getting emotional.

She was remembering about the first title she won. She'd given all, and more, and she'd have collapsed had Mike not caught her. And all she could do was cry, 'Where's Marcy? Damnit Mike where's Marcy—this should've been her win not mine.'" Mike had just held her, firmly, not too tight, let her walk it off; he'd kept her moving so she wouldn't cramp up. And after a few minutes he'd whispered, "It's all right, Catherine, she's watching over you and she's loving the Pac-10 Ass you just kicked."

Catherine looked up when she heard Jamie talking.

"Sounds hardcore to me," Jamie said.

Catherine blinked as the sweat ran down between her eyes.

"Sounds kind of like you don't wanna spar to me," Phoebe said.

Catherine shook her head at Phoebe and felt her eyes crinkle up at the thought of how Marcy would react to Phoebe. She would have liked Phoebe. Marcy was scrappy and a pain in the ass sometimes, just like Phoebe was, but once she decided you belonged with her, she wouldn't let you out of her sight. And Catherine was thinking this was how Phoebe would be . . . but first, dammit, first she was *gonna have to deck her*.

"Well, here's the thing Pheebes. I got all this training. I don't wanna make you cry or anything, because then I'd be hearing about it for weeks, months." Catherine moved closer to Phoebe, so that she was only about six inches away. Close enough to see the little hairs sticking up on the top of Phoebe's head, prickly, kind of a badass haircut, attractive, even in a way. "So go ahead, Pheebes, first one to pin to three wins."

Phoebe didn't waste any motion. She backed up a few feet, then whirled into a high kick, foot aimed at Catherine's jugular.

Catherine moved as fast as a rattlesnake sitting on a red desert rock. She came in under the kick, took a forearm to Phoebe's left hand, and then used all Phoebe's lost balance to completely knock Phoebe's legs out from underneath her. It was over before it started, and they both knew it, but Catherine went ahead and jammed a knee into Phoebe's solar plexus, and waited for Phoebe to tap out.

Jamie didn't move, not even an inch, Catherine noticed. This . . . pleased her. She didn't like to think this was gonna be a sides-taking thing. And it wasn't. Catherine gave Phoebe a hand, and as soon as Phoebe jumped up, she clapped Catherine on the back.

"Damn. Teach me that move, please. Where the hell did you learn to fight like that?"

"My friend taught me, after my roommate, my best friend . . . got raped and . . ." Catherine paused and gathered her composure. *Fuck. This was a fine time for this.*

"I'm so sorry, Catherine," Jamie said. "She's in a better place now."

"Wait, Jamie," Phoebe said, and then she said to Catherine, "Your friend, did she take her life after that?"

Catherine nodded. And that's when Phoebe put an arm around her and patted her on the back.

Catherine took a deep breath and then she faced both Phoebe and Jamie. "Yeah, she did. And I've been on a mission ever since, you know?"

"Yeah, we both do. Jamie runs the riding program at Bryson's and she's, well, it's her story," Phoebe paused and gave Jamie this ever so gentle smile, "But let's just say she's been through some stuff too. So whatever it is you're trying to do, FBI or whatever, I'm thinking I can get behind that, right, right Jamie?"

"It pleases God, so yes."

Phoebe let her eyes move from Jamie to Catherine. "She's kind of a . . . Jesus figure of sorts, best I can explain it, she watches over things here and kind of all over, so . . ." Phoebe chuckled and threw her hands up.

"It's refreshing, actually, to hear God spoken of," Catherine said.

"Good, that pleases me," Jamie said. And then her eyes narrowed. "Listen, Catherine, we're gonna grab a beer after we're done here, come grab one with us."

"Well, I don't drink, but I'd love to talk some more."

"Ah, well, I don't drink much either," Jamie said. She nodded, kind of her trademark sober nod, and Catherine felt at ease, as if she'd been lifting with Jamie and Phoebe for months.

Chapter 21

He reread the email and let his heads fall into his hands. Joey had made it all through three tours. Not a scratch. And he buys his ticket back Home during a milk run, no less? Or no more? As if one reason to go out to the store means more or less than any other; as if one day is any better than any other to die; as if one way was any better . . . stop it. *Stop it Jim. Gotta get a grip.*

Jim hadn't been to church in awhile. But it was one a.m., and he couldn't face another five hours on his own. Not sober. He pulled on a gray Army sweatshirt and a pair of jeans, and wiped his mouth. He probably looked like an old drunk, needing a bottle to calm his shakes. He'd done everything he could. He'd tried praying and all he got when he dipped down deep was static.

One thing he wasn't gonna do was drive to a liquor store. But he wasn't going to sit in his bedroom, shaking, all night either. That's how bad it was and if he was another man, he wouldn't judge a man in his shoes if he just went and swallowed some pills or some bullets just to turn it all off.

Bottle of bourbon used to be the only way. And that's not the man he was gonna be. Not this night.

He took a deep breath, and reached for his wallet. It wouldn't do, to forget it, then get pulled over.

What are you doing and why are you in such a hurry?
I'm dying for a drink, as I lay here seeing men die.
See men die?
Yes sir. In the sand. Man's dying right beside me, and there's the sound of gunfire, and bombs, and I think I just shit my pants, really, and . . .
Please step out of the car, sir.
Step out of the vehicle? But there's enemy fire and incoming artillery, sir. No sir.

Jim took a deep breath, and he tried to stop shaking. It felt like a sob, but he laughed, once, resisting, not surrendering to it, just a sharp "Ha" instead. *Please God, make it stop, and let me not get pulled over in the middle of an episode.* He shook his head.

An episode, like one that keeps repeating on TV a rerun that he, that no one, could erase. He'd give up anything, to anyone, to get free of Pain, hell, from this, of this—sick, sad face.

He checked his driver's license and headed downstairs, pausing at the fridge to grab the orange juice carton and take a few swallows. He was holding his breath so hard, his rib muscles hurt. *No, no.* Not anymore. That was from years ago. That was when he broke two ribs in training. He was okay now. *Pull it together, man. Please God just get me there in one piece.*

He walked outside and couldn't remember if he locked the front door. He turned the ignition on, and then he forgot it was on. So he turned the key to the right again, and only stopped turning it when the engine emitted an angry ch-ch-ch—zzzzz sound.

He groaned because he smelled like sweat and fear. And it was like being in the field all over again, waiting for the pre-dawn scouting mission to start. *No, I'm in my truck, driving to the only church that's open in the middle of the night.* He chuckled and rolled the window down. *And it's Catholic, which I'm so not, but God doesn't discriminate.*

Lights dipped and twinkled as he followed his usual route to work. Everything looked and even smelled different in the middle of the night but each time he tried to focus on just one smell, like gasoline, it took him somewhere he didn't want to go, like behind a line of military Humvees and civilian trucks in a convoy. So he half-closed his eyes and tried to keep his mind blank. Free of anything that would bring it back or take him back there.

The church steeple rose in the darkness, and he carefully steered around a few tree branches that had fallen in the parking lot. When he hopped out of the cab, he bent down, aching from the middle of his back all the way down to his upper thighs, and tossed the branches off the pavement. They landed with a gentle sound of tiny sticks crashing on the grass beneath a stand of tall maples.

He pulled the strings of his hoodie down lower so that the wind wouldn't find the gaps between his skin and the thick cotton. And with a shrug, a shrug at not knowing if he really wanted to go pray inside a Catholic chapel in the middle of the night, he took his first step, and then another one, until he reached the thick, brown doors. *Please, let it be open*, he thought, and it was.

He saw bowls of holy water, and a little self-consciously, he splashed some on his forehead and made the sign of the cross. Some of this made no sense, because he wasn't Catholic, but a church was a place of sanctuary, a safe oasis in a shifting vat of . . . *stop it, Jim.*

He swung around to see who was talking to him but there was no one there.

Don't be afraid, son. Just come inside and feel at home.

But I don't belong here.

Says who?

He shivered, but he wasn't afraid anymore; and the static was gone. He was too tired to actually smile but he felt as if he'd been smiling. He turned the heavy inner door that led from the rust-colored vestibule into the chapel, and the air was thicker, with a faint whiff of incense. He took several steps forward and then kneeled on his right knee and made the sign of the cross. Some things, like swinging a bat, riding a bike, and Catholic rituals, came back easy.

But he wasn't Catholic, not really. Not anymore. So was it wrong to be here? He shrugged, and slid into the pew to his left. He could feel all the muscles in his lower back seizing up, and a crick in his neck forming. He rolled his head, letting it drop all the way back, until he was gazing up, straight up, and watching the angles of the high ceiling approach one another from converging directions.

And then he understood. He wasn't Catholic. Never would be. But Joey was. Jim froze. Joey had been. And Joey would never kneel, nay, genuflect, was the word, in front of a pew again. Not ever. But his wife would. And so would Joey's two sons.

A drunk driver of course. Of course. And he'd done his share, hadn't he? Drinking, driving while drunk, stupid, damn it. Stupid.

His words wrapped around one another, tighter and tighter in his head, cyclonic almost. And now the guilt was gripping his throat. It was like the time he'd gotten stung by an entire nest of bees and hadn't brought his EpiPen on the hike—it buried him. Clear took his breath away. Just like an allergic reaction.

He wanted to unwrap it, rip it off, but guilt had a way of clinging closer once it found its way into you.

Why'd it have to be Joey?

Sometimes it's just a man's time, son. His work here was done.

Why couldn't it have been someone else instead? Why him? Why not me?

Your work is not done. All things will come in good time. Joey made it back Home.

Jim realized he was smiling. Whenever he heard this voice, it always spoke in riddles. Like an oracle from a Greek play. He'd get so distracted, trying to interpret the logic, the message, contained within the words, that inevitably, whatever was bothering him would recede a little.

Crazy sounding really, but it didn't hurt so bad. And damned if the voice always sounded the same. It didn't matter what kind of church he was in, or even if he was in church. He heard it whenever he needed to hear it. So it seemed.

So it was. And is.

Jim smiled a little wider.

Okay, okay. I getcha.

The sound of branches tapping against the ceiling brought Jim out of his reverie. He glanced around, checking the perimeter, and realized there was no threat to assess. Instead, he grabbed a Bible, and it flipped open to Genesis 18. He skimmed it, until his eyes alighted on:

Is anything too hard for the LORD?

All he could see was Joey, standing there with a red bandana wrapped around his head, strumming an air guitar with a gun slung over one shoulder.

And it seemed too hard to let go of it, to let go of Joey. He could see Joey standing there, vibrant, grinning, kind of slouching, with the waves from the desert shimmering in the background. Too hard.

Nothing is too hard for the Lord. Remember that son.

He nodded, and bowed his head, and stopped trying to figure it out. *Maybe Joey was Home. And maybe that was all that really mattered.*

Chapter 22

Wayne Toller carefully shut the basement door. It hadn't changed much since he'd gone three-five. The stairs still creaked on each step. The lighting in the main room, with its gray Berber carpet and faded, light gray walls, cast a dull glow offset during the day by a few stray sunbeams from tiny windows. As a teenager he'd thought it was kind of nifty to call it his bat cave.

That was back when he felt out of place because he used words like nifty when everyone else was tossing around "groovy" and "hip." He hadn't been either. The jocks hadn't slammed his head into lockers. He'd sort of managed invisibility, which was, as he used to joke back when he still tried to make friends, his super-power.

He almost giggled, and he hated when he did that, because then his face would flood with embarrassment. He giggled when he was nervous, and one time, he joked about superpowers, and a row of guys wearing letter jackets had jeered at him. At least they didn't slam him into lockers like they did to his friend Jerry.

He didn't miss those uncomfortable moments, when he had to look up from his desk at a teacher, or pass a note from one girl to the next. He never knew what to say, so he'd look off to the side, and hope they would just keep going, right on past his existence. It had always been easier that way.

He got to the landing, and pivoted to the left, toward the old machine room. The furnace clicked, and shadows flickered from the single light bulb hanging overhead. He ducked beneath a cobweb, but not far enough, and with an agitated flip of his wrist, he dusted the silk out of his face, and wiped several times, to get it all off. Funny, the things that bothered a man, he mused, as he took two more strides, and turned right, into his dark room.

He also shut this door tight behind him, leaning over to grab the cord for the light bulb with a synchronized, almost automatic arm motion. The red light flashed on, and he took a deep breath, taking in the moist, dank air, and the hint of fumes, much faded now, from his equipment. His Dark Room. If he had a home base, okay, even a bat cave, this was it. He was home.

He sat down on his leather stool, which he'd snagged used from a doctor's office, and waited for his eyes to readjust. Idly, he twirled his keys a few times, and then stretched forward and unlocked a tan file cabinet. He took out a black storage case, aluminum alloy frame with steel corners and high impact ABS plastic side panels, and set it down on his lap. He clicked it open, and removed several file folders and slammed the cabinet shut. He turned the key to the locked position and double-checked it. Locked. You could never be too careful. And this time around, he wouldn't use his computer. He'd have to be stronger.

He opened the file folder a tad too fast and cut his finger on the edge. File folder burns hurt even worse than regular paper cuts, and they lasted longer. He cursed under his breath, and moved his finger as if to staunch the blood before it came into contact with the large photograph. And then he saw a flash of skin, and forgot all about the cut. Nice, alabaster skin. So lovely.

He swung around and grabbed his LED headlamp, which hung down from a large hook screwed into the wall. He checked his watch and set the alarm. He should only be down here for an hour, because he promised he'd take the dog out for a walk. Great cover story, walking the dog. Safe. No one would look at him twice. Wish he'd thought of that before, but it was the computer that had done him in. He hadn't been caught for *that*.

He pulled his chair in towards his plank desk, which was several feet wide, and very deep. Then he arranged several photos in a semi-circle, almost like dealing a hand of cards, except he had a run of queens, and he was the king. Wayne giggled. He couldn't help it. This was one thing he couldn't enjoy when he was on the inside, with no space of his own. It wasn't like he stole money from people, or stuck needles in his arms, or murdered anyone.

As his attorney had argued, this was a victimless crime. And he'd been as much the victim as anyone. Wayne shook his head. He'd glanced over at the jury when his attorney had been making that argument, and this middle aged meathead had given him this, "Let me get you outside and tear your head off" look. Wayne had suspected it was all over as soon as he made eye contact. They'd found out later, when they'd polled the jury, that meathead had practically taken over deliberations.

If Wayne were a violent man, full of vengeance and hatred, he'd have understood how angry everyone on the jury had seemed, when they'd announced their verdicts. "Guilty. Guilty. Guilty . . ." rang out all the way down the line, and still resounded in his head sometimes, especially when he was trying to sleep at night.

So this time, well, he'd just be more careful. Wayne sighed, and then pushed all those thoughts out of his mind. *No regrets*, one of my bunkmates had said every night, when they'd been playing cards. He liked that. *No regrets*.

Wayne pulled his glasses down, so that they fit his nose a little better. Then he surveyed his art. And it was art. Some folks didn't see it, of course. But the world would catch up, in time. E-F-W niner five oh. Maybe that would be the name for his book. His book of photos. Oh no. It was stirring again. It. He'd walk now. Walk briskly in the fading twilight, the gleam. Gleam was glam. Glorious.

Now it was time to set up his Dell. The one he'd ordered after his sentencing, with his mother's credit card of course. She'd never noticed it, because he'd never given her the card. It had been easy. Shipped to his neighbor's house, and of course he waited until they left for work, and just happened to be pulling into their driveway like it was his own as soon as the UPS truck made its 10:30 AM Tuesday morning delivery.

He took a deep breath and plugged in the power strip. There was no reason to worry about a five year old computer, but still . . . he sighed when it powered up and blinked a friendly welcome at him. While the software updated, he set up the router. Incredibly easy to plug into the neighbor's source. Ridiculous of him to overlook it the first time, but he was adaptable. He learned. So when they'd taken his computer, he'd realized they'd never think to search again after releasing him on bail. Generous of them, really.

He tramped upstairs, and ducked his head underneath a cobweb. He tried not to swat it away this time. Once you got past the initial distaste for the cobwebs, you could get lost in their intricate patterns, their silk. His mom wore silk, but it was different. Old lady silk, chaste, yet dirtied by her skin, or yellowed. He shivered, and tried not to think about her overgrown fingernails touching his forearm. Talons. She'd always reminded him of a hawk, hunting him for every spare morsel of his freedom.

He got to the landing and heard her shuffling step just outside the door. Poor mum. She must have missed him pretty awfully, and the neighbors? He bowed his head and pushed on the door.

"Hey, Mum."

"Working on your collections?"

He swallowed. Oh right. Collections. "Yep, Mum."

"Sonny, I hope you find another hobby, or maybe take up swimming again." She moved her mouth around, as if trying to get something out from between her teeth. "You really were doing so well, so well before . . ." Her words dwindled away, and then he was in the pool, on the decks, and a family, a little girl, short and curvy, no more than eight or nine, stood beside him. She bent over, and he saw her backside, just a hint of her crack, and it would feel so good, such a relief to—"

"—Great idea, Mum. Great idea." He clapped his hands together, and stood beside his talon-bearing mum, but now she wasn't taking his freedom from him. She was feeding him. Feeding him a morsel sweet and pretty. And then during summer time, he'd join the community pool. It was about a mile away, perfect for a walk.

A walk. Thirty-four houses, twenty-three children. Thirteen girls. Ten boys. "Mom, I'm gonna take a walk."

"Oh. Oh, well okay Sonny. Soup will be ready when you come back. Navy bean. Your favorite."

He twitched, trying not to sneer. Wasn't nice, looking askance at his mom like that.

Chapter 23

Jamie put her arm on Phoebe's seat, glanced over her right shoulder, and backed out of Cassandra's driveway. There was something almost masculine about the way Jamie closed the space between her and Phoebe. Her dad used to do the same thing. It stopped feeling good, like so many things with him, when he would reach over and tossle her hair. Maybe that's why she kept it so short. *One more thing that didn't harken back to . . . him, to them, to the past, their past, the fucked up olden days.*

"Zander. You belted?" Jamie sounded the same no matter who she was talking to, young or old. There was something so egalitarian about her. She didn't kiss anyone's ass. She could take or leave approval and it sometimes knocked people off balance.

Zander made a clicking sound with his tongue. *So fucking irritating.* Phoebe shook her head and sighed. Maybe taking him helmet shopping wasn't a good plan.

"Hey, Jamie? Can we listen to Tyler Slow?"

"Are you belted in yet?" Jamie tapped the brake and turned all the way around. "We can sit here for another hour if need be."

Phoebe thought Jamie was joking. Probably.

The seat belt clicked. Jamie nodded, and headed towards I-66.

"Jamie? Hey, Jamie?"

"Yes?"

"Tyler Slow?"

"The woman you're gonna marry, eh?" Phoebe tossed her head back and let Zander see the side of her face, dimple showing, suggesting a smile. "Sure she's not too old for you?"

"Nah. Hey, Jamie, can you turn on the country music station? Maybe she'll be on soon."

"Sure, you ask me that nicely, you bet." Jamie tapped a few of the small, black buttons on the stereo, and 98.7 came on.

Phoebe wanted to tease him more, but he'd fallen silent. For ten minutes. The only sound was the Firestones rolling over the grooves in the tarmac. Occasionally, Jamie said something but mostly Jamie was silent. Jamie's silences were comfortable ones. She wasn't exactly taciturn, but she didn't waste words. Zander? Different story. He didn't waste silence. *I wonder what he's thinking, or building, or dreaming up this time.*

"You're quiet," Phoebe said. She shifted in her seat and tried to get a better look at Zander. His eyes were peeled on the road. It was raining, and the red, orange and white lights from the cars reflected off the wet pavement. Zander nodded, but didn't answer right away. With his eyes not leaving the road, he murmured, "Yeah. Just watching the cars. I like it."

"Like you watching leaves, Pheebes."

And it was, a moment captured, not so similar to another moment and yet alike for it meant something to them both. Phoebe was watching Zander watching cars just like Jamie had spent so many early mornings watching Phoebe ride.

Phoebe shut her eyes, and she was back on Ginger. It was fall, about three years before, and Phoebe was riding bareback just for fun. Golden light hit the edge of the pasture, right where it joined with the tree line. Phoebe felt the wind on her back, and as she looked up, she saw yellow leaves falling, and she got to thinking about how they flew, floated, fluttered, drifted, danced, wind milled, helicoptered, dipped, bobbed, or just froze completely still. She was watching it, got lost in it, wanted to hold the moment and not let go of it, and that's when Jamie had appeared, or maybe she'd been standing in the copse, standing long enough to watch, with one hand shading her eyes from the glare of the just-risen sun.

Phoebe opened her eyes and almost said something. She had so much more she wanted to say, but how do you thank someone for watching you lose yourself in a moment that stands still? A moment that you intended no one else to see, but once they saw it, you realized you didn't mind sharing it? That was the thing about Jamie. She could stand in places that Phoebe thought she owned, and it was only when Jamie turned to head back to the barn, or walked off the ice, that Phoebe realized some things felt better sharing.

A few minutes later, Jamie glided into a parking spot in front of Ride Hard, Land Safe. Zander hopped out the back and slammed his door shut before Phoebe got one foot on the ground. Zander promptly tripped over the curb and landed ass over teakettle.

Jamie and Phoebe stood on each side of him. Zander moaned, and then gave them both a crooked smile.

"I don't think you're supposed to practice your falls, Zan. It's not like compulsory." Phoebe held her hands behind her and grinned.

"Like a colt who's still getting used to his legs, aren't you?" Jamie's voice shifted from metallic to almost nurturing once she got to the end of the sentence, and then she leaned down and offered him a hand.

Zander reached for her hand, and boom, popped right back up. He was all elbows and knees . . . and hair. He'd asked his mom, or Ms. White to Phoebe, if he could grow his hair out like RG3, and as Zander explained later, his mom hadn't been listening when she said, "Yeah, sure love." But Cassandra White wasn't one to go back on her word; and so there was Zander, age ten, with wild dreadlocks and a few scars already to his name.

Jamie walked through the double-doors first. She didn't exactly stop and hold the door for Phoebe and Zander, but she didn't let it slam shut either. Whatever she did was subtle, Phoebe noticed. The store had an angry vibe, almost an aggressive one. Maybe it was the orange to green to blue to yellow lighting; maybe it was the hip-hop jacked up a few clicks too loud. Phoebe spun around a few times, getting more and more pissed off by the second. She heard the word, "Bitch" over and over again from the speakers, and she wanted to break something. Starting with the fucking disco lights.

And then it changed. Music, lights—it all changed. The volume on the music jerked up, down, up, then faded. Then it came back to the original level, but it sounded like something else entirely. In fact, Phoebe thought she heard a familiar, female voice singing about being a kid in a Chevy again. The disco lights flickered off and a bright, steadier ultraviolet shone from the fixtures above. Phoebe's eyes hurt. Her eyelids throbbed, and that was weird, and she was tired of being weird. She needed a distraction.

Where the fuck was Zander? He was nothing if not a distraction. Like the time he nuked a Gatorade bottle at mom's office. It took him an entire weekend to scrub the break room down. Or the time he put a banana in Phoebe's muffler. He'd fessed up of course, and then, when she'd cursed at him, he'd been standing there, and he was only seven then, and his bottom lip quivered, and she'd stopped yelling and hugged him. *Where was Zander?* Where the action was, of course.

Phoebe looked toward the back of the store and the first thing she saw was some punk wearing baggie, hang off your ass jeans and a hoodie, and sporting a stupid juice mop, chewing somebody out. She pocketed, or sorted this image, just as her mom did with cases, in the *I wanna punch him category*, and searched for the rest of the film reel. She saw things visually, and when she was mad, she'd slow it all down, seeing each bit as a separate image, the way a movie consists of different drawings or images captured on a storyboard.

Next? A dreadlocked little boy, walking fast to keep up with the punk wearing jailer jeans, more being dragged than walking actually. Phoebe gripped her fists and leaped over a skateboard display. She was gonna beat the little punk if need be.

"You trying to steal stuff? Need me to call the POE-lice? I should call the cops. Coming in MY house with dreadlocks? Who do you think you are? Huh?"

"Don't like hearing bad words." Zander yanked his hand away, and snickered. "And your breath stinks. You smell bad, wassup yo?" Zander let his voice sag and then sharpen, and threw his arms up in the air dramatically. A sarcastic, angry edge had entered Zander's tone, and it was unlike anything she'd ever heard before coming from him. He didn't sound or even look ten years old.

"Take your dreadlocks and your slang and go back to the ghetto, boy."

Phoebe heard all this, and she felt her neck getting hotter. She looked around for a fucking skateboard and grabbed the closest one to her. She cocked her wrist. It would shatter the front window in a bunch of pieces. Bitch? Bitch? And now talking like Zander came from . . . you know what? She was going to hit the bastard with the skateboard, right in the juice mop.

But just before she let the board sail out of her hands, Jamie put a hand on her elbow, just tapped it really, and spoke nice and slow. Kind of like a sheriff or maybe like Shane would have talked. "You're going to let go of my brother. And then you're going to measure him for a helmet. When you're done doing that, you'll measure my sister for a helmet." Jamie nodded at Phoebe without taking her eyes off Juice Mop. "Then, you're going to walk to the back, and you're going to get us your three best helmets in each size to choose from. Brand doesn't matter. Price doesn't matter. The sport doesn't matter. That's all nonsense. Your *three best helmets*. And then we'll pay for those helmets and we'll leave. We'll leave you to your music and your thoughts and your anger. But you're going to take care of that, and you're going to take care of it right now." Jamie crossed her arms and spread her legs and didn't take her eyes off Juice Mop.

He opened his mouth once, but Jamie interrupted. "Now, please. Before my sister does something she's gonna regret."

Juice Mop mumbled something under his breath. Phoebe heard, "Whatever, bitches," and she was twitching, but Jamie shook her head, and then extended her hand. "Come on over here Zander. Let's go look at the helmets for a minute."

Phoebe lost the rest of the shopping trip. Jamie did most the talking. She even clowned around and got Zander laughing too. But Phoebe kept throwing the skateboard and hitting Juice Mop right in the teeth. And there was blood, and screaming, and a roaring sound in her head, and she couldn't turn it down, at least not until they dropped Zander back at Ms. White's house in the suburbs.

Phoebe was quiet the entire ride home. When they pulled up in front of her home in Middleburg, Phoebe silently unlatched her car door.

"Thanks. Thanks for the ride."

"Sure. See you tonight? Round seven?"

"Yeah." Phoebe started to slam the door shut and then she thought of what she'd forgotten to ask. "Um, Jamie?"

"Yes?"

Phoebe leaned against the door, holding it open with her body, almost as if hip-checking it. "You like Catherine, like, well, you like her, dontcha?"

Jamie's eyes crinkled up, and she looked in that moment a bit like Anne. "She's good people."

"Oh come on, Jamie. You look at her different."

"Well, Pheebes, if there's anything to tell, you'll be about the first soul I tell, sound like a deal?"

Phoebe was tired. She was probably even being rude. *Damnit why did—*

"—It's okay," Jamie said.

Obviously reading my mind again. Maybe she can read the rest of my thoughts, like wondering why she never hit on me, aren't we best friends, aren't I attractive, oh my God what a weird thought, it's not like I wanted her to.

Instead of saying all of that, Phoebe said, "See you tonight," and she slammed the door shut and watched as Jamie pulled away.

•••

Jamie let her body relax into the SUV's bolstered, or at least sort of bolstered, sort of just beaten senseless . . . leather seats. She'd only gotten leather because it cleaned up easily; then again, asceticism didn't prove holiness. It was okay to buy a more expensive vehicle if that's what you needed. The monk's life, *or nun's* she chuckled, wasn't exactly for her.

And then her mind drifted over to Phoebe. The soul she was here to look after . . . was a handful, no doubt of it.

Yes, I know what you're thinking, and of course you're beautiful, yes you're beautiful too, and no, I don't want to hit on you, never have, never would, you're my best friend, that's enough. And yes, yes, if you must know, I do care about Catherine, I care very much, but I'm not sure if this is her time, our time; so if it's not what's meant to be in this lifetime, that's fine, I'll see her soon enough; and don't worry so much about sex and about who hits on who and all of that, these are just shells, just bodies, and besides, you might not realize it yet, but you're in love with someone and it's not me.

Jamie sighed. She wasn't so sure about Catherine and whose time it was, and that line about being fine with whatever was meant to be wasn't even honest, not really . . . and she had no idea really where she'd end up, where they'd all end up, but she was pretty sure they were all connected, somehow, and probably always had been. And would be.

Chapter 24

Phoebe tossed her bag by the landing and flinched when it reverberated with a thwack. She'd forgotten about the helmet. She chuckled, and bent down to gather it back up and show it to her mom. A dust bunny fluttered up from the refinished wood floor and she irritably swatted it away. *Fucking dust. Dust. Streaming in from the barn, dancing in the sunbeams.* Barn, fucked, fucking . . . Parkings. Fucking Parkings was just like those dust particles. No matter how many times she dusted him away, if she wasn't vigilant about it, about him, he reemerged and repopulated the spaces between the conscious thoughts in her head. Fuck. She'd never be—"

"—Pheebes? That you?"

Her mom's boots click-clacked from the back of the country farmhouse and Phoebe stood up straighter. Her mom still had that effect on her. She didn't want to care but she did care what Helen Thompson thought of her. It wasn't that Helen was hard on her or anything like that. She'd mellowed out, but she was still imposing, formidable.

Her mom's fingers showed on the trim before she turned the corner. She had strong hands. Just like the rest of her. She was still one of the most powerful trial attorneys on the east coast, and even if she sometimes wore a pair of jeans on the weekends, like she was this Saturday afternoon, they were crisp, ironed, stupid-expensive jeans. Probably cost $200.

"Hey Mom."

"You just get in?"

Phoebe nodded, and it hurt. Her neck was killing her.

Her mom reached over and grabbed the helmet. "Oh, good grief, is this a biker thing?" Helen ran her fingers over the helmet. The words "Bitch don't fall" were inscribed in big red letters on the white background, with black skulls drawn around the edges.

"Maybe. But now it's a derby thing. For real. Bitch doesn't, won't fall." Phoebe smiled on one side of her mouth. It was all she could muster.

"You look tired. You gonna get a nap?"

Phoebe swallowed. Her mom read her too easily. Always had, but it didn't matter back when . . . "Yep. I am." It came out sounding clipped, but it was okay. She waved over her shoulder and headed up the wide, circular stairs to her bedroom.

She shut the door behind her and rolled her neck again. She felt all the tension from the skate shop in her upper back muscles, the ones that connected to her neck, and she needed to stretch before she napped. With a tired sigh, she grabbed her laptop and spread it on the thick carpet between her desk and her bed.

Her home screen opened to the Google newsfeed and the first thing she saw was:

A shocking announcement made by the American Psychiatric Association (APA) in its latest edition of the Diagnostic and Statistical Manual of Mental Disorders caused an uproar among right wing pro-family groups and many others, as the APA states it now classifies pedophilia as a sexual orientation or preference instead of a disorder.

She tapped on the built in mouse and scrolled down. She tried to count to ten, the way Cary had taught her. It wasn't fucking working. *I shouldn't keep reading this. I should not keep reading . . . fuck.* Unfucking believable.

Below the article appeared 189 comments. She knew she shouldn't, but she read every single one of them. She kept rereading this one:

True love is unconditional. Christians hate the sin but LOVE the sinner, just as how Christ hates our sin but loves us. Just as I reject the choices people make, yet I accept the people. We need to accept the pedophiles. They can't help it. Who would choose that? Who would want to get off at the expense of a child? These people need help. They have rights. They should no sooner be locked away in prison than a gay man should be beaten to a pulp for simply being.

And another one simply said:

How is pedophilia distinct or different than any other sort of love? Who's to say a child wouldn't benefit from being loved? LOVE IS LOVE. We need to accept people of different persuasions, sexual or otherwise, with open arms.

Beneath that comment appeared a riposte bashing the right wing group that put out this article:

There is a news story going around right now claiming that the APA (American Psychiatry Association) has redefined pedophilia as a sexual orientation rather than a disorder. The news story, which is put out by a right wing organization, does not have its facts or terms right. What has been reclassified as a sexual orientation is Paraphelia - e.g. cross-dressing, etc. Pedophilia has been renamed Pedophilic Disorder, is still a disorder, still illegal, and there is no truth to the story that the APA is trying to reclassify it and therefore make it "acceptable."

Phoebe stood up and gently laid her laptop on her desk. They were denying her story. She felt abandoned, not believed, just fucking not validated.

People have no clue. Sometimes I am like a powder keg. One spark and I'd fucking ignite, goddamnit, just one spark. I gotta do something to release it, before I lose my shit. I gotta, but I shouldn't . . . I gotta. I gotta.

She walked into the bathroom. It was the only way she knew how to release the charge, the pain, the pressure. An old way, not a good way, but there was none other.

•••

Catherine was trying really hard not to slouch in the hallway outside one of her Tactics, Training, and Terrorism classes when Randy Danner almost collided with her.

"Oh, hey, Catherine White is it?" Randy was a bit shy of six foot and like all the other special agents, could pass for thirty-five but was probably closer to forty-five. His hair was salt and pepper, and he was distinguished looking, or almost distinguished looking. His suit was well cut; shoes were shined; but he didn't look like one of her mom's opposing counsel. He was, well, he was all special agent. They had a certain look, the special agents did, and if anything, he had even more of that look. He was one of her class's field counselors, on rotation from the DC Field Office. And the DC Field Office had some major ass-kickers, which is to say Catherine was damn relieved she wasn't slouching.

"Yes sir, thank you sir," she said.

Randy shook his head almost ruefully. "Why you thanking me?"

Catherine wasn't gonna be embarrassed, so she made sure she didn't look down. "There's a lot of us, not sure I'd be able to remember all the names, so thanks for that."

"Well, Catherine, you're doing well in class," Randy said.

Catherine nodded and tried to look unaffected. She wanted to smile a little, thinking back to her first year at Oregon. Then she said, "I have a few professors who would hardly believe that."

Randy laughed. "But from what I saw on your transcripts, good school, good grades, right? You went to Pre's school?"

"I'm so glad you didn't ask me about the football program," she laughed. "Yes, yes, Pre. And yes, my grades improved once I figured out where I wanted to be."

Randy nodded, and was about to walk away when he turned and said, "Wait, you studied harder in school so that you could work with us?"

"Yes, it's absolutely the only reason, at least at first." Catherine felt the lines around her eyes and mouth relaxing. She was thinking about her favorite professor, who had taught comparative religion. Professor Crowley, a damn fine woman. "But then I got fascinated by all the stuff I was learning, and the learning itself became the reason for wanting to learn more, if that makes sense."

Randy's eye flexed a little and then he smiled a slow easy smile. "Absolutely does, yes. I loved school, and still love learning. Wish I had more time to read, but I got kids and a house we're building . . ." A wistful look came into his eyes, and then what followed it was this absolute feel of . . . well, it sure felt like joy to Catherine. "So as much as I miss Plato, I guess raising kids has its merits too, you know?"

"I guess so, yes," she said.

"Well, let me know if you need me for anything all right? I gotta go check with one of your instructors for this afternoon's exercises, but from what I am hearing, you're doing just great."

"Thank you Randy."

He waved and smiled with his eyes again. And then she watched him walk away.

Chapter 25

Maybe it was stubborn, parking in the same ripped up old space next to the Dunkin Donuts, right next to the sign that said, "No commuter parking." He didn't like breaking rules, although if he stopped and thought about it, he always bought coffee. Technically, that made him more than a commuter.

Jim McMahon flipped the collar of his wool coat up and waited for the light to change. It took twice as long when the late winter wind was blowing. He squinted into the sun, more tense than he should have been, before he crossed Braddock. But sometimes, it's the milk runs that killed a man, and when it's not the milk runs or the patrols or a sniper's shot, it's running out to milk at midnight that kills a man . . .

Jim shook it off. *Come on Sarge, check your perimeter, right to left, target opps, escape route, assess and then move straight on through.* Fear could save his life but could fear save a man? Or take his life? He smiled, and tightened his grip on his backpack once he reached the curb. It was the sort of question he and Christopher used to argue about in the barracks. It helped to pass the time. They'd chew tobacco and sunflower seeds and Christopher would flip cards back and forth and over with a smile, sometimes even when he held a losing hand. That's how he wanted to remember Christopher, but most the time, he saw birds and kids wearing Coca-Cola t-shirts.

Jim checked his watch again. He'd packed away the one he'd used in the field and given up military time, but his mind still calculated it. It was like how me computed batting averages as a kid. That was just fun, really. But time, well, time filled the dark spaces, the empty spots; gave him something to think about. It was 17:41, and at this pace, he'd reach the building at 17:49, with another minute, maybe two, before he got to the door.

Parking Lot D. He accessed it as a 45-degree angle. His boots clapped on the gravel. His combat boots—that was one thing he hadn't packed away. It took forever to break them in, and he'd sooner get them re-soled before he'd get a new pair. *Waste makes haste*, Mom said, but waste also made trash. That's why they called them waste baskets. Waste made nothing. It took up space, just like we took up space when we were on the ground. Fighting grounds. Waste. A waste of space.

> *If Waste makes haste*
> *And soldiers always chased*
> *At a dizzying, wearying pace*
> *Was the meaning fractured space?*

At 17:45, he threaded the gap between the disorderly edges of a traffic circle and headed northeast. The pond reflected golden sunrays and tiny waves shivered across the water. Over there, water teased them. Tortured them sometimes. It shimmered on the sand. It beckoned. It was a promise, and just when they started to hope, it disappeared. Heat waved its pseudo promise in slivers, shimmers and light sparkles.

Every time he walked across the green and saw the pond, he thought of where he'd been. He thought of sand, of heat, of tan and brown and a place where there were no ponds and there was no water, except for whatever the army shipped in. He'd think of this and sometimes he would start to freak out but it was always all right because in the next moment he would remember where he was. The waves in the water brought him back and tied him there. So did grass, green, soft, usually wet grass. Grass implied or incorporated (needed, thrived on)—water. And home was water; water was home. *He was home now.*

He breathed in the cold air before he passed through the revolving center door. He was into the stairwell before it shuffled shut. He entered the classroom and was seated in the corner seat closest to the far door—the door closest to the stairs.

There was someone else in there, but he was harmless—a chubby Oriental kid with a hand shoved in an orange bag of Cheetos. His poetry wasn't bad, but it was too ornate. Cut out every third word and maybe there'd be something in it, or add an extra beat for cadence, and maybe he could pay to get it listed in some regional anthology. That's what passed for the publishing intelligentsia in the modern era.

The door swung open and Birkenstocks came in. Jim frowned. Birkenstocks had long hair and wore tie-dyes, which was fine, but he went on too much about blood for oil and Wall Street and then about oceans. Yes, oceans. Whales, salmon, dolphins. Whatever. He skipped half the classes, and then whined to the professor about whatever march he'd been on, but the whole time he'd be staring at Brittany the not Bashful, and she'd bat her eyes—

—And there she was. Brittany with her pajama pants not covering the tattoo just above her underwear line. Of course, there wasn't any underwear from the looks of it, but if she was gonna treat class like a pajama party, then why the thick makeup? *Had to be a Jersey thing.*

Three more people filed in, and Jim gritted his teeth and made himself reread one of the poems he'd written. Every single time someone came in (there was a fourth one, this time a Yoga-Pants Mom), his head jerked up, and he didn't understand it. It wasn't new, to sweep the perimeter. What was new was this sinking feeling he got each time he looked up and it wasn't—*oh.* It was like he was waiting for someone.

At 18:03, she came in at the same time as Professor Jane Hartigan. The girl slammed the far door open so hard, it smacked the door jam. They were late, which was bad enough, but when Hartigan came in through the near door, she paused for the longest time in front of Jim. She was as wide and as slow as a cruise ship—*aw stop it. That ain't nice.* He didn't get a clear look at the girl from the other night. The tough one in camos, boots, and a long black sweater. That's when he realized he'd been waiting for her. He'd been watching for her at the door, and now he was being uncharitable. It had been so long since a girl got to him like that. He hid a smile, and tried hard not to stare at Phoebe Thompson.

•••

He was looking at her. She was sure of it, but damned if she was gonna look back over at him. She wasn't noticing his high and tight blond hair, and his just-right Levis, and those faded, well-worn combat boots. *Damnit.* He saw her looking at his boots. Where could she get a pair like that anyway? Sunny's? Some military store, maybe out west a bit? Maybe she could ask him. Oh hell no.

> *"Hey. I like your boots. Where'd you get em?" Yeah, that would go over well. He'd say, "From Uncle Sam," and then I'd say something like, "Yeah, I used to have an uncle, but then my dad died and we stopped seeing his brother and—oh. You meant The Uncle Sam, as in the military?" And then he'd shake his head, and then I'd ask if he knew any military surplus stores, and he'd be like . . .*

"Ms. White?"

Phoebe looked up, but her eyes passed over again before she could extract herself from a *make-believe conversation about his fucking boots.*

"All set?"

Phoebe rose, all languid and achy. She'd hit the W&OD and rode her blades for hours Sunday, just her and the fifty-mile riders, a few hundreds from the looks of it, and a jogger or two, but real runners didn't run on pavement if they had any sense. She'd heard Ms. White mumble that once. Not that Ms. White talked about running that much. She wished she could be like that, too cool to brag on her shit.

Phoebe took a deep breath. On her last poem, Hartigan had schooled her on excessive fucks. As if there was such a fucking thing. And last night, this poem had seemed like such a good idea. But now? Well, it wasn't like she had anything else ready to go. Phoebe swallowed. Anything else that wasn't—ah forget it. At least this one would get a laugh *and* piss off fucking Hartigan.

Phoebe began quietly.

> *It's just a word*
> *Fuck is just a word.*

She paused, and put her hand on her hip. It hurt to hold her wire ring journal with her right hand, so she waved her right hand instead.

> *Now I don't mean to be defensive,*
> *But I find so many other words*
> *Far more offensive:*
> *Politician, pedophile, pusher, globalization,*
> *. . . GM foods, pollution, discrimination,*
> *War, poverty, fascism, fatism, racism, elitism . . .*
> *Add your own words to this list.*
> *I'm sure there are many that I've missed.*
> *Fuck is just a word!*

Phoebe peeked at Hartigan, who was shaking her head but also smiling. The room was buzzing. But he wasn't—what the hell? Frowning? She didn't need his approval. Just a pause for laughter, and then she'd finish with gusto.

> *See how it stirs the prude*
> *When they hear language colorful and crude!*
> *Sanctimonious hypocrites!*
> *So quick to take offense,*
> *Their lives no more than a shallow pretense.*
> *Watch their self-righteous fury!*
> *So quick to be judge and jury.*
> *Fuck is just a word.*

Phoebe raked her hand through her hair. She didn't care, not really, but . . . everyone was laughing. Well, okay. So it felt good. Even Hartigan laughed at the end of it.

"Well, Phoebe, I see you took another approach to my critique from last week, yes?"

"Yes ma'am."

"Fucking A, man, brilliant."

Phoebe glanced at the student with long hair and sandals. He was a twit.

"Gosh, wow, yeah. Awesome."

Phoebe tried not to roll her eyes at Brittany. For some reason, Phoebe remembered her name from a couple classes ago, when Hartigan asked Brittany to read a poem, and Brittany had actually popped a bubble and said, "Call me Brit."

Even the Oriental guy was laughing. Phoebe smiled, and was about to laugh too, but then she caught sight of Jim—what? Jim. And he wasn't laughing. No. The muscles around his mouth moved, and it was like a frown dimple popped up. He looked annoyed, like a fly was buzzing around his hamburger and he was too proud to swat at it.

"Mr. McMahon—your thoughts?"

Jim whatever his name held eye contact with Hartigan. "Cadence and pace were solid. Had its merits as a comic skit."

"But not your cup of tea?"

"Not everything is everyone's cup of tea. That's not really," he paused and fixed his blue eyes on Phoebe, "my way of doing things, but that shouldn't matter to the person writing it."

It felt like someone had just kicked the wind out of her. *She'd never. Oh. Fuck. All right.* But she knew how to handle that. She'd seen her mom take it, hard, on the chin from a judge in the Rocket Docket. It had been one of the first cases Phoebe had followed her around on, maybe six months after Dad died. Phoebe wasn't really sure what was going on, but she heard the Judge snap, "Sit down Counselor."

And her mom hadn't said a word. Nothing. She'd just moved in slow motion, like she had all the time in the world. She'd taken in every member of the jury, not with this aggressive stare;

no smirking; sure as hell no flinching; just this long, appraising stare. Then she nodded, and with the tiniest, almost indecipherable movement of her left eye, she'd let her eye maybe flicker, maybe wink, and then rest on her daughter's. And something about it had made Phoebe break into a smile.

So Phoebe pulled a Helen Thompson. She stopped, and let her eyes drift over every single member of the classroom. And then she froze, because she realized it couldn't be her mom's move. For an infinitesimal moment, she really fought against it, against riffing on it, and then went with it. She leaned into becoming something separate from Helen Thompson. It was like in derby, adding a move to an already brilliant routine, so that she could later call it a Phoebe Thompson. Because she didn't merely sort of wink at him. A twinkle absconded with her wink, and the twinkle-wink became a complex, understated, super-delicate smile. She couldn't help it. There was something in those blue eyes that made her do it.

Then she sat down.

"Mr. McMahon? You're up next."

He stood lightly, as if he had grown up lanky and only added just enough muscle to fit his frame. He wasn't tall—maybe six-feet, barely. She liked the way the buttons on his Oxford lined up just right with his belt. There was a lot she liked, and now she could watch him without him watching her watch him . . .

"The name of my poem is, 'A Soldier's Tears.'" He rattled his sheet once. It wasn't a nervous gesture. More an authoritative one.

> *Lying on my back*
> *I can feel the chilling mud*
> *For once it's so peacefully quiet*
> *I can hear my hearts gradual thuds*
>
> *Tiny glistening diamonds*
> *beautify the black sky*
> *My breath dances like a pale ghost*
> *as I let out a shuddering sigh.*
> *Well I just really miss you.*

as I lay here all alone
Water swells into my eyes
When I think of never making it home

Her stomach muscles tightened and she checked to see if he was wearing a wedding ring. Was he writing this to his wife or girlfriend? He wasn't wearing a ring. Maybe his mom?

Your face looking down as
my casket lowers in the snow
They hand you my flag folded.
Tears cascade down your face slow.
You see I pull the trigger when I have to,
I do Uncle Sam's will.
I can never show any weakness,
I'm only meant to kill.
I think of all I've done.
Will it be praised or thought as sins.
What will it do to you if I die.
These thoughts have never set in.
But more and more of us are dying and I still don't
understand why.   I'm supposed to be a strong trained
soldier.
Tears can never escape my eyes.
But oh if you could see.
What I have had to do.
The things that I have seen.
All that I have been through.

I wish I could erase the memories.
Tell my brain it's all a lie.
I wish I could just break down.
but I was trained to never cry.
No, crying isn't an option.
When your best friend's shot dead.
The blood paints your face.
When a bullet goes through his head.
Or when a bomb goes off.

Your whole squadron's taken out.
The air fills with shrill screams.
As the remaining survivors shout.
Then another bomb throws you across a field.
the smoke fills your nose.
You quietly thank God.
as you regain feeling in your toes.

You hear a man yelling.
blood decorates his vest.
You walk over as you notice he's an enemy.
with two bullet wounds in his chest.
You look down into his tear swelled eyes you know he is
someone's son. But you already know what you have to do.
As you slowly draw your gun.
Yes people will forever wonder.
The reason soldiers don't cry.
Well it's the truth behind the tears . . . because they will
always tell you why.

Phoebe blinked hard, and closed her eyes to contemplate, well, all of it. When she opened her eyes, he was looking at her, and she nodded, breathing in deeply, and in that moment, felt him, and her, and something she couldn't really explain, but she knew she'd figure it out later. When it was quiet, and she was sitting out by the barn, dark outlines and trees and outlines in the background, scribbling words on paper. No one said anything, not at first. Even Professor Hartigan was quiet. They were all back where he'd taken them, somewhere in Iraq.

And then the fool sitting next to Brittany broke the peace. "Dayam, I guess someone played a lot of GI Joe as a kid."

Brittany laughed. Oh hell, everyone was laughing, tittering really, like scared children.

Phoebe stirred, and her neck snapped around, and it felt like her fingertips were going numb again, and she knew she should or shouldn't—no, should. "Will you shut the fuck up? Just shut the fuck up. How do you know that he didn't live through that? Huh? And what do you know about pain?"

Phoebe rocketed forward in her chair, and the last word she uttered almost sounded primordial, even to her own ears. Pain. It was something that a soldier surely knew about. Something that beautiful man knew about, and now this fool—Phoebe was about to say a whole lot more.

"Okay, thank you Mr. McMahon. And I think we all appreciate your service."

"Fucking right we do."

"Uh, thank you Phoebe. Think it's time for us to wrap things up now." Hartigan said some more stuff about meter and context and postmodern something, but Phoebe was picturing Jim diving to the ground and turning to see his friend's face blown off, and she could smell the blood and the mud. And pain. She could feel the pain. His pain.

Chapter 26

She tried not to bite her fingernails while she waited for him outside the classroom. It was chilly in the hallway, or maybe it just felt cold because the walls and the floors were gray and the custodian had dimmed the lights. It wasn't scary, but the whole postmodern look at Mason worked better in summer. She paced and kept rereading announcements pinned to the corkboards between classrooms, but she'd read a few words, and then lose her concentration. So she kept rereading the same announcements.

She had it all planned out, what she was going to say to him, and it wasn't more than a sentence or two. But it needed to get said. She needed to say it. She'd never heard anything like what he'd read, and she needed to reach out and acknowledge it, and him. The man who wrote those words knew pain. It needed, she needed, he needed—what? Was this crazy? Just because they both knew pain—

—The door creaked and then with a slow whistling sound, opened, and there he was, this man soldier-poet. He waited for the door to glide shut behind him.

"Hey."

"I was wondering—"

"—Oh, you were waiting for me?" His eyes moved down the hallway, and rested back on her.

"Yeah."

"Glad you did," He said.

"Yeah?"

"I am."

"Well." Phoebe tightened her hand around her backpack. *Careful on those reigns, Phoebe.* "I was wondering—can I buy a soldier a beer? To thank him?"

"I'd love that." He smiled, and she smiled too. "But can it be coffee? I can't—I don't drink anymore." His eyes didn't fill with tears but they seemed more luminous somehow, and he lifted his chin a little. "I had to give it up, after I got home. Sober more than a year now." He nodded at her, and she knew he was feeling both proud but humble about it, and for some reason she thought of Ms. White, who was proud but humble too.

And then she knew what to say. "One year?" She said. "That's great. Coffee it is, then?"

His smile got wider. "Sure. Starbucks okay with you? I know there's a place closer, and 'buy local' and all, but Starbucks is farther away, and I could use a walk."

Phoebe resisted the urge to wrap her arm around his, and then she chuckled. She hadn't been around any men or boys older than Zander in the longest time, and she was just not knowing how she should . . . *oh who cares?* She wrapped her arm around his anyway, and started walking, knowing full well he'd follow. And once he started to follow her, she let go, because somehow holding loosely didn't feel good enough. He took it all in stride. As if he had nowhere else better to go.

When they got outside, the moonlight cast an orb over the water, and she stopped for a moment and closed her eyes. "Doesn't smell like grass yet, does it?"

"No, maybe in a couple weeks," he said.

She started walking again. "It helps me walk, when I'm mad, and I got mad in there."

He shoved one hand in the pocket of his long wool coat. His hard jawline flexed a little but he was quiet until they cleared the parking lot, where a few people were milling around. "I liked that you said something."

"But not how I said it?"

He started to answer, and once he realized she was okay and wasn't trying to argue, his jaw muscles relaxed even more.

"It's okay," she added. "We don't need to talk about that."

And then they kept walking some more. The frogs and the crickets weren't out yet, but all it would take was a couple warm weeks. "I like this time of night," she said.

"Yeah?"

"It's quiet, and everything slows down. I can think better. It's when I do a lot of my writing, late, usually down by the barn or sitting on the porch."

"You live on a farm?"

"Yeah," she said. "Out in Middleburg."

"Horse country," he said.

She nodded, and she kept an eye on him as they crossed the green and headed towards the parking garage. Its light flickered on and off, and she read the sign on it that told how many spaces were vacant. "243 spaces, eh?"

"Guess there's not a home game tonight." Jim checked in all directions and then he gazed at her. "You go to games?"

"Oh hell no. Too loud, too many people. Makes me nervous."

They crossed the street and he kept his body between her and oncoming traffic. When they reached the curb, he let her pass in front of him, and then he hugged the left side of the street, closest to traffic. He'd been on the exact opposite side of her until then, as if—she couldn't stop smiling. As if he was guarding her from traffic.

Oh wow. What if he liked basketball and she had just insulted him? "How about you?"

"You mean basketball?"

"Yeah."

"Nah." He shook his head, and she was watching his every movement, not watching the pavement, when she tripped. And for a split second, she thought she was going to fall. But he put a steadying hand on her, and she was pretty sure he held on longer than he had to. She was also pretty sure it felt good.

"Don't like basketball, or don't like going to games?'

"Ah. Good question. It's funny. The sound of the game always annoyed me, even as a kid."

"The sound?"

"Yeah," he said. "The squeaking of rubber on the wood floor. So I never really liked it. But like you said, it's crowded and it's loud, and I'm a country boy. I don't like crowds."

"Or loud crowds."

"Or loud crowds," he agreed.

They took a right on 123, which turned into Main Street, and headed into Fairfax City. It was almost deserted, typical for a Monday night. The stoplights turned red almost like dominoes sliding into place. "My mom's partner hates the new courthouse. She says she got fond of the old Soviet-style one next door to it."

"Mom's partner?"

"Yeah." Phoebe pointed a few blocks ahead and to the right. "Thompson, White & Hansen's offices are over there."

"Is your mom the Thompson in that?"

"You don't know who I am?" She sounded haughty, and almost laughed when she realized it. *He'd probably take it the wrong way.*

But he didn't. He took it in stride; seemed to be his way. "No, can't say I do. Guess I'm not from around here."

"And you're not going to ask?"

His eyes met hers for a moment. She couldn't see the blue in the dark, but she wanted to—she wanted to see the blue. Funny that it mattered. "If you want me to, sure."

She shook her head. "Nope. It's a relief, actually. Everyone else knows me as Phoebe Thompson, daughter of . . . well, never mind. Sometimes I get lost in it, in what other people see me as, and it's like I'm staring into this fishbowl and all these fractal images are reflecting back at me, and they're all distorted and confused and messed up. I know it shouldn't matter, but I start to follow their eyes into the fishbowl. I start wondering what people are saying or whispering or texting about me when I walk past, and then I realize that I'm probably showing up on someone's

Facebook feed again. And it's times like these I swear I just want to learn to live again, free, you know? Without trying to figure myself out through someone else's eyes."

They hit another major intersection, and again he kind of leaped forward and then reached back for her, and this time she was sure he was protecting her. She was also sure it was just his way, but it felt—he felt—like warm cocoa. Not brandy, she thought, in a grim, yet somehow fond way. Her mom's humor was rubbing off on her.

They reached the curb, and then came alongside the Irish bar. Jim shoved his hands deeper in his pockets, and she at least knew not to say something stupid about the way you could smell the beer as they walked past. She wanted to ask him what it was like, not drinking when you really wanted to, but if he didn't ask her questions unless she wanted him to, then maybe that's the way she should treat him.

This was all new. Wanting to know about someone else. Until now, she'd been able to figure out all she needed to know, and it really amounted to answering the threat-insult-harm matrix, as she liked to think of it, or it had to do with her mom's job, or with Anne. When Helen was around, Phoebe mostly just watched and learned. The same had been true of Anne. Jamie too. But she could ask them questions. They were safe like that. He felt safe. Damn, there she was working the threat-insult-harm matrix. *I wish Sascha had stayed local. She always knew what was right.*

"Is it hard?" She blurted it out, then realized she was holding her breath, waiting, worrying that she'd upset him.

"Is what hard?" He took his hand out of his pocket and waved it at the bar. "You mean that?"

"Yeah, I mean—I don't mean to be rude."

"Yeah. It's hard. I drink a lot of coffee and stay busy, and I pray a lot. God's got this, you know? I mean, it's just—well, it's just a substance, really. I am or am not using, putting in my body. That's how I see it. I say to myself, well, today's another day, and yesterday, I didn't, so let's make it today."

She looked up at him and wanted to lean her head against his shoulder but she didn't. Then they came to another intersection, and she could see the library, and then a couple blocks down, the

Starbucks. And she knew he'd lead, and sort of block, but wait for her too, and she realized she was already used to it, to him, to the way he guarded and protected, guarded and protected her—and she liked it.

"And you take it one day at a time."

He paused in front of a streetlight, long enough to unbutton his coat and nod at her. "I do. Sometimes, I take it one minute at a time. Whatever it takes."

"I know that feeling, I know it, all too well, really." She stopped, and didn't know how to finish her sentence.

After he waited, and she still didn't talk, he started to walk, and she fell in next to him. They were silent until he reached the door. Without any wasted motion, he held it open for her, and she passed underneath him, close, close to him, and he looked young, but old too, older in his eyes, but youthful in his smile.

"So, what are you having?" She was all cocky again, and he froze, sort of, hand reaching for his wallet, and then she put her hand on his shoulder. "Remember? I said I wanted to buy you a cup of coffee. So what can I getcha?"

"Drip, biggest they got. Dark roast."

"Make that two." Phoebe tried not to worry about what to do or say next. It was like a kid had taken her parents' M3 out of the garage, and then got it out on the street, and was in for a whole lot more than—she'd never taken a man out for coffee. And now she was paying, and she didn't have a fucking clue.

And that's when he took over. Like he knew. He grabbed his coffee, and hers, and then handed her the creamer, and waited, and it felt better, just following him. It felt new and exciting but he felt old, and comfortable, but if he's so comfortable, why'd she get so tingly when his hand touched hers?

"Where are you from? You said you're a country boy right?"

"Near Charlottesville. Mom's a professor there."

Oooh! "At UVA? Didn't you say she was a writer?"

"Yeah, English professor and writer." He sipped his coffee and then he was grinning. "Thanks for the coffee. Been a long time since anyone's bought me a cup."

She grinned back at him. "Can't say I ever bought a man a cup of coffee before." *But I could get used to this*, she almost added.

"Close to your mom?"

"Oh yeah. Bigtime. She taught me almost all I know, about writing. How about your mom?"

"Same, I mean, we're really close. At least we've been since, well." Phoebe took a swallow of coffee so fast, it burned her throat a little bit. There really was no good way to say this. She looked down and rub-tapped her fingers on her cup. "Well, since dad died. About five years ago."

"I'm sorry for your loss." His blue eyes crinkled up, and she gulped.

"Thank you."

"Lost mine too. He wasn't around much before," he added, when she started to say she was sorry.

"Still hurts. You know? In a weird way."

He was about to shake his head, and then he didn't. She couldn't tell if he was annoyed, and then saw she wasn't minimizing it, or him, but that was her read. He got a thoughtful look. "Yeah, guess it does."

"Not saying I miss mine. I just mean, I don't know." She hesitated. "Jim John? You really don't know who I am?"

"First of all, Phoebe, please call me Jim. It's what my friends call me. No idea why my mom insisted on calling me something out of the Walton's."

She laughed, then felt guilty for laughing, not because of the Walton's but because of what she had to tell him. And she had to. "Okay. Jim. I like that name."

"Thank you. Named after my granddad. You've asked me twice if I knew who you were. I want to say I don't care, and I don't, but it matters to you. Who are you, Phoebe Thompson?"

She studied him again. The threat-insult-harm matrix didn't do a bit of good here. No, that wasn't true. It felt okay. "I've never told anyone before. I mean, everyone's always known, or found out, and then I knew they knew because it would be different. The thing is, if you Google me, you'll see the headlines, and the court case the state decided not to prosecute when, when my mom killed my dad with a golf club after he, he . . . Phoebe shivered, and he saw it, she knew he did, because he leaned in. "He hurt me, Jim. And when mom found out, she did what she had to do."

"Sounds like she's a hero."

"Yeah. I mean, yeah. Mom risked it all for me. And she might have still gone to jail, but the prosecution, the cops, were corrupt."

"So they tampered with evidence?"

She shook her head. "Oh fuck. You're going to find out anyway. He stalked me, and tried to—he attacked me at the safe house. And then one of the women there shot him." Phoebe started to laugh, and then she wasn't laughing. Neither was Jim. He set his coffee down, and took his wool coat, and he wrapped it around her shoulders, and only then did she realize her teeth were chattering. And when he sat down, and just waited, she looked through her tears and then she smiled, not laughed.

She wanted to say thank you, and she kind of did, and he sort of said it was okay, but mostly they were quiet, until her teeth weren't chattering, and then he put his hand on her forearm, nice and slow, and kept it there while he looked in her eyes. "So when you said I knew pain, you understood, didn't you?"

She nodded, and he sat there with her. He didn't say anything for awhile and he didn't move his hand until she wasn't shivering so much. When he moved it, he kept his hand close to hers. His hand was big, with tendons that stood out, and you could tell he worked on stuff. She'd heard once that no amount of scrubbing could get rid of oil and grease. She could see evidence of that maxim sketched in the lines between his fingers. She found these black lines almost transfixing.

She realized she was feeling better when she smelled the coffee again. She didn't know how long she'd been staring at his hand. She looked up and watched the barista rinsing metal containers and buckets. It was probably closing time, or close to it. She smiled bleakly, but knowing her, she probably looked cocky. She didn't think Jim would care one way or another.

"Ready to go?"

She nodded.

When they got outside, she threaded her arm through his. She didn't really hesitate, or think about it. It was kind of old-fashioned, but so was he.

She luxuriated in the clear, cold air as they walked past the bar, the field house, the parking garage, across the pond, and down to parking lot D. It was deserted, windswept, but not desolate. Just her and Jim.

When they reached Anne's pickup, he chuckled. "You like Fords, eh?"

"Well, I guess I do. Got this as a gift, from my coach, well, more than a coach." Phoebe paused, because tears were welling up again. "My riding coach, for five years, we were close. She just passed away, and she left me her truck. Means a lot. Hard to explain why."

He pulled her just a little closer, then released her. And then he led a walk-around of the F-150. "Looks like she's in pretty solid shape. Needs new tires, balancing, and probably, if I'm guessing right, a tune-up. Some spark plugs. How about when you come by and get your Bronco, you drop her off, and I'll make sure she's running right." He put his hand on the rear panel and gave it an appreciative rap.

"Okay. Yeah."

Phoebe leaned against the door and stared up at him. She wasn't sure what she was waiting for.

"Phoebe, thanks for taking this man out for a cup of coffee."

"Sure."

"Can I call you?"

"Oh my God, Jim. You still want to talk with me, even after . . ." She dug her keys out of her pocket and started to turn away from him.

"Of course I do."

"But—"

"We could argue about it for awhile, or you could just type your number into my phone?" He reached into his wool jacket, scrolled to his contacts, and handed her his cell.

She glanced at him. He had laugh lines around his eyes, and his face didn't look so hollowed out when he was laughing.

She stuck her hand out, and tried not to roll her eyes or say something cocky. When their hands touched, she wondered about it. Not whether she was going to type her number in, but whether she could—*no. No.* She couldn't ask him to hug her. And she definitely couldn't kiss his hand. *Oh my God. What the hell?*

It took forever to type her number in. She had to hit the back button five times. Her fingers were cold, but it was more than that. She was nervous, and she felt like stalling. Like they could stand around and talk all night, there in the parking lot, her and Jim, just them, nothing complicated, or everything complicated, just time, and then no time. She sighed and finally hit the save button.

Then she put her key in the door, and it took a couple of turns to get it to take. But it did, and she moved slow. He held the door open for her, and waited for her to get the key in the ignition. The eight rumbled, and she smelled the exhaust fumes and felt the engine roaring underneath her.

He leaned in, and kind of smiled, and she kind of smiled.

"Bye, Phoebe."

"Bye," she said.

And he slammed the door shut, and stood there, ramrod straight, and proud, and beautiful.

Chapter 27

A few hours later, her cell phone rang. She didn't recognize the number, but it was local. Probably someone from the Laydiators. But when she answered, and said hello, a man's voice came on the line.

"Phoebe?"

"Yeah."

"It's Jim. Hope I'm not calling too late?"

She looked at her laptop. It was after midnight. "Oh hell no. I'm always up this late."

"Good. I was working, and then I just wanted to hear your voice. Didn't even think how late it was until I dialed."

Phoebe stood up and stretched. Then she popped open the door to her balcony, and treaded outside. She wrapped her sweater around her shoulder and pulled it tight with one hand, and pulled the door within an inch of closing. She'd never gotten locked outside, but she always thought about it. "You wanted to hear my voice?"

"I did."

"Did you read the headlines?"

"Which ones? The headlines about you and your mom and dad and that cop, the Parkings guy?"

Phoebe lit a cigarette and as she inhaled, she watched the orange ember glow. "So you did read about it?"

"Yes."

"And you're not . . . I don't know."

"Well, I'm here, aren't I? Wanting to hear your voice. I like your voice."

She chuckled. She was being a pain in the ass. And he was still wanting to talk with her. "I like your voice too. I could listen to you read poetry all night."

"Oh, well in that case," he laughed, "Maybe I'll have to call you back at 4 AM when I get this one finished."

"4 AM, huh? That might be too late for even me."

They were both quiet for a moment.

"Phoebe?"

"Yeah?"

"What are you doing right now?"

"I'm standing outside on my balcony, smoking a cigarette. Listening for the frogs and crickets, and trying to feel spring."

"What does spring feel like?"

"Well, it starts with an itch in the back of my throat. And about a day later, I can feel my eyes watering up; and then, a few days after that, I see a blossom, a yellow-green one, maybe on the tree that almost hits the balcony here—"

"—In Middleburg?"

"Yep. We have a bunch of acres. It's just me and my mom. I picked the place out, actually. It's kind of old. Not rundown but . . . I don't know. Not one of the newer McMansions. It's so different than where we used to live. I mean, it's not impressive or anything, you know? But I love it here."

"I never cared for the McMansions. Usually, at least where I'm from, they're not as nice as the older places. They don't have character."

"Or second floor balconies."

"Oh," he said. "You're on a second floor balcony."

"Yeah."

"Wow. My mom's got those in her house, too. But my sisters snatched up those rooms."

"Sisters?"

"Yeah. Two of them. I was the baby."

"Must have been nice, having sisters." Phoebe took a deep breath, and tried to picture what he was doing, and what he looked like as a kid, and then a teenager. "So where do you live?"

"Just off 66. Centreville. I can actually see the overpass from my kitchen window if I," he paused and there was some static on the line. "If I crane my neck just so."

"Sounds scenic."

They both laughed.

"Well, it's funny. I got used to the noise. To the interstate. It's like white noise."

"Built-in sound machine."

"Exactly. But hey, I won't be in a townhouse for long. I'm saving to buy some land. Just not sure where. Depends on where I go for my Ph.D."

Phoebe's jaw hurt. There she went, grinding it. "Where you looking at?"

"Mom wants me to study for it under her."

"At UVA?"

"Yeah. Or I could stay here. They've already offered. And I like the idea of making my own way. Not relying on my mom to get ahead."

"Good."

"Good?"

She rubbed her jaw but the ache was going away anyway. "Yeah. Could get used to having you around." Her voice softened as she spoke. The sentence started harsh, like she didn't wanna admit to it, but by the end of it, she got tired of sounding cocky. He affected her like that.

"If it weren't so late, I'd ask if you wanted to go out for a ride."

Goosebumps rose on her arms. "A ride?"

"Yeah, but I know—"

"—I'd like that," she whispered.

"After work tomorrow?"

"Yeah." She drew the word out.

"Oh, is that not good?"

"No, no, that's not it. It's good. It's just—this is ridiculous. I mean, I am. I was thinking it would be fun, right now. But you gotta work, and I gotta stop doing crazy shit without, I don't know, thinking it through."

"You mean:

Gather ye rose-buds while ye may;
Old Time is still a-flying;
And this same flower that smiles today,
Tomorrow will be dying.

Jim laughed. "Or something like that."

"Who the hell wrote that?" she murmured.

"Beats me. Robert something? I never can remember. Sort of like a one-hit wonder band, it's a poet I can never remember."

"Best one-hit wonder band?"

"Gotta be Thompson Twins." Jim was smiling. She could tell.

"Spandau Ballet."

"Oh no! You might have me. No—wait. 867-5309. What band was that?"

"Oh hell," she said. "I'd have to Google it. But if you don't have the name of the band, you only get half-credit."

"Changing the rules halfway?"

"No. You didn't make any rules."

"Tommy Tutones."

"Ah," she said. "Damnit again."

"Phoebe?"

"Yeah?"

"You're so easy to talk to."

"Mmm."

"Feels like I've known you for years."

"For me too." Phoebe cinched her hood tight. She was cold, freezing really, but it felt more intimate, or safer, talking to him when she was outside. Like she could stretch and breathe and move if he got too close. He wasn't there, but still, she liked having room.

"Can I call you tomorrow?"

"Yeah," she said. "You owe me a ride, anyway. And we got more one-hit bands to get through."

"Do they all have to be from the 80's?"

"Hmm. That's our second rule, I'm thinking—no time restrictions."

"All right. That's a deal."

"Okay."

"I'll call you after work?"

"Yeah."

After she hung up, she tiptoed through the house and into their country kitchen. A warm light glowed from the lava lamp on the counter. Back when they were decorating, and Phoebe was still a kid, her mom had been what she thought was oddly hands-off about letting Phoebe choose things. She'd assumed it had something to do with her mom trying to make up for it all, but after a few years she realized Helen had never cared so much how their home looked, as long as it was clean. And didn't remind her of Great Falls. Or Dad.

Her mom was sitting at the table, sipping tea from a blue mug and reading a stack of papers. Phoebe could see the steam rising from the top, and a tea bag hanging off the side. Phoebe almost cracked a joke about her mom's pajamas but it seemed like a child's joke and she wasn't feeling like a child so much.

"Oh, hey hon." Her mom finished reading her sentence and then looked up. She took a sip of tea, and then half-rose. "Tea?"

"That would be nice." She waved her mom off. "No, sit. I'll get it."

"You talking to Sascha?"

Phoebe grabbed a bag of peppermint tea and smelled it before she laid it into an earthenware mug and poured hot water on top. "Actually no, but I've been meaning to call her."

"Ah." Helen gave a crisp nod and her eyes drifted to her paperwork.

"A guy from class, actually."

Helen couldn't cover her surprise at first. She tried to cover it up by sipping tea and dunking her tea bag up and down several times. "Ah. Well, what's he like?"

"Remember that guy that's working on the Bronco?" Phoebe poured milk into her cup and added a few sugar cubes.

"How can you do that to a perfect cup of tea?"

"Oh my God, Mom. Why do you have to be so fucking Spartan?"

They grinned at one another.

"I remember him, yes."

"Well, he's in my English class. He read—I mean, wrote, then read this poem about war. And how he missed his friend, and, well, then some asshole said something, so I told him to fuck off and—"

"—Who did you tell to fuck off?"

"Oh. Not Jim. This other rich kid, who hates Wall Street and war and people who kill dolphins and grown-ups who work for a living."

"Wow, Phoebe. You sound almost like a Republican."

"Don't get your hopes up. Anyway, I thought you were pissed off at them for shutting the government down."

Helen wrapped her arms around her upper body and shook her head with a rueful laugh. "Okay. I think I got it. Mechanic-poet and did you say, or imply soldier?"

"Yep. So I bought him a cup of coffee. Thanking him. And, I don't know Mom. I really like him."

"Like him as in sipping cider through a straw like him?"

Phoebe rolled her eyes. Her cheeks felt hot. "You disapprove?"

"Whatever gave you that idea?"

"Well, he's a mechanic. Not exactly suitable . . . oh hell. It's not like I'm wanting to be his girlfriend or anything. It's just, I don't know."

"You know, I don't agree with you. Not about whether you wanna be his girlfriend although were I in court I might ask the jury to take notice of your red cheeks."

"You wouldn't."

"Sure I would." Helen pretended to glare, and they both chuckled. "But seriously. As far as what a man does for a living, it's not so much about what he does as it is about how he does it. Know what I mean?"

"I guess, yeah."

"I respect people who work hard. That's all I'm saying."

"Yeah. I get it."

Helen started to flip the page she had been reading.

Phoebe tried to read what her mom was working on, but the words were too small. "Oh. And hey, he's getting his Ph.D."

"In?"

"English. Poetry."

"Oh." Helen reached over and grabbed her pen. She twirled it and then, with a straight face, said, "In that case, hell. Totally unsuitable."

Phoebe gulped half her tea down so that she wouldn't laugh. "Night."

Helen waved, her eyes back on her document, pen now whipping around in circles, and smile lines cast around her eyes.

Chapter 28

It never ended well, reading about predators online. She was looking for him, for all of them, somehow thinking she would find him and stop him. But then she'd gone and read something online, not sure where she started, but she got immersed in an article that said how the Bible endorsed rape.

She'd followed the article all the way to Deuteronomy and she'd only been able to get through parts of it. She got to this section that talked about stoning women whose virginity couldn't be proven, and she was screaming inside, "Right, so when I lost mine, my dad fucked me, no one saved the fucking sheets now did they? So what—God wants me dead? Wants the evil I am purged from the land? For that's what it said: "You must purge the evil from Israel." She'd gone reading more stuff in Numbers and she was on the edge of cutting again, cutting the evil that the Bible had spoken of out of out her body, and then the phone rang.

It was Jamie.

Phoebe barely said a word when she picked up the phone. She couldn't bear to bring up what she was thinking, but she couldn't stand the concept of banalities, of empty words and stupid thoughts. "Hey," she mumbled.

"Calling because I was thinking about you Pheebes. You don't sound so good."

"Fucking world, better off without me, I'm evil, must be purged."

"Stop that," Jamie said, her voice firm and steady. "And turn that computer off, now."

Phoebe swallowed and it tasted brackish, her mouth, her scent, his scent, his mouth on her; it was salt. It was sin. It was him.

"Phoebe, talk to me. You're in pain—why?"

"Oh my God, I read that the Bible endorses rape, and sure enough I read some passages in—"

"—Deuteronomy?"

Phoebe nodded. Her head was a rock, about to fall off her neck; her eyes were amulets, pulling her dead father back to her, his desire the glue of the evil buried inside her.

"As a servant of the Lord, I can say with all solemnity that the entire book of Deuteronomy should be disregarded. It's not God talking, and even if it was, and I'm telling you it's not, but even if it were, the covenants of the New Testament make all those weird, awful sick laws from the Old Testament no longer applicable or enforceable or in any small way meaningful."

"Servant of the Lord?"

"Yes," Jamie said. "Something like that. It's neither here nor there, doesn't matter as far as helping you ignore Deuteronomy."

"Yeah," Phoebe said, "But I thought all the words in there were the Word of God? So how do you know what to pick and choose?"

"Well, I would start off with the New Testament, and just the things we know Jesus said. Because when he came, he brought a new way of living with him. And he also brought a new agreement—that's what a covenant means, okay? He brought a better deal or set of promises with him, and he said that the old ways were no longer the right ones."

"Wait. You're saying Jesus said to ignore the Old Testament?" Phoebe was, perhaps for the first time ever, not pissed off at the Bible.

Jamie laughed. "Not exactly. But understand that it's limited by its time, by the people writing it, and that Jesus gave us an easier, kinder, better set of rules to follow. It's complicated how it all went down, but it's not quite as hard to figure out what to do or who to listen to when you realize that when Jesus announced a new covenant at the Last Supper, he was invalidating the terms of the old covenant God made with Israel—and that's what books like Deuteronomy are all about. The laws God made for a different time, for a different people."

"But those are some shitty laws," Phoebe said. "Like the ones on tattoos and dressing in men's clothing and gays—"

"—Tell me about it. I'd have been put to death probably."

"Yeah, for . . ." Phoebe's words were running past her, and then she replayed what she'd heard. *Was Jamie talking about her tattoos, or was she trying to tell her something?* "What do you mean? For your tattoos?"

Jamie laughed. "Aw, you're telling me you don't know, Pheebes?"

Phoebe blushed a little, and then she started to laugh. "Well, guess I—"

"—Never put it all together?" Jamie's voice was so damn comforting. "I want you to tell me why you're torturing yourself with Deuteronomy, why it's making you so upset, okay Pheebes?"

Phoebe took a deep breath. She wanted to react to what Jamie had just told her; really, she should say something, but there was something commanding in Jamie's voice, something that precluded follow-up questions . . . unless that was just a copout? Oh hell. "As far as you being gay—"

"—I know you don't care, I know we're fine. Just figured you'd wanna know, and it's never come up, has it?"

Phoebe pictured Jamie's eyes narrowing, a flicker of soft light playing off the lampshade in Anne's, no, Jamie's . . . kitchen. Fuck. She should tell her. "Okay, okay. I know this guy, I'm not even seeing this guy, and . . . I'm . . ." Phoebe closed her eyes and she could see him there, standing in front of her, asking her a question and she couldn't hear what he was saying because she was seeing her father in his place.

"You're attracted to this guy, and this is new."

"Yeah," Phoebe sort of whispered.

"And that hurts, because you want to show him, but that's scary, because love and sex means sin, means evil, yes, Pheebes?"

"Yeah."

"Love manifested is good, Phoebe. It's good when you're in love, it's so good, and it's so blessed by God, I promise you He wants you to be happy, he wants you to love and be loved, to make love and have love made to you. I promise you this, I promise. It's okay, it's gonna be okay. He's your soulmate, isn't he?"

Phoebe could smell him, like he was beside her, on top of her, underneath her, and it was all she could do not to groan. "If soulmate means I can feel him in every breath I take, then yeah."

"Yep, that sounds like a soulmate," Jamie laughed.

"Do you have one?" Phoebe gulped a little. She loved Jamie so much, but it wasn't the same . . . she hoped it wasn't for Jamie either.

"In this life, well, I'm not so sure, but I have one yes. I've been with her before, other lives, and she might be here, she might not be, but it's fine. Just makes me happy knowing she's there, in heaven, or maybe even here, somewhere. Nobody else is worth being with is all I know, you know what I mean?"

Phoebe could see her father now, but his image receded and became darker, like an outline, then like a loose outline of a dark image, then it was just a fog-like thing, not even an image. And then she pictured her mom, and it hurt, seeing her mom, knowing that once she'd been her father's, just as her mother had been his. "Jamie? You think my mom and my dad were soulmates?"

"No. No way. He's gone now, he's gone Pheebes, and he's never gonna touch you again."

Phoebe gritted her teeth. She wanted to scream, how do you know, how do you fucking know, but she didn't want to yell, not now, not while she was on the phone with Jamie, because all her anger would go to one of the people she loved most. Instead of screaming, she closed her eyes again and instead of seeing her father, she kept looking until she found a mental image of Jim. He was everything that her father was not. He was safety and he was beauty and he was . . . love.

"Hope you're right," Phoebe said.

"I am. You know I love you, right? And I'm here if you need me, like anytime, okay Phoebe?"

"Yeah, yeah I do. And I love you too."

Chapter 29

The music wasn't loud enough to stop the buzzing in Phoebe's head. It started as a bumblebee, annoying really, and ended up like the roaring of a motorcycle. So she started drinking a little faster.

Beth was talking with Jamie and Sarah. Sarah lived with Beth, but they weren't together, not exactly. Or maybe they were. Phoebe couldn't keep score. Not with those two, but they seemed comfortable. Amicable really, so maybe they were on the outs, acting like a divorced couple, being nice for the sake of—Phoebe shoved her chair back and headed for the bar. It was time for another round, and she was buying. Mom's credit card. She shook her head and stifled a chuckle.

She came back bearing a pitcher. Didn't say anything when she set it down; just refilled four glasses, or three, because Jamie held up a hand before Phoebe could start pouring.

"Wouldn't believe the shit I read today."

Beth leaned forward. "Try me."

"Fuckers."

"Who?"

"Love is love. Children can benefit from any sort of it. Emotional, mental, or physical. Love is love."

Beth's eyes bugged out.

"No."

"Yes," Phoebe said.

Beth leaned forward and rested her head on her hand. She got this look, unlike her standard Jim Belushi imitation, and stared into her Foster's. She took a sip and made a face. "Damn, Pheebes, why you gotta get fancy?"

Phoebe laughed and took a huge gulp. "Fancy? This is one step up from your fucking Bud light."

Beth nodded, and the nod took the oxygen out of their back and forth. She fingered the condensation on her glass. Her bangs hung over her eyes. She swept them back. "Pheebes, Sarah will tell you, I try not to bring my work home with me too much." Sarah must have heard her name, because she shifted her body toward Beth. Jamie, who'd been scribbling plays in one of her ubiquitous green notebooks, finished drawing a diagram, and then looked at Beth.

"That's true," Sarah said. She was blonde, and buxom; hence, her Derby name Golden Grizelda. Phoebe took them all in: Jamie, Sarah, the asshole in the corner who kept his beady eyes on her, the guitarist at the back of the bar, and then she shook it all off. She had to focus on Beth. Otherwise she was gonna shove a fist in the beady asshole's face.

Sarah and Beth smiled at one another and the smile kind of sparkled into something a little more, like a pulse of something. Phoebe shook her head again. Maybe they weren't on the outs.

"Some cases get me. Never know which ones. Reckon the worst was a boy. Think he was twelve. I won't ever forget him." Beth's chin glistened, and she was sweating a little. Messy looking.

"Wasn't his name Ryan?" Sarah wrapped her arm around the back of Beth's chair.

"Yep. He was hard, tough. And we got him out of there. Away from his step-dad, a YMCA director or something brilliant like that. And he—"

"—Ryan?" Phoebe said.

"Yeah. Ryan got out of there. We got him into foster care. Thought we'd done everything, everything we could."

Phoebe snuck a glance at Jamie, who was just sitting there, calm, not showing anything. *Fuck, like she don't care. I feel like she's not with me. All hung up on this forgiveness shit.* Phoebe tapped her fingers on the thick wood and read, *Brittany gives good head* etched into it. She couldn't get away, could she?

"—But a couple months later, I got a call from his mom, his birth mom, and she was crying. She called me all these names, and I was about to hang up on her, but I heard, 'You killed my son,'" and I was like, 'Come again?' And she was crying too hard, really, and then that bastard husband of hers got on the phone, and he said all this stuff, but all I really heard was, "At least with me, he knew how much I loved him, and now you had to hand him over to a son of a bitch."

"What?"

"And then your supervisor called you in the morning, right?" Sarah lit a cigarette.

"Yep. Had to file a 509 report. And I wasn't allowed to attend the funeral. I went anyway." Beth's laugh sounded hollow. "The stepdad gave the eulogy. Said love knew no boundaries. I'm afraid I got myself thrown out of there."

"Of the funeral?"

"Yep."

"Oh my God." Phoebe grinned. "I like your style. Sounds like some old-fashioned justice."

"Guess you could call it that." Beth shook her head at Sarah. "Thought you were quitting, hon."

Sarah exhaled, eyes half-closed. She stubbed it out. "Tell Pheebes what you said?"

"Oh? That. Right. I couldn't help myself. Screamed, 'That's just another word for pedophile, you asshole.'"

"No!"

"Yep," Beth said. "I was saying a lot of other stuff. Really lost it. Then the organ started playing real loud, and it was funny, cuz he must have got confused, started playing a wedding march. I pictured Billy Idol, you know, 'White Wedding' and all, and . . . I started laughing." Beth groaned. "And then I was screaming something about marrying child fuckers."

"Oh my God. Wow."

"Yep."

Phoebe was trying so hard not to look at Jamie it hurt. Jamie was writing something down again. Phoebe checked on beady-eyed asshole, but he was staring at another girl. Then she narrowed her eyes and tried not to feel the muscles around them twitching. Well if she was gonna ignore this, then . . .

"Wayne Toller's out of jail. Talk about child fucker. He served five years. Now he's in this suburban neighborhood in Burke. I drove past his house the other day."

"Um, who's Wayne Toller?"

"Friend of my dad's."

Fucking Jamie was still writing something in her notebook.

"Oh." Beth and Sarah exchanged one of their glances. Phoebe's jaw ached. She'd explained this once or twice, but only to Beth. Each time she told the story, it felt like acid coming back up her throat, like when she ate cayenne pepper, and she could taste the burn again. She downed the rest of her beer and while pouring another she said, "That's the guy who was gonna get in with Dad and Parkings and do me."

"Do me" shot out and she regretted it because everyone flinched, even Jamie. Phoebe felt Jamie's flinch in her own body. Maybe she cared after all. Maybe that hurt worse than Jamie not caring. Maybe she really didn't care and just thought . . . oh fuck it. Stop it. She swallowed another sip of beer, and then pushed back from the table.

"I'm thinking a field trip, a little self-help's in order." Who's in?" The chair teetered, and she had to control her urge to slam it down, break some shit.

Beth stood up and grabbed her purse. "I got wheel."

"Wingman." Sarah said. They were all a little gleeful, but Beth at least wasn't drunk. She could hold a lot of beer.

Phoebe's eyes rested on Jamie, who wasn't saying much one way or the other.

"You in?"

Jamie clicked her pen and clipped it between the round wires in her notebook. Then she met Phoebe's stare. "Walk with me."

The silence burned into Phoebe's shoulder. Her mom always said the first one to speak lost in a situation like this, but she had the feeling she'd already lost—something. Beth and Sarah crossed the parking lot, and Beth held the door open on their Wrangler, like she was being gallant. Phoebe took this all in, and she wanted to, needed to, know, to ask, to demand really, *are you with me, or* . . . but she didn't know what came after the "or." The silence between them sat there, not going anywhere, and Phoebe strained to hear the guitar from inside just so she could stop waiting for Jamie to break it, break the silence.

Phoebe stuck her hand out, the one that wasn't all cut up, and rested it on the passenger side door. She was hoping Jamie was coming. *Crap.* That's what she was hoping.

Jamie tapped the key fob and inclined her head. "You coming?"

"Where?"

"Home. I'm goin home."

"Not—" Phoebe let go of the door frame and threw her hands up in the air, shrugging too. "Come on. It will be fun, come on."

"This isn't what I do. I'm goin home now. Let me drive you home. Come on, Phoebe, lemme drive ya home."

Jamie leaned against the SUV and the expression in her face wasn't exactly unreadable, at least not as cryptic as it had been in the bar. Phoebe stood there, stuck, standing, teetering, which way, not in any damn way. Why'd Jamie have to go and . . .

"No. You come on. What the fuck, you know?" She spun around and kicked at a piece of concrete that was sticking out of the asphalt.

"Why you doin this? You even know?"

"Doin what? What—something to that bastard?" Phoebe tried not to look away, but there was something, damnit, something too holier than fucking thou in Jamie's . . . oh fuck it. Jamie wasn't that way. Just holy, maybe, and that was worse. "Fuck, fuck it. Gotta do something. There's kids and bikes and balls and tire swings in his neighborhood, on his street and you really think he's gonna stop, huh?"

"Don't know."

"That's all you got? Really?"

"There's other ways." Jamie's eyes hadn't left Phoebe's.

Several responses shot through her mind, but Phoebe couldn't choose one. "You're wrong. It's all bullshit. Someone's gotta, fuck, someone's gotta, and if it ain't you, I don't we don't need you. What. You scared? That what it is? Or is it some God thing? Where's God, where was God when, where was—"

"—He never left."

"Bullshit." Phoebe kicked at the block of concrete, and spun around once, and started to walk away. Then she turned back around. "Come with us, please. There. That what you were waiting for?"

Jamie didn't move or speak right away. When she did, it was her captain's voice, quiet and steady. "I can't do that. There's other ways to heal. I know you gotta do what you gotta do, but so do I. And it don't mean nothing; not between you and me. I love you Phoebe. It's all gonna be all right."

"How in the hell can you say that? What do you know about—it being all right?"

"I'll see you soon." Jamie walked behind her SUV and then she put an arm around Phoebe. Phoebe leaned in, and held still for a moment. It felt good, and yet she couldn't feel good yet, not with this other urge, more like an urgent itch than an urge, because urges were—well, they were her Dad and they were Parkings. Those urges were different from what she was feeling now, whatever it was.

She pushed away without touching Jamie. She wasn't so much shrugging as she was shrugging Jamie off. And then she walked away. She did not look back.

Phoebe tried really hard to enjoy what followed. She talked loud. And she talked a lot. She laughed at all of Beth's jokes, and cracked way too many of her own. And it wasn't just the beer; if anything, she wasn't as trashed as she needed to be. Because even as she was spray-painting "Child-Fucker" on Wayne Toller's front door, she could sense Jamie's arm, the one she'd have been leaning on, if she'd been strong enough.

Chapter 30

"How have you been Jamie?" Her neurologist glanced through her chart and then settled down into a circular chair, the kind that a kid would spin around and around on. Jamie thought of Zander with a tender smile. He'd be all over the office, probably tossing the brain model around and using the reflex scraping tool on his tongue. He was doing fine; his bright light shined a lot even from far away.

"Blessed, for sure, thanks Dr. Cooper." Jamie felt Dr. Cooper's pain, not sure about what, so she shifted in her chair and took a good long look, straight in. Cynthia Cooper had aged so much these past few years and today her face was stretched and wan. There was darkness and resignation but not fear, a stage, a moving on, something like that, a lingering sadness.

Dear God please bless her bless her now hold her tight and let her pain be born, be carried, now and forever, amen.

Jamie felt Him there, but Cynthia did not. She could but she didn't.

Do what you can daughter but you must let her tend to you today. You can only bless her and pray.

But I am my sister's keeper.

Yes. And she is yours.

"Any seizure activity?"

Cynthia took a pen flashlight and checked Jamie's eyes as she asked questions.

"Not since the last time we talked."

"Ah, good." Cynthia checked Jamie's reflexes and Jamie barely concealed a wince when the mallet connected with her kneecap. Damn, that was a hard hit the other night at practice.

She is your keeper too. Tell her.

Cynthia scraped the bottom of her foot, which was the single worst thing about seeing a neurologist. It felt like a pin scratching against and poking into the soft part of her foot. Hurt even worse than taking a cortisone shot, not that she'd tell this particular doctor about it. That wouldn't go well. *Why did you get a cortisone shot? Oh. Well. Took a shot at practice. Practice? For what?* Jamie sighed.

Cynthia put the blasted scraper down. "How about headaches?"

"Headaches?"

"Yep." Her doctor gave her an appraising glance.

"Yeah. Well. Been kind of dicey lately."

"Migraines?"

Jamie nodded.

Cynthia pulled her chair closer. "Auras?"

"Not usually, no."

"You having them a lot?"

"Not so much, I mean, no." *Not worth exaggerating or making a big deal about it.*

"When's the last time we had a contrast MRI?"

"What, worried about brain bleed?"

Cynthia shook her head, her lips pursed. "Well, if I was really worried about that, I'd do more than an MRI. Angiogram's the only way to completely rule that out."

Jamie nodded.

"Looks like it's been five years. I'd like to get another baseline one."

Jamie shrugged, and thought about all the tests she'd been through over the years. She was fine. She'd been fine. Cynthia said a few more things, technical things, but Jamie was tired now. She really wanted to go back home and get a nap. Figure all this out, all this medical stuff, maybe in a month or two. She felt fine. Really.

She is your keeper. Tell her.

"Any other concerns?" Cynthia looked up from the order she was scribbling out.

"Are there any activities I shouldn't be doing?"

"Getting that riding bug again? You know that's out of the question, right? Just will take one more hit to the head, okay Jamie?" Cynthia tapped Jamie knee.

"Nah," smiled Jamie. "No riding. Gave that up a long time ago. Anything else?"

"Well, don't go walking on roofs or swimming alone in the ocean is something I tell all my seizure patients."

"Okay."

Jamie took the order and stood up. She put her hand on Cynthia's shoulder and looked into her eyes. "Take good care, Dr. Cooper."

Cynthia's eyes moved, the lines cutting deep wrinkles into her almost grayish skin. She really wasn't looking good, bless her.

"Thank you Jamie. You do the same."

Jamie sauntered out past the receptionist, but she paused in the vestibule. A man sat very still, his hand jammed on his cane. He'd been . . . a physicist. Yes. Jamie could see equations rolling backwards, sideways, forwards, upside down, reflected in his eyes, eyes now yellowing and thick with cataracts. He had been a brilliant man. He was still a good man, and the equations would all come back to him. *Soon.*

"Soon, brother," she whispered, "Soon."

His head jerked up, and he looked off to his right before his eyes settled on a spot just above Jamie. *Please God let me see my Sarah soon.*

Go in peace, brother. She blessed him without speaking. His soul heard her.

Chapter 31

Jim jammed his fingers unscrewing the air impact wrench. It was the third time in an hour he'd jammed his fingers with one tool or another, and this time, he stood up, laughing, and forget to duck under the hoist overhanging. "Hellfire," he exclaimed. Now he had grease in his hair *and* three bleeding fingers. And that's when one song ended and the DJ came on 100.3. "Christine McVie says she'll rejoin Fleetwood Mac if they invite her back." The snarky, deep-voiced DJ paused, waiting for the first notes of "Songbird" to start playing. "Apparently, the rest of the band hasn't gotten the memo. Seems like 25 years is a long time."

Jim shook his head, and reached for a rag. The song never meant anything to him, but when he heard, "And I feel like when I'm with you, it's all right," he saw Phoebe Thompson slamming a door open and scowling at no one in particular, and all he could think about was that moment when that scowl turned into the first indication of a smile. It was that five minutes before the sun came up, somehow even more beautiful than the first rays rising.

There was probably a poem in there, as long as he didn't riff off the song lyric too closely. He'd had to scratch a few poems when he realized they'd snaked into his brain and wrapped around and into a verse. By the time he ripped it out, he'd lost an intangible, a bit of magic, or just the belief the poem had ever been his.

The thing is, he shouldn't have trashed those poems that had a bad line, or doubted if they were really his poems because a few of the words came from someone else. One sentence could be broken, but it didn't mean the entire poem should go. Because if you thought about it, he didn't toss out a truck that had broken parts. He didn't build a new truck or part from scratch, and he didn't simply replace a broken part with a brand-new part. He fixed parts of trucks; he also tended to the entire truck using somewhat imperfect parts, even part-broken parts. He used whatever was on hand to make whatever was already there—better. Nothing was past fixing.

He was a fixer of parts, and a wordsmith of words. He took some broken pieces, added some working parts, and made it work. Maybe that's how God worked. Surely he'd been broken, busted, no good—

"—J.J.?"

Jim frowned and looked up but Ronnie had bent over to pick up a shop rag and his pants didn't cover his skin all the way. It was a rough bit of real estate.

"Um, hey, Ronnie, warn me before you're gonna go and show all that skin."

Ronnie cinched his pants up and set the rag on Jim's work bench. "Yeah, yeah. Just more man parts for my wife to love."

"It's not the parts, it's the presentation that's bugging me."

Still wearing a good-natured smile, Ronnie put his hands on his hips and studied Jim. "You seem a little distracted today."

"Did I . . ." Jim reached over for his clipboard and double-checked a measurement. As soon as he marked it with a grubby pen, he met Ronnie's gaze. "Make a mistake or forget to take care of something?"

"Nope. You're good."

Jim picked up a large wrench and felt its metal grip with his fingertips. He'd never talked with Ronnie about off the job stuff, other than cars and sports, and it really wasn't his way, but Ronnie talked about his wife and kids a lot. That was Ronnie's way.

"Well, good."

"So everything's all right?"

Jim couldn't help it—he smiled, and he knew Ronnie would follow up, but still. "Better than all right."

"Had a good day off then?"

Still smiling, Jim turned to 92' Blazer he was working on, and eyed the tig welder. "Yep."

"And . . ." Ronnie was about to ask another question, but his cell phone rang, and he took a few steps in the other direction before he answered it.

He was off work at 3 p.m. And for once, he actually left on time. The first thing he did after he gunned his engine was to hit the redial button on his cell.

She answered on the third ring. "Already off?"

"I am."

"Was gonna give you shit for working a half day, but realized you probably go in at some ungodly hour."

He loved her voice. It jumped from deep when she was trying not to care, to really high-pitched when she got going on something. "Ungodly?" He grinned, and shifted gears before he turned on Main. "No such thing. Anyway," he continued, when she didn't get on the ungodly bit, "I dig seeing the dawn."

"Same. Miss it. Best time for riding."

"Horses?"

"Yep. So Jim . . ."

"Yes?"

"Coming my way?"

"Soon as I swing by my place and wash the grease out of my hair, I sure am. If you text me your address and still want to go for that ride, I am."

"Done. As soon as we hang up. Guess it's time for me to roll out of bed."

He pictured her—*oh no, man. Don't go there.* "You're not still—"

"—Sleeping?" She laughed her low, sexy laugh. "Nah. Just wanted to see what you'd say. I'm actually accustomed to watching the sun rise too. See you when you get here."

Once he got showered and dressed in jeans and a long-sleeved shirt, it didn't take him long to drive up Route 28 and then west on Route 50 toward Middleburg. The back roads got him out there faster than I-66 would have, and he liked the rolling hills and curves and farms and big estates, most with private driveways.

Most of these estates were too big, really, for what their owners needed, except for the horse owners and maybe the farmers. But even a fifty-acre farm couldn't compete with the agri-business world. It was a sad thing, seeing the self-sufficient farms slowly losing their foothold, kind of like an outmatched army facing an opponent with massive tactical advantages. Not a whole lot you can do about it, but a soldier fights on. This though wasn't his battle to fight.

When he spotted her address and turned off on a slightly rutted road, his stomach leaped. It hadn't done that in ages. It was like something big had changed, or was changing, or on the cusp of changing, and all within less than twenty-four hours. For once it was changing into something good, but that was scary, because one person just couldn't be everything. Not in friendship. Not after losing Christopher. *And not in . . . well, too soon to say.*

Chapter 32

She heard an engine gun from about a quarter-mile away. A V-6, from the sound of it, low geared four wheel drive. So a truck, maybe an old truck-based SUV. Sounded like the sort of thing Jim would drive. Not a Ford, not after what he said about Anne's F-150. He didn't say Fords sucked, but if he had a Ford, he'd have said he had a Ford. Chevy? She wasn't seeing him as a Chevy guy. *Maybe, but just not feeling it.* Certainly not a Dodge. *Junk, that's what Dodges were really, and he was a quality guy.*

Quality. Low geared . . . had to be a truck or SUV, and an old one. Worked on them for a living, so he'd probably have bought something pretty old, but reliable, nothing gorgeous but impossible like her old Bronco. Only one choice left really, maybe two. No, he wouldn't drive a Nissan—too much of an outlier. Had to be a Toyota.

She stood on the porch, leaning against the railing, sure she'd see the 4Runner she then did see, just a moment later, bouncing over a slight gap in the dirt and gravel. Early '90s model, black, and just washed. A car guy's way of saying he cared about the woman he was coming to see. Maybe she was over analyzing it. Phoebe grinned. Nah.

A small cloud of dust followed Jim's 4Runner, leaving the just-polished tires a lighter shade, closer to brown than black, where they'd sunk into the March mud. He wasn't driving too fast or too slow, so he hit the clearing and pulled into a space that her mom's silly Range Rover had left empty early that morning. She was flying to Chicago and wouldn't be back home until Wednesday night, not that Phoebe was counting on her being gone or anything. *Okay, wow. Mom wouldn't be home tonight.*

She rubbed her hand against the white railing, going with the grain so she wouldn't catch a splinter, and then she jumped down from the porch and jogged a few steps to lighten her landing. The brake lights came on, and then the parking lights, and she admired the rear of his 4Runner. It didn't have the tire on the back, which was a good thing. Mounting the tire on the back made getting stuff out through the lift gate too hard. She nodded in appreciation. So far, Jim's taste—perfect.

He leaped out the driver's side and landed with a gracious slide-step after he hit a muddy patch. She could tell he was athletic the way his body moved as if he were expecting the mud, or accustomed to ice. He wore gold aviator sunglasses, jeans, and no jacket over a blue Oxford shirt.

"Hi, Jim."

"Good to see you Phoebe." He took his shades off and tucked them in the front pocket of his shirt. "This place is like a slice of heaven. Reminds me of home."

"Come on. Let me show you around." Phoebe started to walk away toward the fields and then paused, feeling shy all of a sudden. "It's good to see you too. And, hey, I love the old 4Runner. Kind of thought maybe that's what you would drive."

"You did? Really?"

"Yeah. Quality vehicle. Kind of wish I'd gotten one of them and not that damn Bronco."

"Well, I can look out for one for you if you want." He caught up to her, and they started to follow a path down to the fields. He was close enough for her to smell his aftershave, hint of sandalwood, nothing that reminded her of anyone else. She sighed, and then pointed toward the skyline. "See the mountains, just the hint of them, maybe beyond the rise over there?"

"Yep."

They walked a little farther, until they came to a fence post. She leaned against it, with her body angled toward his just a little. "I was thinking of driving out that way, maybe catching the sunset."

"I'm game. As long as we grab some food somewhere along the way."

"There's a sub shop on the way?"

"Perfect. I think I skipped lunch. Kind of distracted today actually."

She put her boot on the lower railing and kicked at it a little. "Distracted? Thinking about those one-hit wonder bands, huh?"

"Um, something like that, maybe." The light dappled the space between them, almost as if bridging the gap. She wanted to go there. It was hard not to, and confusing.

She tried to smile, in between trying to just let go, and go . . . to him. And when she did, when she smiled, he studied her closely. The muscles around his eyes worked, and he was about to do something, but she turned and half-smiled again, and he followed her, hands shoved into his pockets, walking nice and easy, not in a hurry.

"What's your favorite kind of sandwich?"

"Meatballs." She chuckled, no reason why, except it sounded funny. "You?"

"Hard to beat steak and cheese. Maybe a reuben if it's got good kraut and bread that's not soggy."

"Mmm. Steak and cheese has gotta have onions and just be a dripping mess."

"Agreed."

They got to the 4Runner, and he put his hand on the passenger door. "Mind if I drive?"

She thought about how irritable she could get, and then she threw her hands up in the air. "Maybe just this once, but don't get used to it. I like to have the wheel."

"Okay, roger that." He unlocked the door and held it for her. "Kind of nice to think it's something I'll have to get used to."

She pushed off the ground, feeling her leg muscles working, and all she could think of was how she wished he wouldn't shut the door on her, or them, and not just right now. Never. And then she was whispering, "Jim, come here."

He came toward her, his feet still on the ground, so he was below her still. And she took her hands and ran them through his hair, and she was shaking. He didn't kiss her. *She wanted . . . she didn't know what she wanted.* But he didn't kiss her, though he could have. He did something different. He rested his head on her breast, and she sat there, running her hands through his hair. *She had no fucking idea what she was doing, no idea.* And she was whispering that to him, but she didn't even realize it until he raised his head and his voice was mellifluous, kind of deep though, huskier than usual.

"We'll figure it out Phoebe. We'll figure it out."

She let go of his head, and he closed his eyes, sighing, and she knew how bad he wanted her, and it was all she could do not to do all the things she knew how to do.

He sighed again, and opened his eyes. She let her hands fall against her jeans, and then she returned his gaze. Gently, he stepped backwards, and gently, he shut the door, blinking fast, almost as if something was in his eye. She watching his every move, with this reckless, almost feverish attention, wanting more, more of Jim McMahon, but wanting to be sure that all of it was not bad, not dirty, not her being dirty. So when he put his sunglasses on, she weighed it in her mind, and realized no one, *I mean, Dad, just think it, stop avoiding it,* did not put his sunglasses on that way.

And when Jim grabbed his key ring and opened his door, it wasn't the way anyone, any man, Dad, unlocked his door. And that was enough, just two quick bits, two pieces of the puzzle; she said, but thought really, just so loud it was like thinking:

> *I'm putting it away now, I gotta, gotta be here, here, safe, safe, with Jim, not anyone, not Dad, please God. Just me and him, nothing, no one, no man, just us.*

He started the engine, and pulled his seatbelt on, and then he put his hand on the back of her seat and reversed. She took a deep breath, and let him have the wheel, and it felt good when he pulled out and they bounced over the rutted dirt gravel.

She started to talk and so did he, and then they both fell silent, just for a minute, maybe two. It wasn't uncomfortable. She wasn't sure what he was thinking, but he didn't look mad. Thoughtful, not mad. So she wasn't scared. Well, she was scared, but not of him or his thoughts.

"Wanna try to catch the sunset at Skyline drive?" Her voice hit a high note, higher than usual.

"About a half-hour away, right?"

"How did you know?"

He turned right and then smiled. "Figured you might take me out there, so as long as we grab subs in Front Royal, I'm all over it."

"I got just the place. Crazy Carl's." The 4Runner's six whined a little as they headed up a hill, and she chuckled. Her Bronco didn't whine; then again, it was broke more than it was working. "Their Philly sub is a monster."

He nodded, and she waited for him to ask her, and while she waited, she watched the burnt yellow fields drift past. But he didn't ask, or say too much, not until she started to talk again. "I don't even know where to start, you know?"

"You mean, with this first date, or second one, but the first one wasn't really, and you don't know, but really you do, we both do, that this is something, something more, and what are we supposed to do? Because it's easy to talk about our favorite bands, even feels good, but there's more, so much more, we each want to say?"

"Um, yeah. *That*." She laughed, and he did too.

"Why you gotta be so fucking poetic about it anyway?"

"Guess you bring it out in me," he said.

"Mmm." She tapped her fingers on the console near the gearbox, and she left them there. He downshifted into a hill, and his fingers touched hers, and she wanted to kiss them. Something about his hands made her crazy.

And she did. Lifted his hand and brushed the tips of his fingers to her lips. He made this sound, like a sigh, or a groan, and she set his hand back down, and then he lifted it to her cheek and stroked it. His eyes never left the road.

"Oh my fucking God Jim."

"Yeah, me too."

"I don't know what I'm doing. I really don't know what the fuck I'm doing."

He touched her hand again. "Part of me wants to say these things to you."

"What things?"

"Like I understand wanting to go slow, but then it gets away from me, and needing to slow down, and just not knowing what I should do. I know there's all this you're carrying, and maybe if you know what I'm carrying too, it will make it easier. But what if my own stuff is too much, you know, for both of us to carry, me with mine, my past, you with yours."

"Your past?"

His left hand gripped the wheel, and his right hand kept moving from hers to shifting gears, and back again. It didn't scare her, except for how good it felt each time he touched her, and how much she wanted his hand back each time it left. But not scaring her so bad or so much every time, especially the more he did it.

"Yes. War does that to a man. And then there's the drinking, or not drinking, and what that does to me."

"You mean . . ." she paused. She was thinking and she was aware of each one of her thoughts and she was realizing that it helped to think about him. When she concentrated on how he was feeling she stopped worrying about how she was feeling; not only that, but she cared about what he was feeling and thinking and it felt good to care. "You don't know if you can . . ."

"I don't know how honest I should be, either, you know?"

She was trying to fill in the spaces between his words. "Wow. So this isn't just about me. It's not just all my confusion and mess."

He nodded.

"For some reason, that helps. I—I don't know why. But if you can be honest, maybe I can too."

"Yeah?"

"Yeah," she said. "Jim? You know what I . . . did, right?"

"What you did?"

"You looked me up on Google, right? Please say you did."

"Okay," he said. "I did."

"Okay. So you know I'm not exactly . . . well." She hesitated. "Okay if I smoke?"

"As long as you light me one."

While she lit two cigarettes, she thought about how intimate it was, and when she leaned over and put one in his mouth, her hand shook. "I'm not exactly a virgin. And it's just so ugly. So fucking ugly."

"I'm still here, right?" He rolled his window down and so did she.

"Right."

"And I don't think that's really fair, if you're talking about what happened when you were a kid."

"But it was . . ." she stopped and smoked, and it hit her hard, the buzz. She half-closed her eyes, and tried not to see her dad, or feel him, or feel her feeling him. "He was—you know?"

"I do know. And it doesn't mean anything to me." He held the Marlboro between his two fingers, and she thought of the ride from school to Middleburg with her mom, and how she told her mom she'd fucked Dad and her mom had said she knew. Now Jim knew. Jim knew too.

"My mom said the same thing, the night we got away to Bryson."

"The Safe House?"

"Yeah," she said.

"She said it wasn't my fault. And that we were starting over."

"It wasn't your fault." His jaw got real tight. "It really wasn't."

"I don't know." She was so close to shutting down. *So close. And yet his hand. His hand touching her, oh my God it was he was like a drug.* "I feel this thing, it's like I feel it and it hurts, this thing, this . . . us, you, it, wanting . . . When I'm with you, I feel, and I haven't felt anything since, since, he died. And I want to feel but every time I do, it takes me back."

"Oh Phoebe." Her name sounded beautiful when he said it. "We're going to take it slow."

"But I don't wanna take it slow."

"The truth? You're telling it, so I will too."

"Okay," she said.

"I think that we should take it slow."

She didn't say anything.

"I don't want to take it slow. You're, oh, you're killing me."

"Yeah?"

"Oh yeah," he said. "But, well, the war does stuff to you. And so does drinking."

"But you can? You can still?"

"Yeah. At least when I'm drinking, I can."

"Wow. I never thought of that."

"Yeah, well. I didn't either." He chuckled. "But oh man. When you ran your hands through my hair, and then pulled away, it was all I could do to walk away."

She waited for him to keep talking. An electric feeling ran through her and she was thinking of unzipping his jeans and touching him, but she really couldn't do that. She knew just how she would do it but . . . *no*.

"I wanted to kiss you. I want to kiss you."

"Why didn't you?"

The sign for Skyline Drive appeared, and she kept thinking about the kiss that was going to be.

"Needed to be sure I'd stop."

"Well." She laughed, and it was a deep laugh. She had no idea she could sound like that. "Maybe you should try me."

He nodded, and a few minutes later, after she showed the ranger her yearly pass, they glided into a vista. He turned the engine off and he fixed his eyes on her. "I can't think of anything else I'd rather do."

He got out of the 4Runner and came around to her side. She waited, and he opened her door, and put his hand out. She took his hand, and he shut the door behind her.

She got weak in the knees as soon as *no maybe even before* he put his hands on her hips. Everything was so slow, and she fought with all she had to keep it, take it, *make it* stay slow. Slowly, he leaned his head toward her. Slowly, he pulled her closer. Slowly, he ran his hands up her back and up to the crook of her neck. She could feel him shaking, and she was shaking too, and then his lips touched, touched her neck, a plane's wheels tapping the ground, once, jumping back up, then back down again. His lips, soft, wet, on the front of her neck and his hands, strong, bending her backwards, and he was walking, turning her, both of them whispering words, a lot of them, but none of them making any sense really.

Her back was to the 4Runner, and he'd moved her— them—down to the hood, polished, golden light glimmering off it, glittering and swimming in the corner of her eye. Golden light glittering as he swung her backward, or she collapsed backwards, and he whispered, "Oh Phoebe, please say I can kiss you now," and she said yes, yes, yes Jim. When she said his name, she felt it all the way through her, like he was touching her there, all the way there, and she didn't know if she could take it, take waiting, take it, take having it, take not having him, all, all of him, for any longer, take, take having him if she did, so she whispered his name again, please Jim, kiss me, she whispered, and his mouth touched hers, hot, so hot, and wet, and she stopped talking finally, finally stopped.

Chapter 33

The words ran over themselves in her head, barely keeping pace with his, with her, his lips, her hands, his hands, her lips, words, just words that were so much more than letters woven together, symbols, not like in an equation symbols, letters, 26 an alphabet stop it no words. *It's my first kiss*, this, this man, him, his lips stop it no words.

He pulled away from her before she wanted him to, and with her fingers ruffling through his hair, she whispered, "More, please Jim."

She looked down at his profile and she breathed in as deep the air would come. It hurt coming in, not from the quality of the cold air, but how it connected with this thing running through her, this other hurt. It was an ache, this need, that felt exquisite, and when she touched his head, he took his right hand and pressed it right on top of where she ached with this need that felt exquisite, and he traced his fingers from that need, that place, up to her neck.

She took his hand and raised it to her lips, and he groaned. She was not really in control anymore, she knew she wasn't, and she didn't want to be, she just wanted his hand where it was, in her mouth, and she groaned too. It was, she was, way past knowing what to do, and so she stopped trying to make him take her, because she could and if she did what she knew how to do, she would. But something in her just knew, then, at that instant, right before she arched beneath him, to let him lead before she took them too far.

And he imperceptibly shifted. He pulled back, or slowed them down. It was subtle. He took his hand and ran it down her neck and then gripped her shoulder and kissed her. He kissed her for a long time, slow and gentle, tender, just right, and it got slower, the words tumbled slower inside, and she smelled his lavender aftershave again, and felt the warm engine ticking underneath her. And then a motorcycle's high engine gunned, got closer, and she broke apart from his lips and he let go of her and rolled over next to her. He kept an arm wrapped around her, and she laid her chin on his chest, and they didn't say anything for a minute, not while she felt his heart beating beneath her.

"Hey," she said.

"Hey." He ran his hand through her hair, and held it there, cupping the space behind her ear. She smirked, and moved her head as if . . . but she stopped.

And he caressed her head again.

"I could . . ." He paused and squinted toward the mountains, where the sun was heading, but hadn't reached yet.

"Do that all night?"

"Yeah."

She followed his gaze to the faraway mountains. "That was my first kiss," she said.

The smile lines around his eyes creased. "So you have none to compare it to?"

"I don't think I need to. I got this feeling you're not like any other man." She blushed a little. She didn't want to think about any other men.

He reached over and kissed her again, and deeply, but not too long. He was grinning when he pulled away. "I could get used to this. To you."

"To me?"

"Yeah. To us." He had this serious look again, and it mirrored what she was thinking.

"Jim? Can you just hold me awhile? Before we leave? Please?"

He did. He held her and she didn't tell him how scared she was, and how safe he made her feel when the words ran too fast, unpeeling, tripping, tumbling over one another; she didn't say all that. She just let him hold her for awhile.

He kissed her head, and whispered, "The sun and the mountains are about to kiss."

So they watched until the sun passed over and through the mountaintop, and she thought of him going through her, and thought she'd like that, but not yet.

"I'm starving," he said.

"All that kissing?" She was teasing him now, and he took her hand and led her to the door, and they laughed but didn't kiss again.

He started up the engine and headed down the mountain. "Steak and cheese?"

"With onions and mushrooms. And mayo and ketchup."

"Ketchup is sacrilege," he said.

"Then call me a sinner," she said, and the word didn't feel great, and she wanted to reconsider it, but she didn't and maybe she wasn't.

One Week Later

Chapter 34

The phone rang and she knew it was Cary even before checking caller id. "Cary?" It sounded like she was choking, so she tried again, but it wasn't much better.

"Yes, Phoebe, it's me. What's going on?"

"Met someone." Each word hurt, so she'd have to do this one word at a time thing: Cary asking; Phoebe telling as much as she could; and silence, with maybe her therapist's training, filling gaps. "A guy."

"You met a guy? As in you met a guy you're interested in?"

"Yeah," she said. Just that tore her up. The word 'yeah' and its source, and what it meant. Yes to men; yes to the possibilities of it, of anything; yes to kissing and yes maybe to sex no fucking no making love; yes to the nightmare, the nightmares, one after another; yes to the ceiling above her, the stares, the body memories, the sins she did and had done to her. Yes. So she said yeah not yes. But yes winked at her like a misbegotten lighthouse on a pitch black night.

Yes.

"Is he treating you well? Because if he's not, I swear to fucking God, I will bust his head in."

Phoebe gasped, and then, so fast, before she remembered she couldn't laugh, not when she felt this broken busted up—she laughed.

"I'm serious, goddamn it." Cary went on, and then she was laughing too. "Well, so much for my poker face. Guess you got me when I've had too much caffeine."

Phoebe imagined Cary leaning her head back and laughing while taking notes without watching the page. She wasn't sure if Cary had really had too much caffeine or was just saying crazy stuff to make her laugh.

"He is, oh my fucking God yes." Phoebe wiped her eyes. "Look Cary. I said an entire fucking sentence." There'd been many sessions when Phoebe would lose her words, and Cary would have to go back and forth with her, asking a question, another question, another question, and maybe Phoebe would nod, or shake her head, and an entire hour could pass before Phoebe put together even three words. *It sucked, and she was sure it sucked for Cary, but it sucked worse for her because she was the one who hurt too bad to talk.*

"Well good. Maybe we can keep it that way."

Phoebe mumbled something and ran her hand through her hair. And then thought of him, and wished she hadn't, or she wished he was there so she could run her hands through his hair and make him moan. Not that, no, she thought; and then she started talking kind of fast.

"He kissed me Cary, and I asked for it, and it was my first kiss, but not my first time having sex. We haven't yet, and I want to and I know how to make it feel good for him, and I am thinking about him all the time, and touching him more, but then Dad's back, and I am thinking about him too and I can't keep it all separate, this doing what I want I need I should do and doing all these things I shouldn't have done, oh no, not to my dad, not with my dad, I'm dying, I'm dying Cary. And all it was *was* a kiss, a first kiss, nothing more, so much more."

"So it feels good, and of course that would be painful, right?"

"Better than good. I felt it down to my toes when we kissed. I got lost in it, in him, and I want to stay lost you know what I mean? But I can't because what if it feels too good you know?"

"It's supposed to feel good. In so many ways, I am delighted to hear that you've met someone."

Phoebe chewed on her fingernails and tried to stop counting her heartbeats. It was thumping fast. She hated that.

"What's he like anyway?"

"Oh. He's a soldier poet-mechanic, and he writes this stuff about war and it makes me want to run around screaming or crying or getting in fights." Phoebe laughed again, a hard laugh that didn't feel so good. "In fact, I almost got in a fight when some asshole said something about Jim's poem."

"Jim's the guy you kissed?"

"Yeah. Jim McMahon."

"Good grief, the way you say his name, I can tell you care about him. So you heard him read his poem in class, almost got in a fight over it, and then what?"

"And then I bought him coffee. And we started talking. About everything. War. My parents. Mom." Phoebe tapped her fingers on her tattered jeans as she talked, almost in a rhythm. "And you know what else? He told me things, about war, and losing his best friend in Iraq, and getting sober, and he'd never heard of me. He's the first guy I kissed, but he's also the first guy I told about how mom killed dad."

"Nice symmetry in a way."

"Yeah, I guess. It's funny." Phoebe imagined Cary sitting across from her, staring intently at her, and she relaxed her shoulders a little. "I don't know. It's not all about me, about my stuff. I mean, he's got shit. He's got shit from war. I've seen him jump when a truck backfires."

"PTSD?"

"Yeah. Yeah, both of us are kind of a mess."

"He's sober?"

"What, you checking on him Cary?" Phoebe *probably sounded like a bitch, as usual.*

"Just asking."

Phoebe took a deep breath. All their time together, Cary had never seemed like she cared about Phoebe being an asshole.

"All right. He's sober. And I think it's hard for him, I mean, like, he's not made love sober."

"He told you that?"

"Sort of. I mean, I think, yeah. And he said we had to take it slow. For him too."

"How did you feel about that?"

"Honestly?" Phoebe was about to run her hand through her hair, but she stopped herself. "I was bummed. Because I wanted him so bad. And then I was screaming, 'Don't be such a fucking slut' at myself. I mean, what the fuck, what the fuck is wrong with me? I wanted him so bad. And I know how to please men, I know how to fuck them, and make them feel good and now I can't even do that for him so why will he want to be with me?"

"Okay. First of all. You're not a slut. You hear me?"

Phoebe looked down at the wood floors, extra wide boards. "Yes ma'am."

"Second, it's normal to want a man, especially when he kisses you, from the sound of it, extremely well—I mean, it was a good kiss, right?"

"Oh my God . . ." Phoebe felt a rush of desire go through her solar plexus, all the way on down.

"Also, he sounds like he's been incredibly honest with you, which can't be easy for him. And that's allowing you to be honest too, right?"

"Yeah. It really is."

"Okay." Cary was probably smiling. She sounded like she was. "And going slow might feel like torture, but it's probably what I'd suggest anyway."

"But I feel, oh goddamnit. Rejected. How fucked is that?"

"Not unusual at all. This isn't an easy thing to navigate for anyone actually. And when you add a dollop of PTSD, and for both people that sounds like an issue, well, going slow makes sense, don't you think?"

"I don't know. I wish I knew . . . what Cass meant."

"Cass?"

"Ms. White. Cassandra White—you know, right?"

"Oh." Cary made a noncommittal sound. "I do. How does she factor into all this?"

"Back when I first went to Bryson, I met with her and she told me she'd been raped and I asked her how she ever got over it. And she told me it wasn't easy, but she did and I wonder . . ." Phoebe's voice petered out, and she brought her knees up to her chin.

"You wonder?"

"How she got to the point where she thrived, and got it all sorted. I wonder what she meant by that," Phoebe said.

"I take it you look up to Cass? And maybe feel comfortable with her, now that she works with your mom and you see her a lot?"

"Yeah. Guess I do."

"And you can't really talk to your mom about all this."

Phoebe frowned. "Oh fuck no. No way. No."

"Maybe you should ask Cass? I have a feeling she'd love to talk to you," Cary said.

Phoebe could see Cassandra in her jeans and silver-blond hair hugging her husband at a party she'd been to about a year ago. Cass had leaned in when he kissed her, and she looked so at ease, in tune, okay, sexy. "Yeah, maybe, I will."

"How are you feeling now, Phoebe?"

"Better. Like I can be okay until I see you next. Well," Phoebe chuckled, "I think."

"Well, if you're not okay, please call me."

"Okay."

"See you Friday?"

"Yeah."

Chapter 35

Jamie paced and talked with God. It was a warm spring night, right about when the blossoms were about to bloom, or maybe a week or two before it. Could never tell with these Virginia springs. The weather had been all over the place the last ten years and she was thinking it was gonna continue to be a little crazy but she didn't have the inside skinny on the weather. It wasn't part of her job requirement, she liked to think. God had more important things to talk about than the weather.

"Hey, I can do weather," God said.

Jamie laughed. "Fine. You heard what I was thinking there. You got me."

They walked in companionable silence for a few moments.

"Jamie, I want you to reach out to Catherine."

"I thought you said it wasn't our time, this lifetime, or wasn't meant to be, or whatever," Jamie said. She was annoyed with herself, because she felt a momentary surge of . . . something. Felt like hope.

"No, I don't mean to ask her out, Jamie, but hey, knock yourself out." God was laughing again, and she laughed too, but still felt annoyed. She really wasn't looking for any sort of relationship. She wasn't gonna be here for long, not as long as she could tell, and the last thing she wanted to do was make a life she'd be sorry to leave. Besides, Phoebe. That was Job One.

"Nothing wrong with falling in love, you know? And you're not coming Home, not for awhile. You and Phoebe got some really, really important work to get done."

"Oh yeah? Like what?"

"Well, what would you say to the 21st Century version of Abolitionism?"

Jamie didn't get where He was going at first, and it hurt her head, hurt it real bad, trying to concentrate. So He made it easier on her.

"Sex trade, Jamie. It's just as bad, no, maybe it's worse . . . for the soul, not just of the enslaved, but the enslavers. I've had enough. New covenant. Soul death. But that's not enough. We're gonna stop it now, you and Phoebe and Catherine too, maybe a few others, working on that, no no Jamie, shhh, just listen now, I know your head's killing you, so don't worry, you can call her later, just make sure she recruits Phoebe, puts in a word for her, something, something to get her foot in the door."

Jamie put her hand on her head, and walked inside, through her kitchen. She grabbed a glass of very cold water, no ice. *Very quickly, now, Jamie, get to the bedroom, get in bed, lay down, now Jamie . . .*

"Okay, God, I will, just remind me . . ." Jamie closed her eyes and she was gone for awhile.

• • •

Sometimes a man's work was never finished. And sometimes, he thought, with a grim chuckle, he was going to have to declare it good enough. It was sort of amazing, really, that the country club didn't double-check his out of state ID, the one he'd traded for inside. He didn't mind taking it, not really. Once a week, sometimes twice. For two years he'd kept his mouth shut. Sometimes, he imagined he was somewhere else. Although at the end, he really hadn't minded.

And he'd been rewarded. Never whined. Never begged. He hadn't known what he'd use it for, but before he went to the club that first night home, he'd grabbed the ID on a whim. Used it when he checked in, no questions asked. And it didn't take him long to realize how much he'd missed them. When he walked to the pool deck and looked around, well, he'd brainstormed a little. Then, as he swam, a lot.

On the way out, he asked if they had openings and the tired lady at the desk had said for what and he'd said well I just moved here from West Virginia because there's no work and she'd said well, there's always work if you're not picky call Sam in the morning and he'd smiled and said he would.

That night, he'd researched, and waited. Researched, waited, and invested in some very interesting equipment. Wayne Toller rubbed his hands. Very interesting indeed. A few hours of research was all he needed.

It had cost less than $500 total. And all from the safety of his basement. One hidden camera pen, 8GM Micro SD Card: $89; two Coat Hooks with hidden cameras, white: $98; and one AC Adapter Hidden Camera, 16 hours storage: $295. He hummed the MasterCard commercial, then giggled and sang, "Priceless."

Truth be told, he wasn't sure what he needed the pen for, but he'd learned adaptability inside. So much so, in fact, that he'd installed all of this in the men's room. Well, except for one of the coat hooks. Women's room. For old time's sake.

And tomorrow he'd check and see what he had. But for now . . . he sighed, a deep, almost painful sigh. And he reached down between his legs and released the tension.

Chapter 36

Catherine scrolled through her welcome screen and came up on a Virginia phone number and voicemail that was unfamiliar.

"Catherine, Hi, it's Jamie Eddington, Phoebe's friend. Hey, wanna grab a cup of coffee with me sometime soon? Call me when it's convenient, or we'll see you maybe tonight at the gym. Peace be with you my friend."

Catherine was finding it almost impossible not to smile. She almost felt nervous, but that wasn't so odd. In college, or in high school, no one called anyone. It was all in person or over text, so it was just sort of new, she was thinking, having someone call her. It was . . . nice.

Catherine was planning on calling back once she got to the gym, but she saw Jamie locking up her SUV in the gym parking lot when she pulled up. She jumped out of the Volvo and was grinning even before she got Jamie's name out.

"Jamie? Hey, just got your voicemail," Catherine said.

Jamie hitched her duffelbag over her shoulder. She was taller than Catherine by a good three inches, and she had a muscular look about her. It was no surprise she spent a lot of time around horses.

"Oh, right, probably could've just asked you in person," Jamie said.

"Yeah, I'd love to grab a cup of coffee with you, anytime," Catherine added.

"Well, good, hey, you know what? Phoebe's running late, very late today from the sound of it. Walk with me," Jamie said, and she cut across the parking lot toward a shopping center across the road. Catherine could see a Starbucks tucked away near a gas station, sticking out in the corner of a long line of nondescript, non-chain stores.

She fell in alongside of Jamie and tried to keep her mind still. It felt comfortable being with her. Jamie was kind of otherworldly, and yet very much in (if not of) this world. She felt like God was . . .

"Jamie, are you a minister of some sort?"

Jamie grabbed the door handle and held it open for Catherine. "Um, not exactly but I guess you could say I serve Him, I do His work, and I have my flock, or a flock I look after. But I'm not much for established churches or dogmas or divisions between souls. Guess I'm not one for taking orders unless they come from Him. Or at least from on high."

"So you talk . . . to . . ." Catherine ran her fingers around the space between her eyes. It felt like there was a stray hair kind of tickling her skin, and it had just about been driving her mad all day long.

"—God. Yes, I talk to God. Sometimes I talk to my Aunt Anne."

Catherine waited for Jamie to order first, but Jamie sort of waved her hand. "Nope, go ahead, not sure if I want tea or something cold," Jamie said.

After she ordered an iced coffee, Catherine studied Jamie out of the corner of her eye. She was quite imposing, really; would stand toe to toe with the average FBI special agent. She'd have no trouble handling most situations, and from the stories mom told about Anne and Mimi and the whole crew at Bryson House, she'd probably knew what she was doing with firearms as well. Hmnn. And that meant Phoebe was good with guns, seeing who she spent most of her time with.

"Hey, you thinking about shop, aren't you?"

Catherine chuckled. "What makes you think that?"

Jamie drummed her fingers on the countertop and slowly thanked the cashier. Nothing hurried about her motions, and the pace at which she went made Catherine feel relaxed. "Ah, well, you had that assessing all risks and potential threats look about you, kind of like the exact same look my military and police friends get about them when we're grabbing beers after bouts, and you know who else that reminds me of actually?"

"Huh? Phoebe? Sounds like her to a T." Catherine took hold of her iced coffee and pictured Phoebe Thompson glaring around a room, looking near about like she was gonna take a head off or interrogate the quiet but sort of seedy guy in the corner. It was a weird image, like someone was putting it in there come to think of it, because she hadn't really seen much of Phoebe Thompson and she'd never seen Phoebe around men. And yet the image seemed real. Catherine realized Jamie was studying her, but Jamie had a different look to her, like a sheep dog watching his sheep? Catherine shook her head. All these shepherd and flock and even Jesus analogies were getting ridiculous.

"Yep, it does sound like Phoebe. And yet you know what she's studying?"

"Where, at Mason? Mom said she's graduating this year with I think a degree in English," Catherine said.

Jamie nodded. "Poetry, which she's great at composing, but hey, she can always write poetry. I'm thinking she's got other skills, another calling, and I'm also thinking she's already doing the work of a detective or a . . ." Jamie smiled, and her smile made Catherine feel proud, because she knew what Jamie was about to say even before she said it.

"—Or a special agent?" Catherine met Jamie's eye head on and Jamie nodded, but also held eye contact, and Catherine didn't feel the uncomfortable need to look away. She felt something she wasn't sure about, something she sort of filed away to sort out later. "Why, what's she doing?"

Jamie laughed, once, a dry laugh. "Not something she wants anyone's help with, so I'm staying out of the way, just watching from the sidelines, making sure she doesn't come unglued . . . nothing for you or me to worry about. She will come to me, at least I hope, before she does something she shouldn't do. But I know this: when it comes to tracking down people who shouldn't be among other humans, she won't stop until she stops them from doing whatever it is they're wanting to do."

Catherine was watching the light from the windows reflect off the light in Jamie's eyes, and she was thinking about how eyes were the lamps to a human's soul, something she'd read somewhere in theology of the early Christians. There was something mysterious and deep and old in those beautiful eyes, eyes that were about as readable as an oracle, and every bit as unthreatening, at least to those who walked in innocence. *Wow, I'm starting to think the way she does, all full of riddles and roundabouts.* "She's hunting someone or some people down? Really?"

"Something like that, yes."

"Do you think she needs help? I assume she's going after someone who . . . needs going after," Catherine said.

"Nah, she'd just get angry and not come to me when she needed me, like if she got in trouble. She and I sort of had words about it already," Jamie stopped talking as if pulling a car to a quick stop, sort of like a mental shutting off of an engine, and as much as Catherine wanted to open that door, she knew Jamie wasn't going to say much more, not about that.

"Right, so you're not wanting me to offer to help her out or anything like that. You just sort of want me to . . ." Catherine saw a mental image of Phoebe running beside her, dressed in slacks and a blazer, pistol tucked beneath a subtle fold in clothing that only a trained eye would discern, and Phoebe was yelling, "Get the fuck down, get the fuck down right now and don't fucking move," and Catherine got a chill running down her arms. So that's what . . . the future was gonna be.

Catherine looked up, and she knew Jamie knew what she was seeing, and then Jamie leaned forward and put her hand on Catherine's elbow.

"Yes. You're seeing Phoebe as a special agent. Yes. You can help make that happen. Don't need to do much, right?"

"Just mention they're recruiting women and maybe they're forming a sex crimes unit that will focus on . . . computer crimes?"

"Are they really?"

Catherine smiled. "How do you think they recruited me? I mean, I sort of chased them down, but once they decided they wanted me, how do you think they got me on board?"

Jamie's hand had long since left Catherine's elbow and Catherine was thinking she didn't mind whatever that meant; she had long since stopped thinking she'd figure out stuff like that, at least since Marcy passed away. *It didn't really matter, whatever, it just didn't.*

"They need women to run that unit, don't they? And they need motivated women, not just men who lack compassion and understanding and most of all, of pain, of the pain of having been taken, then left, left with nothing, left for dead even."

"Crap, Jamie, you too?"

"Ah, well, Catherine, it's just something that happens. Doesn't touch our souls, not unless we let it, and even if it does, we can bounce back, get up again, realize that no one can really hurt us in a way that lasts once we leave these bodies."

All the muscles in Catherine's upper back had tensed up, but she only realized it when the tension released and the muscles relaxed. "I just hope Marcy's at peace now. I wish she'd had someone to tell her it would get better . . ."

"Your roommate?"

Catherine nodded.

"Our souls our melded back together after we die, and it's like they only start really living once they get back to heaven," Jamie said. "So I'm thinking Marcy is realizing now that eternity is a long time, and pain comes and then it goes just as our bodies come and then they go and yet the light in them only fades to darkness when we let the hurt and the bleeding and the evil done unto us overtake us. Marcy is in good hands. She's in good hands now."

Catherine had a lump in her throat now. "You remember heaven?"

"Yes. Saw it when I was younger. Will see it again, hopefully sooner than later," Jamie said.

The thought of Jamie leaving made Catherine feel sad.

"Don't worry," Jamie smiled. "I'll be around for awhile. Someone's gotta make sure Phoebe gets where she's supposed to be."

Catherine tucked that thought away for later. *Someone's gotta make sure Phoebe gets where she's supposed to be.* The question was why, and she hoped the answer had to do with making the world safer.

Chapter 37

She sees a crowd in the background but they're silent. She looks around, and the team's there. Laydiators. But they're all kneeling down, taking a knee like football players do when someone's gotten laid out and they're waiting for a stretcher. She can hear someone praying, "Please God, please let her be okay," and then she can feel cold, it's cold, so cold, and she's looking, trying to see through the pile of equipment, helmets, pads, and players, but she can't make it out, can't see who's on the ground.

She needs to find Phoebe. Where is Phoebe? Her lost sheep. *Yes, yes, I'll get to her, yes, Pheebes, Pheebes, where are you?* And she's trying not to get overexcited now, because Pheebes is gonna be fine He said she would be but now, right now, she went and got hurt, did she, didn't she?

It's like she's trying to see through a fog. They must have used the fog machine during the break, yes, during the break. But someone's lying on the ice and she must make sure it's not Phoebe.

More noises. An ambulance. Someone's screaming now, and then there's a man and he's whispering, "It's gonna be all right, it will, come here, no, come here, stay here, stay right here Pheebes."

Oh no. Oh no no no. Phoebe. It's Phoebe. Phoebe's hurt.
Jamie sat up.

It was dark in her room, except for a moonbeam that grazed the edge of her curtain. Her head. Pain. She rolled over and felt around for the drawer on her nightstand until she got her fingers on the handle. It was stuck. She yanked on it, but it didn't move, so she gave it a harder jerk, and it came flying out all at once. Cut her finger probably. And a split second later, it crashed on the floor. That really hurt. Her head.

She crawled out of bed. The pills. It will help. She could figure out the dream tomorrow.

Okay. Fingers on bottle. Open them. Water. She stood up too fast. Dizzy. Moonbeam too bright. *Hurts. Hurts eyes.* Into go into . . . bathroom. Yes. Water. Yes. Swallow? Yes, swallow pill. Yes.

She staggered back to bed. Yes. Sleep now. Shepherd flock safe sleep.

•••

When the alarm went off at six, she could almost see straight. She didn't have much of a choice. Horses were waiting and so many people counted on her: a few kids, Mimi, Miranda, and later she'd call Beth. She had a lot of days that started like this, a lot more than anyone else would ever know. There were entire days she could hardly see, and one of those was the day she first met Phoebe Thompson.

When she set eyes on Phoebe, she saw the entire thing play out like a film, a horror film set to old 70s music and an innocent kid, sweet precious child of light, losing so much, so soon. It played out in Jamie's head, and the pain was . . . intense. One of her worst, well, headache wasn't the right word for it. Like having her skull cut in half and yet still held together tightly enough to feel a constant hammering, almost from the inside pulsating out, a hammer-sledgehammer-jackhammer. Oh shoot. No way to describe it really.

It wasn't "just" a migraine. She got those plenty. But the visions, seeing pieces of someone, or parts from their past, or bits of their ripped up torn up souls? No. Whole different type of hurt from seeing that. This had been on a Thursday night; thank God right after she mucked the stalls. She'd staggered home and Anne had run upstairs and gotten her some pills and pulled the blinds and taken her boots off and tucked her in.

She was still sick the next day, but she had to clock in all the same. That was the day she met Zander, God love him. Pure, dear heart, he was. He'd build bridges someday, or draw them. As long as he stayed off the field. A choice. Choices—always had them, and that's what Anne was always trying to teaching Phoebe. But neither Phoebe nor Anne understood God's plan in it all.

He already knew all their choices. And loved them just the same. Phoebe would see that soon; she would. In fact, when she thought of Phoebe lately, she felt something new. Something good. Something she'd seen just a tiny glimpse of that first day, back when Phoebe had caught sight of a bird flying overhead. And she's seen it many times since, but never seen or felt it as strong as she felt it now.

It was love. Yes.

And she wouldn't let anything happen to Phoebe. So long as she was on the ice, Phoebe wasn't gonna be carried off it. That's what that dream was telling her: *take care of your flock, Jamie. Take care of your flock.*

Jamie stepped into the shower, and flinched as the water hit her head. The light in the bathroom was off, and she could take another pill and still take care of things. It was all right. Each day was a gift. Pain? It never lasted. Even when it got like this, she didn't mind, *but please God let it stay cloudy the rest of the morning. And thank you, thank you for another day.*

Chapter 38

Phoebe came around the doorway and entered Ms. White's office gingerly, with one hand resting on the doorframe. Ms. White was standing in the corner, one hand moving, as if she was rehearsing for trial. Phoebe cleared her throat, and waited. It took a few moments for Ms. White to realize Phoebe was standing there.

Phoebe swallowed, and right as she was about to say something, Ms. White looked up and took her glasses off. "Phoebe!" Ms. White smiled, and then gestured toward a brown leather chair. "Please come in. Helen told me you might be stopping by."

"Oh, um, thank you, Ms. White. You sure it's okay? I mean, I can come back if you're busy?"

Ms. White shook her head, still smiling, and shut the door, shepherding Phoebe into her office in front of her. There was something athletic, but still comforting, in Ms. White's brisk side hug. Phoebe sighed, content, for a moment, but wishing she could skip the next few moments, or collapse them into this one. Ms. White waited for Phoebe to sit down and then she grabbed a water bottle from the fridge. "Water?"

"Please."

Ms. White tossed the water bottle in Phoebe's direction, and, giggling, Phoebe caught it. Ms. White was so different from her mom. The idea of tossing a water bottle ten feet, perfect spiral, wouldn't have occurred to her mom in a million years. Ms. White was more like a coach, especially when she was wearing jeans. Ms. White was probably the coolest, weirdest, most unique mom she knew. A flash of orange, purple, and green caught Phoebe's eye. *And of course she was wearing odd socks. Of course.*

"Hey, Ms. White?"

"Yep?"

"Nice socks." Phoebe couldn't stop grinning. She remembered the first time she said something about Ms. White's socks, so many years ago, and her mom had almost lost her shit. It was so rude, but Ms. White didn't bat an eye. Phoebe respected her before she liked her, truth be told.

And now they both grinned because Ms. White remembered too.

"They're becoming my lucky pair, I'm thinking."

Phoebe sat still, trying to think how to ask. She got really busy opening and then closing her water bottle. Ms. White waited, her legs stretched out in front of her, relaxed, and it helped make it seem like not such a thing. But it was a thing, and she had to ask. "Did my mom tell you what I wanted to ask you?"

"Yep. Sort of. You know, you can ask me anything, okay?"

Phoebe sighed. "You remember the first conversation we had? Back at Bryson House?"

A serious look came over Ms. White. "Of course." She nodded. "Of course I do."

"And you told me you'd been raped. And that you got through it. That you even learned to thrive. You said you got remarried, I mean, well, that's obvious, but I remember looking at you, and thinking, how? How could you ever . . ." Phoebe rubbed her fingers against the paper on the bottle. She was dangerously close to crying. She took a deep breath.

"How could I ever?"

"Well, you said the self-hatred fell off like lizard's skin."

"I said that?"

Phoebe wiped a tear away as they both giggled. "Yeah. I was thinking, man, Cat's mom is—aw no I wasn't. I was thinking you were brave, and you were how I wanted to be like you, well, someday."

Ms. White's eyes got all blurred up, and she nodded, like she couldn't talk. "I was thinking the same thing—that you were so fucking brave, that day."

"You were?"

"Oh hell yeah. It was an honor to, well, to work on your behalf. I was thinking that, too. And that is was cruel that I had to interview you."

"Couldn't have been easy."

Ms. White shook her head, and then she leaned forward. Her eyes were still glittering. "Your mom mentioned that you met someone."

"Yeah. Jim. Met him—remember when I gave Zander a ride here and my Bronco broke down? And you had your garage look at it?"

"Ronny! Of course! They're the best."

"Met Jim there. He's in one of my classes, and he recognized me."

"Mmm." Ms. White was listening, letting Phoebe tell it at her pace, and then Phoebe realized she could cut to it.

"I'm scared of sex, Ms. White." Phoebe blurted it out, and then she laughed, shocked she'd said it.

"Aww, that's normal, Pheebes. It's hard, figuring this out—hard for all survivors."

"It is?"

Ms. White got a faraway look in her eyes, and she gazed up and to her right before she answered. "Yeah. It's still hard sometimes. I've been married for twenty years, and most the time, it's fine." Ms. White smiled. "Better than fine. But it's not been easy. For years after I was raped, I had nightmares, and sometimes even flashbacks during sex. Like, I'd see my husband, then, some other man. Sometimes, I swear, I just had sex, not that my husband ever minded, just to prove I could, or he couldn't—the man who raped me—couldn't hurt me anymore." Ms. White folded her hands in front of her, and her knuckles stood out, like she was gripping tight. "I wasn't gonna let them, I mean, him, take that from me too."

They sat there, quietly for a few minutes, and it was a comfortable silence. "I never thanked you, that day, for taking care of me."

"You know, it was an honor for me. Most important case I've ever worked on."

Phoebe nodded. "I'm scared." She could hear the words echoing, as if she'd just repeated a refrain that had been playing over and over again in her mind, but silently until that moment, and now, now it was, because spoken aloud, more real.

"I know, sweetie."

"And sometimes I don't know if the pain will ever go away."

Ms. White was crying too, and seeing her cry helped somehow. She swept her long silver hair out of the way as she passed Phoebe a box of tissues. "I know. But it will."

"You sure?"

"Damn sure." Ms. White stood up and held out her hand to Phoebe. "Come on over here, Pheebes. Let's watch the bird formations."

Phoebe cried a lot harder. The fact that Ms. White remembered that, after all these years, was . . . Phoebe took Ms. White's hand, and they stood there, arms wrapped loosely around one another, and watched the geese flying in formation overhead, heading back to Burke Lake, or maybe farther south, for summer.

Chapter 39

Standing in front of the pharmacist's counter, Jamie smiled at the diabetic in line in front behind her. The woman was close to losing her right foot, at least if she couldn't . . . get . . . *bless you sister. Not much she could do to help right now*. "Go ahead," Jamie said. "Still figuring out my insurance."

"That's so kind of you."

Jamie prayed for a small miracle, and then took a deep breath. So many souls to help, so little time. She had to figure this out, that out, so many to take care of, but first she needed to get some relief for this damn head of hers.

Jamie stared at her prescriptions. Refill on anti-seizure meds. Right. Topomax. It also helped with the migraines. Well, a little. And painkillers, for when she just couldn't see straight. Scary stuff, and there might be a time she'd have to ask for more drugs. If it kept getting worse. Oh, and the sleeping pills. She shook her head. She was so blessed just to be able to take this massive cocktail of drugs and pills and lifesaving . . . don't forget the blood thinners and set up the MRI . . . oh nevermind. That was a one-time thing.

It wasn't getting worse. It was just getting a little wearisome, but it went in cycles, better, worse, worse for a long time, then better again. She'd best be getting busy patching up the fences, stocking up the barn supplies, and maybe Phoebe would call and want to go lifting next week.

Phoebe wasn't mad still, not a chance. Weird that she hadn't called. She always called, or showed up . . . well, she had stopped coming by when Anne died, but she'd gotten over that when she came and got the truck. She didn't feel bad about that night . . .

Does she? Gotta admit I'm missing her. Feels funny to be missing her.

She's well.

Is she?

Yes.

Anything I should be doing?

You were holding what you needed.

But I had to let Anne go. She's with you now. I know she is. Mom told me.

Don't let it go. You're not tending to what you need to and now you're asking for guidance. I told you not to ignore what's most important, what matters, and you're not listening.

Jamie shook her head. Sometimes talking to God was like reading a crossword puzzle in German—upside down. She'd check in later, while she was mucking.

Just then, she felt someone leaving, about a mile away, hard to explain how she knew. But then she heard a siren, and then another one. She was on 29, just off 66, and a long line of brake lights told the story. A helicopter circled over the interstate, but it didn't land, because it was too late.

It wasn't scary to her, because she'd been there; there and back. But it would be so scary for Barbara, that was her name, and for her husband Ray. She had no idea where she got this stuff, but she was getting it more lately. It seemed to come with the headaches and she had to think there was a reason for the pain because God had a plan.

She smiled as she started up her Explorer. She wouldn't mind if His plan involved a few less migraines. As Phoebe would say, *these fucking sucked.* Jamie chuckled. It felt good to cuss actually, especially when Phoebe wasn't here to say it all for her.

Chapter 40

He'd been away since Friday. She'd last seen him on Thursday, but not as long as she needed. Three days. Felt like living in a fucking desert with him gone.

Phoebe hung up and tried to set the phone down but as soon as she did, she had to pick it back up again. Her phone had become a piece of Jim, or of her and him, and it almost left her breathless to be apart from it when she wasn't with him. She really shouldn't call him, not when he was in Charlottesville. She clicked on his number anyway, and he picked up on the second ring.

"Oh Phoebe. I was just about to call you."

"You were?" His voice was making her all turned on, like it always did, and that created this aching chasm down deep, down far.

"I'm on the way back home."

"You are?" She was smiling.

"I wanted, I had to see you."

"Where are you?"

"81. Near Warrenton."

A thrill ran down and through the middle of her. "30 minutes away?"

"'Bout that. I was wondering, want me to bring dinner by?"

"Mmmm. I can make us something. Just come straight," she said.

A half-hour later, she heard his 4Runner and tried hard not to watch for him at the door, and then she stopped caring. No, she never cared. Maybe some women did, but she wasn't, she wasn't *some women*. She leaned against the doorframe, waiting, then watching him walk toward her, slow and easy, almost like he wasn't hurrying, but he'd driven two hours for her, and they both knew it.

He opened the door, and his lips met hers before the screen door slammed shut, and she pulled back long enough to whisper-moan, "Hey there," and he whispered, "Phoebe," but then he brought her close again, gripping her hard now, just as he was hard against her. She pulled into him even harder, and his hands run down her arms, and she wanted to run her mouth down his chest but she wouldn't stop there if she did so she didn't. He would have to lead and wherever he went now, she'd follow.

He walked her backwards, and she let him guide her into the kitchen. She almost ran into the table and she was thinking about when he bent her over the hood of his 4Runner, and how it would feel if he spread her out across the table and took her there, and she laughed, low and she was sure sexy, because she could feel an animalistic side of her coming on so fast, she thought she'd not be able to stop from doing all the things she wanted to do, him to do, to do to him. She made eye contact with him, and let go of him, in letting go wanting to grab again, but not; and she laughed low again.

"Jim?"

He took her by the hand and led her through the doorway into the family room. He stopped, and leaned against the back of a brown leather sofa, hands spread almost as wide as his legs. His hair was a little bit ruffled and his blue eyes sparkled, danced with light, and she just wanted to gaze into them, at him, into him . . . oh Lord. How in the hell had she found him? Jim, her Jim. Jim, my Jim, standing here, *and not an hour ago I was trying to figure out how to make love to him without it killing me and now I gotta figure out how not to fuck him no make love to him fuck fuck without it killing me.*

"Let me just look at you for a minute, Phoebe." He bent his head at an angle, and then he held his hands to his temples and then ran them through his hair.

"Missed me?" Her face cut into a smile, and the look he gave her was so full of heat and longing, same as she was feeling, it made her laugh. It was that low laugh again, that woman in *love wait did I just say I was in love* laugh, deep and sultry, and if she could hear its sultry notes, so could he, and he did, she knew it from how husky he sounded.

"Yes, yes, I'm here, oh Phoebe you're so beautiful. I spent the entire weekend thinking about you, talking about you . . . probably drove my sister and my mom crazy. I just had to see you."

"Mmm. That all you wanted to do?"

"Well," he shoved his hands in the front of his jeans and didn't answer right away.

She stared at his zipper, and let her eyes stay stuck for a long time before she followed the line of buttons up to his cleft chin. This was she was absolutely crazy. She couldn't even remember what day it was, or whether it was AM or PM or spring, summer, or fall, anything but winter was what it was, and that would be the line of a poem somewhere someday. "Well?" She prompted him.

"Well, I thought," and he smiled, spreading his legs a little wider, "I thought about a few other things too."

She didn't move towards him, because if she did *oh fuck*. "Yeah? Like reading me poetry, watching the sunset, sharing a steak and cheese no ketchup no mayo, watching me skate, showing me how to change the oil—"

"—You want me to show you how to change the oil?"

"I do. And I want a 4Runner of my own."

The side of his mouth turned up, and then he smiled wider. "So you're giving me a quest, a magic quest for your next ride? Like a to-do list?"

"Why yes, that's right, I am."

"You know I'd do anything for you, right?" Jim stretched his hands out, and she put her hands in his. He got a dreamy look about him, dreamy and intense, and he stared into her eyes so long, she felt like he could see all of her, all of her fear and need and pain and desire and confusion and what not that word again not that word.

She nodded, and she tried to talk, to say something funny, or light, but she was so close to crying now, and she wasn't really sure why.

"Phoebe? I've never felt anything like this before."

A rush, a thrill, an electric shock almost ran through her, and he must have felt it too, because he brought her to his chest and hugged her so tender, so soft now, like he was protecting her from whatever he saw in her eyes, from whatever they were feeling, or she was feeling, but neither one of them was saying, not yet.

She closed her eyes, and leaned into him. He smelled like a man, but not like any other man. She sighed and realized she was thinking about her dad again, not wanting him—just the opposite but still, there he was, in between her arms and the arms of the man oh no that word again.

"Jim? What is this?"

"What?"

"What is it we're feeling?" She looked up at him, crying now, because it was almost too much, having him close, this close, and not wanting to let go, but not knowing if she could ever get close enough.

"Aw, Phoebe, please don't cry." He took his hand and wiped her tears away, and then he kissed her cheek, and she took her sleeve and wiped her eyes and tried to smile up at him.

"I'm sorry, this had gotta be so fucking awful for you. I wish I could be like everyone else."

"Awful for me? Oh my God, no no no. Are you kidding me? I drove here and it wasn't just to see you or kiss you or God help me, all the other things I was thinking about doing to you." He stopped and they both chuckled.

"Same here—I mean the whole imagining doing stuff to you thing. I even called my therapist to talk through it." She issued a wry smile.

"And I talked to my sponsor. So it's you and me both, in the shit, as it were."

"You just cussed?"

"I did. You have a profound effect on me in more ways than one." He winked at her, and smiled, but the smile faded fast, and she could see tension beneath it.

"Are you okay?"

He nodded. "You? What did you talk to your therapist about? Me?"

"Yeah." She bobbed her head up and down, and then nuzzled her lips against his neck.

"Oh. Not fair." He laughed, and then he turned her into him and ran his lips from her chin, along her neck, and just when she was closing her eyes and waiting for him to keep going lower, he laughed again, and stopped.

"Where were we? Your therapist?"

"And your sponsor," she said.

"And my sponsor," he said.

"Is this fucking with your sobriety?"

He looked at his hands, and she followed his gaze. They weren't shaking. "No, I mean . . ." he paused and then he kissed her neck again, and then grinned at her. "No. I'll be fine. I might lose my mind here in a minute, but no, I ain't gonna drink because of you. No."

"Then what is it?"

"Awwww, man. I can't imagine you want to hear all this."

"Seriously. Can't be worse than my shit." Phoebe took his hand and placed it on her breast, and his lips touched hers again and he kissed her slow and gentle, his hand running down to the top of her jeans and stopping. "My thing, Jim, and I'm just gonna say it because I'm tired of not saying it, is I know how to fuck a man, I know it all too well. And I don't want, I don't want to go there and get lost in that place."

"It wouldn't just be that, Phoebe. I'm not going to let it."

"How do you know it won't? That I won't?"

"Because I know what we have, and I know what I am, and I know what we are. Because when I look in your eyes, my world's okay. When I look in your eyes, I'm safe, I'm safe and if I'm safe, we're safe, and if we're safe—"

"—I'm safe." Phoebe ran her hands from Jim's cheekbone, to his chin, and then she put both hands on his shoulders and she had to know. She had to know what it was. He had to know and since he knew he could tell her. "What is it, then? What do we have that makes us safe?"

"We have love. We have love, Phoebe, we have love and that's what this is, it's love."

"It's love?"

"It's love."

"But what about sex?"

He took her hand and put it on his chest, right about his heart. "No matter where you put your hands, and I'm telling you, I want you to touch me from head to toe and back again, and I go crazy thinking about it," he stopped and his voice got heavy again, because she moved her hand down to the front of his jeans, "Aw Phoebe, I can't think when you do that." His eyes were half-closed. "Oh. That's, you're, feels . . . amazing." He put his hand on hers and drew it to his lips, and then let go of her hand and she told him to go on please keep talking.

"When you touch me, there's love. And it's all I can do not to touch you, love."

Chapter 41

Phoebe heard an engine, and knew it was the Range Rover. "My mom's coming up the driveway, and it's just in time or just at the wrong time. I was about to start something we'd have to finish."

He stood them both up and turned her around, so that his hands cupped her breasts in the front, and then he kissed her neck, and they both groaned. It almost got away from them both, because then she reached up to him and brought his mouth to hers. They were still kissing when the door opened, and laughing, breathing heavy, they extricated themselves, sort of, but he kept his arms around her and she shivered, and that's how they were when Helen Thompson strode into the room.

"Ah. Well. I really must have the worst timing." She paused, face not giving away much, and then she checked her watch. She was hiding a smile, Phoebe knew it, just as she knew that pretty much nothing ruffled the woman they called the fixer. "So. Have you two eaten? I know I'm starved." She tossed her leather satchel beside the grandfather clock. "Jim McMahon I take it? Soldier-poet-mechanic?"

Jim released Phoebe, but not before he kissed her cheek. Phoebe was speechless still, but somehow it seemed like the most natural thing in the world, Jim holding and hugging and kissing her in front of her mom. "Good to see you Mrs. Thompson."

He shook her hand, and finally, her eyes betrayed or suggested a twinkling, maybe even the start of a friendly smile. "I would tell you to make yourself at home, but I must say, you seem quite comfortable indeed."

"Thank you. It's wonderful, your home. Thank you."

Phoebe suspected his eyes were twinkling too, but she couldn't see his face.

"And did you say something about dinner?"

"Well, I was hoping Phoebe had something going." Helen fixed Phoebe with a look that anyone else would have mistaken for a stare, but it just made Phoebe smile. After shaking her head when Phoebe giggled, Helen started walking toward the kitchen. "God knows I'm not known for my cooking, so we might be reduced to bread and butter."

Jim came up behind her and ran his lips across her neck, and just then Helen glanced back at them, and Phoebe blushed because she knew her mom saw it—saw her all hot and turned on. Phoebe waved her hand and laughed, helpless really, and Helen threw her head back and laughed as well.

"Come on you two."

Phoebe felt so fucking happy, she was almost crying again, and she didn't even mind when he wrapped a hand around her shoulders and herded her into the kitchen.

I don't have to hide anything so this has to be safe. I'm safe. We're safe. Mom can see me kissing someone and . . . fuck. Fuck. Not fucking on camera this time. How can she ever forgive me for what I've done?

Phoebe had this awful urge to say something ugly. She thought she did, in fact. But when she searched the room for a sign, proof of what hell she'd wrought, all she heard was Helen's fast-moving words, clipped as usual, rolling like a river tide, and she thought of the time she got the rape kit, and her mom was there talking to her. Words, never stopping long enough for her to worry or feel the metal clamps and the pain for too long, and it hurt, and she knew her mom knew it all, had seen it all, but all her mom had given her was more words, a long line of them, a lifeline of them, and here she was again.

Mom. Safe. And she wanted to hug this giant, this rock, really, of a woman, her mom, and thank her.

"Phoebe?"

"Yeah?"

Her mom was worried, and Phoebe felt stripped of all her barriers. No filter left.

"You okay, sugar?"

Phoebe rested her head on Jim's shoulder, and then she crossed to her mom and gave her a big hug, one that Helen returned only after kissing her on the forehead. Phoebe closed her eyes and hoped Jim wasn't too uncomfortable.

"Yeah, Mom." Phoebe patted her mom on the back and sank into the end chair. "I'm great. I'm just, I don't know." She sighed. "Overcome, I guess."

"Right." Helen opened the fridge, grabbed butter, jam, and orange juice, and kicked it shut with her foot. "I bet you haven't eaten all day. I know I skipped lunch. Jim, can you grab some glasses?" She gestured toward the cabinet above the toaster oven, and while he poured orange juice, she started to cut thick slices of homemade bread they had left over from last night's meal.

Phoebe sat in silence, eyes almost out of focus, sipping orange juice and eating bread and butter. She didn't listen too hard or hear too much of what Helen and Jim were saying, at least until she finished a slice of bread. Then she caught a dry laugh, and Helen's dry laugh usually preceded something pretty damn funny, so she grabbed another slice of bread and kept an eye on her mom as she spread strawberry preserves on top of a layer of butter.

"So when I saw your SUV parked in front of my house, I was actually thinking about something. Every time I go to a bloody function, and Phoebe knows I avoid 'em like the plague, even the ones for charity, someone inevitably finds out I'm an attorney. Doesn't matter what kind, which is funny in itself, because I don't know the first thing about their uncle's will. But still, they ask me for advice."

Helen paused, and Phoebe smiled to herself. This was gonna be good.

"So anyway, I saw your SUV, and I figured it was yours. I mean, not a crazy assumption, right?" Helen lifted her eyebrow in Phoebe's direction.

Phoebe snickered.

Helen spread her fingers wide and formed a teepee with them, and she touched her fingers to her chin as she folded one leg on top of the other. "So when I saw this SUV, thinking, wow, I bet this belongs to Pheebes' soldier-poet-mechanic . . ." Helen waited to make sure everyone was watching her.

Phoebe cast a surreptitious look at Jim, who bowed his head and crinkled one of his eyes.

"Soldier-poet-mechanic? Oh my God, Mom. I'm regretting that expression already."

Getting the prompt she was waiting for, Helen continued, "And I thought to myself, 'Wonderful. Now I can ask Pheebe's young man about the irritating squeak in my Rover.'"

"Your Rover, eh? As in 2013 or 2012 overpriced, what did you call it Phoebe, exactly?"

"Ridiculous."

"Right, overpriced, ridiculous Range Rover?" Jim leaned forward as if to stand up. "Well, of course I'd love to take a look at your vehicle for you, Ms. Thompson."

Helen rested her hand on Jim's forearm, keeping him from actually getting up, and then she gave him a smile that started all starch and stiff, and finally gave way to pure magnificence. Most people thought Helen Thompson was an intimidating bitch, but Phoebe saw her mom as something closer to iron and wine, elegant, strong, and mellowing over time.

One thing Helen also had was great timing. "Well. It's time for me to get my prep in for tomorrow's depo. Night you two. I bet the view's particularly lovely from the balcony tonight. And if you haven't shown him that view, Pheebes, I bet he'd love to see it."

Helen folded her napkin, stood up, and issued one of her no-look waves as she walked out of the kitchen and in the direction of her library. Phoebe heard the door clatter shut and she felt a spasm of desire rush between her legs. He hadn't been upstairs yet, and the balconies were off her bedroom and off the main bedroom. Her mom didn't mind, and that made all of this easier.

"Come on, let me show you that view." She stood up, grabbed the plates, and quickly set them in the sink. And then, before she could think it through any longer, she sent a look in his direction, and there was no doubt in her mind what she was trying to communicate.

Chapter 42

As he followed her upstairs, the boards creaked underfoot, and he said, "You're taking me to your bedroom."

She laughed low and deep. "We gotta get through it to reach the balcony."

When she reached her bedroom door, she let him go in front of her, and she quietly pulled it shut and turned the light on.

He shoved his hands into his belt loops, and leaned against the back of the door. "I like it here," he said.

"First time I've had a guy in here."

"First time for everything."

"Come on," she said. "Let me show you that view."

"It can wait," he said. "Come here."

"Now?"

He nodded.

She stood in front of him, and he bent his head to hers and kissed her. She wanted to take his hand and lead him to her bed, but she didn't. She just folded into him, and let him kiss her, and all she heard was him breathing hard, as hard as she was breathing, and she wondered if it was just a dream, but the sensation of him, on her, his tongue, in her, helped her believe that if it was a dream, it was a dream that would go on until she wanted it to end, and she didn't.

He let go of her and looked in her eyes. "I've made love to you so many times already," he said.

"I know," she said. "And I keep fucking you over and over and for the life of me, I have no idea how to find a moment's peace, either without making love to you or with what will happen if I fuck you."

He stroked her head and she nestled into him, and smelled his cologne, and kissed his neck, and she needed more, and then she was sucking hard on his skin, and running her tongue down his chest, and she was unbuttoning his shirt, and he had his hands on her head. He ran his hands through her hair, and she put her fingers on his chest, and she was tracing a line to the top of his jeans and then someone else was there, not Jim, and she stopped and smiled, the wise, tired, smile of the too-early fucked. It was an awful smile, and it didn't really keep him from seeing that she was trying not to cry.

"What happened?"

She waved her hand at the ceiling, and then she bent down and grabbed her journal.

"Sit next to me," she said.

She sat beside her bed and turned the pages until she got to what she needed.

"Let me hold you while you read it to me."

"Oh, Jim."

"No, for real. Just move forward a little." He nodded, and smiled, and she couldn't say no, so she moved forward a little, and he got behind her, so that his back was to the bed, and he took her by the shoulders and moved her so that her back was up against his chest. His shirt was half-unbuttoned and the idea of seeing more of it was almost making her drunk. But still, he had to know.

"This is what I live, Jim. It's called 'Nine by Nine.'"

I stagger. From here to there and all over the road, path, map or whatever you want to call it—from her to me and here to there and back and forth and nowhere and everywhere . . .
I fall . . . she falls . . .

But before I land, I catch myself and keep moving, moving,
forward and with me it goes, she goes, they go, he goes he
COMES
No.
Stop. Eyes closed. No, no no. Open your eyes because when
you sleep you see them, him, them, talking no walking no,
and worse, worse, what's worse? That's what hurts, the
naked bodies, mine, theirs, his, it doesn't make any sense
when I close my eyes and dream, but until I open my eyes
and see it, it will take me inside of it, them, me, Little me,
my hell, this hell, their hell my hell—when I sleep.
And in sleeping, and seeing, bits, more bits, many more bits
and the bits are broken, and they cut me but I don't bleed.
No blood, nor tears because I held
I hold
it all in, scared, scared of the breaking pieces shattering
whatever's left inside. I'm the guardian of my pain. I'm a
watcher, and I watch this fortress that I built, that he built,
they built, no, they made me build, no, I was too weak to
tear down . . . no, no, it doesn't matter who built it or why it
just matters that I got locked inside and what's even scarier
. . .
(Shhhhhh)
No. Hear me. I speak now.
What's even scarier is that I hid the key and no one, no one
else knows where I hid it. That's worse. No one else is
coming to save me. Here I hide, deep inside, and no one is
coming. No one.
SAVE ME
(Shhhhhh)
Get up. Get up now. Go get the key.
All I have to hold onto is what I have, what I am right now.
I'm the warden, but I need . . . I can't, I hold
can't . . .
please, please God, make it stop hurting. HELP ME.
There's no one else here in this cell, this nine by nine, and
I'm screaming but even if I found a voice for the pain, I
would not could not . . . so tired. So tired of

(whispering)
holding no hiding the key.
(I want to tell someone my hiding place. I do. I want to yell
it out loud so that everyone and yet no one will hear me).
When you release him—
And another one,

And another one,

You confine me. From one man's nine by nine
Go I.

Phoebe took a deep breath and set her notebook down. Jim's chest encircled her, warm, and his arms wrapped even closer around her. "You take my breath away," he said. He sort of rocked her, and she finally shut her eyes and leaned back against him all the way. It was surrender, and she knew in that instant there was no going back, no matter how scared she got.

Chapter 43

"You know what it feels like, Jim?"

"What?"

Eyes still closed, she said, "Like I'm in a storm, it's been raging for hours, days, maybe years, but still I know everything is gonna be all right."

"I'm not going anywhere, you know?"

"Yeah."

He kept rocking her just a little, and he kissed her head a few times. "The key—the one you are looking for, to get you out of jail . . . you said 'you release him.' What did you mean?"

"Wayne Toller. He only served five and now he's out. It's been all I can think about lately." She hugged his arms to her, and sighed. "Well. And you."

"He was one of the men—"

"—Yeah."

She felt his head move up and down. "I want you to know something," he said.

"You'll keep me safe."

"Of course. But that's not it. About the key. Unlocking you from your prison."

"That's why you're here. A prince and I'm Rapunzel, without the long hair." She chuckled. She was so fucking tired.

He nuzzled her. "Not quite. I don't walk on water."

She felt her pulse beating in her neck, and stiffened up. *This couldn't be happening, no it couldn't, no, not after she gave him . . .*

"No, stop Phoebe. It's not that. No." He rubbed her arms and kissed her, again and again, until she relaxed a little.

And now she was so mad she was almost crying, but was too tired for even that. "Fuck. What are we doing here? All this shit about . . . love?" She tore his arms from her and started to jump to her feet.

"Phoebe, no. Please. Listen."

Now he was kneeling and he wouldn't let go of her hand, and as bad as she wanted to rip it away, there was something in his eyes, a light, a glow. "Please," he said. He held both hands out, and she came back next to him and he pulled her to him so that she was lying face to face beside him. "The key. It's not that I can't give it to you, or help you find it, but I am not the key. And I only realized it after I lost Christopher, and lost almost everything. I did. I went on a bender got lost, lost to everything, everyone . . . lost."

He smiled, but he was almost crying, and now she was breathless, waiting to see if he would cry.

"One night, I was up all night back then, every night, because when I slept, all I saw was . . . death. Death and more death, sometimes it was him, sometimes it was just a part of him, sometimes it was these birds eating a kid we shot . . . and I had this whole bottle of pills. More than one bottle. Stuff they gave me to help me sleep, stuff they gave me to help with my back, stuff they gave me to help with my PTSD, more and more stuff. I was done. I'd had it. Couldn't go on anymore. I was ready to go, to let go, the phone rang. But it only rang once.

"I hit the return button and it . . . no one had called. I kept hitting it over and over again, but no one had called. And just when I was sure I was crazy, the phone rang—it did it again, I swear, just when I was sure I was hearing stuff. But . . . same thing. I check the incoming calls and there was so call and no number. I knew who it was. You see, it was his birthday. He was calling to let me know he was okay, wherever he was, he was okay." Now Jim was crying, and she imagined him standing in Arlington, in the rows of white graves, holding his best friend's flag, hat pulled low.

"Your best friend? The one who shot himself, right?" She put her hand on his cheeks and wiped his tears, but they kept falling.

"Yes. Christopher. He was calling me from the other side. Telling me to stay where I was, man my position, finish my job, and stay in the game, as he used to say. 'Stay in the game,' was the last thing he said to me actually. I thought he was talking about our poker game. But he was telling me that night, before he died, to stay alive. I know now that's what he meant. And that he'd miss me, but he had to fold his hand."

"I'm so sorry," she said.

"Thank you. But I know he had to go. He's somewhere better now." Jim touched her cheek, because now she was crying too. "That night, after I set the phone down for the second time," Jim smiled a little, "I got on my knees, first time since Christopher left. Asked God for something, anything, a way to go on. I think I was on my knees most the night. Sun rose. And this peace came over me, first time in so long, and I threw the pills away. And the bottles. It was me or them, living or dying really. And every time I want to go back to it, and that's more days than I'd like to admit, Phoebe."

He stopped for emphasis, and she could see the strain in the muscles around his eyes. He looked as tired as she felt. He stroked her cheek, and she took his hand and pressed her lips to it, and again, he was almost glowing. "So when it gets bad, when I'm locked in my own nine by nine, I ask God to give me another day, I ask for peace, I ask to be free of the birds and the battlefields and the blood and the screaming and the death, the death of the best friend I ever had and the death of I guess my own innocence, or of everything I believed. Because after we shot that kid, after Christopher shot himself, I didn't want to fight anymore."

He turned over and leaned on his elbow. With his right hand, he touched her, starting at her cheek, and sliding, tiptoeing really, down to her chest, and he pressed his hand down between her breasts and he kept his eyes on her, intently watching her open her mouth, just an inch or so, and instead of closing her eyes or moaning, she let him see the desire in her eyes, which were burning, burning hot with it. She put her hand on his and led him to her, down lower, still in contact, looking while he touched her.

His hand reached her belt and she shifted her hips, and she was saying, I gotta have you now, please, please make love to me, and she took his hand and slid it beneath the thin fabric of her pants, down lower, bringing his hand to the edge of her silk underwear, still looking straight into his blue eyes, not looking away, just groaning now, him groaning too, as he slid his hand into her, the tip of her, and then hot, hot, deeper in, and she brought her hips closer. She still kept her eyes on him, and she could feel him, his hips grinding into her now, and they were talking, especially him, saying I love you so much and she was saying the same, and please show me how, please Jim please make love to me.

He rolled on top of her, his hand still deep inside her, and he was groaning, Phoebe, you're making me crazy, and she was crying now, I don't know how to make love, are you going to show me, and he kissed her, he kissed her, his tongue in and out and rubbing hard, hard against her cheeks, her mouth, all of him, all of her, and she could feel him pressing against her and he kept saying I love you, it's gonna be okay, and then he groaned again, and whispered, wait my love, please wait, please wait.

He brought his hand back up to her cheek and she could smell her on his hand as he stroked her and kissed her, kissed her so soft now, kissed her all over, whispering, I really love you and when I make love to you, and I am gonna, oh man I'm gonna, I am gonna and when I do, I don't want to hold back . . . don't want you holding back and we can't do that here and we gotta. So we gotta get. Outta here, ya know. Now let's go, go with me now Phoebe Thompson.

When they got downstairs, Phoebe motioned with her head toward Helen's study. She tapped twice on the door.

"Come in."

"Oh, hey Mom."

Helen was twirling a pen. She nodded and made a motion with her hand for Phoebe to sit.

"Uh, I'm going over Jim's." Phoebe hitched her duffel bag over her shoulder. "Probably get a ride into Mason in the morning."

"Right." Helen gave a curt nod.

"So, I'll see you tomorrow? You're not gonna be in Chicago?"

"Don't think so. I'll text you if I am." Helen set her pen down and stood up. "See you tomorrow." Helen leaned forward and put her arm around Phoebe, and hugged her, hugged her close, and Phoebe put her hand on her mom's hand and smiled. Then she let go, and she almost tripped catching up to Jim, who waved and said good night Ms. Thompson as he led the way out the front door.

When they got outside, Phoebe paused on the landing and lit two cigarettes. She inhaled, deeply, and held onto the railing when the buzz rushed through her. Then she reached up and put a cigarette between Jim's lips, and he squinted, eyes half-closed, and wrapped his arm around her, walking slow, slow and steady, to his 4Runner.

Chapter 44

She had looked so lovely, standing at the door and waiting. Helen had known she was there, but she had needed an extra moment to compose herself before she said *come in*, knowing that *come in* was going to precede something she didn't want to hear. The way he'd been holding her earlier, the way he had looked at her and she at him . . . left no doubt. No doubt. Helen had been brave. *Are you going to show him the balcony?*—brave. He loved her. That much was obvious.

     And . . . her Phoebe. Still tough, all edges and elbows but . . . something different tonight. Phoebe had never known how gorgeous she was but tonight she knew. There was something new in the way her eyes followed him from one side of the room to the other, like she was staking claim to the ground he walked on, and something new in the way she . . . laughed. Deeper. Lauren Bacall. Oh no. Lauren Bacall kissing Humphrey Bogart. Her Phoebe kissing Jim McMahon. Oh. Now she knew; when she looked at him, she suddenly knew she was beautiful. She looked so lovely standing there. So lovely. And Helen had twirled her pen and bought another precious moment. *Uh, I'm going over Jim's. Probably get a ride into Mason in the morning.* A young woman, one she was so proud of. When was the last time she'd told Phoebe how proud she was? *When? I haven't, have I?* Helen put her hand on her neck and gasped.   Her Phoebe was going over Jim's to make love to him.

Helen saw a little girl spread-eagled on her parents' bed, and she staggered to her desk, holding onto the edge as the room got blurry. *No, no. No please no.* And her little girl, her tiny little girl stared up at the ceiling. No no no. Helen squeezed her eyes so hard she saw weird zags of color. Okay. Better that than . . . so she opened her eyes, and then oh no no she was sitting beside her daughter. Feet in stirrups. Nurse, specimen, metal parts inside her daughter . . . vomit rose to her mouth. She ran to the bathroom and got to the toilet just in time.

And she thought she was done with all this. She thought, no no stop thinking. No. And then she saw him she saw Richard. And he was coming toward her and she had one swing, one chance, one chance, and then he was falling he was bleeding and then . . . Helen ran to the phone and hit one on speed dial.

A familiar voice picked up on the third ring. "Hey there, you working late?" Cass said.

"I gotta talk to you right now."

"Sure, sweetie, slow down. What's wrong?"

"Phoebe's going over her boyfriend's house and I think she's gonna spend the night."

"Jim's, right?"

Helen nodded.

"Helen? Still there?"

"Yes."

"Talk to me. You're upset, and I get it. Just talk to me."

"I keep seeing her being raped." Helen could hardly talk, she was crying so hard.

"Oh my God. I can only imagine."

Helen slid down until she was sitting on the floor, her back against her desk. She let her head fall back against the cold wood. Her head was throbbing, so it made it feel better to lay it there. "I wake up some nights, and I see it all over again, but in the dreams, I'm in the room, Cass. I'm in the fucking room, but there's a piece of glass enclosing them and I can't get to her." Helen shook all over, the sobs cascading, probably making her damn hard to understand. "And every time I wake up, I paddle down the hallway, and I open her bedroom door, and I don't always go in. Sometimes I just stand there, make sure she's okay."

"That's a horrible dream sweetie. Horrible." Cass's voice was so comforting. Helen remembered when Cass held her hand and told her they were going to figure everything out, back when they first met at the Bryson House, and Helen had been a little taken aback to have another woman hold her hand. Right now, what she'd give to have Cass sitting there holding her.

"I've done everything I can to keep her safe, Cass. Everything. Took her everywhere with me. Tried to keep that bastard in jail. But it's not been enough. I mean, oh my God. My nightmares are bad, but what are hers' like?" Helen was crying hard again.

"Well, I can tell you something about that if you want."

"You mean, because of your own . . . rape?" Helen sniffled, and tried to slow her breathing.

"Sort of. The nightmares aren't so bad, except if I get triggered. But even when they are bad, I'm used to working through them. And all that expensive therapy is good for something." Cass gave a rueful laugh, and Helen pictured her partner pacing around to try to keep a step ahead of Zander, who was usually around whenever Cass tried to talk. As if on cue, Cass murmured, "No, it's way too late. No, absolutely no. Seriously, I'm on the phone, it's important and—yeah, close the door please."

Helen closed her eyes and sighed.

"Ah, sorry."

"Mmm." Helen rubbed her temples. "What were you saying?"

"Did you know I talked to Phoebe?"

"No! When?"

"Well, she came into my office the other day, when she dropped Zander off. And she asked me about all this."

Helen got up from the floor and wandered into the kitchen. She put the kettle on. "She came to talk to you about—Jim?"

"Yeah."

"What about it?"

"Awww, Helen, I'm not gonna spell it all out." Cass laughed, so friendly and open, and Helen almost smiled.

"Hmm. You talked about sex with my daughter?" Helen opened the fridge door and shut it again without grabbing anything. "Splendid." She was smiling though, and she knew Cass could tell.

"Well. I'm not gonna admit or deny that, but if we did, I'd have told her the same thing I'm gonna tell you. I would tell her it's gonna be okay. I mean, she needs this Helen. She does." Cass's voice got all earnest and serious, and her accent got flatter, kind of like she was convincing a jury of something, but really meant it. "She needs to have a totally safe, totally loving relationship." Cass's voice dropped to a whisper. "She does."

"Like you do?"

"Yeah. Like I do. And you know what that gives a woman, one who's been through this?"

Helen watched the steam rising, and she nodded. "Healing? Right?"

"Right."

"Why's it gotta hurt so bad, anyway?" Helen tried not to scoff at herself. She sounded weak, and Cass was one of the only people in the world who ever saw this side of her.

"I don't know. But it does. Hey—when's the last time you talked to Troy?"

Helen poured hot water over her peppermint tea and sighed. She rarely had time for therapy. Loved Troy, but her time was precious. "Awhile."

"Will you give him a call tomorrow? You need to take care of yourself, you know, partner."

"Okay."

"That's not convincing. I'm serious. You need to take care of yourself. Not just for Phoebe's sake, and not for mine either. Because you deserve it too."

Helen sipped her tea and thought about Cass and Frank and Zander. She had her work, and not much else tonight. "Mmm."

"You ever think about meeting someone?"

"Oh, no, no no no, I'm over all that." Helen almost snorted. "That bus left the station long time ago."

"I wouldn't be so dismissive. And I haven't said this in the longest time to you, so I'm gonna say it again. It wasn't your fucking fault. And you've suffered enough. Someday, you're gonna have to accept that. Someday, you're gonna have to face the possibility of being happy again."

"I am happy. I like my job." Her words sounded unconvincing and Cass was going to be all over her.

But Cass just said, "I love you my friend. It's gonna be all right."

"You promise?"

"Yeah. Phoebe needs this."

"Okay."

"Okay?"

"Yeah." Helen paused. Some things needed saying. Damned if Cass wasn't always making her say them. "I love you too, partner."

"Well, good." Cass's smile came through on the phone, and it occurred to Helen that she really did love Cass, and had never told her before. It felt—good. "Call me again if you freak out."

Helen smiled, and hung up, still smiling. Maybe she'd get a cat. Whole lot easier than a man, that was for sure. On second thought, cats weren't all that cuddly, or were they?

Chapter 45

Phoebe watched the lights shimmer in the distance. "I love this time of night. It's quiet, and I feel safe." She leaned over and turned the radio down a little, but Jim whispered, "Wait I love that song," so she turned it up louder again and pulled two Marlboros out. Then she smiled, because the song was Tom Petty's, "Here Comes my Girl," and even though it was dark inside, she could see the look on Jim's face.

"Yeah, hit me. You know I quit, a few months ago?"

"Mmm," she squinted as the smoke got in her eye. "You saying I'm that kind of girl?"

"Oh no . . ." he looked over and realized she was teasing, so he put a hand on her thigh and while she put the cigarette in his mouth, his hand rose higher, and she felt the shock of the desire shooting through her. She was groaning now, and they both laughed, and he moved his hand to downshift as they hit an exit ramp leading onto 66.

"All I'm saying is you make me crazy, baby, you make me crazy. And I don't regret it, not even if I've smoked more this week than I had the entire year before I kissed you the first time."

"Yeah, that was pretty hot," she said. "I wanted to . . . make love to you so bad that night."

"Trust me, you weren't the only one," he said. "Remember when I was saying goodnight to you that first night, when you bought me coffee?"

"Yeah. Even then, you knew?"

"Yeah," he said. "I came so close to kissing you."

"And I wanted to do this," she said, and brought his fingers to her mouth. She slowly mouthed each fingertip, and again, the desire throbbed in her.

"Oh, Phoebe, I'm gonna crash if you keep doing that," he said, and his voice hit a higher register than usual.

"All right. All right." She let go, and pretended she was angry, and when he looked over in concern, she grinned again, and deep and low, she murmured, "All bets are off when we get to your place. So, how much farther?"

"Few miles."

She fell quiet again, and in falling, fell there, the old place of pain and shame and then she was shaking her head. "Damnit."

"What's wrong?"

"Whenever it gets quiet, I think—I start seeing stuff. You know, flashbacks?"

"Yeah, I know exactly what you mean. I see dead people and you see—your dad?"

Phoebe sighed. "Yeah. Stuff like that."

"I'm gonna be there with you the whole time." He shook his head and laughed. "Well, obviously."

She still felt shaky, almost too weak to move, and she knew they were getting close to his place, because he was exiting off 66. "Can you talk to me the whole time?"

"I will."

She reached for another cigarette but changed her mind. She could see a line of traffic lights in the distance. "I'm sorry—this must seem so fucked up to you."

"It's not. You're wonderful." He focused on the road ahead for a minute. Then he stroked her cheek, his voice tender, right before he turned left into a townhouse parking lot. "I mean, you're beautiful and you're strong and you're everything I ever wanted and I wouldn't have you any other way. Ever since I set eyes on you, I couldn't think about much of anything else. And no one's ever done this to me. No one. Because you're the one. You're the one I gotta have. You. No one else. You."

Jim pulled into second gear, tapped the parking break, and turned off the engine. He turned and stroked her cheek. Then he hopped out his side, and jogged in front of the truck, looking all athletic and crazy fucking hot, and she felt it stirring inside her again, and then he pulled her door open. He ended up with his head against her chest, and they both laughed when she pushed her hands through his hair again, and she pulled him to her and he put his lips on hers, and he stepped backwards, holding her hand as she stepped to the asphalt and they were both moaning now. She wanted it now and she would have if he'd . . . anything he asked, she'd do, she wanted it that bad.

"Let me get our bags," he said, and before he let go of her, he pushed her against the side of the 4Runner and he was kissing her neck now, and touching her and she was touching him, and he let go again, he actually raised his hands up in the air, laughing, and he grabbed the bags and wrapped his arm around her, and they walked up to his door, and she said, "I want a 4Runner, Jim," and while he unlocked his forest green front door, he said, "Anything you want, anything," and then they were inside and he shut the door behind them.

"This is my place, Phoebe," he said.

She took a look around and nodded. "Did they teach you to be neat in the army?"

"Yeah," he said. "Come on, let me show you around," and he started to walk toward the kitchen. Then they both started laughing at the same time, and before she could say another word, he picked her up in his arms and his lips didn't leave hers while he carried her up the steps, and all she could think was *he's carrying me up the stairs like I belong to him*, and she was trying not to cry because it made her so happy to belong to him, to this man.

When they got to the top of the stairs, he took his lips off hers. "Just look at me, Phoebe. Don't take your eyes off me, not for a moment, okay?"

She was almost crying, and he kissed her cheek, and then right below her eye, and staring at her, with his blue eyes glowing again, he carried her into his room and set her down in front of his bed. "Wait," he said, and turned on the light by his bed stand. "Be right back," he said, and she heard his feet on the steps, and before she could see much of anything besides the white walls and the white and blue bedspread, he was back, carrying their bags.

He almost looked shy for a moment while he unzipped his bag. "I, uh, bought some things on the way up here, up to see you, because to be honest, I—"

"—You knew you were gonna make love to me," she said, and she took his hand and put it on her chest. She felt brave and then she felt a lot more than brave, because he was moving his fingers over to the buttons on her shirt and while he unbuttoned hers, she unbuttoned his, and he said please take it off my love and she did, and so did he. She took more things off and so did he, and she never stopped staring into his eyes, not even long enough to watch him take his time, so tender, so slow, his body against hers his body pressed harder against and almost into hers and he never stopped talking to her not when he lifted her up and laid her down and not when he entered her and they became one and not when she screamed his name and not when he screamed hers and the minutes stopped passing everything stopped and all she heard herself say was I love you and she did.

She was still looking into his eyes a few minutes later, and as much as she wanted to jump out of bed and wash him off, she didn't. Not this time. This time it would be different. This time there was love. And she couldn't get enough of it, of him, of his eyes, his skin, his mouth, his chest, his arms, and she kept wanting to make sure he was, she was, they were real. Greedy, she was greedy for him, for them. And from the way he looked at her, and touched her skin, he was greedy for her too.

He was on his side, head on his hand. He ran his hand down her side and along her hip, and she felt goosebumps all up and down her body, wherever he touched her. "I actually liked your poem," he said.

"Then why didn't you laugh?"

"I was too busy watching you. I was waiting for you, and didn't realize it until you smashed the door open, late of course."

"Yeah. Usually am. Always think I'll hit all the lights, like it's divinely ordered," she said.

"Do you?"

"What, hit all the lights?"

He brought her hand to kiss lips and kissed it. "Yes."

"Mmmm. When you do that, it makes me want to do things."

"I've been imaging you doing those things a lot," he said.

"Do you have to work tomorrow?"

"No," he said. "Monday's my day off. Usually I work Saturdays, so that Ronnie doesn't have to, wife and kids."

"That's good of you. And good for me too. I don't want to leave in the morning."

He put his head on her chest. "Then don't. I can't think of anything I'd rather do than spend the day with you."

She listened to his heartbeat. Slow and steady. "Jim?"

"Yes?"

"I feel safe here. You feel safe."

"That's because you are." He rubbed her back and held her tight.

She wanted to tell him how much she loved him, but he fell asleep holding her. She said it anyway because she liked the way *I love you* sounded.

Chapter 46

He flipped through the used car section of the *Washington Post* until he got to Toyotas, but none looked like exactly what she needed. He didn't mind fixing one up, but rust could be an issue on ones that had body damage. Timing belts, clutch, tires—wouldn't be a problem. He smiled, and sipped his coffee, and thought about waking her. Or writing a poem about her. Instead, he grabbed his laptop and ran a few searches on cars.com, and took notes. He'd find her a 4Runner.

Jim stood up and stretched. Most off days, he ran at dawn, and the sun would be rising any minute now. He hadn't asked her if she ran. She looked like she could run all day, and she had the body for it. Not a runner's body, but an athletic one. Not boyish or anything, but she was built for both speed and endurance; bruising hits and, he chuckled, lovemaking beyond compare. That's the thing. She wasn't like any other woman. None that he'd known, and none that he'd—well, he'd never loved any woman the way he loved her. It's like he'd been waiting not just for her, but for a love like he had for her.

And now all he wanted to do was to make her happy. Okay, and to make love to her again. And again. And again.

He turned around and looked for a second coffee mug. He found a dark green one with the yellow Mason lettering. She liked it with cream, no sugar. That was only a couple of weeks ago, and here he was making plans, and all those plans involved her. It was too soon to think of all that, but he was anyway. No one had ever said he wasn't spontaneous enough; if anything, they'd always called him reckless, whether he was prowling centerfield or laying people out as a safety.

It's what made him love fighting, until he hated it. And when he started hating it, he'd hated that side of himself, the one that wasn't scared of much, didn't think things out too hard ahead of time. Maybe that's the way it was when you were the youngest of three, with two older sisters . . . and when he lost it, he also lost something that felt intrinsically true to him, like a piece of him, gone, in a single shot to the head.

And now, in finding her, he'd found a piece of himself that had been missing for far too long. He felt like him again, if not healed. But maybe healing, or at least a little bit more whole. More him. That was it. She made him feel like all of him, like the man he was and could be, had been, or had been on the way to becoming. And it felt, he felt, reborn in a way. Not reborn to God, but to love. To living.

He poured his own coffee, same color as hers, and carried the steaming mugs upstairs. There was no reason to run at dawn. Not with his beloved sleeping in his bed. He reached her and he wanted so bad to kiss her all over. His cheeks hurt from smiling so much.

"Phoebe."

Her eyes fluttered open, and she held her hand out for coffee with a sleepy smile. He had jeans on, no shirt, and he realized as he grew harder that he was wearing too much clothing, but she didn't seem like she was awake, so he leaned against his desk chair and watched her over the top of his mug. She gazed around the room and sipped coffee, and he waited, not for anything much, just a quiet waiting.

She cracked a smile, and man how he loved her swagger. That's what she had; it was one of her defining characteristics. She lifted weights almost for sure.

"Whatcha doing up at the ass-crack of dawn? Thought you took Mondays off."

"Old habit," he said. He didn't mention the undead birds nightmare. "Usually I run at dawn, not today."

"But we were up so late last night." She sat up a little straighter and the sheet dropped away.

Her breasts took his breath away. He wanted to hold her, but maybe she needed space. Maybe he needed it too, but it didn't feel like it. He was in deep, and each minute it seemed like he was falling more, falling not fallen, because he was rising, and in more ways than one.

"You are so beautiful," he said.

She kicked the rest of the covers off and set her coffee mug down. Then she was standing in front of him, and she ran her hands against his chest and then she leaned in, and he hugged her close, skin to skin.

"I love you," she said.

"I know, my love, as I love you."

"I need a shower, and then how about if I throw an omelet together for us?"

"That would be great. I gotta run out to the store and pick up a few things. I'll be back by the time you are done."

Chapter 47

She closed her eyes and sighed. The hot water drummed into her back and she was not in a hurry, not like she usually was. She opened her eyes and reached out for his shampoo. Pert. *Of course.* She'd smell like him all day, and there was something . . . she took a deep breath. *Damn good about that. Almost sensual. Okay, very sensual.* It didn't even matter that she hadn't done her work for tonight's class. And who knows if she could write anything at his place. *Never know until you try.* She shook her head. She almost had a good attitude. Anne would say it was a first for her.

> *Oh Anne, I hope you're somewhere good. Saying goodbye felt so hard, and I didn't say it right. I just stared at you really, tried so hard not to cry, but I did anyway, and you held my hand. Couldn't even hug you. Your body was that broken up at the end.*

Phoebe felt around for soap and it was heavenly. *Oh my God, it's just soap. His soap.* She didn't even feel shy using his stuff.

> *When she first got sick, and couldn't work with me, I was relieved. And I've been carrying that for months. I know it was wrong, but I didn't know. What would Jamie say about*

that? She knew I was done with riding before I knew. No, before I could admit it to anyone. She told me to quit before I got seriously injured. "Head's not in it, Pheebes, and that's dangerous, for you and for your horse." I'd told her to fuck off, and ended up knocking on her door a few hours later, to ask her how she knew. And she'd said the horse could sense it in me, not so much fear, because I was still fearless, reckless even, but me not wanting to be there. And I'd said "I'm sorry" and she'd said "I forgive you, now get out of here because I change my mind," and I'd laughed and wondered why she was so kind to me.

Phoebe stood there, thinking about the last time she and Jamie had talked. Well, argued. Well, she'd argued and Jamie had—hugged her. Refused to go along, for whatever reason. Probably some God thing. God, heaven, what the fuck, where is Anne where is Dad, where are they?

And what did Jamie know about it all? What would Jamie say if she called and asked her? Jamie probably wasn't mad at her. Phoebe was the one who got all hot under the collar. Phoebe was the mad one. And mad about what? That Jamie forgave her . . . the guy that—yeah, raped her. Rape was such an ugly word; sent a shiver of revulsion and shame straight through her, electric really, almost same feeling as when Jim touched her, made love to her, but different. Close.

And to have him close was heaven. Heaven. There I go again. If Dad was there, it couldn't be, he couldn't be; no he wasn't. He couldn't be there. Not with Anne. He just couldn't be.

The water was just now getting colder, and she'd been in there for longer than any shower she ever took at home. That was the disadvantage of living out in the country. She turned the handles off with a quick snap of her wrist. The ones at home shrieked and resisted, and took a few twists to get the drips to stop. And the shower, the walls, the grout, were all perfect white, which was actually a color, at least on a color wheel. She'd looked it up one time for something she was writing. That was the amazing thing about the Internet. Color wheels. But more important, it allowed her to track cases, sick bastards, and crime reports. Her usual Monday morning work. Maybe today she'd make an exception. Maybe not.

She stepped out of the shower and as she toweled off, she thought about Toller. Last Thursday, when she'd checked on him, she'd only seen an old lady cutting the grass around the mailbox with scissors, and she was pretty sure from the trial that was his mom. She'd wanted to kick the bitch's head in. She knew. She had to know, or bake in blindness, the kind that people enshroud themselves in to preserve their stupid lie-worlds. Worlds of lies. Phoebe hated lies.

She heard a door open and close. With the towel wrapped around her, she went to the banister and called, "Jim?"

He paused at the foot of the stairs, hands full of bags. Oh my God he was gorgeous. "Oh, Phoebe, you're just wearing a towel. That's not fair."

She smirked, and let the towel fall to her feet. "Who said life was fair?"

She turned, and heard the rustling sound of the plastic bags hitting the landing, and she snuck a look over her shoulder, just to make sure he was coming. And he was.

He came up to her from behind. "Miss me, did you?" He ran his hands down to her hips, and back up again. "Because I missed you."

She reached back with her hand and brought his lips to hers. This—this was crazy, crazy good, and she didn't want it to stop, and she was saying all those things, and so was he, and she was doing all the things she knew how to do now, and she didn't stop, and she didn't think about it, now not, not so much anymore, not much.

Chapter 48

He worked outside in the garage, reorganizing the tools, garage door open as usual, because it was good to have a routine, and having the door open was friendly, not obvious. And he could watch things over at The Harleys. They left for work at pretty much the same time every day. This Monday was no different. Seven o'clock: Mr. Harley. Seven oh five—the eldest kid. Eight-ten—the youngest kid waited for the bus. Eight-thirty, sometimes eight-forty, Ms.-not-Mrs. Harley. Cow. No. That wasn't nice.

Once they left, he went ahead and started spreading the ten cubic yards of mulch he'd gotten delivered on Saturday. He'd work on the side yard all morning, and at a nice measured pace, nothing out of place, just a guy in his yard. Nobody had to know he was waiting for the UPS truck. Should be here in . . . Wayne Toller pulled his arm up in the air and squinted at his watch. Just a cheap one he'd bought for work.

It wasn't bad so far. Just three days on the job, and the work wasn't exactly backbreaking. Maintenance services sounded better than being a janitor, but it wasn't about the work. It was about the opportunity it gave him. Wayne chuckled. He could be funny. Even when no one else was laughing, he'd be laughing. Or maybe, like the time he split his pants in high school and everyone laughed, they laughed a lot, but then the laughter stopped, but he kept laughing just in case they did too.

He'd gotten the coat hooks installed on Day 2, while cleaning the locker rooms. Disgusting work. But worth it. Now he was waiting on the backordered wall outlet camera. According to UPS tracking, the shredder was definitely arriving.

Yet again, he'd be the only one laughing, just alone this time, once he got everything sorted. His shift was tomorrow, ten o'clock. And he'd be early.

Just as long as the UPS truck showed up as scheduled. Didn't it always?

Chapter 49

"Jim," she groaned, "Stop. I'm trying to cook a omelet."

He kissed her neck again from behind and it felt too good, too good for omelets or anything else, and she was not making sense, not with his lips on her. Was it possible, wanting him so much, oh my God, she couldn't get enough of him. Then she wasn't thinking about the eggs and she dropped the spatula.

It hit the edge of the pan and toppled over onto the floor. Instead of picking it up, she grinned over her shoulder and took his hand and with her mouth, she licked each one of his fingers, one by one, even as the butter sizzled.

"Oh, that's not fair, Pheebes."

"Exactly," she said.

She let go of his hand, and reached for the spatula. With an arch glance, she put a hand on his chest, and ran it down to his belt loops, resting it there. She could unbutton his jeans, and slide hers off and . . . she couldn't stop smiling. This was crazy. Crazy love. Sex, love, sex or love? Yeah, love. And sex.

"Now, really, I know you gotta eat. Right?"

He leaned against the counter and reached over to hand her the peppers. "Mmm, yes."

"So maybe you can let me feed you?"

"Oh, baby, you keep giving me sugar, I'm all over it."

She shook her head at him as she washed off the spatula. Nice clean sink. Gleaming faucets. "Hands-off. I'm serious."

"OJ?"

"Yeah."

"Anything else I can do." He sauntered past her and she narrowed her eyes, trying to concentrate, concentrate on making a fucking omelet. Crazy.

As they ate, and it wasn't her prettiest creation, but he ate fast, neat, but fast, she kept an eye on him.

"Come on, you gotta eat."

She grabbed her fork, and realized she was starving.

"I need you keeping your energy up." He put his hand on her thigh, and she rolled her eyes.

"So after breakfast, you wanna go on a ride with me?"

"Sure," he said. "I'm game."

"Good."

He took a few more bites and swallowed his orange juice in one gulp. "Where you taking me?"

"Well," she hesitated. "Maybe Burke Lake?"

"Love it there. Run there sometimes."

"Me too," she said. "But first, I gotta stake out that bastard Toller."

"Stake out?"

"Yeah."

"That sounds . . . kind of crazy, right?"

She sipped on her orange juice. "No, not at all. He's up to no good. I know it in my bones. Besides, you don't strike me as the sort that shirks from a little bravery. Good crazy, right?"

"Well shoot," he grinned. "Now that you put it that way."

"Exactly. So," she paused and tried not to look too smug. "What's the craziest thing you've done?"

He contemplated his last bite of ham. "Drunk or sober?"

"Oh man. I'm thinking drunk would be a whole lot more fun."

"Yes," he said. "But let's say sober."

She was glad he said so, because she was hammered the night she hit Toller's house. It would be great not to have to share that with him.

"Well, I did some things I wasn't too proud of, you know, Pheebes? After Christopher died."

She nodded, and then felt bad asking.

"But in school, we did a lot of dumb stuff. Country boys. I think we locked this jerk coach of ours in a Don's John for an hour or two. And we might just have rolled it."

"Might?"

"I'd never tell, you know?" He winked at her. "And you don't strike me as—how did you say it? Shirking from a little bravery?

"Yeah. Gonna take a little of that to catch Toller doing what he does. It never changes. Perverts never do."

"Well," he said, "How about if you take me along, and we'll see about that."

She'd been fighting alone for so long. It hadn't felt good to hit Toller's house. But this? Above board. Felt right.

Chapter 50

They threaded through late morning rush hour traffic. Northern Virginia was and always would be a government town, and traffic never so much cleared out as dissipated like mountain fog. They took Braddock straight through, past Mason, past a pet cemetery that always made Phoebe laugh, because she was fucked up that way, and past a long line of strip malls, until they turned right and hit Burke. Phoebe had the wheel, and she said for about the fifth time, "Damn, this shifts smooth. I like it."

He put his hand on hers and smiled. "Okay, okay, I'm working on it."

She gave up one of her slow to develop smiles, always reluctant to go all in, until she hit a certain point, a certain place, where it felt safe to show how she felt. "Good. In fact, can you just trash the Bronco? I'm done with it. Want nothing else to do with it. Tired of fucking Zander calling it my peppermint sled."

Jim laughed. "Good name for it."

Phoebe sighed. "I know. And as soon as I laughed about it, it felt like surrendering. It's funny. Damn thing is ugly; but worse, it never fucking works. Can't have master cylinders blowing."

"Nope."

"That's what it was, right?"

"Yes. But the engine really needs a rebuild. If you want, I can send it on over to one of my friends and—"

— "Yep! Done."

"And between now and then, you got the F150?"

She sighed. "Yeah, but I got a burning need for—"

"Oh I know what that feels like." He took his hand and ran it all the way up her thigh.

She gasped, and then started laughing.

When the light changed, she lurched forward a little until he got to second gear.

"No wonder you broke the sled."

"Oh, blow me."

"Actually," and he was grinning, "Anytime baby."

She shook her head, because the thought of it made her want it, and then she laughed. "Maybe if you take the wheel."

He almost bent over laughing.

She got serious, and pointed off to the right. "His house is in this neighborhood. It's on the edge of a cul de sac, which can be viewed from two other roads and," she paused, focused on clicking through the gears smoothly, "Also partially visible from a tot lot. So my plan is to drive by his house, see if he's home, and take a walk around the neighborhood."

"So," he said, "How many times you been by his house?"

"Since when?"

"Oh, um, we gonna do this the hard way?"

"No, no. I go past at least twice a day. Been coming since a couple days after he got out a couple of weeks ago. All I know is I got a feeling about him. And I saw a sticker on his car late Saturday, after dark, and I was gonna get out and take a look at it, but I had to hightail it over to practice."

"For derby?"

"Yeah. Hey—we got a game coming next Saturday. You coming?"

"Wouldn't miss it."

"Good, because we kick ass, and the team we're playing don't fuck around. One of them has got one coming."

"But you don't strike me as a—what do you call them?"

"Blocker? Nah." She gave cocky shrug. "I'm the shit. The main attraction. The one they all block for. But I can still lay just about anyone out. And when I start shit, usually my girls will finish it."

He surveyed the streets. "I see what you mean. Looks like it's got great sightlines."

"Yep." She hung a left, and then pulled up behind a Ford Explorer parked on the main entry road to the subdivision. She grabbed her phone, and made sure she had plenty of battery power. "Let's take a walk."

He fell in beside her, and she tried to ignore the cut of his jeans and his muscles moving on his neck, down into his shoulders, and the angle of his brow and his dirty blonde hair that felt so good to touch.

"Nice having backup," she said. "Don't have to carry."

"Naturally you got a permit."

"Naturally." She shook her head. Bangs needed cutting.

"How long you been shooting?"

"Bout the same time I started taking martial arts. Since I was 16. Never wanted anyone to lay a fucking hand on me again."

"Do you like it?"

She shrugged, thinking about it. "Honestly? No. I thought I would. I don't hate it or anything. I like knowing how to take care of myself, take care of the people I love, but the whole thing kind of sets off my fight or flight thing. After I go to the range, I need the rest of the night to calm down. It's funny. Never told anyone that." She sighed and checked his face.

He was nodding.

"Why? How about you?"

"Used to be a blast," he said, "Going out in the woods, shooting cans, trees, rabbits. Country boy stuff. But now?" He reached for her hand. "I won't go out of my way to shoot much of anything. And, yes, if you want to ask the next question, 'Does it bring war stuff back,' the answer's 'yes.'"

They walked in silence, past several large colonials squeezed onto quarter acre lots. "I'm sorry for what you've been through."

He squeezed her hand. "Thanks love. Some guys go through lots worse. I got all my body parts, and," he stopped and pulled her to him, "I got you."

She quivered all over. *Literally. This was crazy. I mean, how many times in one . . .* Phoebe nuzzled her cheek against his just-shaved cheek and chin, and she kept telling herself to stop, but it took him letting go for it to stop. Then he just stood there, holding her close, his hands supporting her as she leaned backward a little, and neither one of them said anything. She had so much to say, but if she started, she'd lose Toller.

But Jim was the one who said *let's go find the perp*, or maybe he said *perv*, she wasn't sure, and she still didn't say anything. She didn't know where to start, because until today, she'd just been angry, on the edge of killing a man angry, and now, now there was Jim. She shook her head and tried not to think of how much she loved him, because it was taking her edge off, but she did anyway.

They went another half-block and she turned down a path to a tot lot, just a climbing thing that had a slide, a few swings, and a basketball court a few paces off. Jim leaned against a metal pole.

"Right over there—see the front of his house? Dutch colonial, brown shutters?"

"Yes."

"Okay, and the garage door is open. And . . . yep. There he is." Phoebe nodded at a nondescript middle-aged guy, really no distinguishable traits, not from where they were standing.

"Happen to have a picture of him?"

She reached into her jean pocket and grabbed her cell. Real fast, she scrolled through it, and came up with a downloaded copy of his mug shot, which was in her email. "Yep. Here he is. Looked a little younger there, but mom said he looked pretty much the same at the parole board hearings."

"Wow. Your mom went to those?"

"Yeah. She's hardcore."

"Hey, look? Is that him? Walking to his neighbors'?"

Phoebe saw a UPS truck turn left from the edge of Toller's street. "Yeah. Wonder what—"

Phoebe saw Toller walk over to his neighbor's home, briefly drop out of sight, and when he came back into view, he was carrying a box. "Wonder why he didn't tell the UPS guy they were delivering it to the wrong house."

Jim shook his head. "Can't be stealing it, can he?"

Phoebe shook her head. "Doesn't make sense . . . unless . . . he got something sent there on purpose."

"Why would he do that?" Jim and Phoebe made eye contact and they both started talking at once.

"Go ahead," he said.

"Well, it must be something he doesn't want anyone to know he has, right?"

Jim pushed off from the pole and started off toward Toller's house. "Kind of makes me curious. You said he had a sticker on his car, right?"

She grabbed her cell phone, and got it ready to take a picture. "Yeah."

They came alongside his Honda Civic, and she snapped a picture of the back while Jim ran interference, keeping his body between Toller and Phoebe. "Morning," Jim said, his voice even, but cold, really cold.

"Oh my God," she whispered, a few houses later. "That was Toller."

Jim grunted.

"I think I got a good image of that sticker. Let's check it once we get back to the 4Runner."

Jim was quiet and she didn't like it. He didn't say much of anything and it made the distance they covered interminable. She racked her brain for what to say. Started asking him, or almost started asking him what he was thinking three times, before she asked *what are you thinking* and still he didn't answer right away.

"It's all I can do . . . not to kill the bastard," he said once they reached the 4Runner.

She twisted his keys and realized she was holding them as if they were hers—as if his stuff was hers . . . and it was. And she was . . . what? Proud. But now she was terrified and excited all at once. "Why?"

"Because he . . . was a part of it. Part of hurting you. And I know child abusers are pretty incorrigible."

"Come on," she said. She unlocked the door and waited for him to get in beside her. As she turned the engine on, she clicked on her stored photos, and read the small print. It was a gym in West Springfield, which was a bit farther down Braddock road. "You wanna swing by this place? Maybe, I don't know. Just see where he's working?"

"Yeah. I'm game." He blurted that out, and then she wanted to ask if he was disgusted with her, knowing other men, Toller probably included, had seen her, no watched her naked. Fucking her father. She still got sick thinking about it. And the shame—would it ever go away? How about the nightmares?

When she pulled into the gym's parking lot, she tried to figure out what he was thinking and feeling but as soon as she saw his eyes burning, she got a glimpse into another facet of him. He could kill Toller, and if he'd based his poem on his own experiences, killing was something he'd do and had already done. Toller wouldn't be the first man he killed. It was exhilarating but it was also scary, thinking about Jim killing, not because Toller didn't have it coming to him. Because Jim would go to jail. She'd been through this once, with her mom, five years ago, and that was one time too many.

"Let's just walk around inside again, maybe take a tour. Sound okay?"

"Yes."

"A couple touring the facility."

"Yes."

The county rec center was, no doubt about it, one of the nicer ones Phoebe had seen; with a massive two story weight room, a vast number of classrooms, several racquetball courts, a full-size basketball court, and an Olympic size swimming pool. From the top floor, patrons could view the pool through glass, and the pool ran almost the entire length of the building.

Phoebe improvised up at the front desk, which was manned by two middle-aged women. "Oh, hello," murmured Phoebe. She tried to look confused.

"Yes, ma'am?"

"Ah, well . . . We were trying to arrange swimming lessons for my little sis and we'd called up but to be honest, I can't remember if my mom called here or Oak Hill."

"Ah, yes. Well. Do you remember the name?"

"Oh yes." Phoebe rested her arm on the desk and reflected for a moment. "Right—Wayne Thomas . . . no, no . . . Toller. I remember now, because it made me think of a bell tolling." Phoebe adopted a satisfied smirk, which felt pretty good trying on, like a funny looking hat that fit well.

"Oh, let's see," said the red-haired woman at the desk. "No, no, let me think. No, we don't have any Waynes or Tollers."

"Oh shoot." Phoebe looked Jim's way and gave an embarrassed chuckle. "Well, now that we're here, maybe we should take a tour? This is the closest rec center to our house, and it sure does look nice."

"Of course. We just underwent a major remodeling."

Fifteen minutes later, they were checking out the racquetball courts and the basketball court. Thomas, a muscled guy wearing a blue polo led them down a dim hallway, more gray lighting like Mason's, and at the locker rooms, she split from Jim. Phoebe cut through the women's locker room and when she passed the showers, she peeked in there, just to see if there was a hole somewhere in the walls.

Just as she was about to turn around and recheck the walls near the lockers, she saw a coat hanger set up opposite to the showers. Three hooks. Two were off-white; the third, almost perfect white. She peered at the white one more closely. Holy shit, there was a hole in the top. Like . . . a camera? With a chill running down her spine, she reached into her pocket for her cell phone, but before she pulled it out, she heard a child's voice, maybe two, on the other side of the lockers. She'd have to try again in a few minutes.

She caught up to Jim and the muscled guy who was giving them the tour. Quickly, she pulled the same routine she'd used at the front desk, but this time she altered it a little. "Darn, can't remember his name," she said. "But we did meet with him a couple of days ago. Eric—that's my brother's name—snapped a picture of him for some reason. Damn kid is always snagging my phone, you know?

"Oh? What's he look like?"

Phoebe grabbed her phone, hoping that he'd answer her question before thinking too much about where the photo was taken. She could feel Jim's heat, standing with his arm just by her elbow. His touch was reassuring, which was the last thing she expected to feel.

"Oh—yes. Weird. I've seen him around. But he's not a lifeguard or anything. I think he's a janitor."

Phoebe at this point went all in. "Actually, I didn't give you the whole story. This guy's actually on the state's sexual registry. Hold on—Phoebe grabbed a folded up piece of paper out of her pocket. It was a picture of Wayne from the registry.

"Oh yes," Thomas said. "That's the guy. But I don't think his name is Wayne. Wait—holy shit. He works *here*?"

Phoebe nodded. "Keep him away from kids. And maybe you don't want to tell anyone yet."

"You sure that's wise?" Thomas rubbed his chin and concentrated. "I mean, what if he . . . wow."

"I'd rather not tip him off, ya know?"

Thomas nodded.

"Here's my cell number. Will you call if you see him? Please?"

"Yeah. Funny you ran into me . . . well, weird fact. My sister was abused. If this will help you catch the bastard, count me in."

Phoebe checked the time on her cell. Zander time. "Fuck, it's time for me to pick up my brother. Please call if you see him."

She strode to the locker room and before anyone else came in, she snapped several pictures of the coat hanger. She had no idea what she was going to do with it, with all this information, but she knew who to ask.

Chapter 51

Phoebe held up her hand as they passed the front desk, giving them a Helen Thompson-wave. Then she typed out a text.

Phoebe: Be there in ten. Sorry late.

Zander immediately replied: K. See u and pepp. Sled.

She laughed.

Phoebe: Nope. Got Jim's 4Runner.

Zander: Jim?

Phoebe: Yes. EOE.

Zander: EOE? WTH.

Phoebe: Don't cuss. Oh nevermind.

Zander: Exactly. EOE?

Phoebe: End of message. STOP.

Zander: Don't you mean EOM? Or EOT?

Phoebe: No—yes. I mean—I am done talking to you.

Zander: K.

Phoebe started to put her cell phone beside her. It buzzed again. It was Zander.

Pheebes? Tyler in the car, K?

At this point, Phoebe waved her hand helplessly and handed her phone to Jim. "Please. Take it. Zander's driving me crazy."

He silenced the ringer and gave her a look that showed he was "on the job," so to speak, and she realized this was a cop term, but it sure felt like it fit right. "Zander? You mean, Eric?"

She pulled out of the parking lot and this time, her gear shifts were smooth, but she didn't point it out, and Jim wasn't joking either. "Yeah. Zander White. He's my mom's partner's son. Pain in my ass."

"Just like a little brother."

"Yep." She pulled her sunglasses down to block the sun coming in under the front visor. "You'll see soon enough. But I gotta tell you something. If you look at my pictures, you'll see what I found in the locker room. It's why I went ahead and told that Thomas guy. And now I'm wondering if I should have told him more."

He was quiet as he scrolled through. "Is this what I think it is?"

"What's it look like to you?"

"Well, there's a hole in there, and obviously there's some sort of light coming through . . . it's gotta be a camera or camcorder."

They were going to be at the White's in less than five. Crap. "And look at the other hooks—different color, and no hole. Hey, Jim, can you enter a search, see if you find a place that manufactures—"

"—On it."

As Jim searched on Safari, Phoebe took a deep breath. "You know, I didn't tell him what I found in the locker room. What if someone, well, if he gets back there before we get this to Cass?"

"You're taking it to your attorney? Why not the cops?"

"Oh fuck? Those bastards? You fucking kidding me?"

"Oh, crap." Jim sighed.

And as soon as she heard it in his voice, she wasn't mad. Of course going to the cops made sense most of the time. For most people. And not all cops were dirty. She just didn't know any she could trust. But Cass? She would. Always seemed to.

"Okay," he said. "Listen. It's better that you didn't tell."

"Even if someone else gets their pictures, fuck. I don't know."

"I know. But if Toller finds out now, he'll remove the cameras, right?"

"Yeah, but—"

"—Wait. Here's the camera/hanger thing. Yep. It matches the picture, sure 'nuff."

She felt her jaw tighten up. They had to hurry. Really had to hurry.

"You know, you got damn good instincts. Detective instincts."

She started to scoff. And stopped. *Detective?* Funny. The last thing she'd ever . . . but it . . . well.

Before she could finish her thought, she was rounding the corner to the White's street, and there was Zander. He was going in five different directions, maybe more. And as soon as he got in the 4Runner, he started talking, and swear to God, he didn't stop except to pelt Jim with questions and interrupt his questions with more questions. Phoebe missed almost the entire conversation, her mind on tying up loose ends. And to think a week ago she was taking a pistol to the sick bastard's head over and over again, in her fantasies of course.

Right before she pulled into her mom's office, Zander's voice drifted back to her. Damned if he wasn't asking *what happened to the peppermint sled* and she massaged the steering wheel and tried not to smile too smugly.

"Getting a 4Runner."

"Oh Phoebe? For real? I can get behind that."

Jim shared a quiet smile with her, and then he said, "I'm gonna find one for her. You both okay with black? Or forest green?"

"Anything but peppermint," Phoebe and Zander said at the same time.

"Hey Pheebes? Guess what?"

Okay, she loved him but she really wished he'd stop talking. "What?"

"Cat's gonna take me to the shooting range maybe she said, maybe she will even let me practice on her government-issued pistol, do you think she would, wouldn't that be cool?"

Phoebe groaned. This was actually really interesting, but she didn't want to get drawn into any discussion with Zander right now. But still . . . "Hmnn, which range? Did she say?"

Zander shrugged and leaned forward from the backseat as if to start messing with the damn radio.

"The one out in Loudoun County's good," she said.

"Nah, near the base."

"Zander's sister Catherine is training to be a special agent," Phoebe said.

"I actually interviewed with them before I joined the Army," Jim said.

"You were in the Army?" Zander leaned forward even more and sounded like he was about to ask Jim at least a million questions about it. Phoebe took a quick glance at Jim, who wasn't showing much of anything in his expression, and then she sighed in relief. There was the garage, and there was no way Zander would interrupt—"

"—Don't hit the wall, 'kay Pheebes?"

She glared over her shoulder at him.

Then Jim laughed quietly, and she was smiling a little too.

Chapter 52

As they headed to the elevators, Jim held all the doors. This got her smiling again. She kept smiling even as Zander rattled about colors and tire sizes; in fact, he pinged Jim with so many questions, Jim held up both hands. Then Jim put a hand on Zander's shoulder and told Zander to come see him at the shop where he worked.

Zander was vibrating with excitement and he burst through the doors of Thompson, White and Hansen so fast, he collided with junior partner Carl Hansen. Phoebe tried to summon a polite word or two, and then she told Jim to follow her.

Cass's door was partially open, and Phoebe was too excited to knock before it was too late, and her feet were halfway in, with Jim too polite to follow her all the way in. She chuckled and only then realized that Cass was talking on speaker phone. Wearing a suit for once, a beautifully tailored blue one. She must have had a motion or some sort of scheduling conference. Not a motion—that was on Fridays.

Cass reached over and picked up the receiver, and she held up her index finger. She didn't seem annoyed, but she rarely did. Except when Zander—

—On cue, he tumbled in behind Phoebe, talking before Cass shook her head and made a slashing gesture, face set in a threatening frown.

He got in a half-sentence about the 4Runner, and then shut up, and grabbed a Gatorade out of the fridge. He held one up to Phoebe. She rolled her eyes and whispered "No."

Cass hung up, and then made a welcoming gesture to Phoebe.

Phoebe shifted her feet, and tried to figure out how to get through introductions. "Jim, please come in and meet my mom's partner, Cassandra White. Zander's mom."

Jim stepped through the door, and Phoebe imagined he was wearing a uniform. His back was that straight.

He shook hands and then stepped backwards, hands behind his back.

Zander started to talk. "Jim has a—"

"—Please don't call him Jim," Cass snapped at Zander. "He's got a last name, I reckon?" Cass then gazed at Phoebe and her eyes softened. Then she said, "Jim, I didn't catch your last name."

"McMahon."

"Good. Zander, you got that."

Phoebe had waited as long as she could. "Ms. White, I'm sorry to do this, but we don't have much time. It's an emergency. And it's a legal matter."

"Okay. Zander? Can you excuse us please?"

He mumbled something.

"And shut the door please."

Cass sat down and folded her hands together. "Okay. Before you tell me anything, is it okay for Jim to be in here? Is he also the client? Because otherwise, anything you say to me won't be protected by the attorney-client privilege. And if you're in some sort of trouble . . ." Cass paused and froze Phoebe.

She'd never seen that look before, not directed at her at least and it felt, well, scary. "Oh no, no, it's nothing like that. I have found evidence that's gotta get to someone you can trust, and it's gotta get there ASAP."

Cass leaned forward in her chair. "Go ahead. And let me know if I need to get your mom involved."

"There's no time." Her mom was in the middle of depositions in DC.

Phoebe took a deep breath, and then summarized what she'd found out about Toller. Cass asked a lot of questions, and Phoebe had a passing thought that this was what it had been like when her mom had been in trouble. *No time for that.*

At one point, Cass got that soft look in her eyes, right about when Cass asked Jim, "So your role has been?"

"Backup. Tactical support, as we used to call it."

"Soldier-poet-mechanic, right?"

The side of his mouth went up. "I see you've been briefed."

She nodded, and barely kept from cutting him off mid-sentence. "Okay," she said. "Heard enough. Obviously, you don't want to take this to the police."

"No." Phoebe's jaw hurt. "Got any ideas."

"Remember the Commonwealth's attorney who worked your case? I got her on speed dial." Cass paused, her hand on the phone. "That okay with you?"

"Yep."

While Cass waited on hold, she gave Phoebe an appraising glance. "You might think about going into law enforcement Pheebes."

Before Phoebe could answer, a clear voice with a Southern drawl got online.

"Elizabeth, I know this is probably a terrible time, but I got a hot potato and I need to meet with you right now."

"Can you give me a little more?"

"I got Phoebe Thompson in here and she's got evidence concerning Wayne Toller."

A long silence ensued; seemed fucking interminable. "Do you vouch for it, Cass?"

"Yes, absolutely. And someone's safety might be at stake. We need to move. We need to move now."

"That's for me to decide."

Cass started to speak, but Elizabeth cut her off. "Come over now. I'll get a judge on the phone. Just don't make me look like a fool."

"Have I ever?"

"See you in a few minutes."

Chapter 53

Phoebe didn't share Cass's disdain for the new courthouse. That was one of the many, well, charming things about her mom's partner. She had quirks and issues with *new, ugly Postmodern* buildings, *useless uncomfortable fancy* suits, *incompetent ninny lying bastard* opposing counsel, and a long list of other things. But her authenticity made her trustworthy. Phoebe had been watching and learning from and looking up to Cass for years. And yet the other day was the first time she'd ever thanked her—really thanked her.

Phoebe fell in beside Cass as they cut across the parking lot. Jim kept a few paces behind, except when they were crossing the street. He stood between them and oncoming traffic. *Of course.*

"How's Catherine?"

"Should be graduating next month sometime, and she loves it."

"Good," Phoebe said.

"You ever consider applying? She was just saying the other day that you'd be a natural at it."

"Who me?"

"Yeah, and that was before we knew you were moonlighting," Cass said with a hint of laughter in her voice.

Phoebe thought about it for a moment. "I . . . she said that?"

"Yeah."

Phoebe smiled and clasped her hands behind her. "That's . . . well, I never thought of it." Phoebe chuckled and kept walking beside Cass.

"He's the guy you told me about?"

"Yeah."

"You're glowing," Cass said.

"I am?"

"Sure are."

A few minutes later, they were milling about inside Elizabeth's office. She was standing too, towering above everyone except Jim, who was almost at her eye level. With her heels, she looked taller, maybe by an inch.

"Counselor, good to see you."

"Thanks for seeing us," Cass said.

"I'm on hold with Judge's chambers." Elizabeth then took Phoebe and Jim in.

Phoebe cringed a little. *Elizabeth had seen . . . everything. So had Cass. Fuck.*

But Elizabeth moved, graceful, efficient . . . over and took Phoebe's hand, gently, and put her other hand on Phoebe's elbow. "Ah. Helen's daughter, Phoebe, correct? It's so good to see you. Very, very good." Elizabeth held on for a few beats, and Phoebe remembered that Elizabeth was a mom too.

"And this is . . ." Elizabeth let go of Phoebe's hand, and offered it to Jim.

"Jim McMahon, ma'am. Pleasure."

"He goes with me, Ms. Baldwin."

"Very good," Elizabeth said.

Elizabeth crossed the room, and leaned against her desk, arms folded. "Cass, fill me in. Quick, before Judge O'Brien gets on the phone."

"Yeah right," Cass said, as she quickly outlined the facts.

Elizabeth's eyes widened at the mention of the rec center and the hidden camera. "Definitely cause for a subpoena. A camera in a locker room?"

Cass handed Phoebe's phone to Elizabeth, and the Commonwealth's mouth dropped open. I'll be—"

"—Judge O'Brien here. My clerk said it's an urgent matter."

"Judge, among other issues, we've got a hidden camera installed in the locker room of a county rec center, and apparently, a sexual offender is working at the club under a false identity."

"You sure about that?"

"Upon information and belief, yes, Your Honor."

"And where do you want to conduct the search?"

"The rec center for sure, and also at the suspect's place of residence."

"Counselor, I can give you the go-ahead for the rec center. No cause for a hidden camera to be installed in a locker room, and the added fact that a sexual offender appears to be working there adds a rather urgent note to this, yes?"

"Yes, your honor."

"But without a direct nexus, or some additional proof tying the suspect to the health club, I can't authorize a search of his residence."

"Respectfully, Your Honor, I would request you reconsider that, especially in light of—"

"—Counselor, tell you what. If they find anything at the scene, or some more definitive proof he works there, or at minimum a positive ID from somewhere at the rec center, you can call me back."

"Thank you, Your Honor."

Elizabeth hung up, and her eyes narrowed. "Right. Well, I will call you as soon as I know more."

Phoebe felt the weight of it all pressing on her as soon as they left the courtroom and reached the outside of Cass's office. Everything came back into focus and she realized that it was late afternoon now and the first buds on the trees had somehow appeared. She'd missed it, and now the earliest Cherry trees and forsythia were starting to bloom, or almost starting to bloom. The trees weren't yellow-green or green-yellow yet, but they were covered in raspberry buds, and it all made sense, because March was on its way into April and in more ways than one.

"Phoebe, I gotta go inside and wrap up a few things. I expect we'll hear back in the next hour or two, so I will have my cell on. And I will put a call into your mom—promise I'll get ahold of her, even it's through the back channels."

Phoebe nodded, about a half-beat or two behind now.

"Jim, it's been a true pleasure to meet you," Cass said.

"Likewise." *Jim looked gorgeous, he really did, and wow, his manners.*

"Thank you so much, for everything, Ms. White."

Cass wrapped her arm around Phoebe and whispered, "I'll call soon. You let me know if you need anything else, okay?"

After Cass moved out of earshot, Jim hugged Phoebe to him, and they stood there, her head tucked in below his chin, for at least a minute, probably longer.

"How about a cup of coffee," he said, his head still pressed against hers.

"Mmmm. And this time you're buying."

Chapter 54

Wayne Toller grimaced as he set the code on his safe. His back wasn't made for the janitorial work. So he could do one of two things: he could get in shape . . . Wayne shook his head and stared at his finger, which had gotten partially smashed in the lock mechanism. Now he had the mother of all hangnails. He could even use the gym at the rec center. *Nah.* He tried not to smile. *He could really be funny—see?*

Of course it was just a temporary thing. A way station, a momentary passing in the train route of his life. Very poetic, *Wayne.* Smarter than you look, *Wayne.* That's right. He bobbed his head. He was no ordinary guy after all. His only real choice of course was to quit that job after awhile. Who knows. Maybe he'd see an opportunity . . . wouldn't be the first friend he'd had.

First boy.

Yes.

Wayne shivered a little. No. No. He'd just take the cameras out of the rec center and keep moving. He didn't really need to work. Not with the old cow supporting him.

Maybe he'd keep working after all. Get his own place . . . *away from her prying fat eyes.*

It wasn't kind of him to think like that. But living with her was a whole different kind of prison. Thank goodness for his love shop down here. Wayne grinned. Yes. He was funny.

He heard the boards creaking overhead. Bridge? Or was that on Wednesday? Then voices. Angry? Why angry? Basement door creaked open. More angry voices, and then his mom was calling his name, and a man was saying, "Ma'am, get out the way, right now, or else we'll take you in too."

And she was whining it's a mistake and the police officer barked at her, yes, police officer, because there he was, his mom right behind them, her rolls glistening off her oily calf muscles, jiggling and rolling, icky. And Wayne realized right then and there that this, this house, even this love shack nestled in the old cow's house, was as much a prison as the one he was going back to.

Wayne stood up. He'd never use his combination to hide something after all. But he'd been missing some of the things he'd learned to swallow on the inside. Something leaped about in his lower stomach and down between his legs. Oh. Yes he had.

Chapter 55

Phoebe set the phone down and gave him a bleak smile. She was too tired to say anything more. All she could do, all the energy she could summon, was a nod when he asked *did they get him*? Yeah. They'd gotten him. And now . . . now she felt kind of empty, no not empty, just, oh fuck, fuck, there's always gonna be more Wayne Tollers and who was going to take care of them, keep the kids safe?

There would always be Bryson Houses and therapists and social workers. She'd thought about it. Wasn't her thing. And there's always be decent Commonwealth's attorneys, as they were called in Virginia. DAs everywhere else. And as much as she loved watching the Fixer at work, prowling in front of the jury box and jostling with unruly plaintiffs' lawyers, well, law? No. God no. Not for her. She'd even worked a summer with Jamie. It was great, but honestly? It was because of Jamie. She'd do anything for her—almost anything. No way was she gonna take on that job, and Jamie . . . probably wouldn't want her to.

For so long, she'd thought, maybe I'll do something with my poetry, and for sure, she still could. But teaching stupid punkasses like that shithead from class? And sure enough, he'd been missing from class that night. Brittany had talked with doe-eyed wonder about him, as if Phoebe gave a shit. Funny, come to think of it. Phoebe had minored in criminal justice. Didn't really figure out why. She liked the way the words sounded together. Simple. Not that much in life was simple, but justice for criminals should be.

Phoebe reached up for the cup of tea Jim was handing her, and she closed her eyes when he put it in her hands. The steam rose, turning her face hot and her breath thicker. She was so tired, and she really should be getting home . . . but she really didn't want to go home. He'd have to . . . well, she wasn't asking.

"You okay? You look exhausted," he said.

He sat beside her, and she felt these conflicting needs: one, to have his body close, really close; and two, to find something like white noise for all her senses. To hear, see, feel, touch, smell . . . nothing.

"I guess I should be getting home."

He looked a lot older tonight. Young and reckless and kickass all day, but now, sitting beside her, he was more poet than soldier. "No," he shook his head. "Please stay."

She was going to stay. She had to; hell, she didn't want to ever leave. "But . . . I got no clean clothes." She sounded whiny, for sure.

"I'll wash em'," he said.

"Really?"

Her eyes closed as he was saying yes. Then he was kneeling next to her, and he was kissing her neck and her hand and her cheek and he said let's get you up to bed my love and she didn't remember much more except for the cold pillow and the feel of his chest against her back later, when he crawled into bed beside her.

His voice woke her when it was still dark out. "Pheebes, love? If you want to take the 4Runner today, can you drop me off at work?"

"But it's too fucking early." She was smiling inside.

And he knew it. "Come on, I'll buy you a cup of coffee," he said.

She sat up, rubbing her eyes. "Well in that case . . ."

They both laughed, and then those lines around his eyes got all creased again. "I was thinking you could grab some stuff from your mom's."

He said 'your mom's" as if it was no longer hers and it was funny because she'd never lived away from Helen. She'd not even thought about living in the dorms or with other kids her own age. Not like she had anything in common with any of them. But right now? There was only one place she wanted to be.

"So this is a ploy to get me back here tonight?" She walked into the bathroom and found a new toothbrush waiting for her, still wrapped in a package.

"Yes, totally just a ploy," he said.

She shut the door behind her, smiling, and this time, she saw the smile reflected back to her in the mirror, and the woman she saw there was one she'd never really seen before.

Ten Days Later

Chapter 56

Troy looked dapper, as usual. She saw him regularly enough, at office parties, and somehow it never felt too uncomfortable, mingling with her therapist and her junior partner. Troy and Carl had been together ever since, well, Helen shook her head. In her mind she saw the golf club, not so much swinging through the air, but appearing as a word in a newspaper article, or two, or two hundred, or an infinity of them. She didn't care what anyone thought of her, but it weighed on Phoebe. She could tell sometimes, when Phoebe's shoulders would slump as she clicked through her newsfeed amid her endless research. Like a bird dog, or a bloodhound on a trail—that's what Phoebe was.

Come to think of it . . . The door shut behind Troy, and Helen turned her watch so she wouldn't check it every five minutes. Awful habit that law had given her, because she billed not just by the hour, but by the part of an hour, and sometimes her life was measured in five and ten minutes increments until she realized that she'd lost ten years of her daughter's . . . *stop it get a grip.*

"So Helen, you said on the phone that you'd been having nightmares, and it all had to do with Phoebe?"

She appreciated the way he got right to it. Except for when she initiated it, which was next to never, he skipped small talk;

saved it for office parties, where it belonged. "Yep. Been having the same one, and it's not going anywhere."

"Sorry to hear that. Is it the one you always had?"

"Phoebe and Richard . . ." She tapped her fingers on the leather chair and took a deep breath. She hadn't said his name aloud in years.

"In glass?"

"Yes."

"Helen, will you at least consider meeting with a trauma specialist? Remember the woman I told you about, who does EMDR? It works, I mean, not for everything, not all of the time, but it's the gold standard for trauma."

"Trauma? But I wasn't the one . . ." she squeezed her eyes shut and took a deep breath. This just never got easy. Try again. "I wasn't the one raped."

"True. But you've suffered all sorts of secondary trauma, and seeing the video counts, don't you think?"

His brown eyes met hers, and she didn't look away. It was an old habit, not to look away first, sign of weakness, but right now, maybe she was looking to him to hold her up, so the weakness was strength and the strength, weakness? She was tired, and thinking too much. *Not myself today.*

"But she's been through hell."

"And you haven't?"

It was true. She had. And some days she was still there, and maybe she'd never leave, not if—

"—Helen?"

She peeked at her watch but didn't register the numbers. "But if I had . . ." she said, and then shrugged.

"If you had what? Come on, Helen. You're not blaming yourself again, are you?"

"She's met someone, Troy."

"Ah." He leaned forward, his elbows on his thighs and the crease of his pants shifting but still angled. "She's dating?"

"Jim's his name." Helen felt the tic around her eye return from earlier that morning. "And yes, I have met him and I like him very much." She put her fingertips against her temples but the muscle was still vibrating.

Troy sat and waited. He did that a lot. Felt comforting somehow.

"She's not been home for days. I mean, dammit. I want her to be happy, but I worry and I know she loves him and he adores her. Hell, he actually is trying to get her a truck."

"You mean he's rich, then?" Troy raised his eyebrow.

"Oh no, God no." Helen waved her hand. "He's a . . ." didn't sound right to call him a mechanic, not that there was anything wrong with that. She thought about all he was, and she felt her shoulders relax a bit. "He's a mechanic, and no, not just a mechanic."

"Wasn't thinking anything."

"He's a soldier-poet-mechanic, Troy. It's just not enough to say he's a mechanic. And I think he went through hell in the war; at least, that's what Phoebe said. Now he's finishing up his undergrad degree at Mason. Last class, actually. That's how he and Phoebe met. And he's getting his Ph. D. But he's a car guy, works hard at a garage, rebuilds old engines, and, yes, he wants to get her an old 4Runner and fix it up for her, but he said he wants to surprise her with it."

"Great."

"Yes."

Helen chuckled. "Cass says he's even had Zander over at the garage a couple of times."

"No—for real?"

They grinned at one another. Zander had somehow smuggled fireworks into the last charity function Cass had taken him to, and the outcome had been . . . memorable.

"For real."

"So this, what did you call him, soldier-poet-mechanic . . . sounds like a hell of a guy. Loves your daughter. And they might have more in common than just poetry."

Helen hadn't thought of that. But of course. Jim had been in the war. "You mean PTSD?"

"I do."

"Hmm." Helen was quiet for a moment, and so was Troy.

"So Helen?"

"Yes?"

"You're missing her, aren't you?"

"Oh, gosh, I'm happy for her," she said.

"Right. Of course you are." Troy made a temple of his fingers and rested his chin on it. "Helen? It's normal to miss her. You've been a rock for the last five years for her. Never thinking of your needs. Never thinking that maybe you needed her almost as much as she needed you."

His words knocked the wind out of her, and she sat there, gasping. All she could do was nod, because her eyes welled up with tears.

"You miss her."

"Yes," she whispered. I miss Phoebe."

She sat and stared at her hands, and then reached for a tissue and wiped her eyes. It was so obvious now, but she'd never been good at figuring out how she felt. She dealt in angles and right lines and tactics and strategies, whereas this involved matters of the heart, the province of a poet, or of her Phoebe.

"That's okay, Helen, It's okay to miss her. And it's okay to let her go. You've done your job, mom."

But . . ." Her voice faltered. "I've done my job?"

"Damn well, yes. It's time to let go of that need to break through the glass."

She envisioned the glass enclosing Phoebe and Richard, and the tears falling down her face felt like tiny shards of glass threading her skin.

"She's broken free, Helen. It's time for you to break free too."

"Okay."

"Okay?"

She wiped her eyes again. "Okay."

"Good."

"Troy? Can you write that referral down for me?"

He leaned over and grabbed his white pad. Once he scribbled something down, he handed it over to her.

"So. You think maybe it's time . . . to think about dating again."

"Oh no, no," she scoffed. "Cass was telling me the same thing a little while back."

"And?"

"Oh, Troy. I'm past all that."

"You mean, you haven't suffered enough and you gotta suffer for another, what, five years, before you allow yourself to love or be loved again?"

Helen flinched, and she never flinched, not even when Brian Williams . . . *Brian? Why him, now?* "You're not pulling any punches today."

"Have I ever?"

She chuckled and shook her head. "I wouldn't have it any other way."

"So—you done beating yourself up?" He almost looked severe, *like Cass when she was on one of her fuck this and that tirades.*

"Well, you'll be the first to know if I'm not," she said.

"I'll be here, anytime, you know that, right?"

"I do." She stood up as he handed her the bill. "Thank you."

And as she drove from Tyson's to Fairfax, she thought about Brian Williams, and wondered why she'd said no every time he'd asked her out, and whether he'd ask again. Then she remembered she had a question to ask him—a question her associate would usually ask his associate, but maybe . . . she'd call him later. Just to check on it. Just to check.

Chapter 57

There were only two weeks left of classes before graduation, and Catherine was feeling confident enough; well, almost cocky, but she'd learned from losing a few early cross-country meets at home, of all places, right in front of cheering throngs of Oregon supporters not to take anything for granted. Sure, she was being mentioned as a possible candidate for the Director's Leadership Award, and Randy had told her she was looking at possibly taking honors in academics. She didn't want to assume anything, and she didn't want to ask for special favors . . . but last night, when she'd asked her mom about putting in a word for Phoebe, her mom had actually sort of snapped at her.

"For crapsake, come on Cat, this is how men have been doing it for hundreds no thousands of years, and let me tell you something else, you listening?" Her mom had this fierce look on her face, so Catherine had just nodded.

"Phoebe will make an incredible special agent. She's determined, she's courageous, and she's got this incredible intuition . . . actually, make sure you tell your advisor that there's a Commonwealth's Attorney who will vouch for Phoebe too. I mean, wow, you should've seen the look on Elizabeth's face when Phoebe—"

"—Wish I could've been there," Catherine said. "Zander gets to have all the fun trips."

"Oh my gosh, you're right," her mom laughed. "Zander was right in the middle of all that, wasn't he?"

"So you didn't say, and I thought you would, mom, that Phoebe will make a great special agent because of what her dad did to her."

"Yeah, well, I reckon that's gonna help her get her foot in the door, name recognition and all that," her mom paused. "Is that why you're in, anyway? Because of Marcy?"

Catherine sighed. They'd not talked about Marcy too much, and she wasn't sure if her mom knew the whole story. "Well, it kind of opened up my eyes to a lot so yeah, maybe," she said.

"And you really cared about Marcy a lot, really hurt, didn't it?"

Catherine's eyes were filling with tears, so all she did was nod.

Her mom leaned over and pulled Catherine to her, then kissed her on the cheek. "I never did tell you how sorry I was, or how proud I am of you, or did I, sweetie?"

Catherine put her arm around her mom and patted her mom on the back. "Once or twice," she said. "If not a hundred times."

• • •

The conversation with Randy Danner lasted all of five minutes. Catherine went looking for him after VirtSim, which was this crazy 3D training simulator the FBI used, and it pretty much just made Catherine seasick, but at least she hadn't blown up any civilians. After getting her real legs, her non-virtual legs back, Catherine had found Randy rounding a corner at about a seven-minute mile pace.

As soon as he waved at her, she'd fallen in beside him, knowing, with that athletic confidence she had, that so long as she didn't slow him down, he wouldn't mind the company.

"Mind if I run with you for a few minutes, Randy?"

"Oh my heavens no, at least so long as you don't go and make me run some crazy ass sub-six, sub-five, or whatever it is you're running nowadays mile," he said, and they'd both laughed.

"Okay," he said after they ran in silence for a couple minutes, "You're doing great, and you're not the type to come for hand-holding, so you need to ask me a tough question or you need a favor."

"Yes, I need a . . . well, it's not really a favor actually, because it's something for someone who deserves a look and will be an incredible asset."

"Oh, you got a friend from school you want us to look at?"

Catherine smiled. She'd jacked up the pace just a tad, and Randy was matching her. As always, it was going to be a battle of wills, and he didn't have a chance. She should slow it down, but that wasn't the way this worked. No mercy. It's the only way a good man would want her to play it anyway, and one thing she knew: Randy was a good man. Catherine tried not to smirk, and she accelerated into a hill. This one lasted for a good quarter-mile, which meant she could talk, and he couldn't, not at this pace.

"Not exactly. One of my lifting buddies, and my mom's best friend's daughter, well, you might have heard of Phoebe Thompson? She was in the news a few years ago, in a case involving her father and porn and then that detective got shot at a safe house—"

"—Oh, wait, you mean Judge Thompson's daughter?"

"Yes, Phoebe's graduating from Mason in May I believe, and she's a crack shot—"

"—You've shot with her?"

"Well, I'm basing that off my mom's word, but she's pretty solid, my mom is, so yes, she's a crack shot."

Randy made an assenting sound, or something like it, so Catherine continued, "She's in great shape, got the same education I got, in fact, she was ranked second her year at McClintock, and she's got a 4.0 or something like it at Mason. Plus, well, you know why I joined the FBI, right?"

"You had some personal experience with sexual assault, if I remember correctly."

Catherine sort of shrugged. Close enough. If she talked too much about her stuff, it would distract Randy from thinking about Phoebe. "Enough to wake me up to the need to get law enforcement personnel, motivated law enforcement personnel, and if you don't mind my saying it, motivated female law enforcement personnel—"

"—I get it, Catherine. I have a daughter of my own, and I can't imagine . . ." Randy's breath was coming in ragged gasps now. He sort of waved and added, "Anyway, yes, we need to recruit motivated, intelligent, and tough women. And you're saying that Phoebe . . . Thompson . . . fits the bill."

"Yes, and apparently she helped solve a case and it impressed a Commonwealth's Attorney so much that she will also give Phoebe a strong recommendation, if that will help any," Catherine said.

"Huh? Phoebe was moonlighting?"

"Sort of, yeah."

"Okay, listen Catherine," Randy said, "If you'll take your foot off the gas, I'll make a deal with you." He laughed, and then they got to the top of the hill, and she said, "Oh come on, you were the one who was accelerating. I could barely keep up with you, thank God you're slowing down," and she'd smirked and he'd rolled his eyes, and after they were both done laughing, his eyes had turned serious. And he said, "Tell Phoebe to call me. I'd be happy to talk with her and march her into a round of interviews myself if need be."

Catherine thanked him, and then she spent the rest of the afternoon waiting for a chance to call Jamie. Maybe another cup of coffee, or something like that, was in order.

Chapter 58

He woke up shaking. The undead birds kept coming undead in his dreams, and when he shook like this, it was like he died some too. For a little while, he was shaking too hard to walk into the bathroom. When he did stand up, he had to sit back down real fast, because he was about to fall.

That's when he realized he wasn't all alone. She was there. It didn't help much. It helped a little. He groaned a little, and with his arms still hugging his body, he laid down next to her. He tried to be as still as he could, and not wake her. But he was shaking, a lot.

She stirred next to him.

He tried so hard to stop.

Her eyes opened, and she reached her hand out and put it on his shoulder. "Jim? You okay?"

She could see it; he could tell from the way her eyes looked, like she was wanting to take care of him.

"Jim? Let me turn on the light, okay?"

He nodded, and his teeth were chattering so he didn't say anything.

She sat up and kind of cradled him, let him rest his head on her lap, not asking anything, just warm, her body was so warm. She sat there, rubbing her hands up and down his arms, and then through his hair over and over. "It's gonna be all right," she murmured, and her hands felt so good; she felt so good.

"Wish I could stop shaking."

"I know, I know."

She ran her hands through his hair, and he felt the tingling of it all the way to his toes. He wasn't sure if it felt good.

"Jim? Let's go see the sunrise at the beach."

"The beach?"

She kissed his head. "Yep. Come on. Well, unless you got a problem with sand."

He turned and sat up a little, attempted, feebly, a smile. "Only the kind of sand that's not near water."

She kissed his head again and then she was grinning and pulling on a bra, a shirt, and his best damn sweatshirt overtop her camos. She tossed his jeans at him.

"Come on."

He got to his feet. "You gotta drive, I think."

"Yeah, yeah. Hurry up, already."

Five minutes later, maybe ten, she was pulling onto I-66, and she was talking, hadn't really stopped talking since she'd started. *That was something no one really knew about Phoebe Thompson: girl never stops does she?*

He glanced over at her as she lit two cigarettes. As he took one from her, she asked him why he was smiling.

"You make me smile, that's why," he said. His teeth were only chattering a little, but she must have heard it, because she jacked up the heat.

"So were you having the undead bird dream?"

He nodded, and watched the smoke from his cigarette take a path he couldn't predict or control, just like his time over there.

"Man, I fucking hate dreams like that. I'm always trapped inside this glass, and I can hear my mom screaming, but she can't get to me." She flicked her cigarette out the window, and he watched the orange butt skip behind them out his side view mirror.

"Inside glass?"

Her chin worked next to him. Then she laughed, once, but it was a bitter laugh, and he knew how much it hurt her when she did that. "Yeah. With my dad."

"That's awful."

"Yeah," she said. "And so are the fucking birds."

"They are."

They drove some more. She grabbed I-495 toward Springfield, and then they took I-95S toward Richmond. He kept his window down and let the bumping of the wheels over the tarmac and the sound of her voice quiet his racing heart. She was telling him about derby and about the ocean and how she'd hadn't seen the Atlantic in years, and hitting blockers, and he listened and by the time they hit Fredericksburg, he wasn't shaking hardly at all.

"Coffee? We're going by a Starbucks and they open at four or four thirty, so we can get in and out in ten."

"They open at four? You sure?"

"Yeah," she said. "I checked when you were fucking around."

"We can still catch the sunrise?"

"Yeah. Probably. But you better get me a buttload of coffee."

He smiled. "And if we miss the sunrise, I'll be all mad."

"Yeah?"

He put his hand on hers and stroked it. "Terribly."

She practically screamed around the exit ramp, and they both laughed. "Don't you be crashing my ve-hic-le."

He could see her teeth and that was about it until they pulled into the parking lot. She shoved her hands in his back pocket and kept talking the whole time they were in there, and all the way to Richmond. From there, they were bearing east on Route 64. He just loved the rolling of her voice. Her and the coffee, dark roast, and once they were heading east, the barely-drawn outline of the fir trees. Wheels, and more mile markers, and they hit the first glint of waves roiling under the lights, and the tunnel, and in another 45 minutes, they rolled into the beach and she was asking for more coffee, and he ran in this time, leaving her at the wheel.

In a few more minutes, they pulled up to the far pier and parked in an outside lot. They gripped their coffees and she hugged him close, real close, and they headed into a dawn, pre-dawn really, cold wind and he was safe, he was safe again.

As they walked, hand in hand, to the pier's edge, he thought about all the times they were going do this, and it was all he ever wanted to do. Walk into rising suns with the one woman, the only woman, he was ever going to love again. "Phoebe?"

"Yeah?"

"You're going to be with me always, aren't you?"

"Something tells me that yes, yes I am."

Chapter 59

"Let's take a long walk," she said. She started off and he fell in behind her. "How did you, um, how do you get through this?"

She pulled the hood of her sweatshirt down and tied the strings. It was cold, bracing, and incredibly invigorating.

"Well, the VA offers some shitty counselors. I tried a couple, but I'd get pissed off, you know? It actually made me use more drugs, because they kept sending me to psychiatrists, and those assholes would write more scripts, three different scripts, or four, I lost track. Just was drugged most the time. And the AA just made me drink more."

"Really?" She wanted to get her feet wet but it was way too cold

"Yeah. Kind of ironic, eh?

She heard the military jets even before they came into sight off to her right. "Wow," she said. "Must be on their flight path." Two jets headed out to see.

"Langley," he said.

"Mmmm. So what has helped?"

"With the PTSD?" He was so beautiful. Sun made him even more so.

"Yeah. With your PTSD?"

He walked a few more steps in silence. "God. I offer it up to him. He takes it, not all of it, but some of it."

"I'm still figuring Him out. Why this shit happens, why He lets it, why? Wish I knew, wish I'd get some answers. I ask Jamie all time."

"Jamie?"

"Yeah. At least when we're talking."

"What, you get mad at her?" She swung her head over but he had something gentle in his voice.

"Aw damn, we argued, at least I argued about Toller. Ain't talked since. It's dumb," she admitted.

He didn't say much.

So she added, "But I'll see her soon and we'll be okay. I mean, I get mad at her sometimes and she doesn't really say much. She talks to God, you know?"

"I know. So do I," he said.

"And you're not mad at Him?"

"No," he said. "He didn't pull the trigger. He didn't pull any triggers."

She was trying to listen without unleashing her whys, her doubts, her questions and complaints and petitions for appeal and all the rest of it. The breeze was raising goosebumps on her arms and she was feeling tired now, but she also felt alive and in the moment and then all the stuff she wanted to ask seemed less urgent. He had shit figured out; so did Jamie. Maybe she would someday.

"You hungry?"

She thought about it and wondered why she never realized the simple needs her body had until he asked her about her needs. She was starving. And she could see a diner lit up from across the sand, sandwiched between two high rises, and she could almost taste the bacon and eggs even before they got inside a warm place with a waitress putting up with a couple old guys, weathered, not saying much, nor did they, but it was comfortable.

They were silent while they sat and she was counting the birds, the seagulls, and the planes that flew overhead.

"God made the water and the wind and the seagulls and the beautiful things," Jim said.

"Oh yeah," she said. Eggs had never tasted so good.

"But man made all the ugly stuff. And man turns this world into hell sometimes."

"Guess that makes sense."

He ate the last few bites of his pancakes, and started in on the bacon.

"But what if the assholes get to heaven after they turn this world into hell?"

He swallowed his OJ and shrugged. "No idea. I was just a sergeant. Never said I knew it all, and maybe I never will. I don't know where the bad men like your dad go. It's hard enough to live this life and if I gotta figure out the next one too, I'll end up confused and bitter."

She started to say something else, and then he held up his hand. "Hold on a sec. I gotta . . . thank you. You have no idea how good this feels."

"Being here?"

"Yes," he said. "Being here with you."

The sun was shining on the table now, and she soaked in the light some before she said, "Wish I could make it all better."

"Me too. I wish every time I woke up from my nightmares, we could just drive away, run from it, go somewhere, forget about it for a little while."

"Yeah," she said.

"But we can't and that's gotta be okay. Sometimes we can, and the rest of the time, best we can do is offer it up to Him."

"God?"

He nodded. "Ready?"

"Yeah."

She thought about this, about running from the pain when she could, and taking it the best she could, and how they both had been running alone and facing it alone for so long as they headed back out to the water. It was gonna be a long drive home, and she could ask him to explain it some more. Maybe he had more answers. Maybe. But now she wanted to watch the water and the planes and the birds and forget about it for awhile.

Chapter 60

Jim was up early drinking coffee, reading up on old 4Runners. There were two he liked, decent condition, not priced higher than market average, but also not scary-bargain basement. There was such thing as too good to be true, at least when it came to used automobiles. He had to leave for work soon, but he remembered, with a gulp, that he hadn't called his mom in two weeks. She would be up early, sitting in the sunroom probably, grading papers or maybe writing. *Never too busy to talk to you*, Jim, she'd say, so he dialed her number.

"Hey Mom."

"I was worried about you. Doing okay?"

"Oh yeah, sorry, I'm fine. Good actually."

"Just busy?"

Jim refolded the newspaper in front of his laptop and lowered the top until he heard a light click. "Well, not really. How about you? How's class? Anyone good?"

"Class is . . . what do you mean you're not busy? And yet you're not calling me or your sisters?"

"You all keeping tabs on me?" He was smiling as he stood up and stretched.

"Of course we are. You're not answering my question and I don't like that," she said.

"Funny thing is I am doing really well. Really well."

"Come on. You need to do more than monosyllables Jim, else we'll be on the phone all afternoon."

"You know how I left early a couple weeks ago?"

She sighed. He could hear it and he could see her blinking fast and folding her arms. Always dramatic. "Yes," she said. "Of course I remember. Me and your sisters were all over it."

"Know why I left early?"

She was silent. Just waiting, and the whole thing was funny.

"Oh come on, Mom. I'm seeing someone. Couldn't wait another minute to get on back to her."

"That's what it is?" Her relief was palpable. "We were worried."

"About me going on a bender?" He laughed, because it was sounding bitter otherwise.

"Well, no, yes, I don't know. How is that going anyway?"

"That's the thing about being in love—"

"—In love?"

"Yes."

"So you're good?"

"Yes," he said. "Lot better than I've been. It's just easier, you know?"

"Just don't put too much pressure on it, on her."

"No, it's not like that. I'm not him, you know?"

She sighed again.

"Mom, really. I'm not saying it's all because of her. Or that she's why I am not, why I'm sober. I was already, you know? I was doing good."

"I know you were doing good. It's just . . ."

"Well, it's just what? Dad was a drunk and so am I? Yeah, thanks." He hit the end button, and slammed around the kitchen for a couple of minutes.

The phone rang a few minutes later, and he grabbed it on the second ring. "Really? She told you to call me? Thinks I'm just a drunk, huh?"

"Wow, little bro," Anne said. "You ragin' at Mom?"

"Yeah, she tell you to call me? Or is this one of those coincidences only, you swear, because I just got off the phone with her and—"

"—Oh for goodness sakes. Instead of pissing on my day, call her. The two of you are stubborn as shit and I'm not getting in the crossfire." Anne was gone. Jim laughed. Holy crap, now she'd hung up on him. He hit the redial button.

"Hi," she said. She was sounding kind of arch.

"Mom, you really piss me off sometimes," he said.

"Hmmn. You calling just to tell me that?"

He contemplated hanging up again. But Anne would probably call him. Again. "So, you sicced Anne on me?"

"Oh okay. Listen. I'm sorry. I know you aren't your father."

He relaxed his grip on the phone. That's right," he said.

"It's just he was such a good man, before. When we first met."

"Yeah, but he didn't have a problem before he met you, right? And he didn't find God, he lost Him, right?"

She sighed again. "True."

"I'm not him. Nothing's gonna make me him. Me being in love and settling down—"

"—Settling down?

"Yeah. Planning on it. As long as she is, and I think she is, yeah. You know me. I don't take a long time to make my mind up on stuff."

"Now, see, that's a lot like your dad." She was smiling when she said this. He could tell.

"Guess he had good taste in women, you know?"

"You gonna bring her home?"

"Yeah," he said. "I will."

"Love you Jim."

"You too," he said.

"Jim?"

"Sorry."

He smiled. "I am too."

Chapter 61

It was Saturday afternoon, and the Laydiators were warming up along with The Borg Beauties. They had *Resistance is Futile* duct-taped to the backs of their uniforms. Phoebe took in the noise: the sound of skates and women harassing one another and heavy breathing from most the blockers and the team captains barking out instructions.

Her legs felt good today. She'd hardly worked out the last two weeks *except for all the sex*. She almost smiled, but there was no fucking smiling in Derby. Oh damn, now she was smiling. And he was in the audience. She'd be head jammer the entire fucking bout. Well, in between some serious head banging. She'd start with the CubeQueen, who had it coming after the last bout. Sometime in the second quarter, just when CQ wasn't expecting it; just when Phoebe had worn her down and demoralized the hell out of her— BOOM.

Resistance was anything *but* futile.

The only thing that would make it all more fun would be a banked track, but there weren't any of those within 90 miles. The closest was maybe in Philadelphia. That shit was hardcore. Old school. The speed made it more exciting and the railings and curves made the hits hurt more. She sighed, and put her hands on her hips, touching them a few times to signal the end of the practice jam.

CQ glided next to her, and they exchanged smirks. "You got it coming, Firebird."

Phoebe scoffed and gave her the finger.

Phoebe took three quick strides and skid-slammed to a stop in front of Jamie, who'd been talking strategy to the rest of the team while Phoebe messed around with CQ.

"Oh, and hey. Firebird. You got your marching orders, right?"

"What? Skate fast and score points while destroying and demoralizing?"

"Rock 'em Pheebes," screamed X-traLung.

Two more of her teammates made the Hang 'em high sign with their hands, and Phoebe bashed elbows with her three baddest blockers. Beth of course was one of them. Phoebe had forgotten to tell her . . . she leaned over and put an arm around Beth's shoulder, pulling her close.

"Toller's back in jail."

"Holy shit, that's awesome."

Phoebe patted Beth on the back and traded fist bumps.

"Pheebes!" It was Jamie's voice; Phoebe knew it without having to look in front of her. "Get that panty fixed on!"

Then the whistle blew.

Get through. Phoebe shoved her mouthpiece in and waited for the pack to drift forward. Then she clicked her invisible switch on and turned off all sound, so that all she heard was the push, the rumble, of wheels. She whispered *get through* aloud to herself. *Get through.* She bit down on her mouthpiece and felt freedom taking hold. She was a fast bird soaring, and would *get through.*

Phoebe leaned forward, one eye on CQ, and she accelerated to the left of the pack of blockers and pivots, and with the slightest of shifts right, squeezed between Murderous Marla and Beth, then feinting past Bloody Mary, Spockette, and both pivots. She was through.

Phoebe easily drifted away from the pack, and with several brisk strides, she was around the circle and approaching the pack again as Lead Jammer. She concentrated on drafting behind the other team's two blockers, and split outside, with Beth and Murderous Marla covering her, and she shot past their pivot just as Jamie landed a hip check.

A few laps later, and with several points already scored, Phoebe approached the pack again. She was coming up, and fast, on Spockette, and just when Spockette was about to spread her legs and slow her down, Phoebe lifted one foot, hopped over the near line so that she wasn't out of bounds, and grabbed hold of Jamie's outstretched hand for a gentle, firm whip-it forward.

Phoebe then touched both hips to signal the end of the jam.

At the first quarter break, a few minutes later, Phoebe stood off from her teammates a little. She couldn't handle any distractions, not when she was fucking dialed in. But she did check in long enough to growl, "We're annihilating them. And I haven't even started."

Jamie tapped Phoebe on the helmet. "You mean 'we' dontcha?"

Phoebe was swaggering, if that was possible on quad wheels. "I'm the main attraction. Might as well write that on the back of my fucking shirt. Firebird Main Attraction Thompson."

"Oh, God." Beth threw her head back and laughed.

When the whistle blew once, long and hard, Phoebe pretended her wheel got stuck. There was no way CQ could pass her any other way, and this had to look real. So her skate got good and stuck, and she froze, like she couldn't figure out what was wrong. And then, once she spotted CQ halfway around the bend, Phoebe took a few strides, and then she wind milled her arms, like she was going down . . . nope, just found her balance, and there was CQ, she could feel her almost, feinting no doubt to the inside, and sure enough, going wide, right as the bend cut into the straightaway.

Phoebe waited . . . then crashed into CQ's hip, low and hard, damn hard, clean hit, but barely clean, arguably clean. And CQ tipped back, regained control, and then the edge of her wheel caught the edge of Phoebe's skate, and CQ was going down now, except *no no no*, Jamie had been barreling alongside the other teams blockers, and wasn't seeing CQ going down, and now Phoebe was through, but watching it all around the corner.

In slow motion now. She tried to yell "Jamie watch out" but before she got all the words out, Jamie came around the bend, full bore, head twisted slightly to the side, and she still didn't see CQ, who was trying to get her hands out in front of her before hitting the black concrete, and then Jamie, not looking, or seeing, rammed straight into CQ's foot.

Forever. It took forever. And in that moment, of seeing Jamie go down, while Jamie wasn't seeing the point of contact, Phoebe tried to cover the distance between them. As slow as Jamie was falling, Phoebe thought she could close the distance in the frozen moments, until then she realized that she was also frozen. Or if not frozen, barely moving.

It took Jamie forever. Forever, and yet no time at all, before she got swept upwards, her feet completely taken from her, and she floated, head perpendicular to the ice and then her back hit the ground but only after her head absorbed the full weight of her body slamming into something unmovable.

Phoebe didn't know if the crowd went silent before or after she heard her best friend's head crack against the concrete. The sound, that *sick* sound, was the only one she heard.

Jamie was out cold by the time Phoebe, now on her knees, skidded to a stop beside her. The only thing moving on Jamie was the wheels on her skates, and they were spinning around and around like a crazed windup doll that comes alive in the middle of the night, after all the other toys have been laid to rest.

Kay got to Jamie before Phoebe, and then everyone was taking a knee like football players did when someone got rung up, and then she heard the crowd again, but they weren't yelling or cheering. They were almost completely silent. And then Jamie wasn't still, but she wasn't awake either. She was shaking some, a little all over, and this horrible moaning came from her right before she started to shake, not like all limbs jerking or anything, just a gentle shaking, head rolled back, and that animal moaning and she heard someone yell Call 911 STAT and someone else was screaming, must have been Kay, *get my medical kit NOW.*

Phoebe tried to get closer but Kay barked at her, barked at her and three other Laydiators to *get out of the way no I mean it* and Phoebe could feel her heart beating in her throat, racing really, and the more Jamie shook, the harder, more painful, so painfully fast, beat her own heart.

"Get my medical kit NOW" repeated Kay, and Beth came skidding over with it. "Keep your hands away from her face." Kay put a hand on one of the refs, and added, "You'll get your hand bitten off if you put it in her mouth."

"But—"

"—If you want to help, go meet the EMTs at the door. Tell them we've got possible status epilepticus. Patient has history of epilepsy and subdural hemorrhage."

The ref started to ask another question, and Kay snapped, "Beth. Go with him."

Beth's face was ashen and tear-streaked; she turned and skated away without saying a word.

"Please God, please let her be okay," someone was praying.

Phoebe couldn't see what Kay was doing. She'd ordered a few players to block the stands, and the pads and helmets formed a visual barrier. From somewhere off not too far off in the distance, she heard an ambulance, and then there was motion and movement and noise and then someone was screaming now, really screaming, and it was her, and then—there he was. He was holding her, part hugging, part holding her back, because she was crying and screaming. He just kept whispering, "It's gonna be all right, it will, come here, no, Phoebe, come here, stay here," and someone else, probably Kay, was saying slow, but clear, "Stay right here Jamie, Jamie, stay right here."

Chapter 62

She saw a crowd in the background but they were silent. The team was there. Laydiators. But they were all kneeling down, taking a knee like football players did when someone's gotten laid out and they're waiting for a stretcher. Someone was praying, "Please God, please let her be okay," and for just a moment, she could feel cold; it was cold, so cold. Then she was floating up and over and she was looking down, trying to see through the pile of equipment, helmets, pads, and players, but she couldn't make it out, couldn't see who was on the ground.

The last thing she'd seen was Phoebe screaming *look out*, but she couldn't see Phoebe or anyone else clearly. It felt like she was trying to see through a fog. *They must have used the fog machine during the break, yes, during the break.*

It was light now, much more light. From far, far away, she made out more noises. Maybe a whisper of a siren. And the sound of muffled screaming, and she wasn't sure what the siren and the screaming was because she just felt peace and light, like going Home, and somehow she knew there was always peace, peace remembered, peace rediscovered. From much farther away now, a man was whispering, "It's gonna be all right, it will, come here, no, come here, stay here," and someone else was saying over and over again, "stay right here Jamie; Jamie, stay right here."

And then the world faded.

She was not here—she was there. Which was now *here*. She went there, where time is different. She slid in and now was done sliding out of time. She is out of here, there, whatever and wherever there was and now, now she was here. Here now. Time had folded in on itself and then it wasn't. But she was.

And then it was pure silence and light.

She was not afraid. She waited. She'd been here before so she knew that if she waited long enough, her mom would come.

She tried to get oriented and it was so strange, trying to comprehend her surroundings when the usual dimensions, like time and space, had different limitations. None of the usual rules applied. Looking around and waiting, for example? It lasted no time, and yet time, time as she knew it, would have passed, had she been back there. But here, and now she knew what here was, here there was no elapsed or passed or minutes or years even.

She kept thinking, *but I don't know how to explain this*, and then she heard a familiar voice say, "Stop trying to use what you learned there to explain what is here."

"Anne?"

"One and only."

"I've missed you. I know you visit me all the time. But still—it's been painful and hard, missing you."

"I know." Jamie could feel Anne, almost as if she was hugging and being hugged, but in spirit. It was discombobulating in so many ways, and yet familiar. Jamie then was laughing. "Do you know the name of the team we were playing tonight?"

"Tonight? Ah. Well. Perhaps tonight is not the right word."

"What do you mean?"

"Nevermind, Anne 'said.' Nope, I don't recall who you were playing."

"Well, they were called the Borg. You know, from Star Trek."

"Yes. I recall. And you're seeing a parallel in heaven. Because you're connected to me, us, the One. That's an interesting comparison Jamie darling."

"Yeah. But there's nothing . . . malevolent about it. I still keep, what? Not my body?"

"Not your body."

"But my individual spirit."

Anne was saying yes without speaking again. Jamie was almost used to it already. Jamie felt a lightness in being, not so much a touch but a sense of what it used to feel like to touch or be touched but immediate and so much stronger than it felt back there. As in, the way-back, the way her mom used to call the back of the station wagon, and that was earth, the way-back, or the way-beyond.

"That's another interesting comparison."

Jamie laughed. *"Hey, I could get used to that. Hearing you before you really talk."*

"If you listen real hard in the way-beyond, you can hear us, you know?"

"Yep. But it gets exhausting." Jamie saw another swirl appear. That's what Anne was here, a pink-yellow-green swirl, like an ever-curling candle. This swirl had more green-blue in it.

"Hi, Mom."

"Darling."

"I've missed you, Mom." Jamie was sobbing now, the pain of joy so long delayed, the relieving of a more than decade-old heartbreak, realizing only now how much she'd encased the pain and sorrow in a vat of cold hardness frozen in time. It was now thawing and the thawing left her breathless.

She could see inside her mom's mind, and she watched this cascade of images. Jamie as a baby; as an adorable five-year old kid in Mary Janes and a collared jumper; about to leap off a diving board screaming, "Hey Mom look at me." A little older now, maybe ten, and she was waving goodbye to her mom before she headed off to class from the front office of her school. Thirteen now, and sitting beside her mother's bed, confused, trying to look brave; she was very brave. The next image was a few years later, and she was in a cold metal tube getting another MRI, and she had wondered why she wasn't cold during that one; now she understood. Then she was speaking gently to a child on a horse.

Then she was painting a fence and a butterfly flew past and she murmured, "I miss you Mom" and another butterfly fluttered in sight and the butterflies flew off together and Jamie had started to cry, really hard. A cloud split and a passing shower left the tiniest rainbow off to the west, toward the mountains, and the butterflies had come back into view again. She was sure they were mother and child somehow.

And then she was walking around the estate, pacing as she always did in the middle of the night, listening for everything, God, intruders, anyone in need or creating a need. And she shoved her hands in her pockets and smiled, because her barn jacket was just like one her mom used to wear, and she'd just dreamed of her mom when she napped in her chair in the barn.

"You've been here all these times?"

"And many, many more."

And then she saw one more, a shot of something she hadn't seen yet, but she knew it was her, her and Phoebe pacing alongside one another, Phoebe demanding something in her fragile-hard way, and Jamie chuckling, but her head was hurting so bad. Still, Jamie threw her arm around Phoebe and said, "I'll try to get you an answer, Pheebes, but these things can take awhile," and Phoebe glared, and scuffed her boot on the pavement and snapped, "Goddamn it all, the family's waited long enough."

"This hasn't happened yet."

"No. It hasn't."

"But I'm in pain there."

"Yes, yes, that's how it will be." Her Mom's swirl was still there, but now she was aware of a white swirl as well; and within that swirl was Him. He was a man, dressed all in white, and he had long blonde hair. She felt overcome with reverence and could she have knelt, she would have.

"Jamie, of you I ask much; your mission is great. Your shell has grown attenuated and about this we can do little. But your mission is great, and I will be with you all along. As I have been; even more so."

"The pain will be worse when I return?"

"Phoebe must make it stop; on this, she will work. It is a task most great, and that is why you are with her. This is not your first time with her. You know that, right?"

"I'm always with her," she said, and she saw many different versions of the two of them together; different people on the outside, same souls. Different times, same start and same return.

"Almost always, yes."

"What must she stop?"

"What was she working on?"

"Sex crimes—that's her . . . mission, right? Like modern day slavery?"

"Yes. It is a great mission. It's been going on long enough. It is a lot of you I ask," God said.

"It will hurt worse than it does? Often? I mean," she shivered a little, "Worse than it's been?"

Her mom's swirl was close. It felt like her mom's cold fingers were brushing against her burning forehead. "Much worse darling."

"But mom, the pain—it's . . ." Jamie was crying now. God was there too, but now she was talking to her mom and she could admit it all. She'd never told anyone how bad it was. It was more than she'd ask anyone else to bear; it was part of why she skated, just to get her mind off it sometimes, or forget about the pain for awhile. It was either that or take all sorts of—

"Take them. Take more. Take anything you are offered by doctors. Take illegal stuff."

"But Mom."

"Let Phoebe take care of you. Tell her. You *must* tell her."

"That I'm in pain? But she'll worry."

"It's the only way. She will help you. You're meant to be her guide, Jamie. But the pain . . . she can help. She'll have a way. She'll find one."

"But I . . . oh my God, forgive me," Jamie cried. "It's a lot You ask . . . Mom, it's a lot."

"I know darling. I love you and I will see you soon."

"Time is different here. I love you too Mom."

Her Mom was still there, but she stepped backwards. Now God encircled her, and the light, the happiness of being with Him was almost unbearable. *I love you.* It almost wasn't language at all. It was a knowing, complete and total, a circle that ended in Him.

"I chose this. It's my path and it's her path and I must go help her complete her mission, our mission, so we can get back Home."

Jamie watched something go down, like swirls, one was her, but before, and one was Him, she knew; she knew Him from His voice, the one she heard so often when she walked the grounds alone at night. It was her, but another . . . version of her, and she was saying, "Okay, I can, yes, I can," and a fast-moving progression of images followed. The rape was there. A lot of hospital scenes and there she was on the ground and Phoebe was screaming . . . now she was in the OR and the bright lines were shining overhead and she could hear the doctor asking for instruments. At least seven people were in the room, and she was very cold; she knew it was her under the blue sheets somehow.

"Clamp it."

"You sure, doctor?"

"Yes." She could see inside the doctor's mind, and he was surveying veins and arteries and parts of Jamie's brain on a camera, and then he compared what he saw to about ten other images of other brains he'd seen . . . and found one that matched Jamie's; then another; then a third one . . . yes. Clamp it."

Then the doctor was looking at the camera again, and his fingers were almost impossible to see under the blood.

"Come, daughter. You don't need to see the rest of that. You're in good, capable hands."

"INOVA?"

"Come," He said. "You see, that's what you saw. And you also saw . . ." His light swirled again, and she was holding a child and watching another one race from one edge of a pasture to a barn, and she was laughing, and her head wasn't hurting that day.

"Phoebe's?"

"She's around, of course."

"You realize if I go back, she will ask me about her dad."

"Yes."

"And I will tell her . . . what?"

He didn't answer, but she wasn't frustrated with Him. Well, not as frustrated as she expected she'd be. "Why won't you tell me?"

He didn't answer, and that's when she knew the answer, and it was both the right answer and it was a hard one to swallow, hard, but not hard, because punishments for the hardest of crimes could be nothing but hard; it was hard, and for a moment she doubted, she wondered if it was too hard . . . and then she let that feeling, that thought—go. She stopped thinking about Phoebe's dad, who was no longer, for there was love: she felt more love condensed in that feeling, not a moment, not time, not timed, because there was no way of measuring it, but she felt more love inside, within, even through, within her, within Him, and now given to her, His love, and she knew that was His answer, not just to this question but to all questions. For love meant many things, and even the hardest things that must be done were done with love . . . by Him.

Then He was gone, but not before He said, "Now get your mission done, Jamie, so you can come here and talk more, hurry Home, and stop playing that damn roller derby."

She couldn't help but laugh, then she knew it was time to go because Anne whispered, "It's time, I love you, kiss Phoebe for me and tell her I'm watching and I'm proud, always, always proud," and then Anne smiled and was gone again. And then her Mom's swirl appeared.

"Is it time?"

"Dearest, I will be with you always."

"But Mom—"

"—I know. Jamie. I know. I love you."

"Mom, No! Not yet! Don't go, no, please, Mom!"

"When the pain is the worst, just talk to me, and I'll be there. I promise."

"But Mom . . ."

"I love you Jamie."

"No, Mom, please, please don't . . ."

Chapter 63

"I don't know if you can hear me, but the nurse told me to keep talking to you. Oh, and thanks a lot for giving me fucking power of attorney. You know, they were asking me all kinds of shit the first night. Supposedly you died like three times. Yeah, that's right. You heard me." Phoebe wiped her eyes on Jim's sweatshirt. She had no idea when she'd gotten it and she didn't know where he was right now. Probably at home . . . was it Wednesday? Or Thursday?

"You know what? I'm wearing Jim's sweatshirt. It's dark green, from Mason. I think I'm wearing his fucking sweats too, because it's so cold in here. I love him Jamie. I have no doubt of it. I didn't know what it meant to love a man. And now I do and I never even told you about him, did I? I mean, aside from all the times I've been telling you the last couple days. Have I been? I think I have. He was there that night, when they took you away. I was screaming and he was holding me back. It was killin' me watching you; it was so, so fucking scary. Oh . . . I am crying again. This is crazy. I didn't tell you I loved you, the last time we talked. Damnit. I meant to tell you but I had to go and get all crazy and shit, and all I could see when I was writing "Childfucker" on his front door was the look in your eyes when you hugged me that night."

Phoebe groaned and looked up at the clock. It was ten-thirty, and almost deserted on the floor. So no one was there, not Catherine, not Zander, not Cass, not Jim, and not her mom, no one, they were all gone home she guessed . . . it was just her and the machines and . . . *please be here too Jamie.*

"You said that night that there were other ways to heal. And that we were okay, and that you loved me. And I didn't tell you how I felt about you. I didn't even hug you back. I shrugged, because I was angry, and I felt like you didn't care about my pain, that you wanted me to just forget the hell I've been through. That you wanted me to be something no one should want me to be, that you wanted me to be like you, and you're a fucking saint.

"No, no. I wasn't really mad at you. Maybe you are a saint, maybe you're a prophet, a servant of God, I don't even know what you are, not really. I wish I knew. I wish I knew so I could find you and tell you all the things I need to tell you. I need to tell you about what I'm gonna do with myself; I need to tell you about Wayne Toller; I need to tell you about Catherine and she's got me an interview with the FBI and that was your doing wasn't it? She didn't say, but she smiled a little bit, and then she was telling me stories about how she trained, and oh my God Jamie, I was so excited, but I'm such an asshole, I acted all like it was no big deal, and then she invited me to go to the range with her and that's when I stopped acting like I didn't care, I mean, I just plain forgot to be an asshole, you know?

"So we went to the range, and she's fucking amazing, you should have seen her, even Anne would've had a hard time keeping up with her, all competent and serious, I wish you could've come with us, wish you could have . . . she is beautiful you know, Jamie? Just sayin' the stuff I'd never say to your face because you're a saint or whatever you are and you say you don't care and maybe you don't, but if you do, well all I can say is Catherine gets a little dreamy when I talk about you and I realized that I talk about you all the time, especially now, especially with you gone but not gone, oh my God, Jamie, I am so sorry. I didn't say it. I've been needing to say it to you, and it's like burning my heart up, not knowing if I can say it to you.

"I shouldn't have snapped. But I was so angry, and I still am sometimes, well, I'm angry but now I know what I'm angry about and it's not you, it's not at you, but for awhile I was, it was, oh what am I saying? I was wrong. That's what I'm saying.

"It's just . . . I wanted to think you didn't understand, that you were like all the others, who stare at me, who judge, who want me to forget about it, to shut up about it, because it's just easier if no one talks about any of this. I'm just, I'm just so tired of being quiet, of carrying this fucking truth that no one wants to see, not my shame not my sins but now they're all a part of me, and no one wants me because of it, or that's what I was thinking that night.

"I was thinking that you didn't want me either, that you wanted me to forget it all, and that was a repudiation of me, of what happened to me, to so many of us, dammit Jamie, don't you see? It's always one more repudiation really in an endless string of them. I see it in their eyes when I walk past, or I did, I did until I met him. Him. Yes, Jamie. He sees me.

"And that night, I was sure you didn't see me. But you did see me. You saw a different part of me, didn't you? Not the part-raped, part-dead woman, oh hell, if that makes sense. You don't see that, do you? You see something else, and I've been racking my brain the last few days trying to see what you see in me. I mean, you're my best friend. You said so, well, sort of, didn't you? I'm your next of kin so I must be . . .

"Jamie. You still with me? You were beaten and raped and left for dead, and yet, well, I don't see that when I look at you. I see the sister I never had. I see this woman who I want to be when I . . . grow the fuck up. I've looked up to you ever since that day— you remember that? When I asked you about your tattoo? And Zander was there, and he ran off and . . ."

"He always was a pain in the ass."

"Jamie? Jamie?"

Phoebe knelt on the floor, and put her hand on Jamie's. It felt so cold, underneath all those wires. "Please, please, be here Jamie. I gotta know I made the right decision, because if you're not in there, then I just kept you here for me, and . . ."

Jamie's eyes fluttered, and then Phoebe took her lips to Jamie's hand and kissed her cold hand. "Please be here."

"I never left."

"You heard all that?"

Jamie's hand cupped Phoebe's cheek, and wiped some of the tears away. "Yep. You sure do talk a lot."

Phoebe grinned.

"And who's this Jim? Because I saw you and him and he's the one, isn't he?"

"You saw him?"

"Yes. I saw him and you and I was holding your baby and that's about when I came back. Wasn't gonna miss holding . . ." Jamie's eyes closed, and Phoebe started yelling, "Someone help . . ." but Jamie shook her head and laughed softly. "I'm not going anywhere, Pheebes. And I know you love me. And God loves you too, he told me to tell you some other stuff, but first, the best color for 4Runners is forest green."

"How did . . ." Phoebe gulped. "Yeah, I like forest green too. Is that . . . is that all He said?"

"We've got years to talk all this over. But now, now I want you to call Jim and have him come and take you home. Oh, my gosh, you gotta tell Jim that Christopher's playing cards with God—and winning."

"What?"

"Beats me. He'll know what it means, and I think it's supposed to make him feel better."

Phoebe was too tired to explain. She shook her head.

Jamie squeezed her hand. "And I want you to sleep, for at least a day. I'm here now. And I'm gonna be here for a long time."

"I love you Jamie," Phoebe said.

"Don't forget to call Cass and your mom before you go to sleep, my sister, and I love you too," Jamie said.

Chapter 64

Helen gripped her elbows with her hands and stared off at the budding forsythia and cherry trees outside her office building. It wasn't like her to feel aimless and dreamy. And now that Jamie was all right, Phoebe would be all right.

Ah. Yes. Phoebe. She really was going to be all right. So why did the mere thought of her make her feel like crying? Helen sighed. And then she walked down the hallway and knocked on Cass's door.

"Come in."

"Hey partner," Helen said. She tried to smile, but it was more of a ghost of a smile. Her real mood was too gray, more like a mood sepulcher filled with false cheer. Helen shook her head. That barely made sense. It wasn't the kind of thing she usually thought. No one was dead, dying, or buried.

"You look like hell, partner," Cass said.

Helen sat down and gave up smiling. It was a relief, not having to force it. "Yes, I probably do."

"So I heard that Jamie's gonna be fine."

"Yes, thank God," Helen said.

"Zander was praying every night for her, and he was crying. It was horrible. I had no idea how he felt about Jamie."

Helen wiped a nonexistent thread off her suit jacket. "I think Jamie has that effect on a lot of people. Did you know she made Phoebe her next of kin? And Pheebes was the one who said to keep all the machines going?"

Cass nodded. "Yep. Power of attorney. Lot of responsibility for someone Phoebe's age. Reckon she did fine with it. Really good, actually."

"They're best friends. I didn't realize how close they were, not until I saw them at the funeral together."

"Can't believe Anne's been gone for two months."

"Me either," Cass said.

"So much has changed just, just in that time." Helen waved her hand. She was tired, more tired than she realized. "Never see Phoebe anymore. Almost like she's moved in with Jim, you know?"

Cass nodded. "Yeah. Cat's not even coming home for the summer."

"No, really?"

Cass pushed back from her desk and grabbed a water out of her fridge.

Helen shook her head when Cass held up a bottle.

"Yep, really," Cass said.

"How do you . . . get used to it?"

Cass gulped down some water and then threw her hair back out of the way. "Don't. But then you do. And girls? They come back, I mean, they stay close, when they need you, they do, and it helps having Frank and Zander." A gentle look came over Cass. "I'm sorry."

"What? Because I'm alone?" Helen didn't wave her hand or scoff; in fact, she felt sad and she didn't try to hide it this time.

"Yeah. Because you're alone. You gonna accept Brian William's standing offer? To take you out for a beer?"

"How'd you know about that?"

Cass's eyes were twinkling. "Well, we trial attorneys talk a lot, ya know?"

Oh my God, my heart's beating faster? "Come on. "What did he say?"

"He asked me if you were gay."

Helen's mouth dropped open. "No."

Cass threw her head back and started laughing, and then she was laughing so hard she could barely talk.

"He didn't?"

"Oh my God . . ." Cass stopped laughing long enough to gasp, "No. No. Just teasing."

Helen raised an eyebrow. "Hmmm. Maybe that would be good for my reputation," she said, and then she started to laugh just as hard as Cass was laughing.

Cass wiped her eyes, and smiled. "He asked me to ask you if you were ever gonna grab a beer with him, or something stupid like that. And I told him I would, and then I had to go back in the courtroom. Anyway, partner, God made you two for one another, and hey, you can grab a beer at the Irish bar down the street, what are you gonna lose doing that?"

"Oh all right."

"All right?"

Helen nodded. "Yes. I will call him."

"Now?"

Helen stood up and rolled her eyes, laughing. "Yes. Now."

Chapter 65

Phoebe had no idea what day it was. She was in his bed, and she was alone, and she hadn't eaten anything solid in days. She was sure of that. And she had a killer headache. And yet . . . she smiled. Jamie was okay.

She rolled over in bed and smelled coffee. If he was home, she'd be so happy. She hadn't kissed him last night, or even told him how much she'd been missing him. It was crazy, how much she'd gotten used to the feel of him, the smell of his aftershave, the slightest hitch in his step, the creases around his eyes when he smiled, the grey cast of his eyes when he talked about fighting. Oh, she could write poems about him all morning.

She didn't just miss him. She missed the fact that she didn't really think about him the last few days. It made the space above or around her heart ache a little; and it ached too, thinking she'd done the same thing to Jamie these last few weeks, before the accident. She'd pretty much discarded her, kind of like she'd been ignoring Sascha for most the last two years. No good reason why.

She'd call Sascha soon. Right? Tell her Toller had gotten out, and then she'd tracked him; that she'd met a guy, and then almost lost Jamie . . . and now she was back home. She laughed. *Home? Wow. Have I lost my mind?*

"Good to hear you laughing again." Jim was standing by the door. She shivered a little. It had been so long.

"Time is it?"

"Well," he smiled, and sat beside her on the bed. "I would say it's time to get some loving but . . ."

"But what?"

"Maybe I should pour you a cup of coffee first? Like foreplay?"

She grinned. "Okay. Deal."

His place was clean, like he'd been up scrubbing baseboards all night, probably wearing no shirt because that made extra laundry. She sat at the kitchen table, and tried really hard to find a cobweb or a dust bunny, and when she got tired of searching, she sipped on the French Roast he'd poured for her and looked up at him. He was thinking something, kind of like a question forming, serious look about him.

"What?"

He rested his chin on his hand.

"Jim?

"I just missed you," he said. "Getting so used to having you here, and this had been home for over a year but now when you're not here, it doesn't feel like a home."

She took her time drinking coffee. She had so much to say, but she didn't even know what day it was. Then again, who cared about the time or day or time of day? All they really had was now, sure as anything, now she knew that.

"That's what I was thinking, when I woke up this morning. Well, it is morning, right?"

"Saturday, yep."

"Fuck, you gotta work?" She didn't even try to guard her sadness. She had no doubt what her eyes were showing now.

He took her hand in his. "Ronnie gave me off. I told him what happened."

And then she was talking, no transition or anything, saying, "Jamie went to heaven. She was dead and she told me what she saw when she came back."

He took it all in, and then he rose and grabbed the coffee pot. She nodded when he refilled hers and then he sat back down. "A near death experience?"

She nodded. "You believe in that?"

"Of course," he said.

"Yeah?"

"Oh man. God's . . . well, if it weren't for Him, I'd have folded my hand a few times."

Phoebe snapped her fingers. "Yes. That's it. By the way, Jamie told me to tell you Christopher's at peace. The exact words actually were, 'Playing cards . . .'" Phoebe shook her head and chuckled. "'Playing cards with God—and winning.'"

"Did you tell her about . . ."

"No."

The light enveloped Jim again, the way it had when he listened to her read poetry, and she got it, she got that he was reverent, that he felt the hand of God, somehow she got it, not really knowing what it felt like until she watched Jamie come back from the other side. Now she understood, maybe just a little, of what it was to be loved by, or to love, something bigger; she felt more than just his love.

Maybe.

"She also told me that God also liked forest green 4Runners. And I swear I ain't hinting, Jim. It was just the craziest thing. God knew that?" She was half-expecting him just to stare at her funny, but he didn't.

He was laughing, and then he was kissing her, and he was telling her how much he missed her and she was saying *how about if you show me*. And she really did lose track of time after that.

Chapter 66

"Hey Mom."

"Phoebe! So good to hear from you sweetie."

"Sorry I haven't called in a few days."

Helen smiled at the phone. "It's okay. I see the notes you leave on the kitchen table when you grab clothes, or in my office when you drop off Zander. Hey, isn't he helping Jim in the garage after school sometimes?"

"Oh my God, Mom. It's so cute. He is, and Jim says he's actually kinda helpful. Oh yeah, and Catherine might swing by."

Helen pictured Zander bumping up the walls in the office like a pinball, and she laughed. "Actually, doesn't surprise me."

"What doesn't? Zander or Catherine?"

"Well, either—Catherine is prepping you for the interview, right?"

"Yeah, yeah Mom, you cool with that?"

"With what? You applying to the FBI?"

"Yeah," Phoebe said.

"Yes." Helen laughed aloud. "Oh my gosh, you always loved those cop shows as a kid. It's all you would watch. I mean, any and all cop shows, especially ones with female leads, not that there were many of them, and you were all over them, asking questions, asking if you could get a gun, yes, you were all over that as a kid. Makes total sense."

"Good. And what about Zander not surprising you? I thought you'd at least register a bit of shock on his account," Phoebe said. There was just the slightest bite in Phoebe's voice, but Helen knew Phoebe didn't mean it.

Then Helen grinned a little. "Oh Phoebe, you were the same way sometimes, until Anne got you working in the barn."

"I was like Zander?"

"Well, not as wild. No one is, but you were kind of full of it, you know?"

"Me?" Phoebe was rolling her eyes at the phone, Helen had no doubt of it.

"Well, let's just say you've never taken any shit from anyone, right?"

"Hmm," murmured Phoebe. "What about Dad?"

"Oh come on, we really need to go over that again? It was not your fault darling. None of it. I mean, come on, seriously. I don't wanna ever hear you say anything like that again."

Phoebe was silent.

"You doing okay, love?"

"You know, most the time I am, I really am. It's hard, Mom. Some things you get over but some things, I don't know if you ever get over them all the way, you know?"

Helen stood up and started pacing. "Yeah. I know. I still have these nightmares. Might even talk to a trauma specialist."

"What kind of nightmares, Mom?"

"Aw, really awful ones. Well, always the same one pretty much."

"What happens?"

"In the nightmare?"

"Yeah," Phoebe said.

"I'm watching, and you're in a glass enclosure—"

"—And you see me and are screaming but you can't get to me?"

"Yes . . . how . . ."

"Because we've been having the same dream."

"No," Helen said.

"Yeah."

"Crap." Helen felt dizzy, and rather than try to find her sofa or her chair, she sunk down against the wall, which was almost becoming a habit as of late, this sinking down thing.

"Yeah, I know, right?"

"Yeah. Maybe it's time to break the glass. Bury it."

"Bury it?"

Helen rested her head on her knees. "Well, spread your dad's ashes. We never did that, and we swore we would, or we said we'd do it when we were ready, didn't we?"

Phoebe sighed.

"Only if you're ready."

"Yeah, Mom. Ready as I'll ever be, you know?" Phoebe's voice was a mix of tender and brave. Just the way she always was in some elemental way.

"Where should we spread them? You have an idea?"

"Oh fuck, Mom. It's gotta be at Great Falls, right?"

Helen nodded, her whole body rocking as she then said, "How about on Sunday?"

"Yeah."

"I can swing by Jim's?"

"Okay, yeah, let's do it. Maybe early in the morning."

"It's a plan."

"Mom?"

"Yes?"

"Wasn't your fault either," Phoebe said.

Chapter 67

Helen and Brian Williams had been at the Irish bar for a couple of rounds and that was about the time she realized just how good looking he really was. Helen took a sip of her Porter and felt a smile rising, no, tugging a little, at the corner of her mouth. There was something about Brian's greying temples that was making her, *oh how ridiculous, really*. She gave up trying not to smile.

"So, how many cases have we tried together?" she asked.

"The more important question is how many times does a man have to ask you out anyway?"

"You know what, Brian? I really don't know. It's been awhile."

He took a sip of his beer and she found herself looking at his hands, then his cuff links, and she stopped at his chin, with its solid triangular bottom. When she looked in his eyes, there was laughter there, a lot of it. Someone bumped into Brian's shoulder, so he moved a little closer to Helen.

"I'm glad you finally said yes."

"If I remember correctly, I called you this time."

Now he was smiling. "You did, didn't you?"

"I did. Although to be honest, I have no idea how to, um, well, it's been a long time since . . ." She hoped she wasn't blushing, making a mess of this conversation really.

He put a hand on her leg, and traced a line on it up to her thigh, and she started to laugh, and then he leaned toward her and whispered, "Something tells me you will remember easily enough." He took his hand off her leg, and he laughed too.

"Oh my God, Brian, I wasn't expecting that." She didn't say all the other stuff she was thinking, because she could still feel his hand on her.

"Good," he said. "Surprise has always been one of my favorite tactics."

"Ah," she said, "Just as preparation has been one of mine."

"So aside from hiring a private investigator, how do you prepare to take a man out for a beer?"

"Wait," she said, "You think I'm paying?"

They both smiled.

"And I didn't need to hire a private investigator," she said. "That's what I got junior associates for."

"Oh, I love it," he said. "Find out anything that scared you off?"

"Oh God, can't be worse than what would scare you off," she said.

"And it hasn't, Helen, and it won't, okay?"

She took a deep breath, and fixed him with this look, and it was as steely as it was vulnerable. "Is that a promise?"

"What? That I don't care about your past?"

"Yes."

"Okay. It's a promise. Come on, I already know all this, okay? Just like you know my stuff."

Helen nodded again. Brian's first marriage had ended very publicly. She drank a few more sips of beer. She was going to have to let this go, let Richard go, just let it go. "Okay," she said.

"Okay, now that we got that out of the way, how about if we get out of here," he said.

She reached for her purse, and he put his hand on hers. "Mind if I get this?"

She laced her fingers through his, and nodded.

He didn't let go of her hand right away, and she didn't want him to.

When they got outside, he said, "So, where you parked? Back at your office?"

"I am, yes."

He walked beside her and didn't say too much, which was good. She had all these things she could say, but none of them sounded right, so she just let the cool spring night take them where it would.

They reached the ramp and he took her hand. And then they were at her Range Rover and she turned and leaned against the back of it. Now he was holding both her hands.

"Helen, I don't want the night to end," he said. "Tell me you don't either."

"I don't either."

He kissed her very gently, and she took her hand and pulled his head towards her. His lips were hard then soft; his tongue, soft, but hard. She pressed her hips into his and kind of shuddered, and that's when he whispered, "And I don't want to stop at kissing you. Please come home with me." He bent over and pushed his tongue against her neck and she groaned and he groaned and she was smiling when she whispered, "Okay."

Chapter 68

Zander poked his head under the hood. "Jim?"

"Yep?"

"Need anything? Ronnie's sending me out to Starbucks."

Jim stood up and stretched his back. "Sure, I'd love a coffee."

"Venti? Color of cardboard?"

"Yes, please."

"I'm on it," Zander said, and bounced off.

"Oh, Zander?"

"Yes, Jim?"

"When you get back, if you want, we can go get Phoebe in her 4Runner."

Zander grinned. "You're finished?"

"This morning, yeah. Figure I'll surprise her with it."

"K. It's green, right?"

Jim smiled. "Right."

Zander took a skipping first step, and then jogged off.

Ronnie walked over. "Good kid, eh?"

"Like a little brother, actually."

Ronnie reached over and grabbed a clipboard. "So, you got your girl's 4Runner all set?"

Jim couldn't stop smiling. "Yep. I think she's gonna like it."

"So is this like your version of an engagement ring?"

"Oh, man, I don't know," Jim said.

"Come on, JJ, from the sound of it, she ain't the type who likes fancy diamonds."

"Got that right." Jim set his wrench down on the rack. And then he looked Ronnie in the eye. "Tell you the truth, Ronnie, I was thinking about asking her, but it seems kind of too soon."

Ronnie finished writing something on his clipboard and then tucked the pen in under the clasp. "Too soon?"

"Yeah," Jim said.

"Too soon for you? Too soon for your girl? Or too soon for other people?"

"Well, when you put it like that—"

"—Only people you gotta please is the two of you, right?"

Jim was about to say yeah, but Zander showed up carrying coffee in both hands, so instead, he reached out and shook Ronnie's hand. "Thanks for the advice."

Ronnie looked Jim in the eye. "Any time."

"So we gonna get Pheebes?" Zander handed Jim the coffee.

"Yes, come on," Jim said.

"She's gonna like it, and then she's gonna say I can have it in a few years, when it's time for me to drive," Zander said.

"That what she's going to say?"

"Oh for sure, you know Phoebe. She'll do anything for me."

Jim turned the engine on, and closed his eyes, making sure it was tuned just right. "Yeah, you're probably right about that."

Zander turned on the radio, and kept changing stations. He changed them so many times, it was giving Jim a headache, but it was funny too, and Jim just knew Zander was gonna find *Tyler whatever her name was*. Zander paused. "She almost kicked some guy's ass at this store, you know? Because he was giving me guff."

"About what?"

Zander looked around, as if he couldn't remember, and then he tapped the dashboard. "Funny that you ask that," he said.

"Why?"

Zander turned the dial again. "Well, I guess I was doing something I shouldn't have been doing. But Phoebe was ready to bust the guy's head in when he laid a hand on me."

"That's my girl," Jim said.

Chapter 69

It came and went; she came, she went. He came; she went. Exactly. And a great start to a poem. Great start. And a rotten fucking start to her night.

She was outside, alone now, sitting on top of his 4Runner. She was hiding. Not from him. From them, no, not really, not from him and her. From her, from her shit, the shit she brought with her, like a modern, messed-up, mixed up dowry of pain and sex and shame. *Her lovely contribution to their relationship.*

She never really knew, not ahead of time, when something was gonna trigger her, and it was exhausting, this waiting. And even more exhausting was not waiting but falling; falling into him; relaxing, not worrying; making love to him again and it felt great and again and it felt great and for a little while she forgot . . .

But there was no forgetting, not forever, not even for long. It would never go away, would it? She lit a cigarette and drank a Coke, and the words poured out of her, from her fingers to the pages of her journal.

She didn't realize he was there until he drummed his fingers against the front quarter panel. The sun had just kissed the treetops behind where he was standing, hands behind his back, legs spread. "Hey," he said.

"Hey," she said. "Sun's kissing stuff again."

"Want some company up there?"

She was almost stupid. She almost said no. But her body gave her away, like it always fucking did, no, stop, it's just biology Cary had always said. And now it wasn't just biology that made the side of her mouth turn up, ever so little, in response to him.

He hopped up, and she watched him, greedy as always, for every little movement, seen, unseen, imagined, hoped or anticipated—he made. She sighed, and when he laid down next to her, his head on his hand, body turned toward her, and put his hand on her leg, she trembled.

"Hey," she said.

"You know, I've never made love to you outside," he said.

She actually tried to frown at him. She wanted to be . . . put off, angry, in pain, isolated, rolling in it really, but this man made her curl into him instead.

A minute ago, maybe two, she was sure she was miserable. But maybe all of that wasn't the way it had to be; maybe there'd be oases not of pleasure, but of pain. Like backwards oases, ones you endured rather than forged ahead towards. She threw her head back, and then she laughed, and set her notebook down.

"Outside?"

"Yes."

"Like right here?" She laughed low and deep now, and she envisioned the mountaintop, sun kissing it, Jim's words, Jim's hands, her, her hands on him, and she took his fingers and did what she knew to do to make him moan.

"Of course not here," he said. He pulled her head down and she curled all the way into him and he kissed her. A stray thought, a fear, came into her mind, and she tensed up for a moment, and then she felt, she really felt, him kissing her, and she grasped hold of that feeling, rode it, rode it high and hard, much like another wave she once rode, but this one was one she'd never have to surf alone.

"But I know a better place," he said.

"You're gonna take me to the mountaintop," she said.

He stopped, and his eyes were lit from within again.

"We've already got that magic, more magic than any mountain, than any place can ever give two people. Love. We got love."

Phoebe squinted into the sun and leaned into his kiss. Love. She had—they had—love.

Acknowledgments

This was the first novel I've written since I was called to serve. This was also the first book this lifetime Raz has helped me with, so thank you Raz for the words, the inspiration, and the kick in the pants whenever it was needed.

This was also the first time around this life that I've written while inspired by God. He was with me from start to finish, helping me shape what is at heart a classic love story. It's incredible to write when God inspires your every word: it's a completely different experience than writing just for yourself, by yourself, and of yourself. I cannot claim credit for the story or for the message, but I'm human and I'm sure I got some things wrong, and any mistakes in deciphering or understanding are mine. One thing I do know is I've never enjoyed writing as much as I enjoyed it while I wrote this book.

As a sexual and domestic abuse survivor, I know all too well the minefield that my sisters and brothers must dodge as they negotiate the uncertain process of recovering from the sins done unto them. I wrote this book to help you find your way to the other side, where the wounds have healed, and the sick rat bastards who assaulted you can no longer disturb you when you sleep. I pray you find peace in the same measure I've found it.

I also wrote this book for the proud souls who serve on our behalf. Would that I could find the words to thank you for all you give up for us. It is my wish, my fervent hope, that you will find healing and peace, both in your waking and your sleeping moments. It is my prayer that you no longer dream of the undead, and that the governments of the countries where you reside make it better for you and give you the support you need to live as your sacrifices merit.

As always, I'm grateful to my precious children, Madeline, Jim, and Ben, to thank, for they must live in and among the words ever floating in my head. I am grateful for their patience, their support, and their never-ending interest in my mission, which is to write stories that help guide souls Home.

Thank you so very much, Stevie Eubanks, for the never-ending support, guidance and love; and thank you for the beautiful poems.

I'd also like to thank the lovely Rubylea Demarco from Renegade Roller Derby in Portland, Oregon for walking me through the incredible sport of roller derby. Best of luck in your bouts, sister!

Thank you to Amy T. Monlezun for inspiring the fictional "Tyler Slow," which makes me smile every time I see it in print.

I'd also like to thank A.S. Byatt, whose beautiful book *Possession* inspired me to add poetry to *Wave Rising*.

And thank you to the good souls at St. Mark's Publishing Co., for taking a chance on my work.

E.L. PHOENIX

About the Author

E.L. Phoenix (Elaine or "El") is a truth explorer and a lay minister. She is an adventurer, a charismatic speaker, a lover of nature and animals, and a happy learner. From an early age, she has studied theology, archeology, history, philosophy, quantum physics and modern literature. El is currently on sabbatical from her work as a lay minister to hunt for proof of prehistoric advanced civilizations on all seven continents; in other words, she's hunting for proof of God. She splits her time between Wyoming and Virginia and lives with her three children. El is the author of several books, including the award-winning and best-selling *I Run* and *Ripple*. She is also the co-author of the *Strays Welcome* series.

If you would like to get an e-mail when El's next book is released, please visit: http://strayswelcomeinterfaithministries.com and subscribe for updates, or to subscribe to her newsletter directly, please go here: http://eepurl.com/AGRb9.

Word-of-mouth is crucial for any author to succeed. If you enjoyed this book, please consider leaving a review at the retailer where you bought this book, even if it's only a line or two; it would make all the difference and be very much appreciated.

And if you know anyone who has been sexually abused or has been the victim of domestic violence, please recommend they read *Ripple* and *Wave Rising*.

Stop by and visit!

El loves to talk, and she answers all her correspondence personally. Well, at least for now. She would love to see you, either on her Facebook Page, https://www.facebook.com/strayswelcomeinterfaithministries or via e-mail at farrisburke@me.com

Please also stop by any time at http://strayswelcomeinterfaithministries.com.

Thank you, and peace and love to all of you.

Support Resources

Crisis Support

Universal Emergency Number Nationwide: 911

National Hopeline: 1-800-656-HOPE (4673)

National Suicide Hotline: 1-800-273-TALK (8255)

Rape Abuse & Incest National Network (RAINN)

Direct link to immediate online chat intervention
http://online.rainn.org

Direct link to search all local crisis centers in the US by state or zip code
http://centers.rainn.org/

Survivor Support

About.com Post Traumatic Stress Disorder
http://ptsd.about.com/

After Silence
http://aftersilence.org

After The Rain
http://aftertherain.com

Arte Sana (English/Spanish)
http://arte-sana.com/arte_sana.htm

Dancing In The Darkness
http://dancinginthedarkness.com/

Healing Through Creativity
http://healingthroughcreativity.org/

Incest Survivors Anonymous
http://lafn.org/medical/isa/home.html

Let Go . . . Let Peace Come In Foundation
http://letgoletpeacecomein.org/

Lori's Song
http://lorissong.org/

Male Survivor (for male survivors)
http://malesurvivor.org/

1in6 (for male survivors)
http://1in6.org/men/

Pandora's Project
http://pandys.org/index.html

Project Unbreakable
http://projectunbreakable.tumblr.com/

Recovered Memory Project
http://blogs.brown.edu/recoveredmemory/

Sexual Abuse & Rape Survivor Links
http://aswaterspassingby.org/sexualabuse.html

Safe Horizon
http://safehorizon.org

Survivors Network of those Abused by Priests (SNAP)
http://snapnetwork.org/

Survivors of Incest Anonymous
http://siawso.org/

Witness Justice
http://witnessjustice.org/resources/hotline.cfm

On Gays and Love and God
An Excerpt from *I'll Take the Cows*

God may have inspired all of the books that exist in the Bible, but He didn't write all of them. Even the gospels he wrote or helped write, such as Kings, Songs, Proverbs and parts of Psalms, Job, and Genesis, among others, are limited or constrained by their time periods and more importantly, by the terms of the covenants that appeared in those gospels. Also, whatever God wrote has been respoken, repeated, rewritten, retranslated, and often completely altered by the shifting hands of well-meaning souls over the millennia.

God inspired the Bible, yes. He spoke to the prophets, some better and more clearly than to others. For example, Isaiah, Daniel, Ezekiel, and Jeremiah wrote what they were given, and faithfully transcribed vast amounts of material. Even these great prophets, however, missed some things. It's hard to understand the meaning and intent of the Lord. Very hard.

Moses was perhaps the greatest of the Old Testament prophets, and he contributed greatly to the first several gospels. But it was one of his aids who actually did the writing: a soul named Gadarison. And just as Moses had to use human ears to hear, so too did Gadarison. And these human ears, well, they're limited by a number of factors. Sometimes we just hear things wrong; sometimes we hear things through our own filters; often our own cultural prejudices inform how we interpret the words we are given; and sometimes we put our own beliefs into what we hear, and then when we go to write down the words we're given, well, we add some of our own.

I believe this was the case for Deuteronomy, Leviticus and the other early books of the Old Testament. In each of those books, the aforementioned prophets and scribes were describing a set of laws and also recording history. These books are all limited by their time period. Deuteronomy and Leviticus, among other old gospels, do not completely capture the will or the Word of God accurately; and for guidelines on how to behave, we need not look, shivering and fearfully, to a long-since outdated code of rules. We should listen to the words spoken by the only begotten Son of God instead, and as the Son taught, we should tune into the Holy Spirit directly. We should rely on our own consciences and our own souls to detect the proper pathway to follow.

In addition, there's clear biblical justification for disregarding the laws set forth in Deuteronomy. You see, the Old Testament gospels, especially the early ones, capture promises, also called covenants, made between God and His people. In exchange for agreeing to obey God's laws, God promised His people Israel, which also means, "the promised land."

Over time, the sheer number of laws piled up. There were more than 600 laws and rules and regulations the Jews were following . . . and yet they were still leading unfulfilling lives, which is to say they were constantly breaking not just the little laws, but the big ones, as in the ones set forth in the Ten Commandments. Souls weren't just breaking laws—they weren't finding their way Home, and they weren't loving or finding God.

Jesus came to set humans free—free of the Old Covenants. He brought with him a new covenant, which, to put it simply amounted to this: Love God; love your neighbor; accept that Jesus died for our sins . . . and you're on your way Home. Does it sound too good to be true? Well, a lot of his fellow Jews thought it did. They didn't think Jesus was really a prophet, or the Messiah, the Son of God, and the Jews asked questions like, "Yes, but where's the Ark of the Covenant?" Or, "Yes, but even with all your miracles, how can you prove you are the Messiah?" Or, "Yes, but wait, that sounds so different from anything we've ever heard—it just doesn't . . . sound right?"

The sad thing for so many people is that what Jesus was bringing was some incredibly good news. He was also bringing the people this amazing gift: the Holy Spirit, which amounted to a connection to (or according to some interpreters later, even a piece of God) that would forever exist within each soul born of water and spirit forever after. But before I explain what the Holy Spirit means and how it relates to gay love, I wanted to quickly cover the nuts and bolts of the New Testament's New Covenant.

If you want to learn about the Old Covenants, the best place to start is in the New Testament; specifically, go to the Gospel of Hebrews, which was written by an Essene priest named Barnabus. A teacher and uncle of Jesus, Barnabus was one of the greatest intellectuals of his era, and he not only walked and talked with Jesus for five years—he also walked and preached the good news to Jews and Gentiles for an additional fifteen years after Jesus died.

Barnabus explains the Old Covenants very well. He starts off by setting forth the superiority of Jesus to the prophets who contributed to the Old Testament:

In the past God spoke to our ancestors through the prophets at many times and in various ways, but in these last days he has spoken to us by his Son, whom he appointed heir of all things, and through whom also he made the universe. The Son is the radiance of God's glory and the exact representation of his being, sustaining all things by his powerful word. After he had provided purification for sins, he sat down at the right hand of the Majesty in heaven. So he became as much superior to the angels as the name he has inherited is superior to theirs. Hebrews 1:1-4.

Then Barnabus explains why Jesus had to be human: he had to suffer just as we suffer so that in overcoming suffering, he could show us how to set ourselves free of the fear of dying.[1] Jesus

---

[1] Since the children have flesh and blood, he too shared in their humanity so that by his death he might break the power of him who holds the power of death—that is, the devil—and free those who all their lives were held in slavery by their fear of death. For surely it is not angels he helps, but Abraham's descendants. For this reason he had to be made like them, fully human in every way, in order that he might become a merciful and faithful high priest in service to God, and that he might make atonement for the sins of the people. Because he himself suffered when he was tempted, he is able to help those who are being tempted. Hebrews 2:15-18.

suffered at the hands of man; he was made fully human, and he defeated death.

Jesus was also greater than Moses, and the words he spoke could be trusted as coming straight from God.

> *Jesus has been found worthy of greater honor than Moses, just as the builder of a house has greater honor than the house itself. For every house is built by someone, but God is the builder of everything. "Moses was faithful as a servant in all God's house," bearing witness to what would be spoken by God in the future. But Christ is faithful as the Son over God's house. And we are his house, if indeed we hold firmly to our confidence and the hope in which we glory. Hebrews 3:3-6.*

In the days of Moses, God made agreements with His people, and both sides, or parties to the agreement made promises.

> *When God made his promise to Abraham, since there was no one greater for him to swear by, he swore by himself, saying, "I will surely bless you and give you many descendants." And so after waiting patiently, Abraham received what was promised.*
> *People swear by someone greater than themselves, and the oath confirms what is said and puts an end to all argument. Because God wanted to make the unchanging nature of his purpose very clear to the heirs of what was promised, he confirmed it with an oath. God did this so that, by two unchangeable things in which it is impossible for God to lie, we who have fled to take hold of the hope set before us may be greatly encouraged. We have this hope as an anchor for the soul, firm and secure. It enters the inner sanctuary behind the curtain, where our forerunner, Jesus, has entered on our behalf. He has become a high priest forever, in the order of Melchizedek. Hebrews 6:13-20.*

Jesus was a high priest of sorts in addition to being a prophet and the Messiah, or the promised one, the soul promised by so many earlier prophets such as Moses and Isaiah, Elijah and Elisha, among others. And Jesus took an oath as a priest, an oath that guaranteed the truth or sanctity of any covenants he would later announce to the people:

> *Others became priests without any oath, but he became a priest with an oath when God said to him:*
>
> *"The Lord has sworn*
>   *and will not change his mind:*
>   *'You are a priest forever.'"*
> *Because of this oath, Jesus has become the guarantor of a better covenant.*

What does Barnabus mean when he says that Jesus is the guarantor of a better covenant? That means that we can trust Jesus—we can believe that what He says is the Word or intention of God is true. What Jesus promises us is accurate and real, or to put it in financial terms, if we want to cash a check in, Jesus will make sure that so long as we upheld our end of the bargain and lived virtuously, loving God and loving one another, He would make sure that we would receive the salvation promised.

Barnabus explains why we should listen to Jesus in Hebrews:

> *Now the main point of what we are saying is this: We do have such a high priest, who sat down at the right hand of the throne of the Majesty in heaven, and who serves in the sanctuary, the true tabernacle set up by the Lord, not by a mere human being. Hebrews 8:1-2.*

The earlier priests, from the time of Moses, had to offer up sacrifices up on altars to make good their part of the covenant, or agreement with God. The priests had to make sure their altars were built just so, and that they basically built copies of the sanctuaries that (they thought) were built in heaven.

But Jesus didn't need to use these altars or follow all these practices as set forth in the Old Testament. Why not?

> *But in fact the ministry Jesus has received is as superior to theirs as the covenant of which he is mediator is superior to the old one, since the new covenant is established on better promises. Hebrews 8:6.*

Jesus was bringing a new covenant because the old covenants weren't working, and were now obsolete.

> *For if there had been nothing wrong with that first covenant, no place would have been sought for another. But God found fault with the people and said:*
>
> *"The days are coming," declares the Lord, "When I will make a new covenant with the people of Israel and with the people of Judah. It will not be like the covenant I made with their ancestors when I took them by the hand to lead them out of Egypt, because they did not remain faithful to my covenant, and I turned away from them, declares the Lord. This is the covenant I will establish with the people of Israel after that time, declares the Lord. I will put my laws in their minds and write them on their hearts. I will be their God, and they will be my people. No longer will they teach their neighbor, or say to one another, 'Know the Lord,' because they will all know me, from the least of them to the greatest.*
> *For I will forgive their wickedness and will remember their sins no more."*

By calling this covenant "new," he has made the first one obsolete; and what is obsolete and outdated will soon disappear. Hebrews 8:7-13, quoting Jer. 31:31-34.[2]

There it is—right there in black and white. The old covenants from Deuteronomy and other books from the Old Testament are "obsolete and outdated." For those of you who have been looking for a reason, a clear justification, biblically sound, absolutely logical and doctrinally accurate for why God has not outlawed gay love, here's the passage you've been searching for. And then there's this:

For this reason Christ is the mediator of a new covenant, that those who are called may receive the promised eternal inheritance—now that he has died as a ransom to set them free from the sins committed under the first covenant. In the case of a will, it is necessary to prove the death of the one who made it, because a will is in force only when somebody has died; it never takes effect while the one who made it is living. This is why even the first covenant was not put into effect without blood. Hebrews 9:15-17.

---

[2] See also Galatians 3:21-26. "For if a law had been given that could impart life, then righteousness would certainly have come by the law.

Before the coming of this faith, we were held in custody under the law, locked up until the faith that was to come would be revealed. So the law was our guardian until Christ came that we might be justified by faith. Now that this faith has come, we are no longer under a guardian.

So in Christ Jesus you are all children of God through faith, for all of you who were baptized into Christ have clothed yourselves with Christ."

As Barnabus explains, Jesus "made good" on his promises by shedding his blood on the cross. While this seems anachronistic, maybe even cruel to modern ears, God sealed His agreement with us, His people, with the blood of His son. Jesus died so that we, in a manner of speaking, would gain eternal life much more easily.

The old laws, as set forth in Deuteronomy, concerning what humans can and cannot do are no longer in force. That's why proscriptions on eating certain foods are no longer in effect; and more importantly, Jesus wants us to focus on the deeper, more meaningful issues. As far as what we eat, for example, it's not what goes into our mouths but what comes out of them that matters.[3] Or as far as the laws regarding the Sabbath, did Jesus stop working to make the world better? No—he healed the sick:

> *Another time Jesus went into the synagogue, and a man with a shriveled hand was there. Jesus said to the man with the shriveled hand, "Stand up in front of everyone."*
> *Then Jesus asked them, "Which is lawful on the Sabbath: to do good or to do evil, to save life or to kill?"*
> *But they remained silent.*
> *He looked around at them in anger and, deeply distressed at their stubborn hearts, said to the man, "Stretch out your hand." He stretched it out, and his hand was completely restored. Mark 3:1-6.[4]*

---

[3] See Matthew 15:11; Mark 7:15; The Gospel of Thomas, Saying 14.

[4] "The Father is like that. He labored in the Sabbath, for the sheep that he found fallen into the pit. He saved the life of the sheep and brought it up from the pit. Understand the inner meaning, for you are children of inner meaning. What is the Sabbath? It is the day on which salvation should not be idle. Speak of the heavenly day that has no night and of the light that does not set because it is perfect. Speak from the heart, for you are the perfect day and within you dwells the light that does not fail. Speak of truth with those who seek it and of knowledge with those who have sinned in their error." *See The Gospel of Truth, The Nag Hammadi Scriptures.*

Jesus taught us to look deeper, to search for the true meaning behind all of the teachings earlier prophets had shared.

Indeed, when Jesus was saying goodbye to his followers, he didn't give them a long list of rules. He kept it simple, oh so very simple.

As the Father has loved me, so have I loved you. Now remain in my love. If you keep my commands, you will remain in my love, just as I have kept my Father's commands and remain in his love. I have told you this so that my joy may be in you and that your joy may be complete. My command is this: Love each other as I have loved you. Greater love has no one than this: to lay down one's life for one's friends. You are my friends if you do what I command. I no longer call you servants, because a servant does not know his master's business. Instead, I have called you friends, for everything that I learned from my Father I have made known to you. You did not choose me, but I chose you and appointed you so that you might go and bear fruit—fruit that will last—and so that whatever you ask in my name the Father will give you. This is my command: Love each other.

Jesus told us to love one another, and he gave us a tool, a new tool, that would help guide us: the Holy Spirit.

It is this, the Holy Spirit, or the light within our souls, that should inform how we treat one another. This light, which is pure love, God's love, is inside all of us, and when we look on our brothers and sisters, we should shine light, not darkness, on them. After all, why should it bother us who our brother, or who our sister . . . loves? What, after all, is love? Other than light, shining like a beacon from the Almighty One who made us?

We shouldn't be so scared. God is not scary. Churches should be helping feed the hungry, not scaring the hell out of you with fire and brimstone scorched-soul nonsense. The new laws of the New Testament supersede the old laws of the Old Testament. Even if Leviticus and Deuteronomy once accurately captured the will of God (a position I do not accept but grant for the sake of argument), the laws God gave to his people within that gospel have been rendered obsolete by the New Testament covenants.

For the map Home, look to Jesus, and look within, to the piece of God given to you in the form of the Holy Spirit. That light, and His love—is all we need. For love, is love. And love is good.

www.ingramcontent.com/pod-product-compliance
Lightning Source LLC
Chambersburg PA
CBHW050538260626
47157CB00002B/348